LOVE'S SECOND SIGHT

LOVE'S SECOND SIGHT

DARRAGHA FOSTER

BURNING HEART PRESS

LOVE'S SECOND SIGHT
Darrgha Foster
Burning Heart Press
© 2004-2015 Darragha Foster; first edition previously published 2004; second edition 2012 by Liquid Silver Books. All rights reserved. No part of this publication may be reproduced, stored in a retrieval system, or transmitted in any form or by any means, electronic, mechanical, recording or otherwise, without the prior written permission of the author.
Manufactured in the United States of America.
Cover art by April Martinez.
This is a work of fiction. The characters, incidents and dialogues in this book are of the author's imagination and are not to be construed as real. Any resemblance to actual events or persons, living or dead, is completely coincidental.

ISBN-10 1-5197-5058-7
ISBN-13 978-1-5197-5058-7

CONTENTS

Prologue   *10*

Chapter 1   *12*

Chapter 2   *46*

Chapter 3   *68*

Chapter 4   *81*

Chapter 5   *92*

Chapter 6   *111*

Chapter 7   *121*

Chapter 8	*133*
Chapter 9	*147*
Chapter 10	*150*
Chapter 11	*161*
Chapter 12	*171*
Chapter 13	*179*
Chapter 14	*182*
Chapter 15	*194*
Chapter 16	*200*

Chapter 17	*203*
Chapter 18	*214*
Chapter 19	*225*
Chapter 20	*228*
Chapter 21	*247*
Chapter 22	*271*
Chapter 23	*280*
Chapter 24	*293*
Chapter 25	*301*

Chapter 26	*309*
Chapter 27	*324*
Chapter 28	*331*
Chapter 29	*334*
Chapter 30	*340*
Chapter 31	*357*
Epilogue	*358*
About the Author	*359*

Dedication

For my one true love

Acknowledgements

Love's Second Sight is the culmination of thirty years of adventure and research. Hands-on, sink-or-swim, sometimes even otherworldly adventure and research. I am grateful my path led me to Iceland in 1979 where I experienced a taste of true magic and undying love.

Although based upon stanzas contained in medieval Icelandic texts The Greenlander's Saga and The Saga of Erik the Red, this is a work of fiction. Names, characters, places, and incidents are the product of the author's imagination or are used fictitiously, and any resemblance to actual persons, living or dead, establishments, or locales is entirely coincidental.

Love's Second Sight

by

Darragha Foster

Prologue

"…When Leif sailed from Greenland, he was driven off course to the Hebrides. It was a long wait for a good wind thence, so he remained there for much of the summer. Leif took a fancy to a woman by the name of Thorgunna. She was a lady of good birth, and Leif had an idea she saw farther into things than most. As he made ready to sail away Thorgunna asked to come with him. Leif wanted to know whether her people were likely to approve of this, to which she answered that that was of no importance. Leif replied that he thought it imprudent to carry off so high-born a lady in a strange country. Thorgunna disagreed and stated, 'Then I must tell thee that I am no longer a lone woman and upon thee I charge it. Moreover I see that I shall bear you a son, and that he will come to you one day and be claimed as your heir.' … Leif gave Thorgunna a gold finger ring."
—The Greenlander's Saga

Late Spring, 999
The Isle of Tiree, Scottish Hebrides

Standing at the edge of her world, the shoreline of the Isle of Tiree, Thorgunna glanced at the contract of marriage she clutched, as the chill of her vision subsided.

"All I had to do was bear sons. Nothing more. Nothing less. But now, everything is going to change. I abhor *change*."

Her body and soul vibrating in the wake of the powerful vision,

Thorgunna drew a deep breath, then exhaled forcefully. The brilliant surge of energy past, she again looked at the contract, sighed, and shook her head in disbelief.

"The man I shall love approaches. But so does my new husband. Now what will I do?"

Suddenly her world grew even more complicated than it had ever been.

She scanned the horizon for the sails of the ship bringing her new husband to Tiree. The husband she had wed by contract, but had not yet met. The man who was her husband, but not her love.

"Nor shall love ever bloom between Finn and I. I know that now. How could I expect more from a marriage such as ours?" Thorgunna shivered. "My island has always been my one true love. Nothing else has mattered—until now. *He* will change everything. He *has* changed everything. Damn my sight!"

Thorgunna, filled with the residual deep, heady effervescence characteristic of her second sight, left the shore. To await *his* arrival.

Chapter 1

Eight weeks later

Early Summer, 999

Thorgunna woke just before dawn, drenched in sweat, her bed linens wrapped around her like a burial shroud. Her heart raced frantically, and she gasped, trying to catch her breath—trying to calm herself. "It was just the dream. Just the dream." She exhaled, forcing her body to accept calmness in its dream-induced state of agitation. "It becomes more real every day. Will there come a time when I won't be able to distinguish my waking world from my nightmare? I am weary of these torments of sleep and confusion. I wish the gods would leave me alone. I wish that hellish beastly demigod, Loki, would leave me alone. I don't know how much more of this I can take."

Peeling her bed sheets from her damp skin, Thorgunna emerged from her bedbox like a butterfly from its chrysalis.

"I must discover the winning strategy in this battle played out each night upon the field of my mind. The battle for Tiree. The battle for my soul."

She stretched, reaching for a cup of water on her bedside table. "Fifty-six nights I've waged a battle beyond the veil of darkness. Fifty-seven days I have awakened unable to mourn the death of my husband, having never known him. I have no feelings about the death of Finn MacLean, save those of regret at the termination of the benefits awarded me in the *Condicio Matrimonium*.

"Who killed you, Finn? Who sent your ship to the bottom of the Hebridean sea? Who denied me your wedding gift of skilled Scottish guards to protect my island? If not for those guards, I would never have married you in the first place!"

Thorgunna set the cup down with such force it cracked. "Damn. No husband. No guard. And now, no cup."

She dressed carefully, pinning her black hair back in a utilitarian fashion. Thorgunna emerged from her house not as a woman seeking release from the clutches of a godling-sent nightmarish hell nor as the youthful innocent she truly was. Thorgunna Vagnsdottir, Lady Jarl, mistress of the Isle of Tiree, had no time to dwell upon fears born of nightmares. No time to find an end to her chronic fatigue. No time to seek the means to end her night terrors.

A ship, broken and torn by a summer storm of vast magnitude had sailed into the harbor in the night. Of course, Tiree had many such visitors during the season of summer storms. And they all pulled into Gott Bay as if the horseshoe-shaped white sand cove was littered with lodestones. Custom dictated she offer hospitality to the captain and crew of the storm-ravaged ship, no matter how tired she was.

Thorgunna stopped as a memory surfaced. A fleeting memory from the dream. "Is this the ship bearing the explorer? The man from my vision whom my nightmarish foe uses as a tool to tease and frighten me?"

She recalled the words the hungry beast of her dreams force-fed her every night. Painful, yet promising words spoken through lips both honeyed and scarred. Joyful, yet threatening words. Words accompanied by the scent of salt and leather, leaving the air thick with anticipation.

"Soon, Thorgunna, soon enough, a man shall come ashore. An explorer. He shall explore you, I dare say." Thorgunna shook her head, once again convincing herself the words of her tormentor were lies. "It is the god of lies who haunts me, and therefore everything he says, every night is a lie. If one word is true, then all parts of the *condicio malefactororis diabolus*

between Loki and me are true. That, I must never allow. The woman I become in my dreams must have no sway or influence over the woman I am while awake. My nocturnal contract with the god of darkness must never bleed through into the daylight of reality. Never. No matter who has arrived upon my island in the dead of night."

****

With the sun rising pink and orange across the vastness of the heavens, Thorgunna rode to Gott, the natural harbor in which the torn ship had anchored. The circle of stone-and-thatch beach shelters came into view. Beyond that, a tattered, square-sailed longship lay at anchor in Gott Bay.

She pulled the reins and vaulted off her pony just shy of the rock enclosure surrounding the largest of the cottages, and tried to push fearful thoughts and apprehension aside.

A handsome stranger sat calmly upon a driftwood bench outside the cottage. He displayed nobility in even that simple act. Thorgunna knew he was the captain of the ship anchored in the bay.

She crossed the cattle grid built into the rock wall. Within the enclosure, sheer will alone kept her from turning and running far, far away. Thorgunna, exuding her own nobility while fighting back a raging tide of panic, recognized the stranger all too well. *This man, this tall, golden man, is my true love. Best to put that right out of my head. There can be no true love for me. My island must come first.* He was the man revealed to her by the sight. He was the man used as a tool by her tormentor to try to coerce and trick her into the demon-blessed contract.

Thorgunna was not the only islander to greet the dawn and the weary, storm-ravaged men from off the sea—though she was their leader. Always just out of her line of sight was Thorok, the man chosen by her own father to be her protector.

Flanked by a handful of islanders already offering assistance to the wayfarers, Thorgunna extended her right hand for a traditional clasping of wrists with the storm-ravaged sea captain. *Is this truly the man whose approach I sensed? The man whose scent and laugh have haunted my thoughts even more so than the nightmarish beast that came upon me when news of Finn's death reached Tiree?*

Her eyes downcast, she could not look into the man's eyes. The truth was in his eyes. The truth revealed to her by the sight so many weeks ago, and molded into a lovely cage by the beast in her nightmares.

The man rose to greet her. Tall, with skin as tan as the leather he wore, and with long, thick blond hair, he outshone the rising sun.

She watched with almost hypnotic fascination as their hands met and slowly joined, palm meeting palm for a warm, affecting moment before encircling and grasping each other's wrist. As her fingers clasped his strong arm, she at last lifted her eyes to meet his.

He smiled kindly, as if he welcomed her—not she extending welcome to him.

Feigning a cough, Thorgunna quickly turned her head to hide the blush caused by the light of the man's smile, an infectious smile of mouth and eyes and demeanor more brilliant in its glow than the light of the elusive Hebridean sun.

He was like a mist, surrounding her, filling her. He invaded her with his presence in a way she had not expected nor even imagined. She breathed him in—every part of him. Like strong herbal vapors, he excited her—healed her.

Instinctively, her guard went up. The conditioning and fear instilled in her by repetitive nightmares took hold. Worse, the teachings of her father, who had many enemies, invaded her heart, pushing out thoughts of love and satisfaction.

"When you are at rest is when your enemies will take what is yours," her father had intoned over and over as he trained her to lead the islanders one day.

My enemies, Thorgunna thought. One took Finn from me. Another wants to control my island. The most fearsome desires no less than my soul.

She suppressed a shudder as the sea captain's grip around her wrist tightened, and his index finger delicately and quite intentionally caressed her forearm while his strong, callused hand encircled her wrist. *For the sake of this man's life. For Tiree. I must be strong.*

Gathering her wits, Thorgunna gazed into the captain's piercing blue eyes. So clear, so absolutely clear a blue she had never seen before. Embarrassingly blue. Like a mirror. A mirror reflecting her own dusky complexion, made only darker by contrast with his fairness.

Breathing in deeply, she recognized his scent. Salt and leather. *I do know this man.*

Clasping Thorgunna's wrist firmly, the captain spoke, "The storm took its toll upon us as if we were a child's toy afloat in a horse trough, Lady. These shelters saved our lives."

Still clasping wrists, still drowning in his eyes, his smile, his enticing male scent, Thorgunna forced a weak smile, trying to recall what had been said to her only a moment before to make an appropriate reply. "This island has seen many visitors washed ashore after a storm. We keep these shelters as a monument to our hospitality. Welcome to Tiree. I am Thorgunna. I am the Jarl of this fair island."

Not releasing her wrist, but pulling her slightly closer, the shipwrecked man lifted Thorgunna's hand to his lips, kissing the back of it so gently, but with such unfulfilled hunger, she had to pull away.

The sun had risen, casting a pale light through the heavy gray clouds decorating the sky above Tiree. His back to the sun, standing dead-center in a streak of near-white light trailing a warm kiss across the sand, the wayfarer's head was crowned by a golden halo. A golden man bathed in the glow of a golden streak of sunlight.

Obviously fatigued, he leaned momentarily against the portal leading into the shelter.

"I am Leif, son of Eirik Rautha, of Greenland. Thank you, again, Madam Jarl. Your hospitality is regal. Without chancing upon this island, we would have surely died."

Thorgunna smiled. "I can plainly see your ship hails from Greenland by the square shape and the color of her sail—or at least what's left of it. But sir, your accent is not Greenlandic. You are an Icelander, no?"

Leif laughed. "You recognize Iceland in my speech? My father moved us from Breithafjordur when I was a child."

Breithafjordur, Thorgunna repeated to herself, committing the name to memory. "Icelanders are a proud lot. It reflects in your voice. In your manner of speaking. Most men in realms under Norway's control no longer refer to themselves as the 'son of' their father. Being so far from the throne, I'm sure Greenland learns of changes in court etiquette much later than we do. You truly speak as though you are still a part of Iceland."

"Iceland runs in my veins. But Greenland is my home now. And she is, indeed, a long trek from Norway—but that is precisely where we were headed when a great squall fell upon us, drowning my ship, nearly killing us all."

"Hiring yourselves out as mercenaries?"

Leif laughed again. "Nothing so grand as that. We're not even on a true *iviking*. I'm on a mission to woo the King of Norway into a trade agreement with Greenland. My father wishes his foundling country to be recognized and made a part of Olaf's realm."

"Is your father a pagan?" Thorgunna asked, pointing at the bronze Thor's Hammer pinned to Leif's tunic.

"A pagan? No. Greenland has no pagans. We are Odinists."

"Our king considers all men who do not share his faith in the White Christ, pagans. Does your father not know Olaf of Norway is a Christian? A rather devout and zealous Christian, I might add."

"Lady, as you said, Greenland is quite far from the news of Norway. My father, the Jarl of Bratahild, most certainly does not know his king has converted to the new faith. No priest has ever set foot upon our soil, nor shall if Eirik has his way. In Iceland, there were a few Irish monks milling about the small, secluded islands off the coast, but they feared us, and we left them alone—for the most part."

It was her move, and she knew it. Either I invite this lost captain to stay in the relative luxury of my home, or I ignore tradition and leave him here with his men. How close do I want him when I must shun his affections to save his life?

Thorgunna made her decision after one more glance into the man's eyes. An Iceland-born Greenland-bred giant, he was far from safe. But he was ever so much more a beautiful beast than that which haunted her anyway. "Sir, can you ride to my compound? I'd like to continue our discussion, while welcoming you properly to my island. Your men are welcome to stay in the shelter." Turning to Thorok, who stood just beyond the enclosure, Thorgunna continued, "Bring the captain a horse, Thorok. We shall ride to Gott Hill."

Thorok nodded his usual silent reply, leading his own horse around the shelter to Thorgunna.

"My men are in better shape than my ship, Lady. None are badly injured. All are rested and comfortable thanks to the provisions in the shelter. I am honored, as are they, to be a guest upon your island." Leif stretched. "My legs are a bit weak as we were long at sea, but I believe I can still ride. Is not the motion of a pony under you similar to the rocking of the ocean under your ship? Lead away, madam." Leif nodded toward a large red-bearded man. "Take care of them, Siggi. I'll be back."

The man raised an eyebrow suspiciously, yet replied calmly, "Yes, sir."

****

Leif followed Thorgunna, watching her as she moved lightly across the white sand shore of *her* island, listening to the provocative sound of her keys jingling at her hip like the call of a siren.

By the gods, she is a handsome woman, he thought, admiring Thorgunna's form. She is a buxom, comely woman. Her skin is so deliciously dark. I've never seen such a handsome woman. I envy her husband. He must enjoy bedding her, indeed.

"Lady, may I inquire about the Lord of the Isle?" he asked, his mind lingering on thoughts of Thorgunna, and her bed.

"My brother went off to follow the priests of the White Christ several years ago. My husband, Finn MacLean of Oban, died at sea. We had no children. My father and mother are dead as well. I am the chief property holder on Tiree. I am her Jarl."

Leif's interest piqued. *She is a widow. A young, beautiful widow.* "Tiree. My Gaelic is poor, but does that not translate to 'breadbasket'?" he asked.

"Yes, it does, rather. Tiree is the most fertile of all the Inner Hebrides. We produce fantastic amounts of grain and grain products. You speak a bit of Gaelic?"

"My first mate was born in Ireland. He came to Iceland when I was a lad, and moved to Greenland with us. He taught me."

"You must have made a fine pupil," Thorgunna quipped.

"In all subjects," Leif replied slyly. "Greenland's long winters provide ample time for educating a young man."

They rode across the long, crescent-shaped beach, through the tall grasses and pasture, to a well-maintained enclave atop Gott Hill.

"My home," Thorgunna called.

Leif nodded his head, surveying the structure of the houses and the obvious defensive ring pattern of the dwellings spiraling down the gentle slope of the hill.

Truly, Thorgunna's house atop the hill was better than most he had seen in Iceland or Greenland. Longer than it was wide and built of stone, it boasted shuttered windows and a bright red door with heavy iron hinges. The net-covered thatch roof was cleverly held in place by the tying of fist-sized stones to the net's outer ring, making the structure sound against the ever-present wind off the sea. It was a lovely house.

As they walked the horses to the stable, Leif, always exploring, even if only with his eyes, noted the enclave was more than just a defensible fortress ringed by stone. It was quite obviously the hub of the island community.

The Jarl's house is the sun. It is the bright center of the world to these simple folk. I see a pattern here. The smithy, the dairy, the smokehouse, and the stack yard radiate away like rays of the sun from her house.

A groom ran to Thorgunna and Leif, taking the horses.

Thorgunna turned to Leif, "My house is yours. Your first mate is welcome to visit here, however, I would prefer he sleep with your men to keep them out of trouble. I may have items you need for repair on hand, and you're welcome to them, as you apparently have nothing to trade."

"I have some silver. My purse did not meet its end in the storm," Leif replied quietly.

"What I really need are extra hands in the fields, the brewery, and at the nets. Can you spare a few men, perhaps in rotation—so the repairs on your vessel will not suffer?" Thorgunna asked.

"A good idea, that. I'll talk to Sigurdur and see if he can work it out with the men."

Inside, the house appeared typically Norse, save it was alive with fresh-cut flowers and delicate, vibrant embroidered wall hangings and tapestries.

Leif paused inside the door, breathing in the fragrance of the place. Sweet blossoms perfumed in concert with the stunning spectrum of wall hangings and intricate weavings. *What is more delicious? The sweet flowers or the bare nape of her neck? Which shall I pluck first?*

"Yours?" Leif asked, admiring the work. Admiring Thorgunna.

Thorgunna nodded proudly.

Leif reached up, touching the largest of the tapestries, trailing his fingers across bold reddish words woven against a solid earth-tone background, trimmed in vibrant shades of gold, yellow, orange, blue, and green. He carefully sounded-out and pronounced the woven message.

"This banner commemorates the Battle of the Sheaves. *Sguab choirce gu crios ann an crios Lachlannaich.*" He then translated the Gaelic into Norse, "*Stungull til thess ban i Vikingur magi.* A sheaf to its band in a Norseman's stomach."

"And don't you forget it," Thorgunna responded proudly.

"Aye, Lady. I'll watch myself lest you run me clean through with the poke of a sharp vegetable," Leif replied.

Thorgunna turned a sharp eye to Leif. "A true warrior will battle with whatever weapon is at hand. We had no choice but to defend ourselves with the very stalks of corn we protected. We were victorious."

"No offense intended, Lady. Perhaps you shall regale my crew with the saga of the Battle of the Sheaves whilst we are in repair," Leif offered.

"Perhaps."

Leif studied the great room of Thorgunna's house. It was warm. Without draft.

"A hearth for heating and pit-fire for cooking. Useful that. The way you utilize one chimney to outlet the smoke from both sources is ingenious. I salute your builder," Leif commented.

"I designed. My men built." Thorgunna walked to the hearth. "My bed was always too cold when I was a girl. I like to feel warm, hence two fires and vents between rooms to allow passage of heat." Thorgunna motioned to one of the rooms left of the entrance. "Your bed is there. It is warm, I promise. My private chamber lies beyond that weaving." She nodded to the opposite end of the great room. "I apologize for the inconvenience, but our new pit and shelter isn't finished. Thereby, we must all use a bucket as a privy. Oh, and although I expect your men will be sniffing about my women soon enough, I ask you—please do not take any of my house servants to your bed. It causes problems later. I find my servants lose interest in their work when dreams of foreigners fill their hearts and minds by day and bodies by night. Since I pay them a good wage, I expect good work from them," Thorgunna said, stoking the fire. She turned her head to face Leif, raising an eyebrow, waiting for his response.

Leif, not shocked, but definitely intrigued by her frankness, replied, "I shall watch myself, Lady."

Thorgunna smiled. "After you are rested we shall talk more."

Realizing he had just been dismissed, Leif excused himself, and entered his chamber. It contained the typical Norse bedbox filled with clean straw and a wooden frame covered with cowhide, fine linen sheets, and a large woolen blanket. Again, the room had fresh flowers and wall hangings. And, the room was amazingly warm. "Vents. What a marvelous idea," he mumbled, raising his hands to feel the warm air wafting in from the main room even with his room's heavy privacy curtain dropped into place.

Leif sat upon the bedbox.

"Oh, gods," he sighed, suddenly very, very tired. Though it was still early morning and he wished to explore Tiree—and its Lady—more thoroughly, he simply could not move. His body collapsed and sagged as the hyper-vigilant state it had been in since the storm melted away to the pull of persistent, unquelled exhaustion. "I pray I am amongst friends," he whispered to himself before he crashed into the linens.

****

Lief awoke several hours later, springing from the bed, his heart racing. Confused by the heavy sleep of the near dead, several moments passed before Leif regained composure.

I am intact. Sword, boots, coin. I am also quite alive.

He looked about the room with more rested eyes. Through the leaves of the shutters, he could see a brilliant sunset. "I slept through the day," Leif said. He took a deep breath. His senses became engulfed in the fragrances of the place. Lupines, Baldur's brow, buttercups, and aromatic herbs mixed into the bouquets gave the air a stimulating, yet tranquil aura.

Leif rose, loosening the thongs of his breeches to relieve himself into the conspicuously placed privy. A giggle from behind startled him.

"*Failte*," a delicate female voice called, using a traditional Gaelic phrase for "Welcome." "I am Brigit, Lady Thorgunna's cook and housekeeper. I have barley porridge hot and ready for you to eat."

"Thank you, Brigit. Barley porridge sounds very good. You are not of the Isle, are you?" Leif said, unashamedly lacing his breeches in front of Brigit while taking note of her strong accent and wild beauty. She wore a gathered-waist shirt and cinch, pushing up and exposing her ample bosom. Her skirt had a long slit on one side to allow freedom of movement.

"No, sir. I am from Eire. What you might call a Westman," Brigit replied.

Leif moved closer to Brigit, his blue eyes dancing playfully as he spoke. "I know Westmen. Never would I call you a West*man*. Alas, dear lady, I am forbidden to dally with the Jarl's servants. Too bad that. I've always enjoyed the company of Westmen."

"You, sir, tread upon unsafe ground. Don't you make me angry now."

"Aye. I wouldn't want to raise your hot Irish temper," Leif agreed. "Nor do I wish to countermand the orders of the Lady Jarl."

"There's a wise man. Now, to your porridge, shall we?"

Smiling, Leif exited his room, slipping past Brigit, straining to ignore the sensation of her soft bosom brushing against his chest in passing.

"Well, excuse me, sir," Brigit giggled, stepping into Leif's chamber as he exited.

"No worries, Brigit. Thorgunna just needs to make larger doorways," Leif replied.

A piping hot bowl of porridge smothered with butter and cream awaited Leif in the main room, carefully plated out atop the small table by the hearth fire.

A moment later Thorgunna emerged from her chamber, and served herself from the pot over the fire pit in the center of the room. She joined Leif at the table.

"Thank you for letting me sleep. I took watch after we came ashore, and gods, I was tired," Leif commented, sliding his bench a bit closer to the table.

"Aye. We could hear the lot of them snoring last night. That's how we knew a ship had pulled to harbor. But none were so loud as you alone in your chamber."

"I apologize for my ... for the snoring."

"Don't concern yourself, Greenlander. My father could out-wind a storm."

Leif smiled, changing the subject, "Brigit is a Westman slave?"

"Brigit is not a slave."

"She says she is your cook," Leif replied.

"Aye, that she is. I traded for her, as she was too young to be made off with by Norsemen in my eyes. On Tiree there are no slaves. She was free to leave. However, she chose to stay, and to be my cook."

"What was her value?"

"Twelve kegs of beer," Thorgunna replied.

Leif laughed. "There must be a story there."

"Indeed."

"Will you share it?"

"I am not a skald. My stories are rather dull."

"I enjoy your accent. Please," Leif said, flashing a broad smile.

"I have no accent. You, sir, have the accent."

"Ah, but when you travel to Iceland it will be you who has the accent," Leif laughed.

"When shall I travel to Iceland? Are you a prophet as well as an emissary?"

"Do you not wish to visit Iceland?" Leif asked slyly.

"I'd go for the hot water alone," Thorgunna replied. "As I said, I like to be warm."

"Hot water in abundance, I dare say. Iceland is one big, steaming pot of hot water. I miss that, true enough. Now, about the Irishwoman."

"Very well. If my accent pleases you so, then I shall tell you how Brigit came to be my cook. It is not a grand saga by any means, mind you, nor will it be as refreshing as a bath in one of Iceland's geyser-fed pools," Thorgunna conceded.

"Do tell," Leif encouraged.

*

Through the unshuttered western window a brilliant stream of light from the setting sun wafted in, striking Leif's flaxen hair.

How can I deny him anything? Thorgunna thought, again losing herself to the warmth of Leif's presence.

"The moments after sunset are the best time to tell tales. Lady, do share the tale," Leif said.

"Brigit came to Tiree as chattel of a Rus named Oskar Bloodstaff. Bloodstaff came to buy grain. A simple trade, that. I have no idea why he chose to drag a woman in chains into my circle. My first thought was he wanted to trade that diminutive, downtrodden girl for my barley and corn. But, it was apparent from the start of negotiations the woman was his plaything. Brigit was chained at his feet, and as we discussed the price of my grain he allowed her breasts to distract him. As if they were jumping about like little dogs, he couldn't keep from devoting much too much praise upon them. Bloodstaff is a vile, dirty man. I gathered he wanted to distract me from making a sound contract with him for my grain. I chose to ignore his behavior, and his slave, and stick to business. Then, for a fleeting moment, my eyes met hers. In her eyes I saw a desperate cry for help.

"'Who's your friend, Oskar?' I asked.

"'Payment for services rendered,' he replied.

"I told him 'payment for services rendered' was an odd name for a woman. I then asked Oskar what grand task he had completed to earn payment in the form of one small Irishwoman. He said he had ended a feud.

"I nearly fell off my stone laughing. It was quite unbelievable to me that Oskar Bloodstaff settled a dispute between Irish landowners. Of course, he claimed it was true. I then asked Brigit what the truth of the matter was. Once he allowed her to speak to me, I learned he had slaughtered her entire clan to make their lands available for confiscation by the local magistrate. He meant to sell Brigit into a brothel in Constantinople, along with my grain!"

Mesmerized by Thorgunna's voice, but incensed by the rude behavior of a fellow Norseman, Leif interjected, using the most vulgar profanity one man could hurl at another. "*Argr*. Oskar is *argr*—less than a man."

Ignoring Leif's curse, but privately agreeing, Thorgunna continued, "Oskar had bite marks on his arm. Large, gaping things. Brigit had bitten him! I could tell she was just aching to bite him again, too. To make this long story short, I traded something much more valuable than grain to Oskar for Brigit."

"Beer?" Leif asked.

"Yes, beer. I knew it was a good brew. I had no idea how good it was until the aftermath of my trading twelve barrels for Brigit came to pass. That's when Norway became interested in Tiree. Oskar presented one barrel to Olaf himself, and that's where the trouble started. I now wage a battle to protect the gold. The Tireean Gold. My beer—the grain that produces it, the land that grows the grain, and the good people who till the soil. I'm glad to have Brigit with me, for she is a true and loyal friend, but I wish Olaf Tryggvasson had never tasted my beer."

"You would have your king ignore your accomplishments?" Leif asked.

"Yes! Did I not say the king is a Christian?"

"Aye. You did. What does that have to do with your beer?"

"Olaf is mad for my beer. He would have me chained to the brewery night and day if he could. As it is, he wishes to control Tiree's production of grain and products produced from my grain, and I know ... I know he will try to control Tiree through his priests. I cannot allow Norway to control Tiree. He will start with forced baptism and end with confiscation of my holdings," Thorgunna paused. "I married to secure Tiree's safety. Quite literally, ours was a marriage to protect the beer. I must now protect Tiree on my own."

"I am sorry for the loss of your husband, Lady," Leif replied.

"Would you like to see his monument? The monument to Finn MacLean of Oban, my late husband?" Thorgunna asked.

"Yes, of course."

"Come, then. There is light enough," Thorgunna insisted, leading Leif outside. "It is not far."

She glided down the familiar slope of Gott Hill and led Leif across a grassy, flat field, through her herd of cattle and sheep, to a small stone circle.

"This is the site of an old *dun*. Here lies all that remains of Finn MacLean—at least on this side of the sea. His estates in Oban are managed by a steward. I have the right to make claim. However, to claim my rights as Widow MacLean, I must leave Tiree. And I cannot leave Tiree."

"Forgive me, Lady. I do not know the word *dun*. Is this a sacred site?" Leif asked.

"No. There are many *duns* on Tiree. They are remnants of old stone fortresses and watch towers. The islanders had to protect themselves from the Romans, the Picts, the Scots, and the Norse over the years. Over the centuries! They say Finn liked a good fight—so I put his memorial here."

"An odd way to describe the amusements your husband enjoyed," Leif said. "As if you knew him little."

Covering her mistake, not wanting Leif to know she had married and buried a husband without ever having met the man, she replied, "I knew his amusements quite well, sir."

"Of course, Lady. This monument—it is a portion of a strake and prow of a vessel, is it not?"

"It is. My husband died at sea. This debris washed ashore. We knew it was his ship. See, the strake bears a portion of the MacLean family crest," Thorgunna pointed to a visible, yet quite worn mark on one side of the strake.

"Was your husband a warrior? One who could defend your island?" Leif asked.

"No. He bred horses. And kept fighting men. Amused by stories of the Romans, he actually referred to his private army as his Gladiators. As a wedding gift, I was to receive a small contingent of men who could do more than fight with stalks of corn. However, the gift was conditional upon my producing an heir for the MacLean line. Finn died before we had children. Therefore, Tiree did not receive its army." Thorgunna sighed. "I have considered liquidating the MacLean estate to hire mercenaries, but could no more control Berserkers than the will of the king. Therefore, I return to defending my home, myself."

"Are Olaf and his Church so terrible you need the swords of mercenaries to defend against them?" Leif asked. His eyes no longer looked at hers, but lower, and Thorgunna realized that the wind had plastered the dress against her body, showing off the shape of her breasts and legs to his interested gaze.

"I have not made myself clear, have I? Olaf wishes to convert and baptize the lot of us, and thereby gain control of my island to satisfy his lust for my beer," Thorgunna reached out, taking Leif's shoulders in her hands—having to reach them first, he being much taller than she. "Leif,

Olaf does not baptize with holy oil and blessed water. Olaf baptizes with the edge of a sword. A very sharp, very strong sword."

"He kills converts?"

"No. He beheads those who do not agree to the sacraments of the Church. He controls his converts."

Leif smiled, "I shall have to pray to Odin about this."

Thorgunna shook her head, "Take your pick of my flock for the offering, Greenlander. It won't do any good."

"Blasphemy!" Leif cried, feigning horror.

"I have had dealings with the Old Ones, Leif. They cannot be trusted any more than Norway."

Leif flashed his amazing smile again. "The gods walk Tiree?"

"Indeed, they do." *Especially in my dreams. The gods are the bringers of nightmares and fear!*

"Have they shown dissatisfaction at there being no cairns to them on this fair island?" Leif turned his body, pointing at the open expanse of grassy plain. "I saw none on my ride from the shore to this hillock. Every household invites Odin in. Greenland is no exception. From what I can see, Tiree is the exception. What does Thor think about this?"

"The gods are displeased," Thorgunna replied coolly. She felt a hot bile rise from stomach to throat. *Best not to discuss the gods. Best not to think of the gods!*

"Perhaps you should sacrifice to the thunder god, Thor. Thor—for whom you were named."

"Yes, for whom I was named," Thorgunna agreed.

"And shall you sacrifice of your flock to gain his favor?" Leif asked.

"No. I refuse to follow the old ones. I choose to protect Tiree myself. I respect the gods, but do not pledge allegiance to them. They are a fickle lot."

"You are a brave woman. No wonder you are a Jarl," Leif complimented. "Lady, please forgive me, but the wind chills me. May we retire to your fire?"

"Of course, sir. Please let us go inside. It's getting dark, anyway." Very dark. It is the twilight of the gods, and I am caught in the middle of their battle for survival.

Thorgunna closed and bolted the door behind Leif. Locking out the night. Locking out her fear.

Leif piled several skins together and unabashedly reclined against them on the floor before the fire.

"Madam, I sense a sharpness of wit in Brigit that comes only from too much experience, if you understand my meaning. I've known women like her. Greenland has many such women."

Thorgunna, seated across from Leif, replied coolly, "Men do not cross her path lightly. She may be small, but her temper is worse than the storm that drove you so far off course. She fought the Rus when they had her aboard ship. She fought the Rus as they dragged her to my shore. For every ounce of flesh they took from her, she took two from them. Brigit is special—and under my protection. I'll personally run my sword through any man who tries to force his way with her."

"How very protective you are. I'll watch my step," Leif replied, stretching out. "Are all the men and women of Tiree a part of your flock, Madam Shepherdess?"

"Yes. We may be Norse and under Norway's thumb on Tiree, but I make the laws here. I enforce the laws. Women, children, and animals are protected. On this isle, one may not beat his child or dog. And the taking of liberties with the women of Tiree is punishable by death. If I were you, I'd share that with my crew."

"I've a crew of gentle souls, Lady. There will be no taking of women by force whilst we are waylaid upon your island. Of course, once your women get a look at my men, well, that's another matter," Leif bragged.

Thorgunna shook her head. "Men are always so pleased with themselves. Do all Norsemen truly believe we want only to swoon in their presence and be ravished?"

Leif shot a look of great surprise at Thorgunna. "Don't you?"

As amusing and colorful as the conversation was, Thorgunna was tired. *I must not fall asleep in his presence before this warm fire, lest the beast strike us both down!* "Leif, please make yourself at home. I, unfortunately, must retire for the evening. It is late. I rise early. We shall talk again, tomorrow, hmmm?"

"I apologize, Thorgunna. I slept for hours. Night has fallen, and I keep you awake. Please forgive me and do have a restful sleep. Although I am refreshed in many ways, I am still quite weary. I, too, shall sleep soon. Of course, madam, we could stretch out by the fire and company each other until we are both soundly sleeping. Hmmmm?"

"Good night, Leif."

"Very well, then. Good night, Lady."

****

Thorgunna entered her chamber, proud she had managed to keep so composed while with the Greenlander. *His scent alone shall be my undoing. Here is a man who fills the cup of my senses to its brim and over, and I leave him by my fire unattended! Why do I go willingly into the hell of sleep, knowing what awaits me? I am but a caged animal, all too well accustomed to its cage. The Greenlander makes me uncomfortable. The nightmare, however painful, is at least familiar. Gods help me.*

She extinguished the single oil lamp, turning the soft shadows of evening into a comfortable cage of darkness and dream. Sleep found her easily.

The dream was always the same. By day, she remembered only fleeting details of pain mixed with pleasure and darkness. By night, when her body and mind forced her to sleep, she relived the hell of the nightmare over and over again. Eight long weeks had she suffered. Eight weeks since Finn's boat had washed ashore in pieces. Eight weeks a widow to a man she had never met, never loved, and therefore, could not mourn. Eight weeks in the black arms of night's shadow beast.

****

Surrounded by sunlight, every move slow and deliberate, warmed even past the confines of her soul, Thorgunna surrendered herself to the act of true love. Unseen lips kissing her throat, phantom palms with deliciously enticing fingers cupping her breasts, Thorgunna opened her heart, her mind, her soul.

The body of light, the body of her man of light worshipped her as they made love. He had no face or voice. He cast only an impression of love and the sensual aroma of a man of the sea. Salt. Leather. Sweat. A freshness that comes only from wind in one's hair and at one's back.

"No! Over too soon!" Thorgunna cried, as the pure light of love wafted away into the mists and vapors of her dream realm. Her heart shattered, and her body went numb as a new lover took her into his arms. Hot, seductive, forbidden love.

Compelled by sinister unseen forces, Thorgunna touched her tongue lightly against each of the small white scars radiating out like spokes on a wheel around the lips of this new lover of dark-light and fear.

She brushed her tongue over the disfigured mouth. It tastes foul, she thought, trying to pull away as the hungry lips enveloped her in a long, wet kiss.

"Bring him back," she begged, turning her head away from the skillful, scarred lips.

"You do not need a little boy to amuse you when I can give you divine love," the mouth replied. "You are so strong with the sight. So beautiful in body. Men and gods would wage war for a chance to lie with you."

"I know who you are. I did not call you. I have never uttered your name in prayer. Why are you here? Why do you haunt and plague me so?"

"A killing tide comes in from Norway, dear Lady. I alone can shift the winds, and therefore, stop the tide. You have but to trust me."

"You are evil," Thorgunna said, struggling to free herself from her demon-lover's embrace.

"No, I am not. Evil is one-sided. I am so much more than that. You call upon no god to protect Tiree. But I am in a position to offer myself as, shall we say, the patron saint of your island. By night I shall make love to you in your dreams. By day I shall put Tiree to my own breast and suckle it upon the milk of Heaven."

"I don't trust you."

"Ah, do you trust the Rus traders you bargain with so deliciously well?"

"No. But that is business."

"Acknowledge me and let the trade circle commence! Mine is the trade agreement that will ensure the safety of Tiree!"

"It is considered an honor to sit in my circle. Only those I invite may do so. I have not invited you, nor do I acknowledge you," Thorgunna said.

"You have long waited for someone just like me to help you defeat the armies of change! No single man or even an army of men can defeat change, Thorgunna. I alone can protect Tiree from those threatening to control her. Erect a stone in my honor, become my consort beyond the veil of night, and the priests of Olaf—nay! Olaf, himself, will bother you no longer."

"I dedicate a monument to you, and you will send your mighty army to protect Tiree?"

"Protected Tiree shall be. However, I need no army. I am a god!"

"And should I lie under you in a dream, we would be lovers in this realm only?"

"Aye."

"Nothing more?"

"Not now. There will come a day when you will call me out and ask me to hold you as mortal man would."

"You must be summoned?"

"Again, for now, yes. My interaction amongst humankind is limited. My blood brother, and unfortunately, my keeper, fears, shall we say, my passions."

"I fear Olaf's desire and command that all Norsemen convert to the faith of the White Christ. I think perhaps I fear his love of Tireean beer even more. I also fear you will take me by force; however, Olaf, at every turn, rapes Tiree. There is no difference. You two are one and the same. The Trickster and Olaf, King of Norway. Yes, you are both evil men," Thorgunna whispered.

The Trickster smiled. He stunned her. His radiance attracted her like the light of a full moon or bonfire in the distance crackling through the black of night.

"Olaf will not harm Tiree if you heed my advice."

Thorgunna smiled. She was voluptuous. A bounty of fleshy beauty, an offering worthy of a god. "I do not believe the powers of one little godling can protect Tiree. I am unafraid to face the tide, L—" Thorgunna stopped herself from saying the demon's true name. She knew his name. She knew better than to say it aloud.

"Oh, really? Well, Lady, you should fear the flotsam and jetsam about to wash up on your shores. They come, Thorgunna. The Rus traders. And a band of storm-ravaged Norsemen. Olaf of Norway. I know, Thorgunna," the demon cooed. "I can quell your fears. Call me out. Odin has tied my hands and fetters my will amongst humankind or I would stand before you of my own accord. Please, call me out."

"Beggar."

"I beg to comfort you."

"Rather I should cut off my own right hand than call you home to Tiree."

"Do you not want to know about the coming Norseman? The Greenlander?"

****

The dream continued as always it had. Always the same. Always a shadow of promise until pain and deception burned through the fog. Thorgunna wanted to scream—wanted to awaken the Greenlander sleeping by her fire, but she could not. The dream controlled her. She was a puppet, manipulated by the god of lies. She could not change the tide of the dream, no more than she could stop the tide of change flooding her island.

****

Forsaking reason and sanity, knowing she made a grave error, but being completely unable to stop herself, the dream-Thorgunna uttered the one word she would long live to regret in any realm, "Loki."

As it had every night for eight weeks, the dream shifted from her house atop Gott Hill to her trade circle at Dun Mor a' Caoles.

Thorgunna always sat at the circle headstone, with those of importance to the session arching around her from greater to lesser significance on either side. The stone directly across from her was reserved for the man or woman she wanted as far away from her as possible, the person she trusted the least, but had to have the best eye contact with.

It was a comforting moment. This is where my power lies. No man, or god, can best me in trade negotiations, Thorgunna thought.

Her nemesis sat across from her upon the stone reserved for the likes of untrustworthy business partners. Never had a more appropriate soul took the position Loki now occupied.

Loki gracefully lifted into the air like a bird taking flight, lighting before Thorgunna, boldly taking her into his arms. "The Land Below the Waves welcomes me!" he shouted.

Breaking free, finding strength within the confines of her circle, Thorgunna pulled her lady's knife from under her cloak.

"I did not call you for a kiss!"

"A knife to gut fish with, that. What can you do to me? I am a god!" Loki laughed, then added in a rather vulgar fashion, "I've got a knife for you, however."

"I will not play your games. State your business."

"Ah, no games, then, my sweet. I bring glad tidings. News of a heart made warm and your bed made warmer," Loki said seductively.

"Made warmer by whom? By you? Pain and fear do not make good company in the linens, sir. State your trade," Thorgunna said. She turned her back on the radiant demigod. "What news is worth the price you might exact for telling it?"

"Which leads me to the question at hand, my sweet. Shall I become Tiree's protector? Or do you wish her bounty ravished by the servants of Olaf and his God? What is your word, beloved?"

"I do not trust liars."

"I may be the god of lies and tricks, but what I say now is for your benefit. To protect Tiree. Hear me now, woman. What if we make a contract on speculation? You promise to worship me, and I promise to come when called, for the season only. We can then break the contract or renegotiate the terms," Loki mused.

"What must I do?" Thorgunna asked. I know business, Loki. Do not think you will win this test of wits because you have the blood of Odin in your veins.

"Construct a monument in my honor. It needn't be ostentatious. Just something that says, 'This island is Loki's.'"

"This island is mine."

"No. It is not. It is within the realm of Olaf, King of Norway, and is already his. Unless you heed my warnings."

"What personal profit is there for me in a contract with you?"

Loki smiled. "I offer my love. In your eyes I offer something better than physical love, as well. Protection."

"Consistency could be the biggest lie of all coming from you," Thorgunna said.

Loki moved like shifting smoke around Thorgunna. "Soon, Thorgunna, soon enough, a man, a Greenlander, shall come ashore. An explorer. He shall explore you, I dare say. He comes now, his longship caught in Tiree's warm current. He and his crew are weary. The storm nearly killed them all. His ship is tattered and broken. They shall surely die without your aid. He will need rest, a bed ... your bed." Loki sniffed the air like a dog. "He comes, Thorgunna. I smell his stink from across the sea."

"How am I to pay you for this awe-inspiring prophesy since it is more than likely the case I shall not worship you?"

Loki laughed and pressed his sinewy body against Thorgunna's buxom form.

"A kiss. I want a kiss and your answer. Nothing more."

"How could I kiss you? You are perverse. I know you are the father of a serpent and mother to an eight-legged colt. You change your shape and your sex as you desire to cater to your dark fantasies," Thorgunna cursed.

"Yes, I do get around. It's so much fun when the variety of life is as vast as the universe."

"Be gone," Thorgunna commanded.

"I'll leave you now after you give me what I desire. One kiss. One kiss, and you will know—and remember—the pleasures that await you at my hands."

"Why would I allow you to make love to me when you say the Greenlander will be my lover?" A Greenlander? How barbaric!

"This is why," Loki said, spinning Thorgunna around, pulling her to him and kissing her passionately. A kiss from a god. Physical contact with a being whose parts were more than just human, more than just godly. A kiss from the soul of deceit—not just four lips pressing, wet and warm, but a surge of desire, full of wanton sexual energy.

Thorgunna felt Loki melting into her, enveloping her, pleasuring her, the kiss a blanket of arousal—teasing, promising.

"I alone can protect Tiree," Loki cooed, releasing Thorgunna, who swooned backward, catching her footing before falling.

"And to garner your protection for Tiree, what must I do?" Thorgunna asked, mesmerized by the energy of Loki's embrace.

"Agree to worship me."

"State the terms of worshiping you."

"Commit the whole of the island to me. Construct a monument to me. Sacrifice to me."

"And what is it you require we sacrifice?"

"First and foremost, the word 'we' as in your Tirisdeach, your pathetic islanders, is not quite what I had in mind. You must sacrifice to me. You."

"You wish me to spill blood in your name," Thorgunna confirmed.

"Yes," Loki replied.

"The blood of what beast?" Thorgunna asked.

"I wish your maidenhead be ruptured in my name," Loki replied, his scarred lips twisting into a demonic grin.

Thorgunna raised an eyebrow. "That sounds unpleasant, Loki. And since sacrifices are made before witnesses, terribly public."

Loki laughed, "You are so clever! I do not wish your offering to be a public one. Allow me to restate. You must give me first passage. To sanctify this land and solicit my protection, I must first sow my seed in the dark, rich soil of Tiree. But you already know this. Why question the means to the end?"

"It is my body you will take, that's why," Thorgunna scoffed.

"I need you," Loki said, trailing his skilled mouth across Thorgunna's.

Thorgunna suppressed the urge to vomit. "You speak in riddles, Loki. You say a Greenlander shall be my lover, and yet you would spoil me before even I take him into my arms."

"Think of the magic you can show him in the linens after I've taught you how to make love to a god! A mortal man cannot imagine the pleasure a woman can give when she's been infused with the blood, sweat, seed, and promise of a god. I have given you my terms, Thorgunna. Make your decision."

"I'm a businesswoman, Loki. I would like to present a counter-offer."

"Of course."

"Tiree must be protected from Norway. Our way of life will change drastically should Olaf Tryggvasson convert the Tirisdeach to the new faith against their will. No longer would any part of Tiree be mine to share with the islanders. All would belong to Norway. I cannot allow Tiree to be usurped by the will of a greedy Christian king."

Loki nodded, "Agreed."

"All islanders are free to make their own decisions regarding worship of the gods. Should I agree to make you, Loki, the Trickster, as you so aptly put it, the 'Patron Saint of Tiree,' would not all inhabitants of this Isle be forced to worship you—and only you?"

"I offer to protect the island. If specifically invoked by an islander, I would act accordingly," Loki offered.

I'm beginning to understand, Thorgunna thought.

Oh, are you? Loki replied inwardly, reading Thorgunna's mind.

"Your price for protecting Tiree is a monument and the flesh of my womanhood. What does 'protecting Tiree' entail if the islanders are not included in the contract?"

"Your island would be safe. If your island is safe, would not the islanders be safe as well?" Loki mused.

Thorgunna, long having held trade circles with deceitful, clever men trying to best her, asked her question again, "What does 'protecting Tiree' entail if the islanders are not included in the contract?"

Loki grinned devilishly, "Why haggle over minutia?"

"Tiree is not minutia," Thorgunna scolded.

"No, she is not. But, the details of our contract can wait. I see the longing in you, Thorgunna. The emptiness of your heart. The numbness fed by shattered dreams. The welling desire for my kisses blazing in your loins. I can feel the very soul of your womanhood, urging, begging, imploring me to know you."

Thorgunna blushed, hot and crimson. "Truthfully, my experience with men is limited. Your kiss did engage my senses. It's a good thing I have long been able to set aside my personal desires for the good of Tiree."

"You are Tiree. What is good for you is good for the land," Loki paused. "Thorgunna, my beautiful Thorgunna—I am good for you. Let me make love to you. Your act would be selfless and completely in the best interests of Tiree. When I am upon you, and in you, moving my body against yours, you will know it is the soil of Tiree I plow. And she will be better for it."

Darkness can hide in the light. Darkness can seduce, mesmerize, control, and decay. Loki's darkness masked as light wove a web of deception around Thorgunna, weakening her resolve.

He must have sensed his near-victory, for Loki moved in for the kill. He slid his strong arms about Thorgunna's waist and kissed her throat.

"You bargain with skill that matches my own, Loki," Thorgunna said, neither pulling away nor succumbing to the embrace. "I believe we can make a contract if you allow me to adjust the terms."

"Anything," Loki replied, drunk with the passion of power.

"You protect Tiree for two years. If you keep the wolves at bay and the islanders safe from Olaf's baptism by sword and other as of yet unknown forces that will change our way of life, I will give you that which you desire. A monument and my virginity."

Loki laughed, "Two years?"

Thorgunna nodded.

"That's too long a wait, woman."

"Why? What's two years to a god?"

"The Greenlander," Loki said. I could not stop his arrival, although I certainly tried with that last storm.

"I have no intention of bedding the Greenlander," Thorgunna replied. "Surely he is not my true love."

Loki curled his lip into a beguiling grin. "You fool only yourself, Thorgunna. Your own second sight has shown you this very man, and he is the instrument of your passing into womanhood. However, if you put your word upon it you shall not make love to this man, I agree to your terms. It will be most difficult, Thorgunna. Most difficult and entertaining, actually. Can you do it?"

"My word is law on Tiree."

"I will accept your terms provided you do not give first passage to the Greenlander. I will protect Tiree for two years, at which time payment must be made. A standing stone and the flesh of your body—not once—but as often as I demand it. I see a smoldering passion in you I do not wish to share. Two years hence, you must agree to give me leave to pleasure myself fully in your soft folds."

"What if the call of this Greenlander's maleness is too much for me to bear and I fall back into the tall grass and beg him to ravish me whether I am in love with him or not?" Thorgunna asked.

"Your strength of will and chastity of body must be maintained. Otherwise, the contract between us is void, and Tiree shall fall. You will be made to stand witness to the destruction of your way of life, and then be cast out like so much rubbish for your failure to protect the island and its people."

"And you will then…?"

"Find you—no matter where you are, and take you. Where Ketil failed, I shall succeed. As I pump the last drop of my seed into you, I promise, Thorgunna, I will kill you and capture your spirit. You will forever be mine."

"You know of Ketil?" Thorgunna choked, painfully recalling the man she had killed in self-defense four years earlier.

I was Ketil. "Of course. I know everything about you, Thorgunna."

Thorgunna moved away from the conniving demigod. "No Greenlander shall woo me into his arms."

"Into his arms is permitted. I cannot stop you from loving this man.

And, Thorgunna, you will love him. It will be your undoing, but love him, you will. You must love him enough not to lie with him, however."

"Why?"

"I'll kill him, too. Eventually."

"He's only a Greenlander," Thorgunna replied.

"Yes. Do keep that in mind as he tempts you into the linens. He is a handsome buck, I'll give him that," Loki paused, his depravity and indiscriminate sexual appetite distracting him. "Thorgunna, I do need to ask you a few more questions—before we continue our negotiations and seal the pact, if you don't mind," Loki soothed.

"Yes?" Thorgunna replied.

"Have you accepted the sacraments of the Christ? Baptism? His body and blood in Communion? Perhaps as a young child?"

"No. I thought you knew everything about me, Loki."

"Mere formalities, dearest. Just a bit of that minutia I detest so. Do you have plans to construct a church?" Loki brushed his beard against Thorgunna's throat, pricking her with his wire-like whiskers.

"I would do so only to protect myself from you," Thorgunna replied.

He laughed. "With me you are thoroughly protected."

"That needs to be proved," Thorgunna replied.

"How shall we seal our contract, Thorgunna?" Loki asked.

"I clasp wrists with my new partner and the contract is recorded before witnesses," Thorgunna replied.

"We have no witnesses in this realm," Loki said. "But do take my hand, Thorgunna. Let me help you record our bargain in such a manner you shall recall it for the rest of your life."

"Our bargain is such that we do not require the formalities of custom and tradition. You are a god. Is not your word promise enough?"

"Ah, yes. Of course my word is enough," Loki lied. "I, however, require we seal our contract, Thorgunna. You cannot deny me the opportunity to show you what you have to look forward to."

"I will not lie with you, Loki. I will not be seduced into the linens."

"You may stand," Loki replied, his physical body shifting into a swirling mass of color and lights.

Thorgunna gasped as Loki transformed into his true form—a haze of dancing flames. The son of frost giants and blood brother of Odin moved about her like a wind-borne feather, burning her clothing away with icy blue flames, licking at her nipples and stomach, swirling under her back, across her buttocks and between her legs, stinging her with alternating freezing and scalding waves of unearthly ecstasy before flickering away into the graying skies above Tiree.

Completely overcome by Loki's spirit-being, Thorgunna stifled a scream of panic and pleasure, her internal organs seemingly exploding in rapturous waves of bliss followed closely by the pain of fire's kiss.

Beaten down, tasting blood in her mouth, his snake's tongue trailing across her lips, tasting her sweet life-force, Loki lashed out with his greater serpent, breaching the barrier of Thorgunna's body, spewing its venom upon her and in her like hard rain. "The pact is made!"

Chapter 2

Thorgunna awoke screaming. She sprang from her bed, her heart racing, drenched in sweat. She trembled against the doorframe.

Leif burst into her chamber, nearly toppling her. He had an ax in hand, poised to strike.

Thorgunna caught her balance and shot Leif a look of perturbation. She felt it on her face like an angry mask. "Sir, you are nude."

"Lady, I heard you cry out!" he panted, the privacy drape falling softly into place as he walked further into Thorgunna's chamber. "I assumed you were under attack. I rush to your aid, and you scold me for not putting my breeches on! Really, Lady."

She coughed nervously. *If there is a god upon the island to which a monument should be raised, it is this man's body that should provide inspiration.* She felt faint. Not from the nightmare. From the flush of sheer desire coursing through her as Leif stood unabashedly naked before her. "It was a nightmare. I am prone to them. I should have warned you. I do appreciate your pluck, however."

Leif yawned. "I need a drink." He made no effort to cover himself.

"I am drenched from perspiration of the battle I waged in my sleep. Would you mind?" Thorgunna pointed to the room's exit. "Pull the drape closed as you leave."

Leif smiled. "What kind of man would I be if I turned away from the sight of a beautiful woman changing her nightdress?"

"A gentleman."

"I would prefer to watch you undress."

Thorgunna rolled her eyes. "As you wish. I am too uncomfortable to argue with you." She peeled her sweat-soaked overdress from her body.

She tried desperately to ignore the normal response of Leif's body. His was not the first erection she'd seen, but his was the first she thought she might like to touch. Her lurid thoughts only escalated as Leif crossed his arms and displayed his ample manhood proudly.

"You are a rare beauty, Thorgunna. You make me…"

"I can see what I make you well enough, sir. Please, dress."

Leif chuckled and turned. Thorgunna sucked in her breath at the sight of his taut backside.

She donned a dry chemise and met Leif in the main room with an earthen cup of mead. She pulled a shawl around her shoulders.

Leif, bare-chested, but with breeches donned, took the cup graciously. "Are you cold?"

"Not really."

"Then why hide the curve of your breasts and the other treasures of your body from me?"

"I'm afraid it might get too hot if I leave myself open to your penetrating gaze."

Leif nodded and lifted his cup. "Indeed. I'll drink to that, and to that which haunts your dreams," he toasted.

"An odd thing to say," Thorgunna replied. She sipped from her own cup.

"My mother taught the best way to conquer a frost giant is to give it a hug," Leif said. He drained his cup and refilled it himself.

"Ah, yes. My mother intoned similar advice. Embrace your fears," Thorgunna saluted.

"Aye. Embrace them. Get to know them. Defeat them."

"Melt the frost giant with the warmth of a hug," Thorgunna said.

"Exactly," Leif agreed.

Thorgunna moved to the window and peered out. "It is hours 'til dawn. I see no lights from the homes spiraling down Gott Hill. Even that colicky calf is quiet."

"All the more for us." Leif smirked and poured another. "I'm sure it is not a frost giant you fight in your sleep, Lady. What troubles you so?"

Neither willing nor ready to share her dream-world contract with the devil, Thorgunna changed the subject. "I have something better than mead, you know."

Leif admired Thorgunna's round form against the glow of the embers from the fire. "Tireean Gold?" he guessed.

"Yes, Tireean Gold," Thorgunna said. "Awaken the fire, Leif. I'll bring a keg."

"You do not wish to discuss your nightmares with me, do you?" Leif asked.

"I cannot."

Thorgunna walked across the room, the glow of the newly stoked fire brightening the dimness as Leif stirred the embers and added driftwood to the flames. She returned with a small keg. Leif took it readily, stopping himself from making a comment about her womanly form barely shadowed by the fabric of her shift.

"This is it. My livelihood and the bane of my existence. Tireean Gold."

Leif dipped his cup, filling it to its brim with the amber-colored liquid. He downed the cup's contents in two large gulps.

The beer was unlike any he had ever tasted. "Smooth is too simple a word to describe this beer, Lady. It looks like gold and tastes almost effervescent. It is vibrant and delicious. It is sweet, yet not too much so. I can see why Olaf of Norway covets it so, and why your late husband was willing to defend it."

Thorgunna reached into a leather bag beside the hearth, removing two silver-inlaid drinking horns, "Use this. It is more fitting than an earthen cup."

"Lovely horns," Leif replied, using his cup as a ladle. "Lady, is it not odd we are alone? Even in Greenland there are conventions regarding how men and women may interact."

"Are you afraid of me, Greenlander?" Thorgunna asked.

"Are you not afraid of me? I've been at sea for quite some time. I am a man—and you are—"

"A woman. Yes. I am a woman. I am also a businesswoman, skilled horsewoman, farmer, brewmistress, widow, and the village witch. I can defend myself. I have defended myself," she paused. "Do I need to defend myself?"

Leif laughed. "No, Lady. I shall not ravish you."

"And for that reason, sir, we are without chaperone."

"You had me pegged as a gentleman from the start."

"Yes. Otherwise, you would not be here. You should know this, too. I am never truly alone."

"The large man with the grimace?" Leif guessed.

"Thorok. My 'uncle,' you might say."

"I see." Leif downed the contents of his horn, immediately filling it again. "So when did you defend yourself? The Battle of the Sheaves?"

"I defended Tiree at the Battle of the Sheaves, true enough. I also defended myself on another occasion." *I defend myself each night!*

"Fill your horn and share this tale with me. Brigit's saga left me breathless. Now, do share the saga of Thorgunna's sword!"

"You tease me," Thorgunna frowned. "And it wasn't a sword. I used the knife on my **lyklakippa**. It has been my savior on more than one occasion. I suspect your mother, too, has such a ring of keys at her belt."

"Indeed, Lady. But in your case, I dare say, your keys jingle quite provocatively when you walk as if to say, 'Here goes a powerful woman.' My mother's ring of keys does not sing in the same manner. They serve primarily as a warning for my father to hide."

"You continue to tease me."

"*Nei*, Lady. I don't tease. I am a listener. You are a skilled storyteller. I want nothing more than to lie beside your fire, drink your fine beer, and listen to you speak. After sharing the tale of your battles, perhaps you will speak to me of your nightmares. Speaking evil's name does not invite it to stay."

"You are mad. And I did not say I dream of evil," Thorgunna replied. *Though I do. I do dream of evil.*

"I nearly lost my life and the lives of my crew at sea. I relish the sound of your voice and the sensation of this fine stone floor lined with soft skins against my body. Indulge me, Lady. I am a man whose life was restored to him by a tempest. And it is that storm I shall bless, for it is she who brought me to you."

Ignoring Leif's attempt at seduction, Thorgunna drained her horn. "Very well, Leif. But be forewarned, you may find my company less of a blessing after you hear this saga."

"I do not believe I shall ever tire of your voice, Lady."

Thorgunna smiled at Leif. *His presence makes me see beyond the pain Loki inflicts. In Leif, I see the enlightened side of fear. That which makes one stronger. That fear which renews, not controls. I must not love you, Leif Eiriksson! For if I do, I must love you enough to make you leave Tiree and never return. And then my thoughts return to the vision of your member at full mast, and I am undone with desire. How shall I fight this?*

"Lady?" Leif questioned, returning her smile.

"Yes, the saga. I'm afraid my nightmare left me a bit numb of mind. Let's see ... after my father, Vagn of the Heavy Hand, died, I—being his only heir remaining upon the isle—became Master of Tiree."

Leif laughed, beginning to feel the effects of Thorgunna's potent beer. "Vagn of the Heavy Hand!"

"My nickname for my late father. I loved him dearly, but he was a harsh man. The *Tirisdeach*—the name we islanders call ourselves—worked his land for him."

"I salute your late father!" Leif toasted.

"My father had a governing council. Old men with closed minds and set ways. From the very moment I assumed my role as the island's chieftain, they hated me. I believe they wished I were my father's son rather than his daughter. My brother left the island long ago. He felt compelled to explore the very faith I shun. But to the story ... I pointed out to them every time the council convened, I was Vagn's heir, and I, not they, had the final say in all matters. Quite frankly, I was terrified."

"How old were you?" Leif asked.

"Sixteen. It was only four years ago, Leif."

"Go on," Leif insisted.

"Although I was not wily enough to pick up on the council's plot four years ago, I see in hindsight they wished not to kill me, but keep me occupied with matters of the heart, and thereby, in the birthing straw and out of their way. The council insisted I accept suitors. They said it was my father's will to see me wed. Suitors came from all around the Isles. My father's cousin, Ivar, even came all the way from Gotland to win my hand. I loathe Ivar. He returns to Tiree each summer, always trying to woo me into the linens."

Thorgunna dipped Leif's earthen cup into the keg of beer, transporting and pouring the nectar of grain and clever brewing techniques to her own silvered horn. She drank the contents quickly, delighting in the sensation of the frothiness melting down her throat and the heady aroma loosening her tongue.

"The spring after I turned sixteen, Ketil Arngrimsson came to Tiree. He was the nephew of councilman Loxsson. Ketil…" Thorgunna paused.

"Is this terribly difficult for you?" Leif asked, genuinely concerned at the pained expression upon Thorgunna's lovely face and wrinkle across her perfect brow.

Thorgunna filled her horn, and to Leif's amazement, drank its contents in three hard gulps. "Yes. Ketil was coison poated with honey. Delicious to taste, but bitter once in. No. Poison coated with honey. Oh, my."

"How so?" Leif asked, amused by Thorgunna's burgeoning signs of intoxication.

Thorgunna filled her horn again, pausing before taking her first sip. "I killed him, Leif. He attacked me, and I killed him." She finished the horn. "Gods, I make good beer. But I digress."

Thorgunna took a drunken breath, then continued. "Ketil was my first serious suitor. My first kiss. I should have realized he was nothing more than a usurer hired by the council to keep me preoccupied. After a few weeks of innocent courtship, Ketil and I rode to Caoles, on the northern tip of Tiree. I was forbidden to go off on horseback with a suitor. My late mother's rule. I did it anyway. He insisted so firmly. I was like a fish on the end of his line. He had me trapped."

Leif studied the intense look on Thorgunna's face. "You are a fascinating woman, Thorgunna. I am intrigued by both your grace and iron will."

"At Caoles, he proposed. We sat upon his cloak in the warm sand, and kissed. Nothing more. When I refused his offer of marriage, he became outraged. He then informed me the cloak we were upon was, in all actuality, our marriage bed, as the council had signed a contract of marriage with Ketil in my stead. Shocked and horrified, I pulled away from his embrace. I struck him across the face. He struck back. He then pinned me under him and insisted I give him what a wife should give her husband on their wedding day. I broke free, but he caught me, and struck again. I could taste mouth in my blood." Thorgunna paused again, forming her words carefully. "I could taste blood in my mouth. It was the first time I tasted my own blood beaten out of me by the hand of another. Not the last, unfortunately, but that is a story for another time. Ketil forced me to my knees, pulling my hair, pushing my face into the vile bulge in his breeches. He demanded I give him relief."

"What did you do?" Leif gasped.

"When his beast pushed its way into my mouth, nearly choking me, I ... bit ... down."

"You bit him! You bit him ... *there*?" Leif exclaimed, casting a glance at his own crotch.

"I did. He nearly beat me to death for it, too. But, as I lay in the sand, dazed, my eyes swollen shut, I still had the presence of mind to defend myself. The knife on my ring. I said it is my savior. I use it to cut thread, gut fish. Slice the throat of a rapist. As Ketil came upon me, ready to take me, I loosed the blade and plunged it into his heart. A small blade, I forced it hard to its bone hilt in that black-hearted bastard's chest. My blade—this very blade—tasted the blood of a dying man."

Thorgunna held aloft her **lyklakippa** bearing the knife, waving it about like a victory banner. "This lovely thing ... it has never been far from my reach since. I felt a surge of power and success I have never felt again. I found the act exhilarating."

"Here is a woman who could have been raped and killed and made a part of Tiree's history rather than its future. The Lady should have been a mercenary," Leif laughed.

"Aye! Had I been born a man I might have been a mercenary, indeed. A berserker! My father named his daughter well, did he not?" Thorgunna said, her black eyes dancing.

"Thunder warrior," Leif translated. "Forgive my loose tongue, for it is the drink, but I must have you. You are completely marvelous."

"Yes, I am Thorgunna, Lady Jarl of Tiree whose name means 'thunder warrior,'" Thorgunna boasted, ignoring Leif's seductive words.

"And you say you are not a storyteller!" Leif raised his horn, saluting Thorgunna. They drained the contents of the vessels, immediately filling them again.

"When I was well enough, I banished the council, burned their estates, and scattered the ashes into the sea."

"Remind me not to make you angry," Leif laughed.

"I am a survivor, Leif. I fought my way out of a torrid underworld of deceit by my own countrymen and shall fight against the Hell of the Christians with the same zeal. Tiree is free. And so she must remain. Therein lies the name and nature of my true enemy: *change*. I know it. Change for the worse. Change for the better will not arrive by way of Norway and the Holy Roman Church."

"Norway will back away in fear from you, Lady. Never have I met a more powerful or desirable woman. I thank you for sharing your saga, Lady. You are a strong, beautiful, fascinating woman. I also thank you most heartily for sharing this excellent concoction. Tell me, please, since our tongues have been loosened and we now share more intimate moments of our lives…"

"Yes?" Thorgunna said.

"This is a difficult question, but I am curious. Did not the attack by Ketil leave you scarred and bitter? When your husband reached out for you in the night, were you afraid?"

"I got over it. I had an island to run. I had to press on."

"And your husband?"

Thorgunna looked straight into Leif's eyes, carefully enunciating her reply, "He never knew."

"I am honored you shared with me a part of your life you kept from your husband. You are remarkable. Thank you, again," Leif said.

Leif and Thorgunna, the hearth fire cracking and popping behind them, clinked cups in the keg as they simultaneously attempted to fill their horns.

"I like your beer, woman," Leif said, draining his horn messily.

"I know. All men love my beer. It is magic, you know."

"Yes, the magic of one who knows how to raise flavorful grains. To you, master gardener, Jarl Thorgunna!" He lifted his cup in her honor.

She saluted him in return, draining her cup. "You must regale me with your adventures now, sir."

"I have had too much beer to not embellish my life's story to a greater degree than normal. I'm afraid even a single question might lead to a great many lies."

Thorgunna sighed. "Greenland must be quite wild and uncivilized. I'm sure there are many things to share,"

"Very well! Very well. My father moved us from Iceland when I was twelve. He'd been banished for a killing, and being a man who loves a challenge, took us to Greenland. A more unsettled place than Iceland, I dare say. Soon, many Icelanders sailed to our shores, and over the years, a thriving community has been established. That is why it is time for recognition by Olaf. The inclusion into Norway's trade routes will fill Greenland's coffers."

"That is not a very exciting story, Leif."

"I didn't promise you excitement. I am an emissary for Greenland. I am the oldest son of Eirik the Red. My dreams for my future are more interesting than my life has been."

Thorgunna closed her eyes, drinking in the warmth of the fire and the heat of the body of the man across from her. "You dream of discovery."

"You are a witch!"

"I said as much, did I not? I am gifted with a strong second sight. I can call it out—but more often, it calls me."

"Ah, yes. Second sight. My mother, too, has it. She's the one who told my father there was a land beyond the shoals and mists to the west of Iceland. She told me I would sail even further west, someday."

"I see that as well. But I also see you have a cross to bear and a strong mission in your icy home."

Leif smiled, "A cross to bear? What an odd expression."

"I have heard the priests use it when they sail from Ireland to hold Mass at the ruins of St. Patrick's Chapel. It means you have a burden of the heart which must be fulfilled no matter how painful an experience it may be."

"Hmmm. I shall hire men to bear my cross for me. Perhaps I'll take a strong wife," Leif smirked.

"One's mission is his own. Only you will be able to fulfill it," Thorgunna replied. *Take me seriously, Leif! I am quite clairvoyant.* "Tell me more about Greenland, Leif. I fear I shall not sleep at all the remainder of this night, and having company and good conversation is a blessing."

Leif bowed his head. "As you wish, Lady."

He pushed away the lid to the cask and dipped his horn. "Greenland. Well, it's true Greenland is not as green as my father proclaimed, but portions of it are quite fertile. I believe our population is nearly a thousand souls, many of whom are related to my father. The more children my father begets the more opportunities for growth there are. He is the father of a new nation."

"How many children by how many wives?" Thorgunna asked, giggling.

"My father has one wife according to the rites of Thor. He has many wives according to the code of Eirik. I have two brothers by my mother, one half-sister, Freydis, by Eirik's mistress in Iceland. I have a dozen or more other brothers and sisters by his various lovers. He is able to care for all his women and children, however, so there is no outcry of neglect from any. Mother, however, does threaten to divorce him from time to time."

"Your father is a colorful man," Thorgunna interjected, making a play on Eirik the Red's name.

"He is that, indeed." Leif rolled onto his back. "At daybreak I must see to the repairs of my ship, Lady. Left idle, my men will grow restless and once they discover your beer—well, Tiree may not be ready to have a dozen Greenlandic sailors running amok."

"I've corn to tend near Bhasapol and nets to mend. Many of the field workers are busy with a more pressing task right now. My beer is ready to be kegged for shipment, too. Takes many hands," Thorgunna replied. She fell back, head against the floor, her chest heaving in short, drunken breaths.

"Where's your brewery?" He immersed a finger into his horn, then held the drop over Thorgunna's open mouth. "You're drunk."

"I'm not. This is my beer. It doesn't affect me. And, Leif, my brewery is well-hidden lest I be robbed of a year's worth of hard work," Thorgunna replied.

"How much beer do you produce?" he asked, rolling onto his belly.

"Never enough. I can never keg enough beer to satisfy the Rus, and Norway. The games of chance will soon be afoot, Leif. Traders come to fill their ships with my gold, playing the most insane games of chance with the weather. Who will get here first? Who will get the best trade? Who will test the winds and win? Who will test the winds, and lose? Who will get to Norway first with their shipment and contract with the king for another sailing? The summer storms are the most fierce. Fools, the lot of them. I'm sure much of my beer lies at the bottom of the ocean with the bones of my husband." Thorgunna laughed awkwardly.

Leif, unsure if he should laugh at her joke, ignored the comment of her husband's death. "I know about the storms, indeed. Back on Greenland, my father makes a drink from fermented potatoes. For my tastes, it makes a better lamp oil. His face becomes as red as his hair when he drinks."

"Does he drink often?"

"He drinks often," Leif replied.

"Does he beat his wives or animals?" Thorgunna asked.

Leif rolled his eyes, laughing. "He becomes quite amorous when he drinks. He goes from woman to woman seeking pleasure until he passes out."

"Your father must be hot-blooded indeed if he's able to perform after drinking so," Thorgunna smirked.

"Eirik says Thor enters him when he drinks and that his prowess comes from the blood of a god in his veins."

"Thor is no prize for a lover, Leif. Why do you think he has such a temper? Why do you think a short-handled hammer fits his hand so well? A man and his weapon are often well suited. Small hands. Small weapon. Thor is frustrated over the size of his godhood," Thorgunna said with assurance.

Leif laughed, "You speak so boldly." He glanced awkwardly at his sword.

"It's my house, I'll speak as I wish. And don't worry, Leif, your sword suits you. Quite well," Thorgunna replied. *What am I saying? I am not prone to this bawdiness, at all. It must be the drink talking.*

Leif set his horn aside, shifting his body closer to Thorgunna's. "How do you know Thor's weapon so well?" The fresh scent of flowers perfuming her hair intoxicated him—almost more than the beer.

"I've seen Thor in my dreams."

Leif moved within inches. "Has he made love to you? Surely not as thoroughly as I will make love to you."

"You tease me again, Greenlander."

"Idle play, madam. But I must say—" Leif finished his drink. "—you have honored me by sharing so much of your life with me, Lady." The beer had affected him as beer should affect a man. Liquid courage coursed through his veins.

"I have put too much beer into my mouth and too many words out," Thorgunna sighed.

"You are a remarkable woman, Thorgunna," Leif replied.

"You say that only because you need shelter and a hafe saven for your men while you repair your ship," Thorgunna remarked.

"I do not require a hafe saven for my men. A safe haven, yes. And Tiree fits that bill quite well. However, I would believe you were remarkable under any circumstance," Leif said.

"I'm sorry, Leif. Did I misspeak? I meant no insult."

"Make it up to me," Leif suggested.

"And how could I do that? What's been said has been said," Thorgunna asked.

Leif hovered over her and lightly kissed her.

Thorgunna broke into laughter. "You call that a kiss?"

Surprised, Leif kissed her again, harder.

Thorgunna returned the kiss. She parted her lips slightly, but didn't allow Leif's tongue to slip between them.

Thorgunna enjoyed the sensation of the Greenlander's kiss upon her mouth and his body against hers. He's so clever. I'm too drunk. His thumb moves across my breast as we kiss. I like it. I want more. He ignites a fire below in those places I thought no man would ever inflame. Oh, dear… what in the name of Hel, Queen of the Underworld, am I doing? Is this what it is like to be a normal woman? She rolled her shoulders and moved her ample bosom closer to Leif. His hands caressed her through the fabric of her shift as her arms went around his neck.

*

Leif withdrew slightly. "You are as delicious as your beer. I must have you."

Thorgunna broke off the kiss, moaning. "I feel ill."

"I've never heard that from a woman I've kissed before," Leif replied.

She rose. "You need a bath."

Thorgunna pushed him off and rose on unsteady feet. She shuffled across the house toward her room. I cannot allow any part of the dream to come to pass. I must not allow his touch. His kiss. Him! He is not my man of light. He must not be! For if he is, then the dream is true and the contract is true, and I am bound and chained at the feet of the god of lies. In her drunken stupor, Thorgunna looked hard at the Greenlander lying upon her skins, basking in the light of her fire, rising on occasion to drink her beer. I want him. By the gods, I want him.

"I've not yet been shown the trough! Madam Jarl, I do not wish to breach etiquette, and if I have interpreted your actions of moments ago falsely, please forgive me," Leif began.

"Go on," Thorgunna said. "But be quick about it. The beer has hit me hard tonight."

"You have shared intimate moments of your life with me and returned my kiss. My hands have held no greater treasure than your soft breasts. You make me wild with desire. Moreover, it is a fact you are quite young to be a widow, and I am far from the comforts of my home," Leif began.

"My home is not comfortable?"

"I need a woman in my bed."

"Well, Greenlander, it's nice of you to at least seek permission before you woo my women into the linens. That is, of course, if any of them will have you! I will not see the bellies of my women swell with the progeny of absent fathers."

"I am not so careless with my affections as to leave a trail of fatherless children in my wake."

"Whom, then, do you have in mind as your Tireean consort, Leif?" Thorgunna asked.

"You, of course."

His request writes his own death sentence! I cannot. I must not. "I do not deny a certain attraction between us. But do not think that I give you leave to soil my linens with your salty body, sweat, and seed. I am your host. It is not done."

"Thorgunna, in Greenland we live hard, short lives. We take what we want and make the most of each day. Share my bed whilst my crew and I rest upon this fair Isle. Tell me you have no lover amongst these honest farmers who look to you for support and comfort. I may have to kill him." He felt his resolve weakening just enough to make him drink another horn of beer.

Thorgunna walked to the center of the room near the hearth, nearer Leif. It was an unsteady trek. She felt as though she might swoon.

"I am no man's mistress."

"I did not mean to insult you, Lady," Leif said. In one swift motion, he pulled Thorgunna onto the sheepskins. "I meant the comment as a compliment. You are a rare beauty, and even rarer still, a woman of great wisdom and power. There are so few of us born to a high station. We belong together. I must have you." He brushed his lips from forehead to brow to cheek then lips.

"Your beard is as soft as cornsilk and nearly the same color," Thorgunna said. She involuntarily moaned as an arrow of desire shot from her loins to her breasts. Each part of her body whereupon Leif rested his lips became alive with a tingling, reverberating sensation, chilling her. She curled her toes as Leif trailed his kisses down her chin to her throat and back again, stopping teasingly just below her lips.

"I want you, Thorgunna," he whispered. "I must feel your heat. I need inside you like a ship needs a safe port. Bring me home, woman. Allow me safe harbor within your sweet body."

Her mind a hurricane of drunkenness and her body acting upon instinct, she could not move away. She spread her legs. She responded to his kiss and found their tongues speaking a language unknown to her. *Bliss.* His kisses breached the boundaries of her soul.

Ketil's kiss had been insincere and self-serving. Loki's nightmare kiss had been intense—like a red-hot poker into butter. The desire incited by it, like drowning.

Leif's kiss drew her away with promises she knew were real. As pure and light as Ketil and Loki's were dark and invasive.

Not moving his mouth from hers, Leif ran his hands along Thorgunna's legs, lifting her shift, caressing her. He slipped a hand inside her open bodice to fondle her breasts.

Thorgunna, drunk from the beer, addled by fatigue, blazing with unfulfilled carnal desires, and surrounded by the warmth of the fire and the man beside her, knew she should say the words "…stop … please … no more."

Leif moved his mouth from Thorgunna's, to kiss the exposed dark pink point of flesh on her breast. It was erect. Aroused.

Thorgunna felt lost. Dazed, flushed and unable to form simple words, she could do nothing to stop the sweeping waves of pleasure pulling her deeper and deeper into the warm pool of Leif's desire.

Even as Leif explored her breasts with his mouth and her inner thighs with his hands, she could not fight through the drunken swoon to move away. Finally, one clear thought wafted through her muddled mind.

I don't want him to die! Thorgunna found her mind unable to make her body react in any way except how Leif obviously intended.

As the sensation of Leif's swollen member pressing against her reached her confused and overstimulated mind, she gasped. He'd slipped out of his breeches. *Clever bastard!* Her quim responded with a flood of readiness.

"Yes," she whispered, unable to control the animal passion welling within her.

"I think I shall enjoy my time on Tiree," Leif replied.

Thorgunna was completely lost in the Greenlander's embrace. He could have held a knife to her throat, and she would have never known it. Never had an ocean of desire enveloped her so.

A painful memory surfaced dimming the glow of the moment. A memory of scarred lips kissing her own. Of a serpent's tongue, dripping with honeyed poison, lying to her. *Leif's death by Loki's hand must not ... I must stop ... this ... now!*

Thorgunna pulled away, quickly covering her breasts. Her erect dark nipples peeked out embarrassingly through the linen. She folded her arms across her chest to hide them. Shooting a steely gaze up into Leif's own dancing eyes, she cursed. "You take advantage of my drunkenness, sir. You stripped me of my clothing with the magic of one kiss!"

"You didn't seem to mind," Leif replied.

"We cannot," Thorgunna insisted.

"Aye. We can," Leif replied. He stroked his erection. "We can, indeed."

Thorgunna, the effects of the beer barely lessened, wanted to scream from oppressive anticipation, excitement, passion, and fear.

Leif slipped his fingers between her legs, teasing and pulling her outer woman's lips, parting them to more diligently caress and fondle the treasures hidden therein.

"Your words and your body do not agree, Thorgunna. Your mouth says 'no,' but your body invites me. Lips can lie. A woman's readiness for a man is truthful in every instance. Don't be afraid, Thorgunna." He moved his fingers deeper between Thorgunna's legs, seeking the entrance to her cave of riches, hoping to use her own woman's nectar to smooth his way. "You want me, Thorgunna. I aim to oblige you."

He hesitated as his fingers met resistance as they sought deeper recesses. "You are as tight as a virgin, woman. How long has it been since you took a man to your bed?" He was completely ready to make love to the woman beneath him. His cock had never been harder. He stroked Thorgunna with one hand, and his own sex with the other. "A river flows from you, woman. It shall ease my way and end your drought, no matter how long it has been since a man has filled you." He carefully rolled her clitoris between his thumb and forefinger. Her wetness and heat told him she was ready. Her breaths were short and fast. Her nipples like rock. "I'm afraid, dear lady, should I enter you now I shall climax all too quickly, for I have never felt a stronger need than I do at this moment. I think it would be wise for me to pause and see to your pleasure first."

Thorgunna could not keep her eyes open. All she wanted was him. Inside her. On top of her. Filling her, stretching her. She writhed under his touch. Urged his gentle touch a little left or a little right. She wanted the climax. The reward.

After what seemed like a lifetime of insatiable teasing by the barbaric

Greenlander, she could hold back no longer. Her passion erupted in all directions. She quaked and moaned, and he slid two large fingers into her. All he could. His member was easily twice as thick. He wanted to fill her, but she was not ready for so large a man inside her. Yet.

He scissored his fingers a little and pressed his thumb against her clitoris. She responded with one final shudder. She went completely limp under Leif, embarrassed.

Leif laughed. "No need to feel shame. The flush in your cheeks becomes you. I would like to drink from your well, but I swear that if I do not bury myself inside you this moment I shall expire. He lifted his fingers and tasted them. "Oh, indeed. You are sweet. But the needs of my cock outweigh the needs of my tongue." He ran a finger along her swollen clitoris. "Oh, but woman, your honey calls to me. I cannot help myself. I must have one little taste. I shall crave the sensation of my tongue against you too dearly otherwise."

He knelt between her legs and kissed her labia, then rolled his tongue across her clitoris.

Thorgunna arched her back and gasped. Instinctively, she grabbed a handful of his hair and pushed his face into her quim.

Leif had meant only to taste.

To savor her sweet post-orgasmic nectar.

He found himself unable to stop. He pushed up her hips and spread her labia open with his fingers and inserted his tongue into her. He used the bridge of his nose to titillate her clitoris as he lapped hungrily. He inserted one finger inside her, then two. He moved them like they were his cock and sucked her clit into his mouth.

Thorgunna bucked and shook. Her legs and arms flailed about. She cried out and held on fast to his head as he drew her into a second powerful orgasm.

Even as the final spasms of her climax passed—before she could protest or crawl or fight, Leif quickly rolled her over, slapping her firmly on her backside.

"My turn," he said. "I will be gentle, but I must be firm, for you are so deliciously tight, and I am not a small man. It does not matter ... you will become accustomed to my size and will relish my penis inside you soon enough."

What does he want of me? Drunken. Flushed. Exhausted and her privates still engorged and sensitive, she visualized their position and the answer came plainly.

He urged her onto all fours.

She felt the hard head of his member press against her quim. *He means to take me like a dog!*

"Oh, Lady, you've a fine backside, indeed," Leif said. He lifted her shift and squeezed her buttocks. He rubbed a wet fingertip around her anus, then aimed his cock at her wetness.

Thorgunna shuddered as his hardness teased her opening.

Every nerve in her body tingled with readiness. She wanted this. She wanted him to drive his way into her and make her come again. She pushed back to engage his member.

Then fell unconscious—passed-out drunk on her own beer.

*

Leif stopped dead when he realized the woman under him had passed out.

"Damn!" he cursed. He stroked his hard cock and hit it against her bottom.

So beautiful in the firelight. So desirable. So oblivious. *If I were another man I would take her from behind and then ram my cock into her ass for good measure. Oh, my countrymen have had their way with* women, indeed. It is the Viking way. But I am not like them. I cannot take a woman without her being, at the very least, awake for the act. He straightened Thorgunna's legs and covered her with a wool blanket, leaving her on the floor beside the hearth. "Another night, then, Lady. Sleep well."

The remainder of that night was difficult for Leif. He was completely uncomfortable even though the pallet was better than he'd ever slept on before. The linens smelled of her. Her scent filled the room. "Damn her scent! She fills the confines of my soul with her woman's perfume," he whispered, wanting her. Wanting her badly.

"I'm likely to see her tomorrow and end up beating my member against the wall to end the ache in my groin. I'll smash my head against the same wall. For a moment, then, I shall not want her so."

He did not sleep.

Chapter 3

Dawn never really came to the isle as the dark of another storm blanketed Tiree, rain soaking the already saturated ground.

Leif was alone by the same fire that only a few short hours before had witnessed his failed attempt to mount the Lady Jarl. Thorgunna, he presumed, had awakened from her drunken stupor sometime during the night, and had moved to the privacy of her chamber while she recovered from her inebriated state.

He stirred the coals in the hearth, sparking them anew. "Oh, she's asleep, all right. I hear her breathing from beyond that impenetrable barrier of heavily stitched fabric."

Leif had controlled the urge to relieve his throbbing sexual tension in the folds of Thorgunna's flesh as she lay sleeping by the fire the night before. *Though my conscience is clear, my body is aching.* "I could have used her any way I chose, and she'd have been none the wiser. Damn my sense of morality." He stirred the embers of the great hearth again. "None of my Greenlandic lovers hold a torch to Thorgunna's beauty, or enthrall me as much as she. I could spend a lifetime with any of my countrywomen and still not crave one of them as deeply as I do Thorgunna."

Greenland's women had taught him early how to please a woman just as Greenland's men had taught him to hunt and farm. One learned what one could from whichever teacher was available. The long Greenlandic winters were the proving ground for many young men.

Leif smiled. *I was an apt pupil. Thorgunna's reaction to my touch proved that. By Odin, I want her!*

The heavy wood and iron door of Thorgunna's house suddenly burst open, startling Leif from his lustful fantasies. Soaked and windblown, Brigit entered carrying a large woven bag. Barely breaking stride, she slammed the door shut with a foot as she moved quickly to the table.

"Breakfast, sir. I took the bread from my hearth but minutes ago," she said, laying out meat, bread, and soft cheese upon the table. "Eat well."

The door burst open a second time as Leif's best friend and second aboard ship, Sigurdur—Siggi—slipped quickly into the house and out of the pouring rain.

Brigit stood silent for a moment, then asked, "Well it took you long enough to get here, now, didn't it? I bade you come to Gott Hill some time ago."

Siggi smiled. "I was left in awe of your beauty, madam. I could neither speak nor walk for so very long that I wonder now if I move in a dream."

"Rubbish!" Brigit replied. "You were too sick from drink to arrive before this fine fare had a chance to grow gray from age."

"Will you Irish please stop? I'm hungry!" Leif laughed.

Siggi joined Leif by the fire.

"Are either of you Christian men?" Brigit asked.

"I am when it suits me, lass." Sigurdur winked.

"A blessing for the food—should it be Christian or heathen?" she asked.

Leif piped up. "Heathen."

"Thank you," Brigit replied. Then quoting the Words of the High One, she blessed the food in Odin's name, "The newcomer needs fire. His knees are numb. A man who has made his way over the mountains needs food and fresh linens."

"Will you be seein' to the linens yourself, lass?" Sigurdur asked. Leif slapped his friend's shoulder.

"You've been too long away from an Irish woman, sir. I'm a better man than you even in me skirts!"

Leif quickly interjected before his first mate could egg on Brigit any further, "Thank you for breakfast, Brigit. Will Thorgunna join us?"

"That's up to her, isn't it," Brigit replied, tucking her bag under her arm. "I'll be leaving now. I've work to do."

"Aye, now that's a woman," Sigurdur piped as Brigit pulled open the door, slipped out, and slammed it closed with a great show of force against the wind's best effort to keep it open.

"Did you see the way her breasts move in that cinch? I must give them their freedom," Siggi said. "Let's sit and eat and toast Brigit's fine round bosom!"

Leif nodded. "Aye. Let's eat. Though it feels odd breaking fast without the Jarl present," he said, pouring a cup of beer.

"Her loss. Fine food. Better company," Siggi replied.

Leif shook his head. *Irish!*

The two men ate in silence, listening to the wind and rain.

Leif rose to pull closed the shutters of the one open window as the wind whistled through Thorgunna's house. Angered at being locked out, the wind tried to pry the shutters open by blowing them from their niches in the porthole style windows.

Leif, speaking through a mouthful of bread, broke the silence, saying softly, "I am afraid I may have frightened her."

"Who? Brigit?" Siggi asked.

"Thorgunna."

"You? Frightened her?" Sigurdur choked. "Christ, man. Her own men speak of her as though she is king, queen, and god all rolled into one. How could you frighten her?"

"I held her," Leif leaned closer to Sigurdur. "I fondled her. I could not stop myself. She returned my kisses, and unless she is the greatest of performers to grace the earth, she most certainly enjoyed my touch for I felt her come against my hand—and against my tongue."

"You didn't waste any time hiking up her shift, did you? And I thought I had a fine touch for the ladies. That Thorgunna is a comely woman and no doubt a lonely widow. I'd take a moment or two with her should I get the chance. Ease the widow's suffering with good Christian charity and Irish know-how," Sigurdur said.

"I didn't pressure her into the embrace. I went with my gut. And my gut told me the woman needs a man, badly. I *am* that man." Leif glared at his friend with hard, steely eyes.

Sigurdur recognized the tone of Leif's voice and the command of his stare. Thorgunna was Leif's conquest. The boundary had been drawn.

"How much beer did you put down?" Sigurdur asked knowingly.

Leif continued, "Too much. And she kept up with me cup for cup. I assumed she would comfort me personally, as she is the clan's leader, and a widow. I asked her to be my mistress. And things were going favorably between us until she passed out. I hope when she recovers from the drink she will not be offended by my forthrightness."

"Leifur, your youthful passions will be your undoing. You don't walk into the house of a Jarl, say *How do you do*, put your fingers and mouth to her womanhood, and demand to share her bed. These things take time. You should have waited until tomorrow night to unfasten your breeches and demand sex. What's the matter with you?"

Leif frowned, failing to see the humor. "I am quite uncomfortable of body and confused of mind, Sigurdur. My head is throbbing."

"Ah, yes. I've been there a time or two, myself. I've awakened with throbbing temples in more places than I can count. A beach. A bed or two. A snow bank. Under a bed or two. But never have I put down a pint in a house as fair as this." Sigurdur stretched. "No matter, young Eiriksson! In Norway the king will send a woman to your chamber, for certain. A woman who knows how to pleasure a man. Some plump beauty from the ends of the earth to clear your head. One with an extra little roll of belly and buttock. Oh, I do love a round woman under me. Aye! That's the benefit of being guest of a king! Every king keeps concubines."

"You're speaking too loudly for me this morning, friend. And moreover, this king may not keep concubines, Sigurdur. He's said to be a rather devout and zealous Christian," Leif replied.

"Christian or not, a man needs to fill a woman every now and then just for the sake of spilling his seed, lest he go blind," Sigurdur replied.

Leif had not heard this before. "If I don't have a woman, I'll go blind? I don't believe it. Nonsense." Leif began checking his eyesight by opening and closing his eyes and refocusing over and over.

"Do you handle yourself?" Sigurdur asked.

Leif shook his head. "Not often. And moreover, until this voyage, I never had the need. Since I was twelve many a woman has found her way to my bed. As it stands now, I've not had a woman in over a month."

"Aye, Leif. You need release. Unsown seed can poison your vision." Sigurdur paused, taking a drink. "Better you go out and break open the cinch on that Brigit. She'd be a ripe plucky duck to take to your bed," Sigurdur said.

"Thorgunna forbade me to lie with her house servants."

Sigurdur poured another horn of beer. "She's a clever leader, she is. I guess you'll just have to wait until the woman of the island invites you beyond that tapestry. She's likely in there now panting for want of your touch, but too shy to call your name."

Leif smirked. "My father has that talent. Women cling to him. They beg him for sex."

"I've often wondered what was so special about one red-headed, round-bellied, middle-aged man that makes women fall to their backs before him," Sigurdur agreed.

"I saw my father with a woman once. He made love to her quite vigorously, turning her and prodding her from all directions as if she were a whole lamb on a spit. It shocked me he might be that way with my mother!" Leif recalled.

"You were hiding?"

"Oh yes, quite so. I was barely twelve years old. I made not a sound. My father found pleasure, and with some noise I might add, more than once, and the wench too, but still she urged him on," Leif recalled.

"Your father has good eyesight?" Sigurdur asked, breaking into a loud belly laugh.

Leif shared the joke, laughing heartily. He ceased the jocularity in mid-chuckle as the tapestry separating Thorgunna from the balance of her world opened.

She wore an unadorned linen shift, sheer and revealing in the fire's glow. Not so revealing as to fully display her voluptuous physical attributes, but more teasingly hinting at what lay covered by only one thin linen dress.

Both men swallowed hard and fought to keep their members from saluting the buxom beauty before them. Leif felt a flood of panic course through him like child caught being naughty. *Has she been eavesdropping?*

"I'm sorry, Lady. Did we awaken you?" Leif asked.

"No. I've been at my embroidery," she paused, raising her arms, stretching, the fabric pulling tight across her bosom, outlining her dark nipples and round breasts. "I have the most incredible pain in my temples."

Thorgunna ladled water into her horn, taking a long drink.

"Lady, I am honored to breakfast at your fire. I am Sigurdur. Second aboard the ship—or what's left of the ship." He wiped his right hand against his shirt before extending it to Thorgunna.

They clasped wrists. "Please eat well, Sigurdur," she said. Then turning to Leif, she raised her eyebrows and said softly, pointing a finger just beyond the fire's glow, "Leif, would you mind handing me that bone needle … there."

Leif scanned the flagstone floor, spotting the needle a few paces away. He retrieved it, bringing it to Thorgunna.

"Your eyesight is keen, Norseman." Thorgunna winked.

Leif chuckled confidently, his composure returning. She had been eavesdropping. *No matter. I have nothing to hide.*

Again, wiping his greasy fingers on his tunic, Sigurdur stood, "Lady, I must bid you good day. The men are rested, and it's time to assess the damage and start repairs."

As if on cue, the wind and rain grew harder.

Sigurdur shrugged his shoulders, noting the change in the rain's pattern. "Foul weather or not, we must see to the ship before she goes down in the bay. Thank you for your hospitality, Lady."

"My pleasure, Sigurdur. Oh, and Brigit is likely wandering the shore, watching the storm. She enjoys the rain and wind about her," Thorgunna replied.

Sigurdur smiled and left with a hurried pace into the rain and dark.

"You are a witch," Leif laughed.

"I know men. I know Brigit. She'll enjoy the company of a fellow Westman. Even in the rain."

Thorgunna was so near the fire's glow it appeared to Leif the sheer linen fabric had vanished. Without forethought, Leif reached out and ran his fingers along the curve of Thorgunna's buttocks, whispering, "By the gods, I want you."

"You are certainly one of the boldest Norsemen ever to grace this island. Most offer me marriage before trying to get under my skirts. You plainly state you want me only for a bed wench and expect me to buckle under your touch and give you free reign over my body. I think not, Leifur Eiriksson."

"Pull off your chemise and let me make love to you," Leif responded. His blue eyes danced in the firelight in such a way Thorgunna could not meet their gaze.

Leif lurched forward, lightly pinching one of Thorgunna's nipples through the gossamer fabric. "I need you."

Thorgunna deflected Leif's touch by turning her body away from the fire. "And I need something to make my headache go away."

"I want you."

"There are complications, Leif. I cannot. I must not." She stepped away from the fire, changing the subject. "Will your men work in the fields tomorrow if the storm has passed?"

"Yes, after we sound the ship, whichever of the men are able will assist your men in the fields. Siggi said a few are exhausted beyond a few nights' sleep," Leif replied.

"Leif, it seems I put you ill at ease. Do not let one moment of passion between us ruin what could be a good friendship and perhaps a lucrative trade partnership," Thorgunna said, summoning the strength of will that comes only from great fear.

"Always business, eh? By the gods, woman, I am ill at ease. The sight of you so, in your shift, before the fire, makes my body turn to stone. Moreover, my mind is filled with thoughts of you, without your shift, and I with you beyond that tapestry," Leif said.

"I am sorry to distress you so, Leifur. Although no part of my body is exposed, and this linen is more than suitable attire, I shall wear my apron about the place whilst you are a guest. Rain or no, I've got work to attend to. Will you see to your ship?"

"Aye. To the ship I go."

"We'll talk later," Thorgunna promised, donning a heavy cape folded neatly atop a chest.

She exited her house with such speed Leif thought he should look around to see if the place was on fire. "The only fire is in my loins," he said aloud.

Alone with only the storm for company, Leif finished his meal. This storm is nothing compared to the fearsomeness of that which dashed my ship. I bless that storm in all its fury, for it brought me ashore here, to Tiree. With Thorgunna.

Raising his cup in a mock salute to the storm, he laughed. Then, speaking aloud with only the crackling fire to hear him, "I am lost! A sailor who twice blesses a storm that destroyed his ship because it brought him to a woman. Odin help me!"

Chuckling at himself, he rested his head upon the table against his arms. Still overwhelmed with fatigue, lost in the scent of the woman of the house on the skins, in the air, in the very soul of the place, he nodded off listening to the dance of the pelting rain.

Leif awoke suddenly to the joyful song of his first mate bursting into the house, leaving the door wide open, "Leifur, Leifur … what a time I had!"

"The Irish woman?"

"I met her on the beach. We didn't even speak, and our hands and mouths were upon each other. In the wind and rain! It was glorious. She used her sweet hand to bring me relief when she refused my offer to couple due to her state of innocence. Skillful hand for a virgin, I might add," Sigurdur boasted.

"Good for you, Sigurdur," Leif commented. Then more sternly, said,

"How many men to the boat today?"

Sigurdur held up two fingers. "They rowed out, brave souls, assessed the damage, and will make a list of what we need for repairs. As soon as the weather calms a bit, we'll pull her to shore."

"How many too drunk to work?"

Sigurdur smiled. "All the rest."

Leif laughed. "This beer will be the undoing of my men."

The door burst open. "No man can resist my beer. This much is true," Thorgunna agreed, passing the threshold of her house and quickly bolting the door behind her against the wind.

"No man could resist you," Leif said. "Listening through the shutters are we, woman? Do guests in your house not enjoy a bit of privacy?" He smiled.

"Noisy Greenlanders like yourselves cannot keep private. Your voices carry, even in the storm," Thorgunna replied, returning Leif's smile.

"Lady, forgive me, but I'm Irish, and we Irishmen know better than to be caught in the middle of this type of storm. I'm away. See you soon, Leifur?" Sigurdur laughed, excusing himself.

Leif nodded. "I'll be along."

Thorgunna again bolted the door behind the quickly departing Sigurdur.

"I am more exhausted than I thought. I fell asleep shortly after you left this morning. I'll tell you, Madam Jarl, I think I've had enough of this weather. What do you people do all day while it rains so?" Leif asked.

Thorgunna hung her cloak on a peg by the door. "That depends upon the household. I weave. Brigit bakes."

"And what shall I do?" Leif asked.

"Do you feel less of a man without your ship under you?" Thorgunna teased.

"Aye. Less of a man for that. Less of man for not having you under me, as well."

"By the gods, I wish you would stop that! You make it so difficult to refuse your advances, and yet by allowing your embrace, I could very well sentence you to death. You do not understand with whom you trifle. That said, we should discuss our drunken frolic, shouldn't we?" She loathed broaching the subject, but hid her embarrassment by stoking the fire, her back to Leif. As soon as the only flush in her cheeks was from the heat of the fire and not the memory of Leif's touch, she turned to face the Greenlander.

"I am sorely attracted to you, Lady. From your manner of speaking to the way your hair shines in the firelight—to the power you wield as Jarl, I find you quite attractive and desirable. Please forgive me, Thorgunna, but will you do me the honor of sharing my bed whilst I am upon your fair isle? How long has it been since your husband made love to you? You are far too comely to be without a man's touch against your thighs."

"My husband died but a short time ago," Thorgunna replied.

"Are you afraid you will soil his memory by making love to me? By your words and actions, I believed you were inviting me to hold you."

"Truthfully, Leif, I am bound to another. Before I can even consider your offer, much less give myself to you, I must seek release of that unwanted troth. If you wish, I will summon Unnur, Tiree's comfort woman, to my house. You need not suffer as a man can when tormented by his own desires."

Is she jesting? Leif wondered, approaching Thorgunna, reaching for her.

Leif pulled Thorgunna to him. He held her tightly. He kissed her deeply. She did not refuse the embrace. For that moment, she forced herself to enjoy the man, and not fear the demon who threatened his life—and hers.

"I want no other woman. What must I do to have you?" Leif whispered between Thorgunna's lips as their kiss ended.

Thorgunna trailed her lower lips across Leif's chin. A sharp, hot surge of wantonness shot from her lips to her belly and beyond as their bodies pressed closer, closing any gap between them. She moved her head to his shoulder.

She replied softly, "The price for my love is high, Leif. To have me, you must defeat the will of a god."

Leif pushed Thorgunna away, holding her back at arm's length. "Which god?"

Thorgunna whispered, "You will judge me."

"I shall not judge you. Speak the truth to me now, Thorgunna. There is a shadow between us, and I am beginning to believe it is not simply reluctance on your part, the memory of your husband, your business dealings, or any other earthly apparition. You have invited me to share so much more than the hospitality of your island with each word, thought, and deed, woman. Speak to me now and be forthcoming. I am tormented by you. I must have you."

"I have spoken to no one about this."

"It is time. Who binds you so?"

"Loki. I am haunted in my sleep. Nightmares. While awake I seek the means to undo the damage my dream-self created, and fight against that horrid son of frost giants each night as he enters my dreams to remind me of our agreement. The Thorgunna I become in my dreams made a grave error and contracted with that beastly demigod to watch over Tiree."

Leif's piercing gaze humbled her, as did his words. "Even the most powerful prophetesses in Iceland do not call upon the Trickster for protection. He cannot be trusted." Leif dropped his hands, completely releasing her. "Thorgunna, you may be more than I can handle, after all."

A touch of bitterness in her voice, she replied, "That hurts."

Chapter 4

It pained Leif to see his boat ashore. Though it stabbed less deeply than his hurtful comment to Thorgunna.

"My father says no boat should ever kiss the land once it has made love to the ocean," Leif said, walking with Thorgunna across the beach. "A ship without water under it was like a woman dying a virgin. A waste of a good vessel on both counts."

"How go the repairs?" Thorgunna asked, ignoring Leif's comment. It had been a week since the Greenlander's arrival. Oddly, Thorgunna had expected more wayfaring Norsemen to reach Tiree by this late in the season. None had come. Even the Rus had yet to land.

She and Leif had barely spoken for days. Thorgunna, in fear of Loki's threat. Leif, in fear of Thorgunna's power to summon a god.

Caressing his broken ship, feeling her pain, her desire to be whole and upon the sea, he found he could not concentrate on his lady's needs. He could think only of Thorgunna. He sighed, resting his head against the bone-dry hull of his ship. "But at what price comes her love? What price?"

Though Leif and Thorgunna had maintained a polite, yet difficult, discreet distance, Leif's men had not maintained any distance from Tiree's women. More, they were drinking excessively each night, waking late in the day, and thereby working less before dark.

Leif was unwilling to order his men away from the island women when he, himself, fought to stay away from Thorgunna—especially at night when he knew she was in need of comforting. And protection. *But to share her bed means to share her with a god. How can I live up to a god?*

Love's Second Sight

****

Repairs underway, Leif chose the solitude of the cornfields most days. Thorgunna worked at her brewery in its "secret" location, with dozens of islanders. Working in the rich brown soil calmed Leif's thoughts of his two lady-loves—his ship and Thorgunna.

The island men around him worked tirelessly, rarely speaking.

Leif felt pride in staking weak and wind-blown stalks, giving them a chance to grow strong and bear fruit. With but a short time until harvest, pressure was on to enhance the crop any way they could. Working alongside Thorgunna's countrymen, especially the man called Thorok, was sometimes more of a challenge than saving a windblown stalk of corn. He began to believe Thorok, the Huge and Silent, and another man, Iksan One Hand, who actually had two hands, not one, were his appointed keepers. Where he went, they went. Leif curbed his curiosity about Iksan's nickname. *Do I really want to know?*

"You should have been a farmer. You handle the corn like a man handles a woman," Thorok chuckled, watching Leif lovingly tie off a stalk of corn damaged by the storm.

Ah, he speaks! Leif thought. "I've farmed, to be sure. Never corn, of course. Though we do grow barley. On Greenland one must wear many hats to survive."

"Tiree is unique in all of Scotland in that we can grow corn. Our climate is mild compared to the rest of the isles and the growing season long. Tell me, Leif, why do you sail?" Thorok asked.

"My father wishes his colony on Greenland to be recognized by the king. Given protection. A trade route opened. I don't think Eirik realizes Olaf of Norway is a Christian, however. Do you suppose a Christian king will take kindly to one of his Jarls sacrificing to Thor?" Leif laughed.

"Thorgunna is a Jarl and not a Christian. The king would change that if he could. She knows it, too. Soon enough Thorgunna is going to have to respond to Olaf about her faith. The king will likely accept Greenland into his fold and then send a priest to baptize the lot of you, and an executioner to behead those who don't pray to the White Christ."

"To whom do you pray, Thorok?"

"To whichever god I think will listen."

Men around Leif and Thorok laughed.

"I know very little about the Christ. I pray to Odin for courage," Leif responded.

"And to Frey and Freyja for Thorgunna's bed, I'll wager." Iksan One Hand laughed.

Leif snickered, "I hope to win her heart without divine intervention."

Thorok pierced Leif with a hard, steely gaze. "I will cut out your eyes if you hurt her."

"I would never hurt her," Leif responded.

"Aye, but you put her down like a bitch in heat at your landing."

"I knew rumors would start. We were taken by a passionate moment, but have not yet finished what we began that day. She seems a bit irritated with me, to tell the truth," Leif responded.

"You've hurt her, then," Thorok whispered.

"Not knowingly!" Leif defended.

"I will not allow her to be hurt, young Eiriksson."

"Are you threatening me?" Leif asked Thorok, the two men squaring off.

"Not yet."

"Thorok, let us be friends. I do not wish to harm Thorgunna, nor do I wish to fight you. It would not behoove Greenland and Tiree to become enemies over the curve of a woman's rump."

Thorok smiled. "Wars have been fought over less."

"But let us not invite battle. My time is short on this isle. Soon enough the winds will change and I shall sail. Thorgunna will remain. At this point, as much of a lonely widow as she is now."

"You know so little about her, Greenlander," Thorok said.

"And yet I know more about her than you." Leif smiled, raising his left eyebrow.

Thorok broke out laughing.

"A battle of wits, won by the curve of the Greenlander's brow. Clasp wrists with me, brother. I may kill you someday, but that day is not today."

Thorok and Leif clasped wrists, shaking vigorously.

****

In late afternoon, the sun beginning its slow dip west, the men and women, sweaty and dirty from working in the field all day, encouraged Leif to join them for a swim.

The day had been long and hot in the fields of Cornaigmore, which Leif discovered was the site of the infamous Battle of the Sheaves.

The beauty of the Isle of Tiree astounded him. The beauty of the island's first lady tempted him, and the lake at Cornaigmore beckoned them all to swim and cleanse their bodies of the day's hard work. By the time the work party was at the water's edge, all were stripped bare.

"Come then, Leifur! Loch Bhasapol is magnificent this time of day!" Iksan One Hand called.

"Aye, a swim it is, then," Leif said, removing his clothing and wading into the shallows with the others.

Some of the women giggled as Leif waded into the cool, clear lake. "Ah, the women must see something they like," Thorok teased.

"Greenland grows 'em big," Leif replied.

"Well, then, Leif, are all Greenlander men so well-proportioned?"

an older, yet quite attractive woman asked Leif, wading up to him, her breasts floating just below the surface of the water. As she reached Leif, she gave his buttocks a squeeze.

"Of course," he replied. *What is she doing?*

The woman ran a hand along Leif's hip, over his pelvic bone, her fingers stopping to tug the mass of curly blond hair at his loins.

"Can I help you with something?" Leif asked.

"Aye, you can. Come with me now, and I'll show you what I want." She moved her fingers from the hair, to his flesh, which responded quickly to her touch.

"Get thee home, woman. Leave this one alone," Thorok said. "If you need a man, I'll come to you myself, or you can go to the Greenlander's shelter and take your pick. This man is the captain of that sorry crew. He does not need the likes of you under him." Thorok moved in between the woman and Leif.

"Under him wasn't what I had in mind. Introduce us, Thorok," the woman demanded, ignoring Thorok's rude comment.

"Leif, son of Eirik, this is Unnur. He stays with Thorgunna."

"Thorgunna has a good heart," Unnur whispered. "She shares everything she has."

Unnur's hand worked Leif's member under the water. Leif reached out, stopping her.

Thorok frowned at Leif's refusal of Unnur's touch. If Leif bedded Unnur, and it hurt Thorgunna, there would be even more reason to kill him.

"Come away with me, Leif. See that mound rising from the loch? It's an ancient crannog, the remains of a Pictish water fortress. There's a fine bed of mossy ground amidst the tall grass," Unnur encouraged.

Curious, Leif agreed with a nod.

He and Unnur swam away from the others. They were noticed, but not stopped. Gossip was in short supply on the Isle. This would make lovely conversation around the fire. Wagers were made as to how long Unnur would keep the young Greenlander in the tall grass. Good sport for a little island.

Leif had enjoyed the company of older women before. Greenland had very few choices for love, and affairs were common. Older women were appreciative of the prowess of a younger lover.

Hidden by the tall grasses surrounding the crannog, Unnur moved away from the water's edge, walking away from Leif.

"Come lie with me," she called suggestively.

"Alas, Unnur, I cannot."

"Aye, you can. That is not the soft member of an old man I see jutting out from your body, sir."

"Let me rephrase. I must not. You tempt me, dear Unnur. If I was not a guest in the house of the Jarl, I would use my body as a spit and turn you upon it like a roasting lamb. But, I must not. You do understand, don't you?"

"Then why swim away with me when you now refuse my love?"

"It is not love, Unnur. You perform a service men need. But it is not love. I heard complaints of boredom today in the fields. Will this not give them something to gossip about? They will know by my hasty return we did not couple. You may tell them any story you wish. Say I was too tired from a hard day's work in the fields to make love to you. I don't care."

Unnur smiled. "You are a sly devil, Leif. Thorgunna is a lucky woman."

"She will be, yes." She will be. Damn the specter of that demon, Loki. She needs me. I need her.

Leif returned to the swimming area ahead of Unnur, but a few minutes after his departure from the group.

"That was a quick romp with every man's woman, Leif. For a piece of silver she'll teach you the meaning of life." Iksan chuckled.

"My men take Tireean women to their beds nightly, and the women go willingly, without payment. Why should I be any different? Unnur said nothing of payment," Leif asked.

Thorok laughed. "She doesn't just lie with a man, Leif. She is the bringer of dreams. She'll get a coin from you, wait and see. I've lost a silver coin or two to her, myself."

"He's lost a bloody fortune!" Iksan One Hand chided.

"The women don't mind a woman such as her *working*?" Leif asked.

"No. They bless her name! She pulls her weight in the fields, helps watch the children when a man and wife need some time alone together, and in return, the women of Tiree think nothing of her taking a single man to her bed for a coin or two. Makes them better husbands when the time comes," Thorok replied.

"Practice makes perfect," Leif agreed.

"Exactly," Thorok responded. "She does things with a man he'll never have in the marriage bed. Things the women giggle about over their sewing before the fire, but never share with us. She does a service to Tiree. Why one time when I took her into my arms she let me…"

"No need to elaborate, my friend. I can imagine her skills are many and inhibitions few." Leif dropped the conversation, wondering how long it would take for Thorgunna to hear he'd swum into the reeds with Unnur, and how jealous it would make the Lady Jarl.

****

All thoughts of Tiree's solicitous doxy and the jealousy in Thorgunna he hoped to create vanished as soon as Leif saw the Lady Jarl upon his approach to her home. He slowed his pony to capture the absolute beauty she radiated, standing in her chicken yard, her back to the final glowing rays of the setting sun. The sun illuminated her beauty, reflecting off her shiny black hair.

"A good day in the field?" she asked.

They had not touched since the day Thorgunna confessed to her contract with Loki. He wanted to touch her now. He wanted to press his lips against hers. He wanted to fill her body with his own.

By the gods. I grow tight at the sight of Thorgunna. I am bewitched!
"Aye. We took a swim after. Quite refreshing," Leif said, kicking a chicken aside. "And your day?"

"I buried my gold."

"Excuse me?" Leif asked.

"My gold. My beer. We kegged the lot of it. Ready for Norway or burial at sea. I don't care which after I've been paid. I rode my fence line as far as Happy Valley, tagging areas that need repair with whitewash. Some of the men will ride out tomorrow with mortar and stone and make repairs whilst I ride to Caoles marking breaks in the wall. It is a never-ending cycle of build and repair. I now feed my chickens and shall call my day done and full," Thorgunna responded, brushing the last of the feed from her hands. "It's odd the Rus traders haven't arrived yet. I am beginning to wonder if they will."

"Happy Valley? Caoles? These are places I've not yet seen, I dare say."

"Tiree has many beaches and coves, each more beautiful than the last. You should ride the island sometime. At eight miles wide and twelve miles long, it's not hard to do."

"I'll need a guide."

"Thorok, perhaps?"

"He hates me," Leif replied. "Thorgunna, I must..."

"Must what?"

"I must show you," Leif said, taking Thorgunna in his arms. She did not resist as he engaged her in a long, sensuous kiss.

"I want you," he whispered into her ear, trailing his kisses across her throat before returning to her mouth to satisfy his craving and hunger for her love.

Thorgunna allowed Leif's embrace to bring down her defenses. She melted into his arms.

"Never have I met a woman I wanted more. Let me hold you, Thorgunna. Give me that honor," Leif sighed.

*

Thorgunna rested her head upon his chest, listening to his heartbeat. She could feel the tightness of his groin and perspiration on his palms as he stroked her arms. She closed her eyes. *Should I give myself to Leif, will he be killed? Is Loki lying, or are his threats real?*

Leif went to one knee, not caring what was beneath him as he knelt in the chicken run, his head nestled against Thorgunna's bosom, his arms encircling her just above her buttocks. He moved his face across her breasts like a cat against a stroking hand.

Leif's scent, of leather and earth, and the salt of the ocean embedded in his pores, filled her senses. *I want him, too.*

****

Her eyes still closed, looking deep into the world of her sight, she looked to see if the path, the path to Leif, was safe. It was not.

"I spoke the truth, did I not? The Greenlandic fool at your feet is the one, Thorgunna," Loki murmured in the darkness of Thorgunna's second sight.

"Yes, I know," Thorgunna replied as the internal conversation progressed.

"You want him to take you here, don't you? With the chickens pecking at you while he plays cock-of-the-walk," Loki asked.

"Yes," Thorgunna again replied.

"Do you wish to be free of my invasions into your meditations and sleep? Do you wish to lie with this man, and have him live to see another day? I warn you, Thorgunna, I am in favor with the One-Eyed god again. It took some doing and a bit of reminding him of our loving history, but I have regained status in his single eye. Soon … soon I shall not need his permission, or yours, to walk Tiree. Are you afraid, Thorgunna?"

"Yes."

"Then worship me."

"I cannot. Tiree cannot."

****

Thorgunna opened her eyes. "Leif, I cannot," she sighed.

Leif rose.

"Loki?" he asked. "Or is there some earthly reason why you cannot just lie back and allow me to make love to you?"

Seeing the fear in Thorgunna's eyes, Leif backed away, taking a noble stance. "Loki! Hear me now! I will fight you for the freedom of this woman! Show yourself!"

Thorgunna froze, as if waiting for lightning to strike. Nothing occurred but the clucking of excited chickens.

That's not how to call him out, Thorgunna thought, her heart racing. "You shouldn't take him lightly, Leif. He is a formidable foe."

"Yes, but only in your dreams, my dear. Let him do his worst to me, but let it be while I am awake so I may have the pleasure of stripping him bare naked with his testicles tied by a length of rope to a randy she-goat."

"Why invite suffering, Leif?"

"Because Greenlanders live without the fear of things that go bump in the night and monsters under the bedbox."

"Do not mock me, Leif," Thorgunna warned.

"I do not mock you. I call you to courage, my beautiful thunder warrior."

"I pity you your arrogance, sir."

"You blind me with unquelled passions."

"Your passions may be your undoing, Leif."

Leif shrugged. "So be it. I'll not back down—from you, or Loki."

****

"So be it? So be it?" Loki laughed, nearly buckling over and off his perch far away in Asgard, home of the gods. "If Leif wishes to bear the sins of Thorgunna, so be it!"

Chapter 5

Leif had an uneasy night. He lay awake for hours after dark dreams unlike any nightmare he'd suffered as a child awakened him. He knew it was the place. Tiree. Thorgunna.

He recalled the dream, defensively reaching out for his axe—just in case. It had been too real. Too vivid. *If Thorgunna's nightmares are even half as affecting, then I am truly sorry for her.*

****

He was alone on his ship, lost in thick fog. He could not get his bearings from the birds, or the sky, nor the wind or the stars. He was weak. Confused. Unable to navigate by smell and his own gift of seaman's sight, he felt as lost as his vessel.

Suddenly, there was complete silence. Even in a dead calm, the ocean was far from silent. The fog enveloped him in bone-chilling vapors of death-like stillness. Rising from the mist-covered sea came the throne of Hel, Queen of the Underworld.

She called to Leif, "Welcome. Welcome to my shore." The voice was familiar. The face was familiar. At least half of the face. The left profile of the Queen revealed the progress of death by extreme old age. A maggot-filled eye socket framed by gray hair and even grayer tightly drawn flesh. The right profile of Hel portrayed beauty, youth, freshness. It was Thorgunna's face. Thorgunna's voice.

"Still want me, Greenlander? Come here, then, and take me!" Hel cackled, lifting her half-tattered, half-resplendent gown, revealing legs that matched all-too-well the face and a womanhood most unappealing.

Before Leif could reply, unseen forces catapulted him between the open legs of Hel. With death's own grip, Hel closed her legs around Leif's head, forcing his face—his mouth—into those regions of a woman he would normally relish.

Although the right facial profile of Hel could be construed as lovely to one who had not beheld her left, her nether regions could not share similar praise.

Leif gagged as the fetid odor of every still-born child enveloped him like a will-o'-the-wisp. He stifled a scream as earthworms and maggots slimed their way through the putrid, tainted, long dead womb of Hel, daughter of Loki and Queen of Underworld. To scream would invite the vermin into his own mouth, but he wanted to scream ... wanted to flee the horror of death's grip.

****

Leif sat up, and reached for the pitcher and cup. "Loki's own daughter welcomes me in my dreams. He hasn't the courage to face me himself. How typical of that little sodomite godling. I'm not afraid of you, Loki! Do you hear me, you vile little parasitic being?"

A heavy sigh from Thorgunna's room piqued his attention. She too was restless. Though all nights were restless for Thorgunna. She is plagued by nightmares. I suppose that is her punishment for consorting with Loki. I pity her those nightly torments as much as she pities me my arrogance.

Leif watched the veil of night lift as dawn rose over the Isle. When he emerged from his chamber just as the darkling skies were emerging a vivid blue, he found Thorgunna already awake.

Sitting at her table, one hand toying with a cup, sloshing its contents from side to side, Thorgunna appeared weary and troubled.

"You are unwell, Thorgunna?" Leif asked.

"How did you sleep, Leif?" Thorgunna responded.

"One should not answer a question with a question. I slept well, at any rate."

"Liar."

Leif pulled a stool next to the table, sitting across from Thorgunna.

"I am not a liar, madam."

"Yes. You are. You did not sleep well, for I was witness to your restlessness and furies of sleep."

"I had a nightmare. What of it?" *Damned woman of sight!*

"He'll never leave you alone, you know."

"I'm not afraid of shadows, Thorgunna. And Loki is but a shadow of a god."

"You are a fool, Leif Eiriksson."

"And you? A woman who consorts with the god of lies is wise?"

"I was not mindful of my actions, as they were done while I was asleep."

"And for your nocturnal escapades, I must suffer."

"You suffer?"

"Yes. It is the actions of Thorgunna, Queen of the Night, that keep me from you, the woman I desire too fervently, Thorgunna, the Lady Jarl of Tiree."

"The Thorgunna I am in my sleep is a troubled businesswoman with the wrong partner. I would never have agreed to…"

"Agreed to what?"

"Never mind, Leif."

"But I do mind, Lady! I mind greatly!"

"I do not wish to discuss my business."

"Always business first, aren't you, Lady?"

"Around you it is the safest choice."

"For whom?" Leif asked.

Thorgunna stared directly into Leif's eyes, speaking softly, but with heartfelt conviction, "For you."

"Lady, when I am in your presence of late, I find I am desirous of tying you to a post to beat the truth from you. You weave a maze of half-truths and shadows about me. One minute teasing and tempting me. Another shunning and doing your very best to drive me from your bed."

"I cannot drive you out of that which you have not entered," Thorgunna replied.

Leif tossed his head back, shrugging his shoulders. His unbound long blond hair cascaded down his back, nearly reaching his buttocks. He moaned, rotating his neck and arching his shoulders.

"Are you in pain?" Thorgunna asked.

"Yes. You pain me. You burn me with your fire and sting me with your ice. You are the womanly embodiment of my beloved Iceland. And, dear Lady, you are just as mysterious in your interior as is that great island of my birth." Leif paused, pulling his hair into a loose ponytail and knotting it. "I am surely mad to have closed my senses to the call of a woman who needs me more than you, in hopes you would sing my name."

Leif rose. "There is a woman, Thorgunna, who speaks only the truth to me. She is a rare beauty. I have ignored her long enough. I must make haste to her side now, for standing center of a war waged between two beautiful women is not a safe place for me to be, indeed. I must choose. And I choose her."

Thorgunna frowned. "Which woman?"

Leif leaned forward, gently kissing Thorgunna on the cheek. "My ship, Thorgunna. She needs me."

"Away with you, then, sir. And good riddance!"

Thorgunna held her chin up. Leif laughed at her.

"You're waiting for a kiss, aren't you?"

"Of course not!" Thorgunna cried.

"Yes, you are. My Thorgunna runs hot like a geyser this moment, and the next shall become as cold as a glacier. The Lady of Fire and Ice." Leif slipped past Thorgunna, not looking back. Not kissing her.

Leif hailed Thorgunna's stable boy, mounted his pony, and rode hard to Gott Bay. He prodded the pony with his heels. "Run fast, horse. Burn her from my heart and mind. She is naught but sweet poison, and I have for too long dipped my tongue into her pot trying to taste the nectar. What a dangerous woman she is. And yet, I long for her. I am possessed. I am not whole without her. Fool! Leif Eiriksson, you are a fool!"

The longing in his heart became a great wail of mourning as his ship came into view. *My broken lady. My dearest love.* Leif dismounted. "No. Thorgunna is my dearest love," he whispered tying off the horse.

"Sigurdur!" he called. Time to work. Time to forget—about her. For now.

****

Thorgunna, still seated at her table, felt angry. Angry at Leif. "How dare he talk to me that way! How dare he! I am the Jarl of Tiree. I should have him stoned. Flogged."

She burst into tears. "Yet, I am nothing without him. Therein lies Loki's curse. If only there was a way, a way to love Leif without…"

She rose, moving softly to her wash basin. She rinsed her face and soothed her tired eyes, barely quenching the heat of her cheeks and forehead. The cool water did lift her spirits, if only a bit.

She raised her head to view her reflection in her looking glass, a convex disk of highly polished silver. She slowly revealed her reflection to herself by lowering the linen towel used to dry her face. Her piercing brown eyes gazed back at her as she stared at her reflection in the mirror.

"I no longer wish to be torn between two loves. It is time I chose.

Tiree? Or him?" She dropped the towel, looking at herself with conviction. "I want both."

****

Thorgunna rode to Gott, approaching Leif a bit apprehensively.

Leif lay upon the white sand beach, under the raised bow of his ship, a measure in his hand. Shirtless, wearing only his woolen breeches, the sweat dotting his chest glistened like crystals growing from a hard outcropping of limestone. He was alone.

Leif heard the rider's approach.

"Lady," he acknowledged, before pulling himself deeper under the bow to work. To hide.

"How go the repairs, sir?" Thorgunna asked from horseback.

"Slowly, thanks to the randy women of this island. They fill my men's minds, bellies, and beds, leaving little of them for work." Leif paused. "Are all the women of Tiree so lustful?"

"They just might be. Will you be taking the time to find out?" Thorgunna asked.

"I had hoped. Now, I wish only to speed the repairs of my ship. I have ordered the men away from your women after this day, until the strakes are hammered. They are not happy with me. I am their captain. So be it. Oh, and do not enter the shelter, Lady, lest you see more of my crew's interests in your women than is proper."

Thorgunna dismounted. "Leif, slide out and face me."

Leif rolled out onto his shoulder. "Yes?"

"Don't be angry, Leif. Please."

He pulled himself up to his feet. "And why should I not be angry, Thorgunna?"

"I do not mean to hurt you, Leif."

"I am not hurting." Leif took an arrogant stance, hands-on-hips.

He takes my breath away. "I do not mean to confuse you. I would like to explain. I would like to gain your trust. Would you come with me, to Caoles, and to the Stone?" Thorgunna mounted her horse.

"I have work to do."

"Please, Leif."

"You warm to me now, only to dowse me with frigidness later, woman. I tire of fire and ice."

"Trust me, Leif. I need you to trust me."

Standing alongside her horse, Leif ran his hand along Thorgunna's leg, feeling the soft leather of her riding pants.

"Rarely have I seen a woman in a man's breeches. It is oddly arousing, and quite fetching."

"You would go on horseback with me, then? And talk?" Thorgunna asked, carefully avoiding use of the word "ride."

"Yes, I would ride with you," Leif replied.

"Our language is odd, is it not, that one simple word such as ride can have two meanings. We both know you refer to going on horseback when you say ride, but if a stranger entered our conversation, what would he think?" Thorgunna smirked.

"I would ride, Thorgunna," Leif said, continuing to caress her leg.

"You're scaring my horse, Leif."

"You tease me."

"I might. I use humor as a defense in awkward moments," Thorgunna admitted. "Take one horse or two?"

"I'll go astride your horse, with you. My pony is grazing," Leif said.

Thorgunna pulled forward, and Leif climbed aboard her chestnut pony, holding her waist, smelling the perfume of her hair and body. Her bare neck enticed him to kisses. "It is no wonder Norsewomen wear their hair long. Your bare neck is quite a distraction."

Thorgunna laughed. "All the more reason never to wear my hair pulled back again. I do not wish to distract you."

They rode east around Tiree until the little island of Gunna appeared before them.

"What island is that?" he asked, pointing towards the speck of land in the inlet.

"Gunna? It is a place for isolation of sick livestock. From there it is but a pull of the oars to Coll, our closest neighbor. Thorok has a home on Coll, though he seldom goes there," Thorgunna replied.

"Gunna? *The Warrior*. Like you?" Leif asked.

"Named for me, although I've only been in two battles," she replied.

"The Battle of the Sheaves and…" Leif questioned, recalling the tapestry hanging from the rafters of Thorgunna's home.

"It was here, at Caoles, I passed my knife into the heart of Ketil Arngrimsson," Thorgunna said sternly.

"I'll watch myself!" Leif laughed.

"You do not seem to be the kind of man who would force a woman, Leif, or you would have taken me when we lost ourselves to our ill-timed passion."

"I won't force my way, though I have considered it more than once as you lay in your chamber and I in mine. I know you do not sleep well, Thorgunna. And now I find my slumber disturbed by visions of Hel herself forcing me to pleasure her."

Thorgunna pulled the reins up quickly. The horse stopped and she slid off. "You dream of Hel? I knew you were vexed by a strong nightmare, but that I did not know."

Leif nodded. "I did."

Thorgunna, crestfallen, sighed. "There is no escaping him. Leif, if you are dreaming of Loki's own daughter, then perhaps it is better we do not continue this conversation. Further, you should move from my home. There are many comfortable homes on Tiree. Unnur Grimsdottir has a large house. I could introduce you."

Leif bowed his head respectfully, suddenly flushed. "I met Unnur."

"Oh? When?"

"Ah, you are jealous. That gives me hope for your affections. Dearest, Unnur is nothing but a poultice upon a wound that will not heal until properly treated. Please do not think me unkind," Leif said, deliberately trying to mislead Thorgunna.

"I am not a free woman, Leif. I have a king, the Rus, and even a god biting at my heels. It would seem only natural in the course of my life that you turn to another with your body when still dripping honey from your lips when you speak to me."

Thorgunna walked away. *Damn! I determine to share my life with him and he has already given himself to Unnur. I had not expected this.*

"Thorgunna, wait!" Leif called urging the pony towards the angry woman before him.

"Get off my horse. You can walk back to Gott. It's not that far," Thorgunna demanded.

Leif dismounted, the pony taking the opportunity to graze the tall grass. "I have hurt you. I'm so sorry. My need was great and overshadowed my wisdom. I have insulted you as my host and as a woman."

What is it in the soil of Caoles that causes men who walk upon it to hurt me so? "Did I not make it clear to you that I killed a man not far from where you now stand?" Thorgunna said.

Leif put his hands upon Thorgunna's upper arms, spinning her around to face him.

"I killed a man not far from where you now stand," Thorgunna repeated, this time quite emphatically.

"Kill me, then, Thorgunna. I await your blade." Leif stretched out his arms, tightening his finely muscled, tanned chest and stomach.

By the gods he is handsome! Thorgunna removed the symbol of her status, her ring of keys from her waist. She loosed her blade. The same knife that had killed Ketil.

"You want to die today, Leif Eiriksson? Is it a good day to die?" she asked. *What kind of game am I playing?*

She carefully traced the tip of the blade across Leif's chest, circling his nipples, running it across the ridges of his stomach muscles.

"Strike when ready. A true warrior does not torment his victim," Leif responded, his arms still out, his stance firm.

Thorgunna, blade in hand, moved behind Leif. She let the knife caress his spine from shoulder to hip. The blade bit, causing a ripple of blood to flow from the scratch. Leif shuddered, but made no sound. It was a clean strike. The blood flowed freely from the wound and dripped onto the soil.

He is enjoying this, Thorgunna thought. But not as much as I!

Thorgunna reached around Leif, loosening his belt, untying the laces of his breeches, which fell to his hips, exposing the top of his buttocks.

She traced the knife over the curve of Leif's rump.

"Thorgunna, strike now or I will be forced to defend myself. And, dear Lady, my weapon is sharper than yours," Leif whispered.

Thorgunna moved to face Leif. He held in his right hand his fully aroused member.

"Your flesh may be sharp, Leif, but not so much as my blade. I told you it has tasted blood. It hungers for more. It hungers for yours," Thorgunna whispered.

Holding her blade just above his swollen shaft, threatening to put the sharp edge upon it, she continued, "Defend yourself, Greenlander. You have crossed every boundary, tested my patience, and defiled my island with your carnality. I shall not yield my weapon to you."

Thorgunna raised her hand as if to strike a blow to Leif's manhood. As her hand came down, Leif caught it, and slapped the knife away.

"No more. Your jealousy over nothing proves to me only one thing. You want this," he said, placing her hand, not her knife, upon his erection. "I did meet Unnur. She offered her services to me, but I refused her. Thorgunna … torment me no longer. I beg of you."

Thorgunna encircled her fingers about Leif's thickening member, feeling its warm circumference, running her hand along the shaft, its length.

Their eyes meeting in a bizarre showdown of wits versus desire, neither willing to break eye contact, Thorgunna continued stroking with her hand. With each stroke of her hand, her rage grew. Rage fueled by sleepless nights and untapped passions.

As Leif's breathing quickened, so did Thorgunna's assault. Her hand moved quicker as all her hurts, all her pain, welled into her hand and were released with each stroke.

"I am angry with you," Thorgunna whispered, burying her mouth under Leif's chin, biting his throat, her anger still moving her hand in forceful, even motions.

"Don't be. Thorok has threatened to kill me if ever I hurt you," Leif replied, nearing climax.

"I loathe you," Thorgunna cursed. She bit harder.

Leif winced. She had drawn blood.

Leif could not reply, for a moment later Thorgunna drew more than blood as his body responded to her attack. Erupting, surging, his seed spilled upon the earth, washing the ground with the oldest of magic.

"You killed a second man at Caoles today, woman," Leif panted, holding onto Thorgunna while his head cleared. "Am I bleeding badly on my shoulder? I feel it trickling down my back. See here, woman! There is a puddle of my blood at my feet!"

Thorgunna backed away, resting against a boulder. "I should have put my knife to your manhood. At least then the satisfaction would have been mine."

Leif gathered his clothing together. "Lady, I am perfectly willing to give you the satisfaction you truly need."

Thorgunna looked at her right hand, now tired and weak from its battle against the Greenlandic giant. *That was exhausting. Completely exhausting.*

She studied Leif's seed glistening on the trail before her.

The control had been hers. I could have killed him. Leif knows this, too. But instead, I merely defeated a swollen beast, not the whole man. Thorgunna shook her head, clearing her thoughts.

She had won this battle, a prelude to the war she knew she could not avoid.

She spoke, wiping her hand against her riding breeches, "I have been both blessed and cursed by Loki. He said you would come. He said you would want me. He said I could care for you, but to lie with you was to invite death. Death for me. Death for you, and death for our way of life here on Tiree. He would have us bow to him and suckle on his unholy shape-shifter's milk. He wants Tiree."

"I will fight that evil being and make love to you before his broken corpse," Leif cursed. "How can you trust the threats from the god of lies?"

"Spoken like a true berserker, Leif. But I fear the curse Loki set upon me is even too much for you to conquer. Loki's war is waged in my mind, a most difficult place to do battle," Thorgunna replied. "You're a good man, Leif. Too bad you don't want to marry me."

"An absent husband, I would be. You need a man in your bed every night, Thorgunna. You are too much woman to have remained alone for so long."

Thorgunna smiled to herself. "Truthfully, it has always been my preference to have an absent husband."

"I cannot offer you more time than the season allows. But while we have this time, I offer all I am to you."

"I am paralyzed by too many choices. Always I have looked first to what was good for Tiree. When I have put my own interests first, I have been attacked, assaulted, beaten, and burned."

"I will not hurt you."

"You already have. By your very presence I am tormented. I want you, Leif. Through the fog and nightmares and idiotic kingly decrees I produce beer for only him, I want you. You are the only constant light in my life. I have trusted no one fully enough to share my burden. And yet, though I long to bare my soul and cast off the yoke of secrecy and humiliation in which Loki has bound me, should I give myself to you, you may die. Therein lies my true burden."

She dug her foot into the sandy soil, imprinting the spot next to where Leif's seed had kissed the earth. "I'll have to plant something here now. There is no better catalyst for growth than a man's seed, in a woman or a corn field."

"I have never heard of such a thing," Leif laughed, envisioning all the men of Tiree fertilizing the corn like spawning salmon. "Thorgunna, I do not dismiss that I had a nightmare. But it was only one nightmare. I do not dismiss that Loki may have once been a powerful being in the pantheon of gods my father worships. Truthfully, my prayers have always been half-hearted. But I do not believe he has power over you, or me. Or Tiree. Let me make love to you. Here. Now. Once I am deep within you, moving with you in the oldest of dances, you will know Loki is a liar, and that to couple with me is no prelude to a sentence of death. Kiss me, Thorgunna. Kiss me."

Thorgunna fell into Leif's arms, their lips joining. Every part of Thorgunna's body responded to Leif's embrace. His skillful hands loosed her belt, allowing access to her bosom hidden under her man's over-large tunic. His touches set her ablaze. Her nipples responded to a degree she had never imagined, as Leif cupped and caressed one breast, then the other, still kissing her.

"Oh, Leif. I cannot. Not now. I must go to the Stone. Thorok is to meet me there, and he is probably livid and ready to do you bodily harm for keeping me so long away from his protection," Thorgunna said pulling away. She straightened her tunic and tightened her belt. Her erect nipples revealed her true desire and feelings.

"There's time, Thorgunna. There's always time when a man and woman want to be together." He bent his head, lightly kissing the rise of fabric pulled across Thorgunna's bosom. "A young widow such as yourself must still remember how passion can be quelled in minutes when the fire burns as hot as it does right now, between the two of us."

Thorgunna took a step back. "Leif, please. I want to. I do. But not right now, right here. It is not time. Please, we must away." She mounted the pony.

"As you wish, madam. But do remember this—I will step beyond that tapestry barring you from the rest of the world and make love to you until we are completely and utterly spent. Nothing will stop me." Leif hopped up behind her.

****

Loki reacted to the spilling of seed by Thorgunna's angry hand like a child being given a first taste of a honey cake. It made him giddy, elated.

"Seed and blood upon the soil of my island! Spilled in anger! Come blood and seed and sweat of brow, Thorgunna. Tiree is now sanctified to me!"

Loki laughed, anticipating the arrival of night upon the island. Sweet night. A veil of disguise for a myriad of evil acts.

****

Thorgunna, concentrating upon nothing but the path from Caoles to the Stone, felt the ripple of Loki's laugh strike her like a fist. She refused the call of the sight. *I refuse you, Loki! Do you hear me? I refuse you! Though you cackle like a hen and strike like a serpent, I shall not fall into your fog. Not while awake. And if ever I find the solution, never again whilst I sleep.*

Leif, pressed tightly against Thorgunna as she urged the pony on, sensed the chill and loss of concentration run down Thorgunna's spine. He clutched her tighter. Protectively. Lovingly. He felt her body relax.

He sighed. "It took the bite of your blade against me for you to trust me. I would have allowed you to cut sooner and deeper had I known."

****

The way from Caoles to the mysterious Stone was well-marked. Thorgunna's pony seemingly knew the path without so much as a turn or twist of its reins. The white sand beach of Caoles turned into marsh-like tall grasses wherein Leif spotted calves hiding while their mothers grazed. Terns and gulls swooped defensively at the pony as it padded through a nesting ground.

"Damn birds! Thorgunna, press on. The birds are pecking at my head as they dive at the pony!" Leif called.

"We're almost across. Hold on, Leif!" Thorgunna replied. She urged her horse to gallop.

The tall grasses and crags with hiding livestock and birds' nests gave way to another pristine, remote beach area, flanked by thick, green pasture.

"Who is this man, Thorok, to watch you so?" Leif asked, as the large, solid man came into view.

"He protects me. Too bad he cannot defend me against the armies of Olaf, the Rus, and one determined god. The likes of you, however, I think he can handle."

"Your watchdog and faithful hound," Leif laughed.

Thorgunna laughed. "Yes, he is faithful. Faithful to me. Faithful to Tiree."

"What is the Stone, Thorgunna?" Leif asked, glad the pace of the pony had slowed and the wind was no longer forcing his words back into his mouth each time he tried to speak.

"Once we're over the hillock, you will be able to decide for yourself what you think it is."

Leif kissed the back of Thorgunna's neck.

"Stop that. Thorok will know we almost … Thorok will know."

"I don't care if he knows."

Thorgunna hailed Thorok as they reached the top of the grassy hill.

From below, standing upon a pink-shelled sandy beach, Thorok waved.

"Hello, Thorok!" Thorgunna called. Then to Leif, "This is a holy place on the island, Leif. Behave yourself."

"Lady, you're late," Thorok said softly, helping Thorgunna from her horse. "And, you, Greenlander, are bleeding."

"I stabbed him. He deserved it," Thorgunna said, walking quickly away from the glaring Thorok and defensive Leif.

Thorok, taking three long strides, caught up to Thorgunna, taking her arm, assisting her as she walked to the Stone. The Ringing Stone—*Clach a' Choire*—lay before them.

"Thorgunna, you wear a man's scent," Thorok whispered.

"I did not lie with the ruddy bastard, if that's what you're implying."

"You have the smell of a man's pleasure and woman's need about you. The Stone should not be rung with his scent upon you," Thorok replied.

"Ah, hello? Where are we going?" Leif called, trying to catch up.

Thorok turned slightly, and with eyes alone, commanded silence from Leif.

"Aye, Thorok. I'll wash up at the loch," Thorgunna replied sarcastically.

"You obviously brought him to fruition, but you, Lady, he did nothing for you?" Thorok asked.

"Thorok, you are asking me questions you have no right to ask," Thorgunna said firmly.

Thorok stiffened his already tight stance. "You and Tiree are my life. I will ask these questions and more if I see fit to do so."

"Yes, Thorok. And no, Leif did not touch me," Thorgunna lied. "I'm not sure why I touched him. He doesn't deserve me."

"That much is true," Thorok replied stoically.

Thorgunna reached into the little loch behind the Ringing Stone, separating it from the sea, washing her hands and face. Leif caught up to her.

"All right, what is this Stone, and why the pomp?" Leif asked.

Thorgunna smiled lovingly at Leif. "The Ringing Stone—*Clach a' Choire*—is that which binds Tiree to the whole of the world. The seasons change now, Leif. The Stone must be struck so its music, its song, can usher in that change. It's an old tradition. One started long before the Picts and Scots and Norse came to Tiree."

"A rock that sings?" Leif asked, amused.

Thorok replied, pushing Thorgunna ahead, "Aye. It sings. Now shut ye up and show some respect for the old ways of the Isle. Ye shouldn't even be here, 'cept she brought ye."

"And why are you here, Thorok?" Leif asked.

"I go where the Lady goes."

"You did not ride with her to Caoles today, Thorok."

"No, I did not. But not for a moment should you think I don't know what occurred at Caoles. I smell you on her, Greenlander. I smell her desire for you. I hate you for it. I'll kill you someday, you know," Thorok replied, his voice low and threatening.

"Aye. With your breath alone you'll do me in, old man," Leif countered.

Thorgunna turned to the bickering men, "Please don't put your arrogance before the wind. When I strike the Stone I want only hope to ring out, not dissension."

"Yes, Lady," Thorok replied.

Thorgunna and her faithful dog, Thorok, Leif thought.

"Leif, this boulder before us, it seems out of place here on this shore, does it not?" Thorgunna asked.

"Yes, very much so. It is large and round and smooth, while all around us are shoreline crags of sharp, uninviting rocks sitting upon this lovely bed of crushed shell."

"It was placed here long ago by a tribe or clan now lost in antiquity. See these cup marks? A thousand hands over a thousand years have struck *Clach a' Choire*, to make it sing."

"A thousand hands over a thousand years," he repeated.

The stone had fifty-two cup marks. Leif counted them as he observed the ringing ritual, Thorok watching him as if he were prey.

Resting on smaller stones, *Clach a' Choire* sat only inches above the shell-kissed sand of the shoreline. The thousands upon millions of little pink shells made the beach glow with color.

"This place is lovely," Leif commented.

"Babies are brought before *Clach a' Choire* and put in the path of the song as the father strikes the Stone. It's a baptism of sorts. A baptism into the folds of Tiree. The dying, too, are sometimes brought here to have their final sensations be the sound and vibration of the Stone."

Leif nodded. "I apologize for my former attitude. I was unaware of your custom and tradition surrounding the *Clach a' Choire*," he said, pronouncing the Gaelic poorly, but carefully. "What god associates himself with the Stone?" Leif continued.

"All gods," Thorgunna replied.

Taking a stone the size of both her fists into her hands, Thorgunna reverently struck the ages-old boulder. The clang was soft and tinny, yet vibrated like a ripple in a pool of water.

"It is a bell," Leif marveled.

Thorgunna struck *Clach a' Choire* again, the first tone melting into the second as it, too, surrounded and enveloped the listeners.

A third time she struck the Stone. The hardest blow. The loudest clang of the rock-bell.

"*Ceud mile failte*," Thorgunna called.

"*Ceud mile failte!*" Thorok repeated.

Mentally translating the Gaelic into Norse, Leif said softly, "*Einhundred thusand velkominn*. What are we welcoming a hundred thousand times?"

"Summer," Thorgunna replied.

Chapter 6

Thorgunna dropped Leif off with his men before riding to her house atop Gott Hill. Brigit awaited her, hands on hips.

"You went off on horseback with young Eiriksson today!"

"I did," Thorgunna replied, pouring a cup of frothy beer for herself.

Brigit touched Thorgunna's chin, pushing her Lady's face up so their eyes met. "Well?"

"I do not have to report my day to you!"

"No, you don't. But you could share it!"

Thorgunna moved quickly to her room. "You should go plant something up at Caoles. The ground has been sanctified. I marked the spot."

A sudden feeling of dread crossed Thorgunna. *I sanctified the land with Leif's blood and seed. How could I have been so stupid?*

Brigit screeched, leaping towards Thorgunna. "What occurred at Caoles, Thorgunna?"

Thorgunna and Brigit fell onto the floor laughing, as Brigit landed squarely atop Thorgunna. "Tell me!" the Irishwoman cried.

Shaking off the feeling of dread pressing through her soul, Thorgunna responded, "I believe we came to an understanding, at the point of my knife. Get off me with those sharp elbows of yours."

Brigit rolled off Thorgunna. "Oh dear Lord, you didn't kill him, did you?"

"No, of course not. I wanted to. I wanted to hurt him as he hurts me," Thorgunna stopped, realizing she did not wish to discuss this, and thereby admit her descent into jealous rage.

"But?"

"Instead of slicing the root of the tree, I took it instead into my right hand and planted its seed. At Caoles. I marked the spot." Thorgunna repeated. "I did not receive any physical pleasure from the act myself, but I did feel in charge of the situation. I have not felt in charge since the night the dream first came. It was a good feeling."

"Thorok went mad when he found you went on horseback alone with the Greenlander."

"Good. Perhaps Thorok's rage will keep my Norseman in line whilst I figure out how to juggle."

Brigit giggled. "Juggle?"

"I juggle the amorous advances of a very desirable man, the impending trials with the Rus, the inevitable priests of Norway, and the carnal desire of a god. I am juggling, Brigit. Thorgunna, jester of Tiree!" Thorgunna paused thoughtfully, "Perhaps I should seek council in these matters."

"From whom? The *Tirisdeach* elders? The priests? The law speaker on Coll? I can hear him now, 'A hundred men to choose from for protection, and you call Loki. What's wrong with you, woman?'" Brigit mimicked.

"Aye. I do not need to be scolded. Even by you," Thorgunna said.

Thorok burst into the house. Stunned to find Brigit and Thorgunna lying on the floor in a twisted knot of legs and arms, he froze in his tracks.

"Do you ever knock?" Brigit asked, looking up at the big *Tirisdeach*.

Thorok stood silently for some time, looking down into the depths of Thorgunna's eyes as if she were at the bottom of a well, for any sign of hurt, anguish, or pain.

"Is there any reason I should not kill him for you?" he finally asked. Thorok, a very large man, sporting a full beard and shoulder-length dark reddish-blond hair, towered over her. Yet, Thorgunna was his queen. And he was her most loyal subject.

He extended a large hand to Thorgunna, offering to pull her from the floor. "I held my tongue at *Clach a' Choire*. I was angry, so angry he soiled you. He is lower than the dust, Lady. When you can have your choice from a hundred men on any isle in the Hebrides, why defile yourself with that *Greenlander*?"

Thorgunna accepted Thorok's hand. He easily lifted her to her feet. "You're a bit impertinent, Thorok. You should watch yourself. And as for me, I am fine."

Thorok pulled Brigit to her feet. "I'm not happy the Lady is consorting with young Eiriksson, Thorok. But let us keep in mind it is her choice. Just as it was her choice to marry Finn MacLean by contract. Let's give the grieving widow a bit of leeway, shall we? How long shall Thorgunna remain a virgin? Until she's fifty?" Brigit scolded.

Thorgunna threw up her hands. "I decide when and with whom I shall *fokk*!"

"Thorgunna, your language," Brigit gasped.

Leif burst through the door, left ajar by Thorok. "Well, I should hope you do choose the time and place to *fokk*, Lady. Only I'm very cold, having not worn a shirt riding, and this wound on my shoulder blade needs attention." Leif twisted his body sideways to show off the gash caused by Thorgunna's blade.

"I'll patch that up for you, sir. Better not let Thorgunna at you again. She's likely to cut through and through next time," Brigit said, pulling Leif into his chamber.

"When you're finished with the ministrations of a woman's touch on your scratch, will you be coming to the beach? We can always use extra hands at a time such as this," Thorok called.

"Well, I suppose so. What am I to help with? Shall I have Siggi gather my crew?" Leif replied, wincing as Brigit applied a salve to the love-bite of Thorgunna's blade, and glad Thorok could not see him flinch.

"Come to Gott when your mommy says you're well enough. Wear a shirt!" Thorok called. Then turning to Thorgunna, "I'll be going to the shore now."

"Hmmm?" Thorgunna said, rousing from deep thought. "Shore?"

"The fire, Thorgunna. Did you forget about the fire?"

Thorgunna sighed. "I don't know how, but I did forget. I'll be along shortly."

"Don't be so preoccupied with the Greenlander that you forget your responsibilities to Tiree, Lady," Thorok admonished.

"All my life I have looked only to what was good for Tiree. I sold myself into a loveless marriage for *her*, Thorok. Don't tell me I am shirking my responsibilities!" Thorgunna exclaimed. "How terribly presumptuous of you!"

"I struck a nerve, didn't I? Only the truth would sting so, Thorgunna. Remember that." Thorok turned without waiting for a reply from the fuming Thorgunna, firmly slamming the door behind him.

Damn! Thorgunna thought. *Damn!*

"Your pet rebels, Lady?" Leif asked, stepping from his room wearing his tunic and cape.

"You task me, Eiriksson. You task me. Never before has Thorok so much as raised his voice to me. And now, both he and Brigit scold me," Thorgunna said sharply.

"And that's my fault?" Leif held his arms out. "Come here, Thorgunna. I'll let you order me about. I'll be completely docile and subservient."

Brigit emerged from Leif's chamber wiping her hands on a scrap of linen. "Better you come along to the beach, Thorgunna. I'll be your escort. God Himself only knows what you'd do, left unattended with this ruffian right now. The air is so thick between the two of you it could be sliced, buttered, and served on silver." She shooed Leif away, "You, go now. You've had quite enough of the Lady's attention this day."

Leif bowed, his eyes tilted upward to meet Thorgunna's gaze. "Indeed. Any more attention from our Madam Jarl and I might bleed to death."

"I hate him!" Thorgunna cried.

Brigit straightened Thorgunna's hair. "No, you do not. You should. But you do not. Now, shall we go to the beach?"

Thorgunna nodded. "Yes. Duty calls. Again."

"There's a good Jarl. Come away, then! The night before the longest day is upon us!"

****

Leif looked wistfully to the hull of his ship at the west end of the beach. Still stripped and bare, it looked like weather-aged bones washed up on shore.

"Will you be allowin' your crew to come to the fire?" Thorok asked, handing Leif a brick of peat. "Stack the bricks on my cart. We'll need hundreds of them."

"Is it necessary that she watch?" Leif asked, referring to Thorgunna, astride her horse, still and silent in the distance.

"Yes. It's custom."

"Odd custom."

"She's watching."

"Yes, Thorok. That much is obvious. She watches us work!"

"No, Leif. She's watching the horizon and the skies and sea."

"Are we to be invaded?"

"In a most wonderful way, yes. *She* comes now. Thorgunna will sense her arrival. It is then the fire is lit."

"Who comes?"

"Are you daft, man? Summer! Summer comes. Thorgunna will know when the actual moment strikes. It is one of her many gifts. To Tiree."

"Curious."

"Only to an outsider such as yourself."

"Always making me feel welcome, aren't you, Thorok?"

Thorok smiled. "I haven't killed you yet, have I?"

"Then, yes, Thorok. My men will attend the fire. Unless your solstice celebration is one festivity I should forbid them from attending."

"Old traditions die hard here in the Isles, as you witnessed at the Stone. Tomorrow is the longest day, the first day of summer. Tonight we light a fire to welcome it. Tomorrow we go to the fields and prepare for the harvest. Your men will enjoy the games tonight, and the prizes won tomorrow," Thorok said softly, continuing to cut squares of cured peat as fast as Leif could stack them.

"So, you burn throughout the night, playing a game, then toddle off into your fields at dawn to prepare for the harvest in some manner that involves prizes. I must have details if I am to play the game well and win a prize, Thorok. How, exactly, does one prepare for harvest on this isle?" Leif asked.

"We sacrifice a virgin," Thorok said, his eyes meeting Leif's.

Leif held his breath for a moment. "You kill a woman?"

"Or a man."

"Does Thorgunna approve of this?"

"She holds the blade."

"Who is to die?" Leif asked, concerned.

Thorok stood. "You're too serious, son of Eirik. Do you think us so barbaric we would make blood sacrifices?"

"You seemed quite sincere."

Thorok, slapping Leif on the back, laughed, "I was joking! We burn the fire tonight and drink until we are heady. At dawn we go to the fields, harvest enough ripe ears to feed us all, slaughter a sheep, and while it is roasting ... well, that's the best part of the longest day."

Leif smirked. "You while the time away with a companion?"

Thorok smiled. "Or two or three."

"Come, help me, Eiriksson. We need to stack the fire high. Its light must shine all the way to Coll and beyond. It must be a well-made fire, able to burn all night. Tomorrow comes summer. You work well today and I may not kill you."

Leif raised his left eyebrow suspiciously. "Well, thank you, Thorok. That's very kind of you."

As the day passed and the sun set, Leif, his crew, Thorok and several island men stacked bricks of peat and driftwood into a towering pyramid of combustibles.

"Yes, this will be a grand fire," Leif agreed, wiping sweat from his brow as he and Thorok admired their handiwork.

"When does she put the torch to it?" Leif asked, glancing back at the motionless Thorgunna atop her chestnut mare.

"When she is ready, she will light the fire." Thorok replied. "We're in luck tonight. The skies are clear. The gods are happy."

"Let's hope the gods are happy enough to leave us all alone," Leif added. *Especially Loki. Especially tomorrow, when I take Thorgunna to the corn.*

Thorok nodded in agreement. "Divine intervention is not always welcome, true enough."

Leif slapped the big islander on the back. "So when do we start drinking, Thorok?"

"After the fire is lit, we drink. And eat a tremendous amount of food. The women and men then square off, choosing partners from across the flames for the harvest tomorrow. Many babies go to the Stone in early spring. You seem eager to partake in our solstice celebration, Greenlander."

"I am, indeed, Thorok," Leif said. "My father always said that to honor your hosts you must respect their customs. One good debauch and my men may have the delights of this fair isle burned from their hearts. Then, I'll get my ship to sea."

"You might get more work from them once they've drunk and rutted themselves dry, but you're still going to have to wait until the storms pass. Don't let a day or two of calm fool you. Beyond the isles lies a treacherous open expanse of waters constantly churning from the breath of the gods blowing down upon it."

Leif laughed. "Sounds like you want to keep me safe, Thorok. I didn't know you cared."

"That doesn't mean I'm taking you to the fields, sir!" Thorok cried, feigning shock.

****

From the edge of the grassy expanse separating Gott Bay and Gott Hill, Thorgunna's horse whinnied nervously. "I feel it, girl," Thorgunna comforted, patting the pony's shoulder.

"You look lovely, dearest," a frighteningly familiar voice cooed from behind.

Thorgunna's breathing ceased. Her heart stopped. "Loki," she whispered.

Invisible hands slid around her waist from behind—hands pulsating like the slithering body of a serpent. The nape of her bare neck, the neck she wished she could instantly cover with her thick black braids much too securely pinned into a bun, stung from the touch of twisted, unseen lips. She knew the lips. They bore the scars of deceit and misfortune.

"The One-Eyed god has released me," Loki cooed.

"I don't believe you," Thorgunna sighed.

"Believe it, dear one. Soon enough I shall be as human, as flesh and blood as your long-dead friend, Ketil. But where he failed, I shall be victorious."

The sensation of the hands and lips upon her body vanished.

"I'll never worship you, Loki. Do what you will to me, I shall never become yours. Nor shall Tiree!"

Thorgunna's horse reared. She tightened her grip on the reins. "Calm down. Don't be afraid of shadows, girl." She patted her mare, calming the beast.

Thorgunna dismounted, holding the lead rope of her frightened mare. The specter of the god followed her. "Really, Thorgunna, why continue on so? You and I both know I am your last hope for the survival of Tiree."

"There is always hope," Thorgunna replied angrily, calming her nervous pony.

"Yes, hope found under the puny body and inadequate prowess of that Greenlander, I assume. You are losing yourself in him, Thorgunna. He will be your undoing."

"Better to lose myself in him than to consort with you."

"But he shall soon leave Tiree. I shall stay. I alone can defend your isle from the minions of king and Christ."

"Go away, Loki."

"Of course. Of course. Just remember, I'm never too far away. Remember that if you follow your heart and allow that pup first passage, it will be an enjoyable moment for you both, but it will be his last."

Thorgunna shook her head, burying her fears that Loki's words were far more than mere lies and tricks. "Go away, Loki. I tire of your lies."

The invisible hands trailed up her body to her breasts, squeezing them roughly. "You're mine. Every part of you is mine. Your body, your soul, your life, your island. Mine. Remember that, Thorgunna."

"How could I forget?" Thorgunna whispered.

"That's a good girl. Now, go to your faithful flock. They await you."

"Summer has not yet arrived."

"For you, it never shall."

"I hate you, Loki."

"Good. Your hate shall be the bed upon which I ravish you for all eternity."

"I'll kill myself before I allow you to have me."

"Do you think that will make a difference to me? You kill yourself, and I'll place you upon the throne of the Underworld as its Queen."

"And displace your daughter?"

"I'll give her Tiree."

A brilliant flash of light streaked across the dusky-sky, illuminating the already pink glow of early evening to a shocking white glow.

"It's here, Thorgunna. Summer is here. I shall enjoy my time in the sun with you. Oh, yes."

Thorgunna closed her eyes, breathing deeply as the invasive hands of darkness unleashed her bosom, and the breath of Loki faded into the breeze. From the bottom of her soul—still *her* soul—she called forth composure, calm, and a smile joyful-looking enough to hide the terrors and torments of her life from the people of Tiree. From Leif.

Chapter 7

Leif hung back and watched what could only be described as a *Tirisdeach* ceremony. Thorgunna approached slowly. Her movements were firm, yet graceful. A torch awaited her, planted in the sand like a beacon of promise.

Loki's threats and lies notwithstanding, summer is here. Nothing can halt winter from turning into spring, and nothing can stop the arrival of summer and the harvest. Not even him. Especially not him. Even he cannot stop Thorgunna from welcoming summer to her island.

The throng exploded into applause as Thorgunna triumphantly raised the torch and touched it upon the stack of peat and driftwood. It ignited brilliantly. The party commenced. The solemn rabble raised their voices in song and filled their cups as keg bearers broke open cask after cask.

Leif watched Thorgunna with interest. She is regal. Powerful. Desirable. I am humbled by her.

Siggi shoved a cup at him. "This shall be a paramount celebration, don't you think so, Leif?" Siggi asked, surveying his prospects for the evening. "I mean to have a go with that Brigit if I have my way."

"I think the real celebration comes tomorrow. At least for me," Leif replied, watching Thorgunna. Watching Thorgunna watch him.

Leif held back from the revelry as night fell, and the stars came out to decorate the solstice eve like millions of candles arranged against rich, black cloth. It was truly a lovely, magical evening. With his own inner senses tingling and his body aching to hold the Lady Jarl, Leif knew, deeply knew, that she was soon to be his. If he could drag her away from her countrymen! "In all things, Thorgunna is the key to the well-being of these poor farmers. She is not only their leader, she is a part of the land itself. No wonder even a god wants her. But I shall have her first," he said to himself.

Leif caught on to the game played by the men and women through the flames easily enough. Women were on one side. Men on the other. They chose through the leaping, dancing sparks of fire. They chose who would be their partner in the fields. Their partner in harvest.

Which woman is casting eyes upon me? Which man is looking right through the light, unlined summer chemise of a Tireean wench, feasting on that which he'll have the next day in the fields?

Leif drank the fine golden beer—perhaps too much. He downed every cup offered him by the women of Tiree. Unnur. Brigit. Thora. Magda. Kristjana. All fine buxom, luscious women. Though none were as beautiful or as titillating by her very breathing alone as Thorgunna.

The more Leif drank, the more women he saw giving him an inviting nod. The way the potent brew affected him, he was certain every woman of the island wanted him to plow the field ... her field. His cock twitched at the thought of heaving into them, one after the other. *I could do it. I can go all night. I am my father's son. I have enough to go around.* He caught site of the Lady Jarl in the firelight. His lurid imagination dimmed, and his manhood deflated in shame. *I truly want only one woman of this fair isle. She who stands now like a goddess in the glow of the flames, but who has not looked my way but once for hours.*

Leif looked through the leaping flames to Thorgunna, who was holding the hands of a child, playing a game perhaps. The flames of the solstice fire sent dancing sparks into the heavens to mate with the thousands of pinpoints of light in the night sky. No storm brewed this night. As clear an evening he'd never seen.

I need her, he thought. No. More than that, I'm falling in love with her. My need for her is stronger than the base craving to have her under me. My need for her is embedded in my heart. I love you, Thorgunna. I love you.

"Eirik's son? Leif?" Thorok said.

Leif snapped back to reality. "Thorok, I'm sorry. I am watching Thorgunna and the child. What game do they play?" Leif asked.

Thorok, who had not wandered far from Leif's side all evening, replied, "She's using the sight to give the child something to think about."

"She's scrying?"

Thorok nodded.

"Oh, I must have her read my fortune as well," Leif said.

"You may not like what she sees," Thorok replied.

Leif stood, straightening his tunic. Thorok followed.

Is he going to accompany me all night? Leif thought. Thorok moved alongside Leif, not breaking stride. *Apparently so!*

A young woman holding a baby stopped Thorok, taking hold of his arm.

"Watch your daughter, Thorok. I've things to do!" the woman demanded as Thorok rounded the women's side of the flames, placing a red-haired little girl into Thorok's arms.

Thorok took the child, cradling her lovingly.

"How many children do you have, Thorok?" Leif asked, admiring the baby.

"Eight on Tiree. Four on Coll. Maybe one or two on Mull. I've never been back to check."

"How many wives?" Leif laughed.

"No wife. I'm saving myself for the right woman," Thorok said, winking.

"One of them will pin you down, Thorok. You know it will happen."

"Aye. But not today."

They approached Thorgunna. The baby squirmed in Thorok's arms, tightening her little brow into a frown, letting out a mighty roar.

"Your daughter isn't happy, Thorok. Better you had go find her mother and have her press that baby to her breast before the child cries the sky down upon us," Thorgunna said.

"Aye," Thorok agreed, frustrated he could not hold his protective stance between Thorgunna and Leif.

"He would not leave my side this night. Bless that screaming child," Leif whispered. He sat next to Thorgunna on a long plank set out upon stones.

"Do you only tell the fortunes of children?" he asked.

"I can influence children with my visions. Help them see a clear path," Thorgunna replied.

"You look lovely in the firelight, Thorgunna. What do you think you'd see if you held my hands and looked into my heart with your woman's inner vision?"

"Give me your hands," Thorgunna replied.

Leif extended his hands to Thorgunna, who turned them palm up. He moved his head closer.

"Will I be harmed if I kiss the Jarl of Tiree in public?"

"I'll kill you myself. Now be quiet and let me see what there is to see."

Thorgunna studied Leif's palms. Each ridge, callus, and scar told her a story. He had large, strong hands. Dirt from the fields remained embedded under his nails. She looked at the fingers which had given her so much pleasure his first night on Tiree.

Thorgunna laughed softly to herself. She closed her eyes and plunged into the darkness of the sight.

Leif felt a bit uncomfortable as twenty or so *Tirisdeach* and some of

Leif's own men had gathered around the couple.

"Apparently my reading is not to be a private affair," he whispered.

"Shhh," Thorgunna said, squeezing Leif's hands, drawing them in, placing them over her heart.

"I like this game, Thorgunna," Leif whispered, entwining his fingers with Thorgunna's.

The joyful noises of celebration subsided as an eerie silence enveloped the beach. An occasional snap and pop from the fire were the only sounds to penetrate the veil of night.

"Am I required to cross your palm with silver before you speak?" Leif joked to break the absolute stillness of the night.

Thorgunna made no reply. She was far away—in the realm of prophesy and prediction, metaphoric truths, visionary revelations.

****

Thorgunna walked among the rows of corn near Loch Bhasapol at Cornaigmore. The stalks were quite tall and laden with ripe ears. *That's a good sign*, she thought. A path opened up. She followed it to the toppled standing stone of *Clachan Mor*. Blood stained the stone as if a sacrifice had been made. Thorgunna felt a trickle of warmth run down her legs. *It is my blood. I am bleeding. From what? My woman's flow?* Leif's cloak lay beside the stone. Leif's bloodstained cloak. Then she knew it was not flow, but virgin's blood that trickled down her leg, staining the stone, the earth, and the cloak. Looking closer at the cloak, there was more than just blood. A navel cord graced the fabric with its presence, too. *I shall bear his child*, Thorgunna realized. *But will he live? Will Leif live?*

Thorgunna opened her eyes and stared into Leif's. I love you, Leif. I love you and will give my life to protect you from harm.

****

"What did you see, Lady?" Leif asked skeptically.

"I cannot tell you. It is something that must be shown," Thorgunna replied.

"Lead away!" Leif replied, holding fast to Thorgunna's hands, not allowing her to move them from over her heart.

"Go enjoy the fire, Leif. What must be shown can wait until dawn."

The crowd laughed, dispersing. There would be no story from Thorgunna's scrying tonight. She had a secret. They knew it and respected it.

The fire burned throughout the night. Leif sat back, drinking the beer, watching the men and women of Tiree move about Thorgunna.

She is their central figure. The hub of their wheel. The queen of the hive. What would happen if she left? What would happen to the lives of these simple folk should I whisk their Lady Jarl from them and make her my wife? Leif wondered. *And always there is Thorok. He's watching me now. I see him through the flames, his cup raised to me. Is it a toast or a threat? What is it that makes him behave like a loyal dog, ready to spring at the master's orders?*

It then occurred to Leif only two things could make a man act so. The first would be fear. The second would be love.

I cannot separate her from Tiree. Damn me for falling in love with the one woman I can never make my wife. In spite of my feelings, I must leave Tiree. I must leave Tiree without her. Thorok is in love with her. He'll take care of her. She'll be safe.

As Leif wandered the beach, watching his fellow Greenlanders drink Tiree's beer and fondle Tiree's women, he clearly saw the urgent plea in their eyes as they looked up at him with red eyes stinging from smoke and brew as he passed by. *We're men of the sea. Greenland's future lies with* us. *We must away, Captain. We must away! Before the women of this fair isle trap us into contracts of marriage and more!*

Greenland's future weighed heavily upon his mind. His father's dream of recognition and acceptance by Norway for the country he'd founded. Eirik was an outcast. Greenland was not a part of Olaf's realm, and therefore attracted no traders and few settlers from beyond Iceland. No wealth streamed in by way of ship and man. Eirik wanted heathen Greenland recognized, accepted, and blessed by a Christian king.

Leif approached Thorgunna, taking her by the arm. "Walk with me," he commanded.

Thorgunna glanced toward Thorok, then back to Leif. "All right."

Holding Thorgunna by the elbow, Leif led her away from the fire, away from the revelers.

"He's following us, isn't he?" Leif asked.

"Always. But he'll keep his distance," Thorgunna remarked, smiling.

"Thorgunna, I've come to realize you are a very important woman on this island."

"And what does this mean to you?" she asked.

"As I see it, you are Tiree."

"Go on," Thorgunna said, taking Leif's hand.

"I am only now beginning to understand your apprehension about Olaf and the coming of the Church to your island. If Norway usurps your power, then Tiree will lose its heart. Oh, I'm sure the island will produce fine grain and the people will go on living, but without your guidance, they will never be truly happy. Thereby, I find I am troubled. Once we've made love, I'm sure an attachment will develop between us. But I must leave Tiree. I cannot stay."

"Oh?" Thorgunna took a deep breath, holding it, to stifle the welling sense of hurt adding to the churning broth of troubles in her belly.

"My father desires Olaf to acknowledge Greenland and establish a trade route. With that trade, comes the priests, I fear. My father still clings—and passionately, I might add—to the old ways. He does not relish new thoughts. Progress, to him, must wear a cloak resembling the past."

"What does this have to do with our making love?" Thorgunna asked.

"You will want me to stay with you. Marry you. I know this. You're a woman, after all. The most startling woman I've ever met, but still, you're a woman with a woman's heart." Leif paused, turning to face Thorgunna. "I must complete my mission to Norway for the sake of my father and my country."

"I have not asked you to make love to me. Nor, I might add, have I asked you to marry me or stay on Tiree. In fact, you have been hounding me for sex from your first hour on the island! And as for your commentary on womanhood, I fear you know very little about women except where to aim your erection!" She moved away, her fists clenched. Thorok, watching in the shadows, smiled.

Leif followed Thorgunna. "Thorgunna, I have misspoken," he began.

"I'll say!" Thorgunna replied haughtily.

"Thorgunna, I have not expressed myself well. What I am trying to say is—"

"Leif, you are an arrogant, ill-mannered little boy!" Thorgunna cursed.

"That may be so, but at least I am honest. I want to make love to you, right here. With Thorok watching, if need be. My desire for you is insatiable. But know this, when my ship and the weather are ready, I must leave Tiree. I fear my leaving this safe haven is only the beginning of my true journey, but leave I must. I am my father's eldest son. I am the emissary for his foundling country. He is relying upon me."

Thorgunna turned away, walking quickly to the safety of the fire. She called, without looking back, "And what of the others whose loyalty and trust you should cherish, sir?"

Leif returned to his lonely station across from Thorgunna, just out of the fire's glow. *I am a fool. I am a damned fool. I love her, and still I shun her, offend her, and drive her away. I don't deserve her.*

****

Dawn blossomed promisingly. Warm, sunny, and bright.

The Lady Jarl had fallen aglow, her head and body framed like an icon on a page of holy text in the rays of dawn. Brigit felt compelled to cross herself, saying a prayer for Thorgunna.

"Holy Mother, protect my Lady. Protect her and bring her into your arms that she may understand true love. I pray most ardently now, Holy Mother, for I am certain Thorgunna shall fall this day into the arms of the Greenlander. If ever she needed You, that time is now."

****

Facing east, welcoming the first day of summer, Thorgunna allowed herself to escape in the warm glow of the rising sun. For a moment she felt the fleeting sensation of absolute freedom she'd cherished as a child.

Leif approached Thorgunna, interrupting her memories of youth. "Do you take a partner to the fields?" he asked, hoping Thorok was not too close at that particular moment.

"I have not yet selected my partner," Thorgunna replied. *I've never gone to the fields with a man.*

The beach grew deserted as the final couples sauntered off. Only the children, watched by the very old women, broke the stillness. The great fire had burnt itself to embers, glowing red and orange against the white sand of the beach.

"Your choices are few, Lady," Leif whispered. His arms went about her waist, turning her. "It is time. You know it. I know it. Thorok must not know it, and that's a blessing."

"What choices do I have, Leif?" Thorgunna asked.

"To make love to me here, on this long stretch of beach, or take me to the fields and let me hold you in celebration of an end to winter, for Tiree—and for you."

"I don't want you to die, Leif," Thorgunna whispered, searching for the depth of Leif's emotions hidden in his crystal blue eyes.

"What?" Leif asked.

"Aye," Thorgunna replied.

"Perhaps you'd like to share something with me, Thorgunna. What exactly, are you talking about?" Leif asked, taking a commanding stance.

Thorgunna frowned. *He reminds me of my father standing there. Firm. Dead set. Unbreakable.* "When my husband died at sea I lost the protection of his private army for the Isle as well. You know this. These people are farmers, Leif. Should Norway storm Tiree to shackle their faiths and my brewery, I am left defenseless."

"Farmers make excellent warriors when their home and way of life is at stake," Leif replied.

"Aye. They would fight," Thorgunna said grimly. "And they would die. And Norway would control the isle and force us into submission to the Church."

Leif struggled to find the correct words. Slowly, as if dawn lit not only the sky, but his mind as well, he spoke, "It is not that you hate the Church and Norway, it is that you hate forced conversion and control. Yes?"

Thorgunna nodded. "Since I was a small child the priests have chastised me for using my second sight to advise and guide the islanders. My father nearly beat to death one young acolyte who punished me for scrying. Eventually, my father paid those priests enough money to have them overlook my talents as my brother and I were tutored. The priests eventually left Tiree, taking their only convert with them. My brother, Helgi. Then my parents died, and I became Jarl by my own hand. I am a wise woman, Leif. I can read and write Latin. I cannot be bested in trade. And yet in my dreams, I fell…" Thorgunna paused, eyes downcast, looking almost ashamed.

"Tell me, Thorgunna," Leif insisted.

"I fell into a contract with the devil that damns me, and damns you and damns Tiree in the guise of protection."

"The untapped passion of a widow is stronger than the idle threats of any half-god," Leif said, smiling.

"My passions could be my undoing as well as your own." Thorgunna sighed.

"With the force of my passion for you alone, I can defeat Loki. Make love to me, Thorgunna. Today, this first day of summer."

"I want to. But I am tangled in a web of lies and do not truly wish you to suffer my fate."

"I am willing to walk into the fire for you, Thorgunna. The desire I have for you burns hotter than even the tricks and lies and boasts of Loki. I know him for who he is. He cannot fool me. He cannot tame me. He cannot harm me."

Surprising herself, Thorgunna pulled Leif to her, kissing him deeply. In the darkness beyond her closed eyes, she saw only what should be there. Nothing. Emptiness. Loki waited for her in the night of her heart.

In all the days since Finn's death, the first dream, and Leif's landing, the dark had not been a safe haven or a place of rest and renewal. But now the dark, the dark of the stillness of her sight, revealed more than any vision she had endured since childhood. There was nothing to fear in this dark. No razor-sharp lies. No jagged threats. No enemies hiding.

As Thorgunna broke the kiss, feeling safe and filled with the promise of ardent first love, she forgot that, unfortunately, shadows can hide in the dark. Clever, willful shadows.

She whispered, "It is time to reveal to you that which I saw when I held your hands before the great fire. The secret of the field."

"Godling threats or not?" Leif asked, squeezing Thorgunna.

"He's lying," Thorgunna replied.

"That is his nature."

"I have been blinded by fatigue, fear, and duty. Today, if only this day for the rest of my life, I want to put my own interests first."

"I'm not going to die, Thorgunna. At least not by the hand of Loki."

"Yes, I know."

"Then, take me to the fields. Loki, Norway, and responsibilities be damned. Take me to the fields, Thorgunna."

Chapter 8

The early-morning dew still wetting the machair—Tiree's native wind-swept tall grass—Thorgunna and Leif mounted their ponies, and rode west. Thorgunna turned her horse north as the corn fields overtook them. Row after row of tall, healthy stalks of corn flanked them as Thorgunna continued north, driving her horse directly into a field, following only a pathway she could see. Leif followed, not questioning her lead.

At last, Thorgunna pulled back, urging her pony to stop. She slid off, nodding for Leif to do the same. Tying the ponies to a jagged outcropping of rock amidst the furrows, Thorgunna then tied Leif off, in a manner of speaking.

Ripping the hem off her chemise, Thorgunna blindfolded him, her hands trembling to tie the knot.

"Well, this is unexpected. I'm quite stimulated by your behavior, Thorgunna. Are you going to tie me up, as well?" Leif asked.

"Don't be silly," Thorgunna replied.

"I am quite serious."

"Do hold still while I tie this mask, Leif. And uncross your wrists. I'm not going to bind you further. A secret is best revealed with a bit of anticipation, don't you think?" Thorgunna moved in front of Leif to check the blindfold.

Leif leaned forward, somehow knowing instinctively how close Thorgunna was to him, whispering, "Lady, I have felt nothing but anticipation since first I laid eyes upon you."

"One more little surprise won't hurt, then, will it?" Thorgunna pecked Leif's lips, taking his hand to carefully guide him through the rows.

"And what, woman, is the secret of the field?" Leif asked, quite amused, becoming more than just a little aroused at being blindfolded and led through the cornfield.

"All will be revealed in time," Thorgunna replied, pulling on Leif's tunic, urging him forward. "I told you my vision is something that must be shown."

"I'll trip and fall, and a strong stalk of Tireean corn will pierce me through the belly," Leif complained. "I know about the Battle of the Sheaves, after all."

"The corn obeys me Leif. I made it promise to pelt you lightly if you misbehave as opposed to running you through for your barbaric Greenlandic ways."

"I should remove this blindfold and swat you like a spoiled child," Leif replied.

"You'd enjoy that," Thorgunna laughed.

"Yes, I would. We'll have to consider something along those lines next time."

"There hasn't been a first time and already you speak of a next. How presumptuous of you," Thorgunna said.

"I can't tell if you're smiling, Thorgunna."

She turned, lightly kissing Leif. "I'm smiling."

At last Thorgunna released Leif, having led him some distance through the corn. She untied his blindfold.

"We're here," Thorgunna proclaimed.

Leif found himself surrounded on all sides by green and golden stalks of ripening corn in a clearing perhaps twenty feet in circumference. At the circle's center was a megalith—a standing stone. Toppled and broken into two large slabs of solid rock it was still an impressive sight.

Several smaller stones ringed the perimeter of the clearing, most half-buried by soil and overgrown by spreading stalks of corn.

"Who made this?" Leif asked, running his hands along the sleek, precise square line of the cuts which had freed the beast from some long forgotten quarry.

"That depends upon whom you ask. Oral tradition says it was the Picts, the race from which my mother descended. There are several standing stones about Tiree. This is the largest, even toppled."

"This is amazing. Where's the quarry?" Leif asked, still marveling at the precise cut of the stone.

"We've a quarry on the west end of the Isle. These stones were cut from the very heart of Tiree, for Tiree rests upon a foundation of this stone. We've unearthed things around here. Odd things. *Frightening things.* When we turned the fallows for the corn, we disturbed a burial site," Thorgunna whispered, as if to say it aloud would bring bad luck.

"What things?" Leif asked, sensing her excitement.

"Bones, of course. And stone idols. Little idols in the shape of a round woman with large breasts. We found two."

Leif slid his arms around Thorgunna's waist, "It is a wise man who worships a round woman with large breasts." He put his head to Thorgunna's ample bosom, his hands stretching out at her waist to caress the curve of her backside.

Thorgunna, lost for only a moment in the tingling surge of pleasure at Leif's touch, took a step back, continuing her archeological discourse, "We left the idols here since it is where someone took great care to bury them. Would you like to see one?"

Leif smiled slyly, nodding, "Aye, I'd like to see the goddess of Tiree."

Giddy as a child, Thorgunna lifted a loaf-sized stone from the perimeter of the clearing, nodding for Leif to join her.

Within the hole were two small stone statuettes, crudely hewn from gneiss. They were identical, or at least there was an obvious, careful attempt by the ancient artisan to make them exactly alike.

About four inches in height, each idol was of a woman, identified solely by the huge breasts; the idols' carved hands pressed to a round, perhaps pregnant belly. The thighs of the woman-idol were heavy, giving the overall appearance of fertility and wealth. There was no discernible face. It could have been any woman. Leif knew once he coaxed Thorgunna from her shift, that she, in her beckoning fleshiness, would resemble the statuette, though in truth she was already worshipped by her people.

"I find these statues quite remarkable—and arousing," Leif said honestly. "I'd love to bed the woman who modeled for them."

Thorgunna laughed. "Never before have I heard such a lurid statement!"

Leif turned to face Thorgunna, holding out one of the statues to her. "I've thought worse when in your presence."

Tenderly, Leif kissed Thorgunna's throat, pulling upon the leather ties to her tunic with one hand, fondling her breasts with the other.

They joined in a long, passionate embrace. His kiss was so seductive, so hypnotic Thorgunna failed to notice Leif's clever hands had completely removed the front lacing on the V closure of her dress.

Leif's mouth moved to Thorgunna's cleavage, now spilling out the front of her shift.

"Leif, please," Thorgunna said. *I'm afraid.*

Not looking up, Leif replied, his tongue dragging across the soft folds of Thorgunna's breasts, "It is time, Thorgunna. I told you I wanted you for my mistress, and you refused me. I have stopped myself many times from entering your chamber at night and taking you by force. I mean to have you, and this place beckons me to do so. This is a place that has seen and heard the acts between man and woman long before we came here, I'm sure of it. Enjoy this, Thorgunna. It's been too long for you and much too long for me."

Thorgunna raised her arms to deflect Leif. "We mustn't."

Leif clutched Thorgunna's hands. He held her wrists. She held the goddess. "Let me worship you, Thorgunna. This little statue is you, don't you see that? *You* are the goddess of Tiree."

Thorgunna squeezed the little stone figure in her hand, trying to call upon some protective force now eluding her. *Is it time? Is it time to allow a man, this man, beyond the pain and grief? Past the fear?*

"Leif." she began. Her words were cut off as Leif involved her in a deep kiss, his tongue probing, caressing hers.

"I don't want you to die. He'll kill you if we…" Thorgunna sighed.

"One of Loki's threats?" Leif asked.

"Yes."

"He is a liar. However, for a chance to hold you, I'd face him unarmed in battle." Leif kissed Thorgunna tenderly. "It is time you came out of mourning. Step out from the darkness with me. Please. Do you trust me, Thorgunna?" Leif asked, stepping back.

"I do. Yes. I trust you. Fool that I am."

"Then, trust me now. Don't be afraid," he said.

In one movement of his strong hands, he ripped open Thorgunna's tunic from the end of the V opening at the bodice to her ankles, leaving her body vulnerable to his gaze and touch.

"Leif!" Thorgunna cried, desperately trying to hold the torn fabric closed.

Leif shook his head. "You're mine. Not Loki's. Bugger that little son of a frost giant. I want to see you unclothed before I take you. Hold your arms above your head. Rest your forearms against your head. Oh, yes, that way…"

Thorgunna did as Leif ordered. *Why am I allowing this? I know why I'm allowing this. I love you, Leif. He said I would love you, and I do! But still, I should kill you where you stand rather than let the likes of Loki torture you for all eternity.* She closed her eyes, unable to concentrate on anything as the heat of Leif's callused hands ignited her flesh to a smoldering blaze. She felt her skin erupt in goose bumps of both exposure to the cool breeze and arousal as Leif's hands trailed over her shoulders, breasts, and belly, exploring the folds of her body, her roundness, her sensual voluptuousness.

"By the gods, woman, you are a prize worth waiting for. Your markings about your upper arms invite me to kiss and caress," Leif whispered, continuing his tactile exploration of Thorgunna's body.

"My tattoos. I wish mother had never given them to me," Thorgunna replied.

Leif knelt, sliding his arms around Thorgunna's hips, kneading the flesh of her buttocks, his mouth at her belly, his tongue in her navel.

Thorgunna shivered. The keys attached to her shift by a penannular brooch jingled as Leif moved his hands about her thighs, forcing her legs apart.

I've a knife on that ring, she thought.

Leif was ahead of her. "You won't be needing this. Don't think about killing me to protect me from Loki's wrath. I feel it emanating from you, Thorgunna. I can smell it on you. I'm not Loki, Olaf of Norway, nor am I Ketil or Finn. I'm Leif, and I'm going to make love to you," he scolded, breaking the small dagger off the ring, tossing it aside. "Spread your stance, woman," he ordered.

Thorgunna held her ground.

"Do it!" Leif commanded.

"I cannot," Thorgunna replied.

Leif stood. "Lady Jarl, you've met your match. Until I leave this island, you are mine."

"I do not want you, Leif Eiriksson! I do not want you!" She wept.

His eyes glaring into hers, Leif thrust a hand between Thorgunna's legs, pushing past the outer lips of her mound, driving across her flesh, a finger dipping into her womanhood.

"You want me all right," Leif said, continuing to caress Thorgunna as he had done the eve of his arrival, spreading her own wetness about her mound, his fingers drenched. He pulled her tightly to him, kissing her hard.

"Your body doesn't lie. I want your lips to speak the truth as well. Admit you want me," he whispered, holding her firmly, still manipulating the flesh between her legs.

Thorgunna broke. She began to weep, releasing all the fear, all the anguish, all the loneliness with each stroke of Leif's hand, each touch of his lips upon hers.

"Yes, I want you," she mewed softly.

"I knew that all along," Leif said.

With a gentle passion that surprised even him, Leif kissed Thorgunna. He dropped to his knees before her.

His tongue went to that spot his hand had just been.

Leif pulled away. "This won't do. Over there," he commanded, pointing to the standing stone. "Sit at the edge. I want your legs over my shoulders. Since I first tasted you, I have wanted no other honey against my tongue."

Thorgunna's face went ashen.

Leif shook his head. "Don't be afraid. Surely your husband must have pleasured you. If he did not, then he was not worthy of your love. I cannot believe that you must be drunk to enjoy the sensation of a man's mouth on your lovely quim."

Thorgunna's mouth dropped open in alarm. *There was no marriage bed! I don't know what to do!*

Leif scooped Thorgunna into his arms, setting her upon the toppled stone, her cloak and torn shift acting as a blanket under her.

"Your legs upon my shoulders, now."

Overwhelmed, Thorgunna complied.

Embarrassed, she hid her face in her hands as Leif licked and tasted the soft folds at the seat of her womanhood, pulling her engorged bud into his lips, sucking it, his tongue darting in and out of her, his whiskers burning her tender inner lips.

Leif sighed contentedly as Thorgunna quivered under his ministrations, yet returned from the brink of his own emotions when she startled as he slid his fingers into her.

"It has been too long for you, indeed, Lady. You'll enjoy a bit of reawakening. Enjoy it as much as I."

Gently pushing Thorgunna over, her back to the stone, her torn clothing now like an altar covering, Leif proceeded to seduce, titillate, and worship his fleshy goddess.

Thorgunna dropped the little stone idol she had been holding so tightly as she became lost in Leif's embrace.

Picking the goddess up, Leif raised it over Thorgunna as she lay supine upon the stone.

Silently, his eyes not leaving hers, he traced the idol across the slope of Thorgunna's right breast, stopping to let it kiss the nipple before traveling up the side, then under, then to the left.

Thorgunna's nipples responded, hardening to dark pink points. It could have been the dead of winter and her nipples would not have been more erect.

"Beautiful," Leif murmured as he took the statue and ran it over Thorgunna's belly and thighs, just avoiding her woman's mound with each pass.

Thorgunna brought her arms across her bosom. Leif pushed them away. A hand went modestly across her thighs. Leif slapped it away.

The stubble of his beard burned across her skin from neck to knees as Leif continued staking his claim, his own tunic removed and breeches cast aside.

Dragging the goddess across Thorgunna's goose-pimpled flesh, he continued his assault. He was in control, a position it seemed he rather enjoyed.

He raised her knees, opening his path. Leif slid the idol between Thorgunna's spread legs, carefully caressing her inner thighs, dipping the goddess deeper, briefly baptizing it with Thorgunna's own nectar.

Thorgunna reached out to touch Leif.

"No. You lie still," he directed, brushing her hand aside.

"Leif, let me…"

"No words now. No words," he whispered. He kissed her over and over.

At last Leif climbed atop the stone of *Clachan Mor*, still holding the fertility goddess. He moved between Thorgunna's legs, the weight of his hips going squarely against hers, he sought out that part of her he had so long desired to explore fully, deeply, and completely.

Leif thrust forward, inward, expecting easy access and rapid, turbulent passion. A widow lay beneath him. A woman used to the weight of a man upon her and in her. He had done what he could to ease his passage. Yet there was firm resistance. His spirit unhampered by the boundary between his flesh and hers, he guided himself past the blockade, and dove deeply.

Thorgunna gasped as Leif pushed his way into her, tearing her flesh as he had her clothing. So powerful was Leif's entry into her body she could almost hear the rupture of her maidenhood as Leif breeched that most holy of barriers, thrusting intensely, then withdrawing, then plunging in again like a sword hot from the forge into pristine snow.

Hesitantly, Thorgunna responded, moving her hips in rhythm to Leif's thrusts, mesmerized by the wet sounds their bodies produced at the peak of the union, falling into an erotic pattern of movement atop the fallen stone.

For a fleeting moment her thoughts turned to Loki. Loki's curse. Loki's wrath. But only for a moment. Leif's passion was more powerful than the will of the malicious little godling. Leif's ardor and passion swept her into a magnificent symphony of body rhythms and rapturous union.

She raised her legs, and Leif mounted higher, riding her slowly, deeply, pressing against the crest of her womanhood, arousing her to new heights.

"Thorgunna, I am ready. Let me hear your pleasure that I may release," Leif murmured, his throat constricting as he forced his body to act contrary to the demands upon it. "Remember when you had no inhibitions due to the drink? You cried like a banshee when you came. You rewarded me."

Hear my pleasure? When I was drunk what did I do? Oh, gods … what did I say? Thorgunna wondered—but not for long.

A moment later the smoldering fire in her loins sparked, ignited, then erupted like the previous night's bonfire, spreading flames of pleasure throughout her body. She cried out, unable to contain the guttural vocalization of orgasm as its fire coursed through her.

Leif knew he could now allow his own release. Quickening his pace, the full weight of his body behind each thrust, he too exploded in orgasm. Just as Thorgunna relaxed into a puddle of warm, exhausted flesh, Leif pulled back and away, completely out of her, using his hand to bring his final release.

Thorgunna watched with fascination as Leif spilled his seed upon her belly and breasts as opposed to deep inside her.

****

Still shuddering with the force of his orgasm, Leif opened his eyes, expecting to see only a satisfied woman beneath him.

There was that, yes, but something unexpected caught his eye. There was blood on his penis, and upon the hand which held his still-pulsating beast.

Hopping off the stone, off Thorgunna, his naked, muscled backside to her, he spoke, "You should have revealed you were having your woman's flow, Thorgunna."

Thorgunna sat up on her elbows, "I am not in flow."

Leif turned. "Here is your blood, woman," Leif replied, extending his hand. "Look, your thighs too, are stained."

Thorgunna laid back again the slab. "The truth is, Leif, until a moment ago, I was unknown by man."

"A virgin widow?" Leif replied, laughing. "A woman's flow is nothing to hide or be ashamed of. I would have made love to you anyway, but I would not have had to withdraw. Nor would I have put my mouth to you."

Thorgunna, holding her torn shift about her, approached Leif. "A widow, I am. I married by contract. Finn MacLean died at sea while en route to Tiree, before we had ever met, much less consummated our nuptials. I have never known a marriage bed."

Leif sighed. "I took your virginity."

"Aye," Thorgunna replied.

Leif rolled his neck, wincing. "This is unexpected." A sudden, painful throbbing at the back of his skull unnerved him.

"Are you in pain?" Thorgunna asked.

"My neck is stiff, nothing more," Leif replied, worried a contract would now exist between him and Thorgunna.

"It is said that the blood of a virgin heals all ills," Thorgunna said softly, invitingly. "Are you in need of healing, Leif Eiriksson?"

He made no reply.

"Leif Eiriksson, are you in need of healing?" she asked again, brushing her still-tingling nipples along his spine.

Leif felt his loins stir. "Damn my readiness," he muttered. "I am in dire need." He lifted Thorgunna onto the toppled standing stone in a sitting position, standing between her legs, kissing her deeply.

As they kissed, Leif slid two fingers between Thorgunna's legs, exploring his conquest, bringing his fingers away stained with her bright red blood.

Without breaking their kiss, Leif wiped his fingers on what had been his blindfold, tucking it under his leather wristband. First blood. Virgin's blood. It was within a Norseman's rights to claim a trophy, often the woman herself, with first passage.

Fully aroused by the conquest, the anticipation, and the blossoming feelings in his heart, Leif then thrust into Thorgunna as she sat atop the ancient fallen standing stone, her legs wrapping around him, pulling him in, urging him to new depths.

Only a moment passed before they climaxed simultaneously; Thorgunna held fast onto Leif with her legs, rocking in rhythm to the ancient music of his thrusts, refusing to release him as he once again forbade himself the pleasure of spilling within her.

Leif pushed away hard, withdrawing under Thorgunna's protest, covering her thighs with his seed. Almost apologetically, he whispered, "I must not father a child with you, Thorgunna. I shall leave Tiree one day soon, and sail to Norway."

"I would love your child," Thorgunna said, hurt.

"If I stayed on Tiree with you sharing my bed, I would give full rights to any child of your body, but I am not staying on Tiree, and we must not beget a child."

"With me in your bed as your mistress or wife?" Thorgunna asked defensively.

Leif frowned. This was what he feared. A contract signed by the taking of virginity. How should he answer?

"To marry is a decision I cannot make when I am blinded by desire and passion. I want you. Is that not enough for now? In fact, I want you often. You are worth battling a god for, woman. Every lovely bit of you, inside and out, I would fight for."

"I should feel complimented, and yet I can only think about lighting your funeral pyre."

"Don't worry about me."

"But I will, Leif. I will worry about you."

"Learn not to."

"Harder to learn than Latin, that." Thorgunna paused. "Leif, if we make love again," she asked, hoping, "Must you always withdraw?"

"Yes. When you are in flow I need not pull away. If you were nursing a babe, likewise. A man's seed will not grow in a woman during those times," Leif replied.

"And you know this, how?"

"The woman who first took me to her bed taught me many things. I was a good pupil."

"I'll bet you were!" Thorgunna laughed. "I know little except what has been gleaned from the whisperings of women who've drunk too much beer by the fire late at night—and in the nightmares of passion Loki subjected me to. What can you teach me, Leif Eiriksson?"

"I'm not sure we have that much time together," Leif replied.

Thorgunna reached for her knife. It felt more secure to her than Leif's strong arms. At least she could control the blade.

Chapter 9

Loki clenched his fists so hard his fingernails broke the flesh of his palms. He was too angry to bleed. He had seen too much. Too much from his vantage point high above Tiree, high above the world of men.

Loki leaped off Odin's throne, the *Lidskjalf*, his fiery nature popping and crackling as his rage stewed and grew, threatening to explode with cataclysmic force.

"No, no, no, no, no, no!" he cried. "That willful, disobedient woman! I've set too many plans into motion for her not to truckle to my will!"

Loki kicked at Odin's throne. "Damn your shackles, Odin! Damn your arrogance in thinking I am the one who must be contained!"

Calming himself, pulling the flames of envy into their hiding place in the shadows of his lithe, handsome human form, he knelt, leaning over the parapet of Odin's tower, stroking Odin's wolves, watching the sexual union of Leif and Thorgunna in the midst of Cornaigmore.

"That Greenlandic pup plows Tiree's rich soil. He defiles the land. He takes what is rightfully mine. Tiree is mine. Tiree must be mine," Loki hissed. "What to do now? What to do? I must persevere. Indeed. To lose my hold on Tiree because I could not stop that bothersome son of Eirik the Red from breaking ground on my island is more than I can bear! I am a god! The blood of divinity courses through my body, and I shall not be denied!"

Loki looked at the old, wise gray she-wolf. "You understand, don't you, Freki. We share the animal instinct to survive, don't we, girl?" He paused, stroking the wolf's head. "I loved you once, you know. To run with you, across the vault of Heaven and into the bowels of the underworld was bliss. Someday soon, when the others are gone, and I rule from Tiree, you and I, we shall run again. As mates. I promise you, old girl."

Freki looked to Geri, her male counterpart.

Loki reached out to touch the strong, white male. "Oh, don't worry about Geri. I'll love him, too. But first I must again yoke the Lady Jarl. I shan't permit her virgin's blood to mix with mine at the final battle. It shall be her blood, and Leif's, and the blood of their kin who shall perish when the last god standing dies under my sword."

Freki and Geri moved away from Loki. "Where do you go, my beloved wolf cousins?"

The wolves snarled as they backed away from the befouled throne of Odin, and the demigod who soiled it by his breath alone.

"Fine! Go! When Odin falls the two of you shall burn, too!"

Loki climbed back onto the throne—rather, Loki slithered onto the *Lidskjalf.* "Every day another god fades into obscurity as baptismal fonts overflow across the Northlands. I need only one cairn, and I shall live on, even after the other gods are dead. And die they shall, at my hand."

He smiled.

"I shall find a way to control Thorgunna, gain Tiree, and thereby fulfill my destiny as the harbinger of the final battle." Loki fell back in the throne, laughing. "I shall fulfill my destiny not as prophesied, but as I shall write it!"

The words of the *Voluspa,* the prophesy of the gods, ticked through Loki's dark, diseased mind. "Ragnarok, the final battle, is at hand. And only I shall remain when the long winter passes. First, I must set myself to the task of ridding the nine worlds of the Aesir gods' oppressive rule. Then, I shall neuter Thorgunna's bull and force her to set his head and heart before the very stone she shall erect in my honor. Then, I shall deal with her…"

Loki, bloated with diseased carnality and desirous of power no man or god should ever covet, cackled and shook as he delighted in his devilish plans. When causing destruction, wreaking havoc, he was at his best.

Chapter 10

Although exhausted from the activities of the night before the longest day, and broken from the activities of the longest day itself, Thorgunna had not slept well, again. Leif lay beside her, naked and snoring. It was the first night, in all her life, that she had shared her bed. She had no nightmare, for she had not been able to drift into deep sleep with the presence of another next to her.

It is one of life's jokes, I fear. Here I long for a man to lie beside me, and hold me, as all women do, and now I find I cannot get comfortable next to the hard, warm body of a man in my bed, she thought.

Thorgunna rolled onto her side, her back to Leif. "I need to build a bigger bed," she whispered, feeling Leif's protective arm slide around her waist. "However long it takes to grow accustomed to this man beside me, it is worth the effort. I love you, Leif. I love you."

Comfortable, feeling safe, still aglow from the fire of Leif's passion, Thorgunna looked back on her day, recalling the whirlwind-driven gamut of emotions she had traversed to reach the one moment in her life that would never be repeated. The loss of her virginity.

Fear. Apprehension. Embarrassment. By the gods I must have turned red from head to toe when he tore open my shift! And yet, I relish that moment. He took control of my fears and tamed me as no man has ever done. And once under his control, well, I ... I wonder why I waited so long to know the pleasures of a man atop me. Thorgunna giggled. "Or under me!"

The entire day and night had been lost to their shared passions. Thorgunna's mouth was numb from Leif's kisses. She was caked with sweat, soil, and seed. And yet, she had never felt more beautiful.

Wide awake, as the second day of summer dawned, Thorgunna replayed their final coupling before fatigue and the chill of the solid stone overtook them, driving them home to Gott.

"Go atop me," Leif had encouraged. "Swallow me with your body, woman. Then move as your own body tells you to. Yes … yes…"

She watched herself, as if she were a bird on high, mount Leif carefully, tentatively. She recalled how quickly she responded to his upward thrusts, crushing their pelvises together, his member filling her more deeply than ever it had in any of its prior opportunities.

As Thorgunna replayed the sensation of Leif's blond, wiry pubic hair meeting her own silky black-haired mound, she felt a stirring in that place of her body he had filled so well.

Quietly, so as not to awaken Leif, she whispered, "It was much like going on horseback. The same movements. No wonder the Norse use the same word for *sex* and *ride*."

The flower of orgasm had blossomed simultaneously atop the great stone in the cornfield. Thorgunna summoned up the memory of that moment when she fully immersed herself in the hot rain of Leif's passion, driving hard against him in the wave of ecstasy.

Leif had not pulled away. He couldn't pull away. I felt his explosion inside me. He poured life into me. He gave me his love.

Thorgunna touched her belly. A strong wash of second sight flowed into her as she became aware she was no longer alone. Nor would she ever be from that day forward.

"Thank you, Leif. Thank you," she whispered.

****

Brigit was loath to disturb Thorgunna. She stood outside the door to Thorgunna's home. With news. Bad news. A ship had arrived at Gott Bay. A ship Brigit recognized all too well. A ship and crew well known to the isle, and to Thorgunna.

Ivar the Rus had come to trade.

"God help us all," Brigit prayed, seeking strength to enter.

"He won't help you. But I can," cooed a honeyed voice from behind Brigit.

Brigit turned, raising a questioning eyebrow at the stranger behind her. "Do I know you, sir? You're certainly brazen to take my prayers to the Lord God so lightly."

"I've come to help your Lady."

"It is hard for a stranger to walk upon Tiree without me knowing him. I do not recognize you," Brigit said, wrapping her cloak a bit tighter around her shoulders.

"Always your head in the hearth or up to your elbows in your mortar and pestle, are ye, lassie? I've been about the Isle for quite some time now. The better part of spring, and now I am here to enjoy this fine summer day."

"Whoever you are, and wherever you've been hiding yourself, it gives you no right to scoff at a prayer to the Almighty. Especially not my prayers."

"No time to quarrel over religious differences now, Brigit O'Saltee."

"Fine. Then leave me be so I can announce the arrival of Ivar to the Lady."

"And disturb her slumber? She worked hard yesterday, little one. She rode hard."

"Don't be crude and vulgar with me. Your name, sir. Give me your name."

"Always the good girl, aren't you? Your Da would be proud indeed."

"Leave my father out of this, sir. He's with the Lord."

Loki's face took on an almost angelic glow. "Do you recall his dying words to you? The last words he spoke through the blood and spittle as Oskar slit his throat?"

"Who are you? How do you know my father's last words?"

Loki smiled. "Does it really matter?"

Brigit turned, unwilling to delay the news of Ivar's arrival any further.

A fast, hard hand darted out, catching her arm, pulling her in like a fish caught on a hook.

"Unhand me, sir!"

"What is the penalty for rape on this island, Brigit?"

Brigit struggled against the stranger, hitting him with her free hand.

"Oh, don't worry, little one. I have no intention of raping you. Now stop the struggle and answer my question."

Brigit ceased her struggle. "The penalty for rape on Tiree is death."

"Yes, it is, isn't it? Thorgunna's own law. Her law written in the blood of Ketil Arngrimsson."

"It's a sound law."

"Yes. With that law you can help Thorgunna, you know."

"Unhand me. You're hurting me."

"I'm sorry, dear one. Just hear me out. You must kill in the guise of self-defense to protect Thorgunna."

"I will not kill."

"Brigit, sweet, Brigit," the stranger moved his face close to Brigit's, sniffing her hair, breathing in the perfume of innocence. "Thorgunna contracted with me to protect Tiree. I enlist your aid in that sacred mission."

"How?"

"That bit of flesh you carry between your legs is more deadly a weapon than even Ivar's breath. Use it to ensnare. Seduce. Trick."

The stranger pulled Brigit to him, wrapping his strong, sinewy arms about her.

Looking into his smoldering black eyes, she felt the seal affixed upon the door to her soul break, fall to pieces, and turn to dust under her feet.

"Who are you?"

"I am an angel."

"No, you cannot be a being of Heaven. You are a fallen angel."

"Does it matter who I am when I give you the means to protect your Lady and your home?"

"What must I do?"

With a warm, wet kiss, Loki put his will into Brigit. As if drowning in poisoned honey, Brigit succumbed to the too-sweet yet bitter flavor of Loki's ignoble plot.

"Now, go ye forth and alert your Lady of Ivar's approach. See now, he pulls his skiff to shore. The door is open. Enter and alert the Lady of Ivar Horseleg's arrival. When the time comes, you shall remember what it is you must do. Until then, I shall be but another passage through the mists rolling off the sea to you."

Brigit, breathless and shaking, lifted her chin, begging for another kiss.

"Ah, you like my kiss. Does it penetrate you? Fill you? Leave you wanting more?"

"Aye, your kiss, stranger, my angel. Give me another."

Obligingly, the hellish angel of fire and light kissed Brigit, delighting in and feeding upon her innocence, leaving his venom in the mournful wound upon her soul.

As Brigit entered Thorgunna's house, she remembered nothing. Nothing save the warm tingle against her mouth, reminding her of the buzzing of bees.

Thorgunna heard the door creak as it opened.

"Brigit?" Thorgunna said, rising.

"Thorgunna," Brigit called through the tapestry. "A ship has pulled to port."

Thorgunna emerged from her chamber wrapped in her shawl.

"Lady, forgive me. But the news is of great importance. Ivar the Rus has landed," Brigit said.

"Oh, gods. The man comes later than expected and at a most inopportune time."

"Indeed," Brigit replied.

Thorgunna stood thoughtfully for a moment, quickly devising a plan to keep Ivar away. "My guard is down. I cannot allow him too close. He'll best me. I must gather my wits. Brigit, send Thorok to confirm a trade circle for tonight, at dusk. He can go set the stones and torches. And a fire in the center. I want a fire between Ivar's stone and mine. I do not want Ivar brought here under any circumstances. I'm not prepared for the likes of Ivar. I need some time to … to strategize," Thorgunna commanded.

Leif emerged from behind the tapestry and said groggily, "My men. My ship. What kind of man is this Ivar the Rus?"

"He's come for his beer. You needn't worry about him pirating your men or ship. It's highly unlikely he'll even acknowledge you. That's his way. Rude to the end," Thorgunna reassured.

"I shall stand at your circle," Leif announced.

"You may stand at my circle, Leif. But do not interrupt or speak. You will be in unfamiliar territory, where I am truly the guide."

"Unlike yesterday," Leif said, chuckling.

Thorgunna blushed.

"Red is a good color for you, woman." Leif darted behind the tapestry.

Composing herself, Thorgunna continued, "Brigit, have Thorok keep

Ivar drunk. If he demands an audience with me, make it known that if he sets so much as a foot on Gott Hill, I'll run him clean through."

"You'll excite him with a message like that, Thorgunna. Don't worry. I'll take care of everything," Brigit said. *And I do mean everything.*

****

The day was clear, and Thorgunna preoccupied. So businesslike was she, Leif felt rejected, and spent the day at his ship.

He watched Ivar. He watched Ivar drink. Ivar watched Leif watching him. However, the most Leif heard from the Eastern Norseman was a rather vulgar belch as Ivar plodded by the damaged hull of Leif's lady.

Just as well. His breath would likely do me in, Leif thought, watching Ivar wander the crescent moon-shaped beach all afternoon, his horn never empty. Without decorum, Ivar spat and belched, scratched his privates, and pissed where he stood.

"Where's my Thorgunna?" he called drunkenly whenever a native islander was within earshot.

In late morning, Brigit came to Gott Beach with food for Ivar and his crew. She deftly maneuvered through the hands of Ivar's shipmates reaching out to touch her as she passed loaves and cheese around, until Ivar himself got hold of her.

"Take me to Thorgunna, woman. Why has she not yet arrived? I grow weary of waiting," Ivar said.

"She'll call you to your tradin' at the time and place she names, and no other time shall she give you this day. She's busy," Brigit responded, pulling away.

"Give us a kiss, woman. You're looking well this bright morning," Ivar demanded, again taking Brigit by her clothing.

"Quit treating me like a common bar wench, and I'll kiss you, Rus!"

Ivar opened his breeches, displaying his flaccid, yet long, thick penis for all those on Gott Beach to see.

"Kiss this," he laughed, thrusting his hips forward.

Brigit held her breath, planting a light kiss on Ivar's lips. "Now do up your pants, Ivar. Your member will grow as red as your face in the sun, and then where will you be, hmmm?"

"Come away with me, Brigit. You've grown up since last I was upon Tiree. A comely woman you've become. Come away now, and I'll give you the ride of your life," Ivar bragged.

Brigit pulled away. "When *that* time comes Rus, it will be of my choosing."

"What's the matter, little girl? You afraid of a real man?" Ivar said, shaking his partially aroused member at her.

"I'm not afraid of the beast you carry between your legs. But hear me now, Ivar, the time to ride that monster will be mine for the choosing." Brigit stood her ground, her eyes fixed firmly on those of the Rus. He backed down, tucking his penis away into his breeches.

"You're a different woman altogether, aren't ye? My Thorgunna knows a good thing when she sees it."

"Yes, she does, Ivar. That's why she avoids you!"

Ivar laughed. "A quick wit she has, my Thorgunna. But not so quick as you."

"I knew I belonged with the Jarl when I first saw her."

"And so you stayed after she freed you."

"Aye. I stayed for her, and because I was waiting for you to come along again," Brigit teased.

Ivar moaned, "I'll have you, you know."

Brigit smiled. "No, Ivar. I'll have you."

Turning away from Ivar, Brigit left the sandy beach of Gott Bay, leaving Ivar to his beer.

"He's a dreadful beast," Thorok said to the Irishwoman as she passed him.

"Yes, he is. And I've never met a man I wanted more," Brigit replied.

****

Leif, ignoring the slobbering Rus trader and his drunken crew, hammered soundly at the new strakes along the hull of his ship, chuckling to himself, drawing the attention of his first mate.

"That good, eh?" Sigurdur asked, turning away from his own hammer. Leif smiled.

"The sex, with the Lady Jarl, it is good, then?" Sigurdur asked.

Leif beamed. "Sigurdur, the Jarl was a virgin until I fell upon her. I took her that first time and a half dozen times more over yesterday. She is fresh and sweet, and for an untried woman, does not hide her passion." An unwelcome thought crossed Leif's mind, clouding his victory over Thorgunna's innocence.

"She is a widow, no?"

"Yes, she is. She married by contract. The man died at sea before ever setting foot on her island or rump in her bed," Leif replied.

"Ah, so you alleviated the widow's grief?" Sigurdur teased.

"Oh, aye. The only grief she feels now is for that bit of girlhood I have forever taken from her," Leif laughed.

"And what of a contract betwixt the Lady and yourself for making first passage?" Sigurdur asked.

"There will be no contract. She is my mistress, nothing more. I restrained myself before," Leif paused, allowing his emphasis on the word "restrained" to sink in, "before the breeding process could take place." *Except for the time she climbed atop me,* Leif thought.

"Restrained yourself?" Sigurdur shuddered. "I can't do that. You're a better man than I, Leifur Eiriksson."

Solemnly, Leif replied, "It was necessary. I cannot have a contract of marriage with a woman I shall never see again once we set sail from this island."

Sigurdur gazed at his captain and friend for a long moment. "You're lying to yourself and me."

Leif turned to face Sigurdur. "Now why would you say that?"

"It was not the laugh of a sexually satisfied man I heard a moment ago. It was the laugh of a fool in love."

"I love only taking what I can from her body under me," Leif replied.

"By the gods, man! Ask her to come with you when we sail, or you will forever regret it."

"We have met at a crossroads, Sigurdur. My path takes me to Norway. Her path ends at the edge of Tiree. She cannot come with me, nor can I stay with her. These simple people need her. Without her, there is no Tiree. It will sink into oblivion without its Lady Jarl. Nor can I stay here. I am not of this land. I would never fit in," Leif replied.

"Trying to convince me, or yourself?" Sigurdur asked.

"A little of both," Leif admitted. "Look at that man—Ivar. A thousand men such as he clamor for Thorgunna's favor. Her bed will not grow cold from lack of a man after I leave."

"You're right, Leif. The soldiers of Norway will fill her bed. The days of Tiree's separation from the Church and Norway, are numbered," Sigurdur said softly.

"All the more reason I cannot stay. My mission depends upon winning the favor of our king. To stay on Tiree would be to dishonor my father and Norway."

Sigurdur reached out, placing a hand on Leif's shoulder, "Then you shall be without the woman you love for all your life, Leif. Are you ready for that?"

"I have no choice." Leif turned back to his work, his head down, refusing to discuss the matter further.

Chapter 11

Thorgunna opened trade negotiations at *Dun Mor a' Caoles*. A fire roared in a pit in the center of the circle as she had commanded. It cast an eerie glow upon the circle of men and women representing Tiree and the men of Ivar the Rus.

Older than oral history, *Dun Mor a' Caoles* enclosed the traders with defensive walls of stone hewn by unknown hands, for protection from some long-forgotten interloper upon the Isle.

Thorgunna drew strength from the stone blocks and the shelter it provided. There was but one entrance, wide enough to allow only a single man to enter at a time. The thatch roof was in disrepair, and she left it that way purposely so smoke from the fire wouldn't choke the gathering. If a little rain came in, the quicker the trading would go.

A large, dirty man with bad teeth, Ivar the Rus' white-blond hair above his beet-red face gave him a comical, yet unfortunately forbidding appearance.

Ivar took the place accorded to him—directly across from Thorgunna. He saluted the Tireeans before sitting.

"Cousin, it is good to see you again. You kept me waiting today. Nor was I invited or escorted to your home. Rather, your servants bade me drink away the day on the beach. I do not understand your lack of hospitality, nor do I understand your delay in convening the trading," Ivar said, undressing Thorgunna with his eyes. Never one for tact, he added, "By the gods I would take you right here if you would just give me one word of encouragement. You're looking well, Thorgunna."

"Ivar, because you are kin to my father, I will forgive you your poor manners. But let me remind you, as I have on many occasions in the past, ours is to remain strictly a business relationship. Now, what do you bring this trip?" Thorgunna replied.

Leif appeared from beyond the fire's glow, standing on Thorgunna's right. A position of great importance.

"Who's this? Oh, I know. You're the beached whale," Ivar insulted.

"Ivar, this is my guest from Greenland. Leif, son of Eirik," Thorgunna replied, motioning for Leif to take a seat close to her, but outside the main circle.

Ivar grunted, "How go your repairs?"

Leif nodded. "Well enough, thank you."

"Been there, sir. I pray your repairs are sound," Ivar said.

"Thank you, sir," Leif said.

Ivar shifted upon the stone, feeling uneasy. Feeling deceived. Blind to the truth. He whispered to his first mate, "That Greenlander is too close to the head stone. Too close to my Thorgunna. Something is going on. What is it? What is being kept from me?" He raised his voice to the gathering. "Leif, son of Eirik, I am Ivar Hestleggur."

"Nice to meet you," Leif replied.

"Lady," Ivar continued, turning his full attention back to Thorgunna, "I bring greetings from Olaf, King of Norway."

"The beer is ready. But I cannot trade it for greetings. What else have you? Something of value, perhaps?" Thorgunna replied.

Ivar's face grew even redder as a few of his men laughed from beyond the glow of the fire.

"Lady, when our king sends his regards, do ye not wish to pay heed?"

"No, I do not wish to pay heed to Olaf."

"Unwise, Lady."

"Ivar, if you have nothing to trade for the beer, then be off. I will not waste my time discussing religion and politics with you."

"I'll take the beer—by command of Olaf himself, I'll take it. But there's something else I am to take as well. Trade for it, I can," Ivar chortled.

Thorgunna held her face still, suppressing a grimace. "What trade do you wish to make, Ivar?"

"Olaf approves of strong bloodlines staying strong. You and I are kin through our fathers. Olaf has confided in me he wishes our family line to grow, in strength and numbers. He wishes us to wed," Ivar said, smiling as devilishly as Loki.

Concentrating upon how cold her feet were, not on the eyes of her people upon her or her building rage, Thorgunna held her reply. "You said there was trade involved, Ivar. I'm a businesswoman. What benefit is there for me in marrying you?"

"It is the will of your king, is that not enough?"

"Not really, no."

Ivar laughed. "That's what I like about you, Thorgunna! There is a trade, indeed. Shall I continue?"

"Please do."

Ivar smiled, displaying his rotting, yellowed teeth. "You become my wife, strengthening Tiree's ties to Norway, and I leave, two days hence, a married man, with a clean sword."

"What will soil your sword, Ivar? What happens should I not agree to marry you?" Thorgunna asked.

Thorok moved defensively behind Thorgunna. She heard his hand go to the hilt of his own sword.

"I've a priest aboard my ship, Thorgunna. A priest to baptize you and marry us according to the rites of the Holy Church. I'll taste the communion wafer from your mouth on our marriage bed, I will." Ivar rose. He continued, "Should you not agree, well, then it shall be either Christ's blood that flows into a cup for these good people, or their own blood flowing from them. These simple farmers do nothing you do not do first. You shun the Christ; they shun the Christ. They are sheep, Thorgunna. They follow you, their shepherdess, without question. Tiree's furrows will run red by your refusal to marry me. Are you ready for that?"

Thorgunna's posture turned rigid. "If I refuse to marry you, you destroy Tiree. I can only assume you have ships to port on Coll or Mull, waiting for your word to attack. No wonder it took so long for you to arrive. An armada takes time to mass. I see your plan, Ivar. We are too much alike, you and I. Our blood comes from the same line. I know how you think. Whether I marry you or not, you'll tell Olaf what he wants to hear. Olaf cares only for his drink, not the souls of the people who brew it. And you—you're not committed enough to anything but your own purse to put your sword against the necks of the unrepentant. You'll not destroy Tiree."

"Destroy Tiree? *Nei*, wife. I would bring the peace of Christ to your island. Some *Tirisdeach* might find that peace in a grave, but peace it would be. I am sincere in my adoration of king and Church, Thorgunna. My sword has been blessed in Olaf's service in the name of the Christ. Marry me, accept the Church willingly, command the *Tirisdeach* to do likewise, or I will use force to accomplish the conversion of Tiree. I shall become favorite of the king! I convert the heathens, portage the beer, and bed the witch who brews it. Take this to heart, cousin. Either you submit to me in holy matrimony, or I will—and I do not jest—I will force every last islander to bend his knees to the Christ, one way or another."

Thorgunna stood. She took a deep breath. "Ivar, leave me to my thoughts. I have much to consider."

"Come along with me tonight, Thorgunna. I'll make you forget everything," Ivar offered, vulgarly thrusting his hips forward.

"I have seen and heard enough! The Lady said 'Leave.' Be off. The sight of you offends me," Leif said.

Thorgunna, alarmed, turned toward Leif, frantically calling for his silence with her eyes.

Ivar drew his blade.

"Ivar, stop," Thorgunna said to the Rus.

"Give a boyish, shipwrecked Greenlander the right to speak in the circle now, Thorgunna? Even that idiot, Thorok, does not enter our discussions."

Ivar approached Leif. "You're a brave lad. But you don't know your place."

"I know my place, all right," Leif responded, stepping between Ivar and Thorgunna.

"Ah, what is this? Damn me for my late arrival, you've quelled your grief at Finn's passing in the arms of a child, haven't you? I'll have to kill him," Ivar said, pointing his sword at Leif.

"Ivar—" Thorgunna began.

Leif raised his axe, posturing defensively. "Come then!"

Ivar backed off, laughing. "Don't test me, boy. What care I that the Jarl has taken a lover? I'll fill her with enough seed to destroy anything of yours that grows in her belly."

Disgusted, Thorgunna cringed. "Ivar, please, let me to my thoughts."

"I grieved when word of your marriage reached me. I later rejoiced when I heard your husband had died before landing upon Tiree. I must have you, Thorgunna. The king wills it so. Now, get ye to the boat, wife. I would try you tonight," Ivar demanded. "At dawn I shall fly the sheet from our marriage bed from my mast as the mainland lords do to let their people know you have been blessed with seed."

"By the gods, she will not!" Leif lashed out.

"What's this?" Ivar laughed. "Do I hear a man's voice coming from a boy's body?"

"Thorgunna may hold her tongue in your presence, but I cannot. You will not force these people to the faith of the Christ, nor will you marry this woman!" Leif cried.

Softly, Thorgunna held her hand out, touching Leif's shoulder, "Why, Leif? Tell him why I cannot marry him."

Leif turned his head, his eyes meeting Thorgunna's. He could hear her heart pleading with him to speak the words, to give their love voice.

He replied, but only within his own heart, as the words choked him. *I do love you, Thorgunna. I love you.*

To Ivar, he said nothing.

Thorgunna, crestfallen, let her hand slip away.

*

"Come with me now, Thorgunna," Ivar demanded, laughing at Leif. Leif lowered his head.

"I will do no such thing. Be gone and end your lamentations for lack of my company, or I shall call out the Trickster to haunt you. He wants me too, you know," Thorgunna replied.

Ivar shuddered. "Witch."

"Yes, and what of it?" Thorgunna smirked, reaching inside her shift, drawing forth a talisman engraved with the symbol of the Norse demigod, Loki.

Leif backed away. "Why are you wearing that?"

"Didn't know your bed wench was a witch? In Norway she'd be burned. The Christian God doesn't allow women to call upon the old gods to empower *their sight*," Ivar said.

"Thorgunna is not a bed wench. Moreover, we are not in Norway. Thorgunna will not be burned for witchcraft," Leif replied. "It is not she who is empowered by her sight, but the gods. This woman wields more power than even Olaf, himself."

Ivar laughed heartily. "Not your bed wench? Never took her in a bed, I wager! I suppose you plowed the field like dogs, outside, in the mud. The mongrel Greenlander and his bitch!"

Leif replied defensively, "Do not speak so."

Ivar laughed, "You're not worth the fight, little man. I'll deal with you another day." He stretched, lewdly scratching his groin. "I need a woman. If you won't willingly come with me this night, then give me a woman from amongst the *Tirisdeach*."

How can he demand such things? Thorgunna thought. "Any woman of this island who wishes to go with you, may. I do not control the will of the people. They are not slaves. Nor am I. The king can go bugger himself if he thinks otherwise," Thorgunna replied.

"They're all sheep! And I need a plump, furry one tonight. What woman here will have a go with me? I promise no hurt, only a bit of fun aboard my ship."

Brigit stepped into the circle, as if guided by unseen hands. "I'll take you on, Rus. But not upon your ship. I told you the time would be of my choosing, and now I state the place as well."

"Brigit, no—" Thorgunna began.

Brigit nodded to her mistress. "I go freely."

Ivar scoffed, "Aye, she's ripe, but too thin for my mood."

"You call this thin, Rus?" Brigit ripped open her bodice, exposing her fine, round breasts. "I am a virgin, Ivar. I offer you first passage to ease your *disappointments*," Brigit nodded toward Thorgunna and Leif.

Thorgunna's entourage gasped, astounded and confused by Brigit's actions.

Ivar's men sniggered and jeered as Ivar approached Brigit. "I'd have

Thorgunna before all other women, and I will have her soon enough, but you will certainly ease my suffering this night." He leaned forward, slapping Brigit's breasts with one foul lick from his putrid tongue where her delicate white flesh rose above her cinch.

She backed away. "Meet me at Vaul when the moon is high," Brigit commanded.

Ivar spat on the ground. "I'll be there, all right, you wee *wummin*. But Vaul's a big place. Name the spot." He turned to Thorgunna, "Not such a bad night for trade after all. Your servant gives her maidenhood to me to save you from having to lie under me. Will only happen this once, you know. Unless you want to pass along all your virgins to me."

Thorgunna said nothing. She could not. Not to Ivar.

"Brigit, a word, please?" Thorgunna asked.

Brigit went to Thorgunna, holding her torn shift closed. She kissed Thorgunna lightly on the cheek. "Have no fear. What I do is for the good of Tiree."

Thorgunna pulled Brigit away from the fire into the recesses of the *dun*. With just enough light to see her eyes, Thorgunna looked deeply into Brigit's windows of the soul. "Do not attend Ivar."

"I must."

Thorgunna's own soul froze as she realized the woman before her was not the same woman she knew and loved. *Something has changed in her. Something has taken the light from her. Someone. No! Not Brigit!* "Brigit, have you been plagued by a nightmarish man who speaks with a honeyed tongue and kisses with scarred lips?"

"Nightmares? No. Not nightmares."

"But something or someone has approached you. Do not lie to me, Brigit! This is important!"

"He said he was an angel sent to protect Tiree."

Thorgunna felt her blood run cold as the ice deepened and compacted against her heart and soul. *Loki*.

From the circle, Ivar called impatiently, "The directions, lassie. Which part of Vaul shall we make our own?"

From the shadows, Brigit replied, "Follow the low stone fence, Ivar. Near Vaul Bay is a hillock surrounded by a rock wall. I'll be waiting."

Ivar laughed. "I know the place, Brigit. Keep her in the corner there, Thorgunna. Prepare her well! Share all the pointers you've learned while rutting in the dirt with that Greenlandic swine of a lover you've taken."

Ivar's foul laughter trailed off into the night as he exited the *Dun*, his men following.

Thorgunna bowed her head. Holding Brigit tightly, she closed her eyes, calling the sight, demanding the sight to do her bidding.

Like a thief in the night, he was there. Waiting. Cackling with delight. Ready to pounce, cut, hurt, devour.

"Loki! Release whatever hold you have upon Brigit."

"I warned you, Thorgunna. I warned you not to give that Greenlandic cur first passage. Gave him entrance to my treasure trove, you did."

"I love him."

"Love him well, Thorgunna. Your selfish act has condemned him. Condemned you. Condemned Tiree."

"No!" Thorgunna screamed, falling out of the vision with such force she could not breathe.

Brigit, filled with Loki's venom, held Thorgunna as she swooned from the impact of the vision. Holding Thorgunna's face in her hands, Brigit pressed her lips against Thorgunna's, inserting her new serpent's tongue, locking the Jarl in a wet, forbidden kiss. Too dazed to pull away, Thorgunna allowed the momentary, yet shocking embrace.

****

Leif, oblivious to Loki's possession of Brigit, watched with interest as the women embraced. Aroused, he guiltily shifted his stance to hide the bulge in his breeches. *Now there's a sight to ignite a man's fire!*

Brigit broke the kiss abruptly, leaving Thorgunna to fall like a cornhusk doll to the floor, in the darkened far corner of the *dun*. Brigit dashed from the ancient fort into the night, laughing.

Both Thorok and Leif rushed to Thorgunna.

"Thorgunna. Thorgunna? Are you well?" Leif asked, scooping her into his arms, helping her to her feet.

Thorgunna cast a forlorn, bewildered look at Leif. "I am damned, Leif. I am damned, and with me goes Tiree."

"What are you talking about? Brigit can handle Ivar," Leif replied. "I must say I am surprised by her actions tonight, but she does what she must, and perhaps what she truly wishes to do."

Thorgunna raised her chin to look Leif in the face. "I need Thorok."

"Thorok?" Leif asked, hurt.

"I am here, Lady. What is your will?" Thorok replied.

"Follow Brigit. Do not be seen. If Brigit…" Thorgunna paused, gathering her thoughts. "If Ivar tries to take her by force, if Ivar hurts her in any way, kill him. At least then he will not be killed as a marauding agent of the king, but as a rapist. That is within my right," Thorgunna commanded.

Thorok nodded. "As you wish, Lady."

"Take me home, Leif. Take me home," Thorgunna begged.

Chapter 12

Ivar, with a waterskin filled with beer and a mind clouded by too much drink, made his way across the swampy lowland preceding the area of Tiree known as Vaul. Sheep mouthed their objections as he stumbled over their sleeping bodies. Cows wisely moved out of his way. Ankle deep in muck, he cursed himself for agreeing to bed the wench at Vaul. "I know better. She chose this area of Tiree just to spite me!"

Climbing the mossy crags, Ivar lifted himself away from the low-lying wetland, spying the hillock surrounded by an old Pictish fortress in the bright moonlight.

Ivar crossed the machair and flower-strewn rocky outcroppings to the hill. Looking up, he smiled. The moon was high. By its light, he could see his quarry.

Brigit waited. Completely nude, her white body reflecting her smooth, satiny beauty under the bright half moon, she beckoned the Rus to her.

Ivar approached, dropping sword, axe, belt, and water skin. He pulled off his tunic and loosened his trousers. He exposed the reason for his nickname—Horseleg—to her. He gave his cock a good shake.

"I promise ye, one time to break you, and the next three or four to pleasure you. Have you nothing to say before I put you down?"

Brigit shook her head.

Over Ivar's shoulder, she saw Thorok's strong frame, hiding in the shadows.

Ivar, unobservant and obsessed with his own sexual prowess, intended to use the Irish wench badly.

Before Ivar could pull Brigit to him, she pulled Ivar's mouth to hers, nearly leaping into his arms.

He is foul, she thought, forcing her tongue into his mouth, *and not very bright.*

"Oh, yes. You're as sweet as honey. A virgin always wants the likes of Ivar Horseleg to bring her to womanhood. You are ready, aren't you?" Ivar cooed, fondling Brigit.

Brigit winced as Ivar's big, dirty fingers forced their way past the tuft of red hair between her legs.

Then, quite suddenly, Ivar stopped, pulling away. "Oh, I had too much drink today. My head is swimming." He sat back without grace, onto the rocky soil. "Are we having an earthquake?" he asked, laughing.

Brigit took a step back.

Ivar felt a tickle at his upper lip as a drop of blood from his nose trickled off his moustache.

"I'm bleeding!" he cried, trying to stand. His vision blurry and equilibrium quite lost, he could not rise. "I've been drugged. Poisoned! What have you done to me?" he demanded.

Brigit donned her shift. "It's poison, all right. You'll be dead in a moment."

"From your kiss," Ivar coughed.

"Yes."

"Give me the cure." Ivar coughed deeply, spewing blood.

"I took the last of it so I could hold the poison in my mouth before transferring it to you."

"I am a Christian. I must be shriven," Ivar gasped.

"Go to Hell, Ivar," Brigit said.

Ivar lunged blindly at Brigit, striking her with closed fists before succumbing to the numbness in his extremities caused by the fast-acting botanical poison. Again crashing to the ground, his body convulsed violently. His chest went still as his breathing slowed. His lips turned a vivid shade of blue.

Thorok emerged from the shadows.

Brigit, stunned from Ivar's blows, her face already swelling and lips bleeding, nodded at the large, silent man approaching her.

"What took you so long?" Brigit sighed.

"He's dead?" Thorok asked.

"Not yet. His heart has slowed, and his breathing will fail him in time. The poison is strong, certainly strong enough to put him under, but not strong enough to wield death with one blow. I intend to hit him upon the head with a great rock and say he raped me. You must carry me to the midwife's cottage, then summon Ivar's priest from aboard his ship. I shall seek confession, and ask forgiveness for my wanton, sinful behavior in agreeing to go with Ivar. I shall say he was bitterly cruel to me. That he raped me as I pleaded with him to stop. I shall say that in self-defense I smashed his drunken head with a stone, killing him. Only God, and you, will know the truth. And before God I swear, I do this only to protect Thorgunna and Tiree."

"Ivar's men ... they will want proof you were raped. I will be accused of causing Ivar's death."

"You and he would do much damage to each other if ever you had fought. No one will suspect you. You do not look like a man who has been in a life-and-death struggle with a powerful man such as Ivar. I must appear to have been in just that situation, however. That's where you must help me," Brigit paused. "I want you to rape me, Thorok."

Aghast, Thorok took a step back. "I cannot. I will not."

"When I stand before the priest I must reflect the injuries of a woman ill-used by this Rus. It needs to be a most convincing fabrication."

"You stand before me barely clothed, and because of my deep respect for you, I am not aroused. A man cannot rape if not aroused by lust or power. No, Brigit. I cannot do this thing you ask of me."

"Thorok, you are truly an honorable man. But hear me out. It is a pity Ivar fell before hitting me further, for now it is you who must strike me. You must bruise me in places that will show. My face. My arms. And because the Rus will want proof I have been violated—and they will, Thorok, you know this—I must be bruised in that place only the midwife will examine."

Thorok shook his head. "What you ask of me is against all I stand for. I have never harmed a woman."

"If you do not harm me now, thereby creating an alibi for Ivar's death by poison given him by my own lips when he had not attacked me, and I was here, in front of witnesses of my own accord, the wrath of Olaf will descend upon Tiree, and *she* will be lost."

"I cannot rape you. Brigit, I'm not sure I could even make love to you. How can I strike you, and take you forcibly? I cannot. A woman's first time should be gentle and pleasurable. That I would give to you willingly under different circumstances."

"It must look like rape, or the consequences will be great. I want only pain to show in my eyes when the priest looks into them for the truth." Brigit kneeled before Thorok. "I am going to arouse you. I will then lay my body over the wall of this enclosure. The rocks will bruise my belly and breasts. Take me quickly. As unpleasant as I know it shall be, I want you to tear my flesh in evidence that Ivar abused me."

Thorok sighed with regret as Brigit took him into her mouth. He was a man. A man cannot be handled so by a beautiful, nude woman, and not become aroused. As he closed his eyes, tears streamed down his cheeks. He had fought many a battle, but none so brutal as the task before him.

****

A great, urgent thud at Thorgunna's door roused her from the mournful stupor of one paralyzed with rage at the choices she had made. The choices Brigit had made. Keen of hearing, she had listened to the voices on the wind, waiting to hear the cry of Brigit as Ivar took her, or the cry of Ivar, his blood spilling out from a quick slice of Thorok's blade.

"Ah, it comes, Leif. See? The knock on my door is not calling me to Brigit's to select a warm loaf from the hearth, but to tell me she has fallen and is lost."

Thorgunna opened the door.

An islander Leif did not know by name, his old eyes downcast, stood at the threshold.

"Brigit?" Thorgunna asked.

"Aye, Brigit. The lass is with the midwife." The islander paused. "Lady, our Brigit has been raped. But there is more. Ivar is dead."

Thorgunna nodded. "Thorok?"

"It was not he who killed the Rus. Brigit, herself, killed him as he plunged into her. Cracked a rock upon his skull, she did. We sent his men to fetch the corpse."

Feeling as though her own right hand had been severed and her life's blood had spilled onto the ground, Thorgunna ran blindly into the night. In the light of the now blood-red moon Thorgunna found her pony. She mounted it and rode it hard, west from Gott Hill to the home of Aud, the midwife. To the Reef.

Once underwater, but now a low grassy plain flanked by an antediluvian fossilized coral reef, the Reef was a great flat expanse of good grazing land between Balephetrish Bay to the north and Traigh Bay to the south.

Leif stopped the islander from leaving Thorgunna's home. "Can you take me to where she rides?"

"Yes, of course. I could ride to the Reef blindfolded," the man replied.

"No need to don a mask, old man. Let's ride. Just get me to Thorgunna," Leif responded, mounting the man's pony.

Ivar's priest had beaten Thorgunna to the midwife's door.

So had Thorok.

Thorgunna vaulted from the pony, slapping the mare on its haunches, sending it away.

Thorok stood silently, his eyes lowered as Thorgunna slipped into the thatched cottage of Tiree's midwife. That alone told Thorgunna something was amiss.

"Brigit," Thorgunna cried upon seeing her friend's battered face. "What did he do to you?"

"He beat me, and he raped me. What else is there to say?" Brigit responded. "I smashed a great stone upon his head as he pulled away from me. I killed him, Thorgunna."

"I hate myself for allowing you to go to Vaul," Thorgunna cried.

"It was my choice and the will of my angel, Thorgunna," Brigit responded.

"Priest!" Thorgunna called. She wiped tears from her eyes. "I trust you not, sir, but Brigit undeniably does, for she subscribes to your faith. I must ask you this, and I expect a truthful reply. Did this woman kill in self-defense? As you are undoubtedly aware, a woman may give herself to any man freely on this island, but rape is punishable by death."

"Aye. She has confessed this to me. Your island midwife attests Brigit was indeed broken in a most foul manner. May God have mercy on them both."

"And Ivar's men?" Leif asked, entering the midwife's house.

"I will give them a full report. It is only my command that keeps them from running you all through to avenge Ivar. They await me now at Gott Beach." The priest paused, "Be at peace, my child," he said to Brigit, making the sign of the cross over her.

"Thank you, Father. I'll make my acts of contrition and show my penitent heart to our God, and his angels and saints," Brigit replied softly.

Thorgunna slumped onto the midwife's chair. "Ivar is dead. What will this mean to Tiree?"

"You will not be forced to marry Ivar to save the *Tirisdeach* from forced baptism," Leif replied from the entrance to Aud's.

Thorgunna looked up. "I would have never married him, Leif."

"Thorgunna," Brigit whispered through her bruised lips.

"Yes," Thorgunna said, drawing closer to Brigit.

"My pain is less than that which you will suffer."

Thorgunna pulled back, aghast. It was not Brigit's eyes or lips speaking. It was not her friend. It was the shadow of her tormentor. Eyes ablaze, lips scarred, voicing harm not love.

Mentally casting her command, Thorgunna looked into the fiery eyes that once shone Brigit's brilliant Irish green.

"Leave her, Loki. Leave her now." Thorgunna growled.

Brigit returned like a cloud uncovering the sun. "I will be fine, Thorgunna. Any suffering I feel now is much less than that of my countrymen should Ivar have forced them into accepting Christ. I am a Christian, a Christian with strong faith, and I know, through that faith, Ivar and Norway are wrong to force conversion. Christ comes through love, not war," Brigit said softly.

"I am so sorry, Brigit." Thorgunna wept.

"It was my choice, Thorgunna."

Thorok entered, brushing by Leif abruptly.

Thorgunna rose. "Where were you when this happened, Thorok? I told you to kill him if he hurt her! The hurt is done, and by her broken hands does Ivar lay dead and bloating on the beach at Gott!" Thorgunna screamed, facing Thorok.

"I was late to Vaul," Thorok replied.

"You were late? *You* were late?"

"I came upon Ivar and Brigit just as the stone crashed upon his head. There was naught I could do for Brigit, and she'd already killed Ivar."

"I cannot see you right now, Thorok. Please leave."

Thorok looked sheepishly toward Brigit, who, with her eyes alone, expressed a silent thank-you. "I'll go then," Thorok said. Oddly, he passed Thorgunna to reach Brigit, kissing her lightly on the forehead. "I'm sorry," he whispered.

"Oh, now something is not right here," Thorgunna said, as Thorok left the midwife's cottage.

"I want to sleep now," Brigit said.

Aud, the midwife, the oldest woman on Tiree and she who had birthed nearly every baby for sixty years, ushered Leif and Thorgunna from her house.

Chapter 13

Her home did not feel safe. The fire did not feel warm. The beer was flat. The bread, stale.

Thorgunna collapsed into a chair, resting her head against the table, sobbing. "Tiree is dying. Tiree is lost. I have sold my soul to the devil, and he has come to collect."

Leif pulled a chair next to Thorgunna's, reaching out to comfort her. Somehow.

"Lady, I am at a loss to understand how a specter of your dreams can haunt you by day and impose control upon an entire island. Loki is real, of this I have no doubt. But is it not he who has always deceived the gods with seemingly disastrous situations with one hand, while offering them a solution to their problems with the other? I cannot believe your island is lost to you. Loki craves Tiree, does he not? Why would he destroy it? What he does, he does only to trick his victims into a sense of hopelessness and despair. Thereby shall he gain access to your soul."

"What are you saying, Leif? Loki has invaded Brigit's spirit. And she's a Christian! Is there no protection from the whims of gods?"

Leif stroked the growth of beard on his chin thoughtfully. "You know, as I see it, Brigit is first loyal to you, then to Christ. Perhaps that is why she became a pawn of the Trickster, and a murderess."

"Brigit did not murder Ivar. She killed him in self-defense! A man would never understand this! Men are not subject to rape!"

"I'm sorry, Thorgunna. I know this is a sensitive area for you. It's true what you say. Men cannot be victimized by rape in the same manner as women. Men can, however, be humiliated and brutalized by a *futhflogi* enemy, an enemy who flees from the sex of a female. I have heard of such things. I apologize. Brigit killed in self-defense."

"Brigit killed because Loki told her to. I don't know how or when, but I know, Leif. I know. And now I must understand why Loki wished Ivar's death by such a means."

"Was not your agreement with Loki to protect Tiree?"

"Yes."

"And is not Loki shackled by the will of Odin at present?"

"I had believed so. I am no longer certain of this."

"Loki fulfilled his obligation to Tiree, Thorgunna. I would assume he did so using Brigit as a weapon because he is fettered from long-term physical interaction with humankind."

Thorgunna looked up. "You don't understand, Leif."

"What do I not understand, Thorgunna?"

"If it is true Loki acted according to the *officium pactum* by killing Ivar, then the whole of the contract itself is real. Not a dream."

"And?" Leif asked.

"There was a price, Leif. A price I had to pay."

Leif raised an eyebrow. "Go on. It would be nice to hear the truth."

"Loki was to protect Tiree for two years. At the end of that two-year period, an offering would be made. An offering of flesh."

"That does not seem unreasonable for a god."

"An offering of the flesh of my body."

"Your shorn locks?" Leif smoothed Thorgunna's thick black hair over her shoulders.

"My maidenhead."

Leif swallowed. "Oh, really."

"Since I allowed you first passage—which I do not regret, Leif—the contract is now null and void."

"I see that as a plus."

"There's more. He said I could lo—" Thorgunna paused. "He said I could have a relationship with you in all ways but one. Into your arms would be permitted—but not into your bed."

Leif frowned "I do not know which is more frightening. The words we do say to each other, or Loki's wrath. What will he do? What shall we do?"

"It won't matter what words are said between us, for he will kill you. He will mold Tiree into his sanctuary. He will haunt me, even after death."

"Lies."

"Leif?"

"He is the god of lies. His threats mean nothing," Leif said.

"Then why am I so afraid?" Thorgunna asked.

Chapter 14

At Gott Bay, Ivar's men had left the body of their captain laid out on a makeshift pyre. Not a one of them knew Ivar's funereal desires. Those details were left to the priest. The priest who held reign over their right to vengeance against Brigit for the killing of Ivar.

Ivar's priest had informed the Rus sailors there could be no retaliation against Tiree for Ivar's death, for Ivar had raped Brigit, and she had killed in self-defense. The law of the island was the law to be obeyed in this case. "Only Olaf himself can order retaliation. And he's not here. Forgive Ivar his transgressions and forgive Brigit for the action she took in her own defense."

"She offered herself to Ivar, Priest. He had no need to rape her. Ivar liked the ladies too much to ever ruin his chances of bedding one for sport. Ivar was not a rapist!" Rurik, Ivar's first mate, exclaimed.

"Nevertheless, the Irish servant of the Jarl suffered a grievous rape and beating while in the company of Ivar. You cannot tell me Ivar's anger with Lady Thorgunna could not have been a catalyst to violent behavior on his part. I know Ivar better than you think," the priest responded. "Now, row me to the ship. I need to pray. On the morrow we'll decide how to commend Ivar's remains to God."

"Row 'im out," Rurik ordered. A young Rus lad with bright blue eyes, a bad complexion and long, unruly straw-yellow hair snapped to action, offering the priest his strong arm for support as the old man climbed into the skiff.

Ivar's sailors, never men to pass on an opportunity to drink, sat by a fire on the beach, guzzling large quantities of beer, toasting Ivar. Toasting Norway. Toasting Brigit for her strength. Toasting the possibility that Ivar's seed now grew in that fine, strong woman. Toasting the passing of their friend with beer that would have been paid for out of the king's own purse—but was now gratis thanks to Thorgunna, who made the gesture only because Ivar was kin to her father. The sailors could now pocket the silver the king sent for the brew, and collect their portage costs as well once in Norway.

So drunk on Tireean Gold and the amount of coin in their coffers, the Rus, not a one of them, took note when the body of Ivar, stone cold and still for hours, moved.

A soft moan escaped Ivar's lips, followed by little bubbles of spit and blood. Then a hand and arm moved. His eyes fluttered open.

I am alive, he thought.

For the most part, yes, replied a voice within Ivar's thoughts.

"God?" Ivar stumbled to ask aloud, finding the sound of his own voice the most wondrous song he had ever heard.

"For the most part, yes," replied the voice, now fully audible.

Ivar turned his head to face the direction from which the voice came.

"Who are you?" he asked.

"I am your new friend. The Irish bitch poisoned you, then smashed a rock against your head. Really, Ivar, the women you pick for thrusts. Your taste is almost as bad as my own."

"I was poisoned?" Ivar asked. "Oh, yes. I remember now."

"If you wish, I can remove the poison and the death it slowly carries. Heal that cracked skull of yours as well. Make you whole again, I can."

"Are you a demon?" Ivar asked.

"Not exactly. I am Loki. I want to help you."

"Help me what?"

"To live another day. To take what is yours."

"Thorgunna."

"Aye."

"What will I owe you in return?"

"Does it matter?"

"No. I've been dead. You can do no worse than that. Take the poison from me," Ivar agreed, pushing himself into a seated position.

"You may find this awkward, but it is the proper procedure for removal of poison," Loki said, taking Ivar's bruised face into his hands.

"What do you mean to do here?" Ivar asked, not relishing the intimate touch of another man.

"Trust me," Loki replied, putting his mouth to Ivar's in a illicit kiss, forcing Ivar's mouth open and his own serpent-like tongue down Ivar's throat.

The men became locked in a passionate embrace. Ivar struggled against Loki as the god pulled him in with the strength of ten Rus traders. Loki literally sucked the shadow of death from Ivar.

Ivar squirmed uncomfortably as Loki closed the gap between their bodies. Loki pressed his sinewy, lithe, yet powerful body against Ivar's coldness. Ivar felt a flash of heat burn its way up his body from his groin, cascading out to his extremities, bringing life force and godly healing to his being.

Ivar, afraid to move away, yet afraid to stay, succumbed to the kiss. Humiliated. Titillated. Fully aroused and poured out as if he'd been with a woman. He shivered as the forbidden orgasm brought on by the kiss of another man quaked through him.

At last Loki released the Rus. Ivar flushed bright, shifting his weight as he sat, hiding the bulge of hardened flesh and male flood at his crotch.

"I am less of a man for this," Ivar mourned, mortified that the embrace of another man had aroused him so.

Loki laughed. "A man takes pleasure where he finds it. There is no shame in your loins twitching at my healing embrace. I am a god, after all."

Ivar made no reply. He could not. He must not. To do so would be to admit he had committed an abominable sin in the eyes of Norse society, and the God of Olaf.

"Time to kill the bitch, then?" Loki sniggered.

"You must never reveal this, godling. Never," Ivar bade, glancing toward the dim firelight from his men's encampment up the beach.

"Who would I tell?" Loki replied.

Ivar nodded. "First things, first," he said. "Where's my sword?"

"Have mine," Loki offered. "Forged upon the anvil of Brokk, master dwarfish craftsman, it is a good sword. Though he later sewed shut my mouth, I cannot fault his craftsmanship."

Ivar took the weapon from Loki. "I have a bone to pick with that Greenlander before I attend my audience with the Lady of Tiree."

Loki laughed, "Then you'll need this, too!" He proffered a large dagger bearing a solid bone handle.

"That'll do the trick," Ivar said, taking the dagger, stroking its refined edge lovingly.

"Go to her, now. I shall reward you richly when you bring that sword back stained with her blood."

"And the Greenlander?" Ivar asked.

"Do with him what you will. Make it painful."

"I shall make him suffer."

"Lovely! Now, be off!" Loki commanded.

****

Ivar stole silently through the encampment of his men with the stealth of one able to walk between drops of rain. He felt invigorated. Strong.

Potent. Aroused. He watched Thorgunna's house from afar with the night vision of an owl. He stalked her like a rabid wolf, unafraid, uncontrollable, and unstable.

Thorgunna had fought sleep for hours after Brigit's attack. But at last, she could no longer remain awake. Her head resting upon her arms at the table before the fire, she looked so peaceful Leif was loath to carry her to her bed lest he awaken her. As he gently lifted her into his strong arms, he could plainly see she was dead to the world. In a manner of speaking.

He carried her to her bed. "Please, no nightmares for her tonight. Let her have one restful night," he prayed, not knowing or caring to whom the winds blew his request.

Leif sat for some time in the lessening light of the fire, awake, yet riddled with fatigue. "I'm too tired to sleep. Too tired to think. And the beer has gone through me."

Leif considered urinating into a jar rather than exiting Thorgunna's home, thus leaving her unprotected. He laughed. "She would scold me for not using the pit. I might as well do something to please her in this time of crisis. I can't say the words she longs to hear, but I can piss in the appointed place." Then he chastised himself, "I'm talking to myself. The first sign of insanity."

He exited the house in the dark of the night and dashed to the newly finished pit and shelter. He carried a small oil lamp. The moon had waded behind some clouds. It was utterly dark, his light barely enough to find his way.

From his vantage point midway up Gott Hill, Ivar held back a burst of excitement as Leif entered the pit, the glow of that little clay lamp illuminating the stretched skin privy in such a way Leif's form was clearly visible.

"Such luck!" Ivar whispered, carefully, quietly, sneaking up the hill, his blade at the ready.

His back to Ivar's approach, Leif did not hear or have any premonition of danger as he urinated. He knew nothing, suspected nothing, until Ivar's dagger plunged into his right shoulder from behind, through the skin wall of the shelter.

Too shocked to cry out, Leif froze as if entombed in ice, dropping to the earthen floor of the shelter, his breathing slowing, his lungs filling with blood.

"Such is the death of a Greenlander! To die while pissing, face down in the dirt! Die well!" Ivar laughed.

The wind kicked up around Ivar. He hated that about Tiree. This time, however, the incessant breeze carried a message. Loki's honey-drenched voice gave praise to his puppet with the sword. "Nicely done. Now, quiet yourself and move on to the home of the Lady. She is waiting for you."

"Then I shan't keep the Lady waiting," Ivar said, loosening the leather thongs of his breeches.

Thorgunna's door was ajar. Her fire had burned to a few glowing embers. It was nearly as dark inside as out. But Ivar could see. He saw with eyes flaming from rage, desire, and cruelty.

Ivar slipped a hand past the heavy tapestry curtaining off Thorgunna from the rest of the house, the rest of the world. He entered the Lady's sanctuary, a sword in one hand, his hard, pulsating member, alive with the breath of Loki, in his other.

With one leap Ivar was upon Thorgunna, the razor edge of Loki's sword slicing into her throat. "Move and I will cut you clean through."

Thorgunna immediately called upon every fiber of her being to remain rigid. Gathering her wits, her mind racing for options, Thorgunna remained perfectly still, her breaths short and shallow.

"Thought I was dead, didn't ye? Well, I'm not. I aim to show just how alive I truly am," Ivar threatened.

Thorgunna made no reply. She felt the ultra-sharp edge of Ivar's sword kiss her throat, drawing blood. A slow, frightening trickle of her life's blood began to puddle beside her.

"Sweet," Ivar chided, lapping at the red line meandering down Thorgunna's throat and shoulders. "Too bad it's not your virgin's blood I taste now, cousin. That would have been sweetest of all."

Ivar reached to Thorgunna's bedside table, taking up her stitching. Wadding the homespun fabric into a tight ball, he shoved it into Thorgunna's mouth.

She dared not fight back—yet.

"I'm going to bind you now, woman. You scream, cry out, or move against me in any way, and I promise you, I'll slit you open and befoul your corpse in such a way your own people will retch at the sight of you. Do you understand?"

Thorgunna nodded.

Ivar laid his sword alongside Thorgunna, making sure she could feel its cold, hard steel against her body. He ripped her linens and tied Thorgunna's hands above her head, looping them through the boards on her pallet.

As if answering a question, Ivar spoke aloud, responding to Loki's windborne praise, "Yes, it is well done. She will be well done now, won't she?" He laughed. "I've wanted to do this for a long, long time, cousin." He ran his tongue across Thorgunna's face. "Sweet."

He bit her cheek, tasting her flesh as he had her blood.

Thorgunna winced with pain, but remained still. *His breath is dead,* she thought frantically. *He is dead! He is dead and has risen to do me harm!*

Ivar placed a large hand on Thorgunna's belly, gathering the fabric of her shift. Using the sharp point of the sword he easily shredded the fabric, exposing Thorgunna's breasts to his mouth, his hands, and his steel.

He smiled, kneading the flesh of her belly. "I feel it, cousin. I feel the seed of that Greenlander growing within you. You didn't know it yet, did you? But I, I now know many things. The dead know all. Afraid for your unborn child, Thorgunna? Yes? Good. Do be afraid. Before I'm through with you this night, your womb shall be ripped open and split in two from the depths my love will take you. Now to those legs of yours." He chuckled and used her own shredded nightgown to bind her ankles to the footboard, her legs spread wide.

Thorgunna grunted her resistance, struggling against the gag and bindings, bucking her body in anger.

Ivar pressed his weight against Thorgunna's chest, making it hard for her to breath. His member, having been fully erect and pulsating with a life of its own, now seemed an even more fearsome threat than his sword. Vilely, he knelt over Thorgunna, slapping her breasts with his sword of flesh.

He leaned forward, forcing his member into her mouth, pushing the gag deeper into her throat, mocking the act of fellatio. "That'll be next, Thorgunna. I'll cut your tongue out and stuff something bigger down your throat and choke you to death." Ivar moaned sadistically, moving his battering ram against the cloth blocking Thorgunna's cries. Blocking her airway.

Thorgunna wanted to bite down, but could not. She needed to cough, but the spasm stopped in her chest, unable to escape.

For a moment, Ivar pinched Thorgunna's nose shut. "I could kill you so easily," he said, his maniacal laughter spewing fetid saliva and rotting breath into the very air Thorgunna struggled to draw breath into her lungs.

Near panic, Thorgunna fought to remain conscious. Where was Leif?

Surely he would have heard Ivar by now!

Ivar, his tongue hanging out like a panting dog, rolled off Thorgunna's chest. "He's not coming, if that's the question I see in your eyes. I left him in mid-piss, my blade in his back. I see your desperation. The 'where's my lover to protect me' plea in those black eyes of yours. He's not coming."

Her eyes flashing, Thorgunna looked at Ivar with a hateful glare that clearly relayed the message her lips could not mouth: *Get off me!*

"I like this. You can't give your commands, now, can you?" Ivar spat to the side and positioned himself to take Thorgunna. His large, dirty body reeked of the grave. Thorgunna shuddered as the clammy touch of Ivar's hands positioned his stone beast.

"You fight me now, or do anything but what I instruct you to do, and I will start with your tongue, then work my way down. The sword is otherworldly, woman. It can slice you in half by my wish alone."

Loki, Thorgunna thought.

"Yes. It was he. The god, Loki. I took him into me. Now, I'll show you where I keep him," Ivar said, thrusting his hips, pushing his swollen, grotesque shaft deeper between Thorgunna's legs.

Responding defensively to Ivar's force, Thorgunna tightened every muscle in her body, concentrating every fiber of her being into impenetrable, solid determination, literally locking tight the entrance to the castle treasury.

"You're not broke in, woman! That Greenlander must be a small man to have left you so tight. Well, Ivar's going to teach you how to take a real man."

"No, you shall not," Leif cried from behind him, cracking his battle axe hard against Ivar's backside.

Ivar sprang from Thorgunna's bed, but could not sustain the vigor of a god with his spine split in two. He collapsed on the floor, his body split open, blood spilling from him, wetting the room with its crimson rage.

Leif smiled weakly at Thorgunna before joining Ivar on the floor, unconscious.

Thorgunna frantically pushed the gag from her mouth with her tongue, spitting it onto her bare chest.

Taking a long, deep breath, she screamed for the one man who would always hear her cries for help, "Thorok!"

Twisting her body, painfully contorting in her bindings, Thorgunna tried to see the carnage on the floor of her chamber. She could not see the dying men. She could hear only one chest struggling to rise and fall. "Thorok! Thorok!" She cried again.

Thorok, accompanied by Iksan One Hand, burst into the room.

Both men stopped in their tracks, struck silent by the horror of Thorgunna's chamber. Once a pure ash-washed room, it was now red with blood splatter and stinking of death.

Thorok coughed, nearly vomiting. "Lady, are you injured? The blood, is it yours?" he asked.

"Leif! Help Leif!" she cried. "I'm not hurt. It's Ivar's blood!" she screamed wildly.

"By the gods, what has happened here?" Iksan One Hand asked, untying Thorgunna's bindings. She leapt from her bed to Leif's side, stepping over Ivar like so much rubbish.

"Ivar was not dead. Or if he was, he was helped to life again by forces I choose not to name." Thorgunna gasped. Her hands were stained with Leif's blood.

Iksan knelt beside Leif, studying the wound made by Ivar's blade. "I need to staunch this bleeding," he said. "Get me coals from the fire." Then softly to himself, "By the gods, this is bad. A jagged-edged blade. It looks as though Ivar chewed through Leif's flesh."

Wearing only remnants of her blood-soaked torn chemise, Thorgunna dashed to her hearth taking hot embers up with a pair of iron tongs.

"All right, then," Iksan said, removing Leif's clothing with one great rip of the fabric.

"Oh, gods," Thorgunna shuddered at seeing the full extent of the deep, jagged wound piercing Leif's shoulder blade.

"It's a good thing he's out," Iksan said, pushing an ember directly into the wound. Leif's body convulsed, tightening as if in rigor mortis, then went completely limp in Thorgunna's arms.

"This one's dead. Although I thought that before," Thorok said of Ivar, turning the Rus over. "I'll get his men. This time, maybe they'll not let a dead man slip past them."

"Keep Leif on his side, like so," Iksan said. "I need to stitch this up. Thorgunna, Leif's wound is severe. To what gods does he pray? Perhaps it's time to call upon them," he said, positioning Leif to keep his airway unobstructed.

Thorok handed Thorgunna a blanket from the chest at the foot of her bed. "Cover yourself, Lady."

Thorgunna gratefully wrapped the blanket about her. Ivar's drying blood had become sticky and uncomfortable against her skin. Looking about her chamber, now a disheveled, red-splattered battle zone, Thorgunna shook her head sadly, "I don't know. I think he prays to Odin. I don't know!" she cried.

Iksan nodded, "I'll need a thin bone needle and fine hairs from a horse's tail. I haven't stitched a wound like this since I went on *iviking* as a mercenary in Byzantium. Many years have passed since I last dressed a battle wound. I'll need tar and a poultice of ash and boiled cow's urine, as well." He paused. "Thorgunna! Please! If you wish him to live you must muster your strength and wits about you! Damn, I wish Brigit were able to help me now. I need a good nurse!"

"I'll go, Iksan. Thorgunna is in no condition to..." Thorok began.

"No! I'll go. Thorok, get Ivar out of my house. Save Leif, Iksan. Do whatever it takes. Save him! I'll be right back," Thorgunna said firmly.

Unnoticed, Leif's eyes fluttered opened for a moment. In that moment, he saw Thorgunna, alive, and Ivar, seemingly dead in a pool of blood—his eyes staring right back at Leif with a sinister glow.

Chapter 15

A great fever fell upon Leif in the first week after his attack. Thorgunna dared not leave his side. Ivar's ship sailed, hull full of Tirean Gold and the body of the Rus for burial in his homeland. A proper Christian burial. Something strong enough to keep the dead in the grave.

Brigit, recovering, hovered about, trying to console Thorgunna. Thorgunna shut her friend out as she sat silently as if in prayer, wetting Leif's brow with a cool cloth, changing his bandages, applying healing ointment to the wound.

"Thorgunna?" Brigit said.

"Aye," Thorgunna replied. She looked at Brigit. The purple bruises on her face and arms had yellowed. She would heal. Physically.

"I must share something with you," Brigit said.

"Yes, I know you must," Thorgunna replied, her hand trailing along Leif's arm, feeling the heat of his fever, the dampness of his flesh as it sweated out the poison of infection.

"I did not speak the truth the night Ivar died by my hand," Brigit whispered.

"Do you think I do not know this?" Thorgunna asked.

"I know you are aware it was not Ivar who took me by force. But I assume you do not know who did."

"That is so. The facts have been well hidden from me. They are swaddled in deception," Thorgunna replied. "Did one of Ivar's men join him?"

"No."

"Then tell me the truth, now," Thorgunna commanded. "I'm too tired for any more lies."

"It is true I killed Ivar—thought I had killed Ivar. But I did so by poison. After the poison I cracked a great rock upon his skull to assure his death. I failed."

"Who was it that beat you so?" Thorgunna asked, gently stroking Leif's brow. *Even in this unending sleep, he is beautiful.*

"I did most of it myself," Brigit replied.

"You could not rape yourself. You were stained with blood and seed," Thorgunna said frankly.

"The blood was mine. The seed was Thorok's. I begged him to take me so I could claim I killed Ivar in self-defense," Brigit admitted.

"Thorok," Thorgunna sighed. "Thorok could not do such a thing."

"He wept and pleaded not to do the things I asked him to do. I wanted only to protect you. I wanted to save the *Tirisdeach* from forced conversion and you from marriage to Ivar."

"You were beaten black and blue," Thorgunna said. "How could Thorok hurt you so?"

"I begged him to strike me, to take me harshly and quickly so I would be bruised and torn. It was a perfect plan."

"Until Ivar failed to stay dead," Thorgunna added.

"Had I killed him, Leif would not be lying here, the sleep of death upon him."

Thorgunna did not respond. She fell silent, deep in thought. *Loki would have found a way, Brigit. Loki would have found some way to take Leif from me. Ivar was merely a pawn, as were you. As am I.*

"Do not blame yourself, Brigit. Ivar's resurrection came by unholy means. I am afraid a greater foe than Ivar or Olaf of Norway is now walking amongst us. Please leave. Don't be offended, but if Leif is dying, I would like to spend what time he has left with him, alone," Thorgunna said.

Brigit nodded. "I must seek absolution. My faith is tested because I fell under the spell of the devil himself. I don't recall meeting him, Thorgunna. I recall only the acts I committed on his behalf. I'm so sorry."

"He has tricked us all, Brigit. Seek out the priest on Iona if you must. I shall not stop you from renewing your faith, but please don't bring one of them here. Good night, Brigit." Thorgunna crawled onto her bed next to Leif.

"Good night, Lady."

Thorgunna held Leif, wanting desperately to see the richness of color in his eyes, hear the music of his laugh, feel the magic of his touch. Kissing him lightly upon the lips, she whispered, "I love you, Leif. Please come back to me."

"How touching," came a voice from the shadows of the room.

Thorgunna held her breath. Her heart stopped. "Loki."

"Yes, 'tis I," the demigod replied.

"You've been freed by Odin?" Thorgunna asked, knowing she was not asleep, knowing Loki was in her waking world.

"More or less. My spirit is free to roam the nine worlds, but my body … well, my body can only be corporeal for brief, fleeting moments. I use those moments to my full advantage," Loki replied.

"You gave Ivar life," Thorgunna coughed.

"I did."

"He tried to kill me."

"Oh, yes. I know. He would have succeeded if he'd just taken one more moment on the Greenlander. One good twist of the knife handle would have done it. Oh, well."

"I despise you, Loki. I hate what you've done to me, to Leif, and what you want to do to Tiree," Thorgunna cursed.

"I thrive on hate, Thorgunna. Watch your emotions. They will be your undoing."

"Why are you here?" she asked.

"You know why. It is my nature to cause the problem with one hand and bear the solution in the other. Leif said it. He's wiser than I thought. All you need do to gain the solution is pay my fee," Loki replied.

"I have given you too much already," Thorgunna said softly.

"What is his life worth to you?" Loki asked slyly.

"His life? Everything," Thorgunna responded without forethought.

"Then give me everything, and his life is yours. You don't need to give it to me all at once. A piece here. A piece there," Loki whispered.

"I know what you want, Loki. You want to live forever. How vain." Thorgunna choked on her words.

"When a god is worshipped, he lives forever."

"Any tribute I pay to you would be false."

"But it would be tribute, nevertheless. I do not relish vanishing into obscurity with the other gods. I want to continue my reign on earth forever," Loki said. He stepped toward Thorgunna and Leif.

"Not too close, Loki," Thorgunna warned.

"Not too close, or what? You amuse me so. Now, which shall it be? Leif alive, or Leif dead and rotting?"

Thorgunna closed her eyes. "He could heal without you."

"He will not heal. He will die. Look, he dies now." Loki waggled his tongue and hissed.

Leif's body seized. Rigid and stiff, his breathing ceased.

"Stop it!" Thorgunna demanded, lunging at Loki, striking him with closed fists. "You're killing him!"

"He doesn't need much help in that respect. I'm just reminding him of what he's supposed to be doing. Dying. It is his stubborn Greenlandic upbringing that keeps him alive."

"Bring him back! Bring him back!" Thorgunna cried.

"And you will…?"

"I will worship you," Thorgunna said mournfully.

"Then, he shall live."

"What must I do?" Thorgunna asked.

"How does one worship any god?" Loki asked.

I don't worship, Thorgunna thought as she pulled off her shift, to offer herself to Loki in exchange for Leif's life. She wept. "You wanted me once. Is not giving myself to you freely an act of worship?"

"Oh, darling, Thorgunna! We're way beyond sex. I don't need you for that! You can be much more creative, if you really think about it."

"A monument?"

"Yes. That's a good start to a new contract between us. I'd like one on the southern end near the farm you call 'Moss.' Nice area," Loki said. His broad grin stretched the scars around his lips like thorns on a rose.

"And rituals?"

"No, not really. They bore me. An offering or two and perhaps a day of feasting in my honor would be sufficient, for now," Loki replied.

"Fine. Anything you want. Just bring Leif back to me," Thorgunna spat, donning her chemise.

Loki moved gracefully toward the supine, rigid body of Leif. Like fog rolling in from the sea, Loki leaned forward, kissing Leif gently on his forehead. "I do so enjoy this part," Loki teased, locking lips with Leif, drawing death from the Greenlander, swallowing it himself, feeling its power ebb and flow in his semi-corporeal form. Arrogantly, Loki cupped his hand over Leif's groin and laughed as he gave it a squeeze.

"Stop that," Thorgunna whispered.

"He's not really my type, anyway. I've had my fill of rugged, chiseled, blond Norsemen. Come to think of it, maybe one more…"

"No," she replied, her voice firm and unwavering.

"It is done, however. He shall live."

Thorgunna watched in amazement as Leif's body relaxed and his skin tone brightened. "He'll need to sleep now. But don't worry. He'll awaken, I assure you," Loki said.

"I pray you will be a distant, invisible god, like that of King Olaf," Thorgunna said.

"Oh, I'll be around. On the morrow, set your stonecutters to the task at hand," Loki commanded, vanishing.

"I have sold my soul to the devil for Tiree, and now for you, Leif." Thorgunna wept, watching the final flickers of Loki's hellfire fade.

Chapter 16

Thorok knocked softly on Brigit's door. Never locked, it danced open.

"Just a moment!" Brigit called.

But it was too late. Thorok had entered Brigit's cozy cottage built in the shadow of Gott Hill to find her standing nude in her wash tub.

Never embarrassed by nudity, Thorok pulled a stool next to the tub.

"Thorok, have you not the decency to let a woman wash without an audience?" Brigit scolded, continuing to bathe.

"They're healing," Thorok replied, taking note of the fading purple and yellow bruises covering Brigit's supple body.

He held his clenched left fist, that which had struck Brigit, in his right hand. So numb with grief was Thorok that his stronger left hand was numb and seemed to be detached from his body. He fought back tears.

"Yes. They are healing. I am fine, Thorok. I am better than fine. As God is my witness, I am overjoyed that Tiree is free of Ivar and her people free to come to Christ in their own time," Brigit sighed.

"I heard you're sailing to Iona. Before you go, I need to speak to you. I need to make amends," Thorok said, gently trailing his fingers over the smooth, white flesh of Brigit's arm.

"Amends? No need."

"I cannot live with myself if I do not replace the violence and destruction of my actions against you with ones of tenderness and warmth. My soul dies, Brigit. My left arm is numb to my elbow. I cannot sleep, for I dream of tears and blood, and I awake with my heart in my throat, my bedbox drenched in my own sweat. The aching in my chest grows stronger with each passing day," Thorok whispered. "I cannot breathe sometimes, nor can I speak, for the numbness in my jaw prevents it. I am too saddened to continue living without begging your forgiveness."

"What you did, I asked you to do. There is no need to suffer. I do not suffer for your actions. Why should you?"

Brigit stepped out of the tub, wrapping her thick, curly red hair in linen to keep it out of her way while she dried herself.

Thorok moved his hands from his lap and spread his legs slightly. "I am aroused by the sight of you, Brigit."

"Aye?" she asked, drying her breasts and belly.

"Aye," Thorok responded.

"And what shall we do about your arousal, Thorok? We have bathed together in the loch on more than one occasion and never before have you so much as glanced my way. We are not lovers, Thorok. We are partners in crime."

"I've looked at you before, woman. I refused to acknowledge my lust out of respect for you, your position in our society and…" Thorok paused. "I am looking now, Brigit. I want to make things right between us."

"How?" Brigit asked. She turned to dry her legs, exposing her round, firm backside to Thorok.

"You're teasing me, woman," Thorok scolded.

"No. I'm not. You entered without asking while I was bathing. This is the only time I'm going to have to get washed. I'm going to finish up whether or not you're here."

"I want to make love to you. Really make love to you. A woman such as you should not have but one sexual experience, and that one unpleasant. Let me find forgiveness in your bed," Thorok said.

Brigit pulled the linen from her head, shaking her fire-red hair, the curls flying in all directions.

"You would make love to me so my memories of your body against mine are pleasurable as opposed to painful?"

"Aye."

"My memories of that night are not painful. You did a great service for Tiree by helping me cover my crime against Ivar. I respect you now, more than ever. Do you truly want to make love to me only to influence whatever thoughts I may have about you in the future?"

"Aye. Give me that chance. I beg you."

"What would Thorgunna say?"

"She has never interfered in my affairs."

"I doubt she will now, either," Brigit said, climbing nude atop Thorok's lap, wrapping her legs around his hips, her lips to his.

Chapter 17

By the very first light of morning, Leif's steady, even breathing and good skin tone reassured Thorgunna that her love would live.

Only thoughts of carving out a standing stone from the breast of Tiree and dedicating it to Loki interrupted her feeling of well-being at the recovery of her lover. She snuggled against Leif's warming body, slowing her breaths to match the rise and fall of his chest. "He shall live. He shall live."

Not summoned, but unstoppable, the sight wafted in, enveloping Thorgunna and Leif. Compelled to look beyond the waking world, Thorgunna allowed the vision to penetrate her spirit.

She saw herself standing alone before a great ring of fire. She could see her home. Leif's ship at Gott Bay. The fields of corn and barley. The Ringing Stone. She watched as Leif boarded his ship and ordered his crew to set sail. Her heart sank as he did not look back at the Isle. He departed Tiree—and only looked forward. A great whirlwind picked Leif up from his ship, carrying him high into the sky. Another figure appeared in the sky with Leif. Thorgunna knew who it was. The apparition stabbed at her soul, wounding her. It was the enemy she had fought so long and so hard to avoid. It was Pope Gregory V of the Holy Roman Catholic Church. The Pope held out his hand to Leif, who kissed the Pontiff's ring.

"Damn!" Thorgunna cursed, witnessing Leif's conversion to the Church. "In his adoration of the new faith, he will forget me." Suddenly overwhelmed with grief, Thorgunna wailed like a banshee warning of an impending death. Death would to come to Tiree, after all. The death of her dreams to spend a lifetime with Leif Eiriksson. He had a new mistress.

A new Virgin to love.

Thorgunna awoke from the vision suddenly, startled by a great crashing noise.

It was Leif, trying to make his way past the heavy tapestry. Though looking a bit lost for his long confinement, Thorgunna had never seen a more beautiful sight.

"Oh, Leif!" Thorgunna cried, dashing into his arms.

"Ivar…" Leif asked.

"Is dead. Dead and gone. The ship sailed for the Ruslands over a week ago."

"Before I fell unconscious, I swear I saw him alive. His eyes, shining with hatred for me."

"Ivar is dead, Leif." Thorgunna sighed.

"What of Norway? Will Ivar's death herald new assaults by greater foes?" Leif asked, sitting.

"The king will know soon enough Ivar died on Tiree. Killed twice on Tiree. I'm certain my battle is just beginning."

"He stabbed me as I pissed. Very uncivilized of him," Leif laughed. "Oh, I cannot laugh. It hurts to laugh."

"You should lie down. Rest," Thorgunna urged.

"I've rested enough. Did Ivar harm you?"

"No. You prevented that, and I thank you."

"My beautiful Thorgunna. I missed you so while I was with the dead."

Thorgunna offered her lips to Leif. They kissed as passionately as their first kiss, renewing and strengthening the bond between them.

Leif broke the embrace, moving to sit in the great room by the fire. "My ship … my men…?" he questioned softly.

"Your ship is nearly repaired and your men are well. I'll send a rider to fetch Sigurdur. He has prepared your crew for the worst, but will now rejoice at your recovery."

"How does Brigit fare?"

"She is healing," Thorgunna replied. She went to Leif, kneeling before him.

Leif studied Thorgunna's face. There was something different about her.

"I'll get you some food. I have nothing in my larder. Brigit will have broth and flat bread. Move closer to the fire, Leif. Do not get chilled," Thorgunna said.

"In a moment," Leif replied, pulling Thorgunna into a second kiss.

"Thank you," he whispered.

"For what?" Thorgunna asked, delighting in the embrace.

"For healing me."

I only paid the healer, Thorgunna thought.

"Thorgunna, I'm not too hungry just yet. Will you lie with me here before the fire?" Leif asked, sliding off the chair onto the fur-lined floor.

Thorgunna snuggled into the skins beside Leif. "Oh, I am tired," she sighed.

Safe in Leif's embrace, comforted by his strong will to live, Thorgunna finally fell asleep.

Blessedly, she did not dream.

Hours later, Thorgunna awoke refreshed and content in Leif's strong arms. In that moment, she felt there was no safer place on earth.

Quietly, so as not to disturb him, and pangs of hunger from a very empty stomach rousing her, Thorgunna rose and quickly made the trek down Gott's gentle slope to Brigit's house. She threw open the door to make the happy announcement of Leif's recovery and found herself completely overwhelmed with nausea.

"Oh, gods, Brigit! What are you cooking?"

Thorok nodded a greeting as he slipped past Thorgunna on his way out.

"Thorok? Here? What is that awful smell?" Turning away from the entrance, Thorgunna retched, heaving several times.

"That smell is nothing but lamb broth. A smell you've delighted in for years! Are you ill?" Brigit asked.

"Oh, aye. I am," Thorgunna coughed.

"Come, sit," Brigit said, helping Thorgunna to her fire.

"You're looking much better, Brigit."

The Irish woman smiled. "I am quite well."

"Why's that?"

"I believe I am with child." Brigit didn't speak, she sang.

"From that night alone, you are pregnant?"

"Thorok came to me, begging for a chance to atone for the hurt he had caused. I agreed to give him that opportunity. He made love to me gently and passionately. I am certain my good Irish soil was quickened by his seed. I felt a stirring deep inside my belly as I sat astride him, riding him like my own horse." Brigit blushed, giggling.

"Indeed."

Thorgunna broke out in a cold sweat, heaving.

"Thorgunna, you do not look well, at all," Brigit replied.

When composed enough to speak, Thorgunna sighed, "I have great news, Brigit. Leif lives. Perhaps it is the excitement of the moment or the stress of the last two weeks making me ill."

"Thank the Lord, Leif lives," Brigit said, crossing herself in prayer.

Brigit studied Thorgunna for a moment. "Lady, since you took the Greenlander to your bed, have you had your flow?"

Thorgunna shook her head, but then nodded in realization. "I have not flowed since before their coming. I am with child." She sat thoughtfully for some time, toying with the bowl of lamb broth, swirling the brown liquid to keep the meaty sediment from sinking to the bottom of the bowl. *I am pregnant with Leif's child.* "I felt the child take root within me. It was a most magical sensation welling up within me as I straddled him. That must have been the moment of conception."

"I wonder if all children born on this isle next spring were conceived when the woman went riding!" Brigit joked.

"Thorok coming back?" Thorgunna asked.

Brigit smiled. "Oh, dear Lord! I hope so!"

"He has many children and many women love him," Thorgunna cautioned.

"Aye. He is a popular man," Brigit agreed.

"Do not be hurt if he does not marry you."

"I do not expect him to marry me. Without expectation, there can be no hurt," Brigit replied.

****

Thorgunna returned home with the lamb broth. Leif had positioned himself before the fire, reclined against a stack of skins. He had draped a thin veil of linen over his body.

"Making yourself at home?" she asked, offering him the broth.

"Clothing is uncomfortable against my skin. I wish I could see the wound," Leif replied.

"It is healing. Iksan put a coal to it to stop the bleeding. The flesh of your shoulder has been pierced, burned, and stitched. It will hurt for awhile longer, I wager."

"Does Sigurdur come? I really need to check on the men," Leif said.

"He'll be along," Thorgunna lied. "Do you plan to leave so soon?"

"Aye. We must. We've been upon this island for what—eight weeks?

Longer?"

Thorgunna moaned, holding her stomach as she caught another strong whiff of the broth. *How could I have ever enjoyed this? It is foul!*

"Thorgunna, are you well?" he asked.

"You come back from the dead to me, and plan your departure in the same breath."

"I must. Greenland depends upon me," Leif replied.

"Then, I am truly unwell. I would come with you," Thorgunna said, sitting.

"You cannot leave your people. I cannot take you from them. There are no born leaders. Your island would suffer greatly without you."

They'd be better off without me. Thorgunna sat upright, and in very formal speech said, "Leif, may I speak to you regarding something of great importance?"

Leif nodded. "Why the formal tone?"

Thorgunna continued, "Forgive my timing, but there is something which must be said."

"Please, continue," Leif encouraged.

Thorgunna looked directly into Leif's deep blue eyes surrounded by their long, flaxen eyelashes. She hesitated for only a moment before saying softly, "Though you intend to sail from Tiree, and what I have to say will not stop that, I must tell thee I am no longer a lone woman, and upon thee I charge it."

Gingerly, Leif sat upright, the linen fabric wafting off his body, leaving him nude.

"You are carrying my child?" Leif asked.

"I am pregnant. The child is yours. I have been with no other man and have not had a monthly flow since before you arrived. Your strong Greenlandic seed grows well in the soil of Tiree."

Leif said nothing, the moment as pregnant as Thorgunna.

Thorgunna broke the silence, continuing, allowing her sight to speak through her, "Further, I see that the child I bear shall be male and that you shall accept him one day as the son of your body. I shall send him to you when he's old enough, and I intend to follow as well."

Leif fell forward, his large hand going over Thorgunna's belly. "My son," he murmured.

"Your son," Thorgunna replied.

Leif gently urged Thorgunna back onto the furs, his hands lifting her shift, caressing her stomach. It had no rise to it save for her own voluptuousness.

"When the boy comes to me, I shall accept him as my heir," Leif whispered, his mouth going to Thorgunna's navel, his tongue trailing down, wordlessly encouraging her body to respond to his kisses.

Thorgunna sighed, welcoming his touch.

"My son grows within you. I find you more beautiful now, than ever I have before," Leif whispered. "I want to make love to you."

"And I, you," Thorgunna replied.

Leif dipped his head, feasting greedily, taking his fill of the flesh hidden in the sensual crevices of Thorgunna's nether regions. His tongue urged her woman's nub to bloom from its hood, ushering Thorgunna into a realm of sexual fulfillment she had never dreamed possible.

She exploded, nearly smothering the Greenlander as she rode the crest of her orgasm. She shivered as the chill of ecstasy subsided, but was instantly set ablaze again as Leif thrust his member deep into her. He burst in orgasm immediately, his own passion swelled at the thought of not having to withdraw at the height of pleasure.

"And to think but a day ago I lay dying," Leif said.

"Your spirits have indeed risen," Thorgunna agreed.

"Although it is unlike him to be late, I bless Sigurdur for his absence."

"I didn't send for him. I lied."

"Do you intend to chain me to your hearth, woman? And keep my countrymen from me always?" Leif asked.

"For as long as I can, yes."

"And whilst I lie chained at your feet, what treatment will you bestow upon your slave?" Leif asked.

Thorgunna smiled. "This, perhaps," she replied, moving her head to Leif's still-aroused member. "An instrument of torture I heard the old married women laugh about over the fire. Your treatment will be humane, I promise," she said, licking his shaft like a cat cleaning its paws. "Tell me what to do to pleasure you. I want to do this right, and never have I done this before."

Leif lay back, moaning softly, his hands going to Thorgunna's black hair. "Do as you will. You'll learn quickly how to coax the bear from its cave."

Thorgunna took Leif into her warm mouth, circling her tongue around the tip of his thickening maleness, pushing the foreskin back with her lips, exposing the sensitive tip to the warmth of her tongue. She stroked the base of the Greenlandic beast with a hand while allowing the head to dive into her mouth. She could taste her own ardor mixed with his salty passion on his flesh.

"I find it quite unbelievable you have never done this before. Thorgunna, please, lie back. I need you now, woman," Leif moaned.

Thorgunna waved a hand, cutting him off, continuing her battle with the monster, now fully under her control.

Leif shuddered, trying to pull away, to warn Thorgunna that his seed brimmed, but she did not stop her rhythmical washing until the throbbing, pulsating beast was fully at rest.

"By the gods, Thorgunna," Leif moaned, dizzy from the force of the orgasm.

Thorgunna looked at Leif with a commanding glance, "Are you certain I cannot accompany you?"

Leif fell back against the skins, "Aye, but for your sweet mouth upon me I'd sell my soul to a devil to stay here!"

"That would make two of us, then," Thorgunna said, rising to rinse her face in the washbowl.

Turning, Thorgunna looked closely at the lounging body of her lover, whose back was to her. The wound upon Leif's back opened like a mouth yawning, pulling open Iksan's tight stitches, revealing the charred flesh beneath them. A slow trickle of blood oozed out from the smiling gash like spittle.

"Leif, your back is bleeding," Thorgunna said, taking the washbasin and a clean linen wrap to Leif.

The Greenlander made no reply.

Quickly, Thorgunna moved to mop up the flow of blood, using her fingers to push the wound closed. Carefully, she pulled on a stitch hanging loose where once it had held fast the flesh of Leif's shoulder blade. The open mouth of the wound literally snapped at her fingers like an angry dog.

"By the gods! Loki, no!" she cursed, fighting the snarling edges of Leif's charred flesh to close the gash.

"How dare you shoo away the patron saint of the isle," Loki sneered from the depths of the wound.

Thorgunna spat, her hands still fumbling to staunch the bleeding, "You said he would heal!"

"And he will, once you have addressed a more important issue. An issue as close to my heart as Ivar's dagger was to his."

"I cannot build a temple to you if the man I love lies dying!"

"I am a god who demands the faith of his children be proven, and often."

"Loki, release Leif from this accursed wound of yours, and I will erect your Stone. I will honor you!" Thorgunna pleaded.

"First, me. I must come always first," Loki insisted.

Leif's skin took on a blue tinge.

"He is dying!" Angry and desperate, her eyes firmly fixed upon the demigod, Thorgunna reached for her knife.

Still gazing directly into the wound, into the image of godly terror, Thorgunna sliced open her left palm, holding the bloody hand aloft. "I give you my word in my own blood you will be worshipped on Tiree."

Loki rose like a mist from the wound, swirling into his strikingly beautiful human form.

With desperation shielding her, and surprising Loki, Thorgunna approached the fire-god, offering him her cupped hand, pooled with her own blood.

Loki smiled a devilish smile. A fearsome, haunting, twisted smile. "Offering accepted," he snarled, dipping two fingers into the pool forming in Thorgunna's hand. He licked the blood from his fingers, cooing seductively as if aroused, "You are sweet. So sweet is submission. So sweet the blood of the conquered," he purred.

Thorgunna glanced toward Leif. "Now, heal him," she demanded.

"Place your bloodied hand upon the wound. Your own life force shall give him the strength he needs to heal, and drive away the curse I implanted upon the dagger," Loki replied. Loki vanished into a thousand pinpoints of dark light, his howls and cackles trailing off like a will-o'-the-wisp into the gray morning sky.

Thorgunna's blood ran cold as she placed her left hand over Leif's shoulder blade. As her own blood seeped into the gash, she could feel the slash on her hand healing and the strong laces of Iksan One Hand's needlework re-closing the wound.

Such a waste of power on such a nasty little godling, Thorgunna thought, amazed at the sight of her healed hand.

Chapter 18

When the sun was high, Leif awoke, remembering little. But loving more than ever he had before.

As he carefully dressed, watching Thorgunna as she dozed on the skins, he felt as torn in his heart as he was on his back.

He stole from the house, pulling himself gingerly atop his horse. The pony whinnied with discontent at being removed from grazing.

"Don't fret. The grass at the beach is as sweet as the grass here." He urged the pony toward Gott Beach.

"Sigurdur!" Leif called, riding up to his ship.

"Leif! You're well! Oh, thank the Lord, you're well!" Sigurdur exclaimed.

"Hello, Sigurdur. It's good to see you, too. Are we set to go? The ship looks new again."

"Aye. A bit more to be done before we stock her and push her out to sea. Thorgunna forbade visitors while you were unconscious. She kept you to herself, she did. I never worried for your recovery, though. You're too ornery to die at the hands of a Rus."

"I am healed," Leif replied simply. He shrugged his shoulders. "Yes, I am quite healed. A bit stiff, but that will pass."

He surveyed his ship. New strakes, a new high prow, new sail. "Pitched and ready, she is. I've missed her."

"The song of the open water is beckoning to you stronger than the cries of your lady beneath you," Sigurdur surmised.

"Aye, Sigurdur. I must go now, or I will never leave this place. My ties to this island are now much stronger and deeper than ever I had intended them to be."

Sigurdur nodded. "She's pregnant?"

"She is."

"Many a belly of Tiree's women will rise and pop as the days grow longer. Brigit too, but not by my hand, more's the pity."

"Ivar's child?"

"So it is said. That bastard. I'd turn the babe out if it were me," Sigurdur spat.

"Aye, so it would be in Greenland and Iceland if a child came from a rape. But here, on Tiree, I doubt the custom continues. These Norse are too steeped in other traditions."

"Indeed. A strong Celtic influence weaves its way through these people. I suppose it's only natural, they being so far from a proper Norse parliament," Sigurdur agreed.

"Yet, they are Norse, and Thorgunna is the law speaker. No governing body will ever serve this place as long as she remains," Leif said. "And she will remain. I will not take her with us, though she did ask to come."

"Who shall raise your child?" Sigurdur asked.

"I think I'll ask Thorok to uncle my child. He's in love with Thorgunna, you know. He'll never say it, but he is."

"Does he love her more than you do?" Sigurdur asked under his breath.

"No one can love her more than I," Leif replied softly.

Sigurdur looked up at Leif. "Don't you think you'd better let her know that?"

"And make our parting even more unbearable for her?"

"No. To make your parting sweeter by the anticipation that you will reunite one day."

"Lie to her? I cannot guarantee we shall ever meet again," Leif replied.

Though she did say my son would come to me one day—and that she would follow, too.

"Just tell her you love her, Leif. Give that child of yours something more to grow on than the flesh of its mother and father," Sigurdur said.

"Aye. I'll tell her. As always, Sigurdur, you are a voice of reason. Now, let's sound the ship, shall we?" Leif dismounted, casting a glance up the beach to Gott Hill. To Thorgunna's home. The home where his son would be born.

Thorgunna awoke with the single-minded purpose of fulfilling her responsibilities to Loki once and for all. She pulled her hair into a tight bun, dressing quickly.

She dashed to the stable, not taking the time to saddle her pony. "This is surely the most unpleasant and distasteful act I have ever committed. Murder is less foul than ordering a stone be cut and erected in the name of Loki."

Thorgunna leaped upon the beast bareback, holding fast to its mane, about to urge the beast to full gallop, when Thorok hailed her.

"Hold there! Thorgunna!" he called, approaching the stable atop his own pale horse.

"I must ride to the quarry, Thorok. Do not stop me," she replied.

"Why would I stop you, Lady?" Thorok asked. "I awoke early this morning in a pool of my own sweat. Something is wrong on the Isle. I can feel it. What is it, Thorgunna? What is it that is amiss? Do you sense it?"

"Aye. I can put a name to the trouble, Thorok. I cannot stop it, but know its name, I do."

"Why the quarry?"

"I want the stonecutters to carve out a standing stone as large as you in height and girth. It must be portaged inland to Moss, and its base secured in the ground near that ring of Pictish stones half buried in Allrud's pasture. Will you help me? Will you see to the cutting of the monument and arrange for payment to be made to the stonemasons?"

Thorok nodded. His horse whinnied and reared.

Calming the pony, not looking up, Thorok questioned Thorgunna, "May I ask to whom we are dedicating the stone? Should not we ask a blessing upon the rock before the masons take their chisels to it?"

"No. You may not ask. And no, I do not want the rock blessed. In fact, tell the men to spit and piss on it as they carve it out of my island. What I command is a chore which must be done—but no one specified how it should be done," Thorgunna replied.

"As you wish, Lady." Without another word, Thorok rode north toward the home of the stonecutter and his sons, leaving Thorgunna to her thoughts.

The stonemasons lived in an area of Tiree called "the dunes," and rightfully so. The terrain consisted of windswept, shifting sand dunes which covered so sparsely and randomly the area was also known as Bald Man's Bluff. Since Sigfus, the mason, had lost his once-thick red hair as a young man, he aptly, although inadvertently, built his home in what others considered a most humorous location. The bald man of Bald Man's Bluff.

"Sigfus!" Thorok called. What an odd house they have constructed. Open to the wind and sea and abutting Beinn Hough. They must be insane to leave their front door open to invasion and their rear against a hill of rock. "Sigfus!" he called again.

"Bugger me! It's Thorok! What brings you to the dunes?" Sigfus Andresson hailed as he stepped from his house.

"Thorgunna wishes a monument be placed at Moss," Thorok said plainly.

"Aye. My sons and I are in her service. Tell me more of the Lady's wishes," Sigfus said. "And Thorok, tie off your horse and come inside for a drink. The weather is foul, and my ale is sweet," Sigfus invited.

Thorok smiled. It was sunny and warm. "Thank you, sir. I shall take you up on your offer."

Inside, the four strong sons of Sigfus gathered around Thorok as though he were visiting royalty. "How is the Lady? She does not often ride to the dunes. We do not often ride to Gott. What is the word, Thorok?"

"The Lady is well. She wishes the good masons of Tiree to chisel out a standing stone and set it at Moss. Are ye up to the task, laddies?"

"A'coorse we are, Thorok. Will the Lady meet us at the quarry to bless the stone?" Sigfus asked through his ale.

"There will be no blessing asked for this monument," Thorok replied.

"Hmmm. That will not please the god to whom it is dedicated. I know my stones, Thorok. A blessing must be placed upon it before we lift it from the heart of the isle," Sigfus responded.

"Thorgunna was quite insistent. No blessing. Nor will she divulge the name of the god this stone will honor. And, there is more." Thorok paused. "As you carve the rock from the earth, you are to defile it with the fluids of your body."

"What?" Sigfus choked.

"Aye. She wishes the stone washed with your own urine and spittle."

"Thorok, is the Jarl unwell?" Sigfus asked.

"No, she is strong and quick of mind. She says she is being forced to erect this stone, but no one told her how it should be done. Are you up to the task?" Thorok asked.

"My sons and I do the Lady's bidding. Always have. Always will. We'll cut the stone as she has directed. Boys! We start at dawn," Sigfus agreed.

"The Lady will be pleased," Thorok said. He finished his ale and dropped a handful of coins on the table. "She would have the work take precedence."

****

Thorgunna, exhausted and suffering from the plight of early pregnancy, tied her pony to the trough outside her house, hoping to make it inside before succumbing to what appeared to be a bout of nausea blowing in like a summer storm. Slamming the door behind her, she dashed to her bed, and literally collapsed upon it.

"I have no strength. This will never do," she said aloud, sliding her foot coverings off, wiggling her toes once they were free of their leather prison.

"Thank you for the stone, Thorgunna. You have assured that your Greenlandic bull will live. Well done," Loki said, stepping from the shadows.

"I am too tired to deal with you. Go away," Thorgunna sighed, turning her back to Loki.

"I am free to come and go as I please, Thorgunna. And I please to stay here, with you, for the time being," Loki replied, crawling onto Thorgunna's bed next to her. "Even a god needs a bit of comfort every now and then." He trailed his slender fingers down Thorgunna's bare arm, tracing the design of her tattoo.

She shivered. "Don't touch me."

"Afraid I'll soil the precious blossom within you?"

Thorgunna made no reply.

"Do not be so alarmed by my more frequent visits. I get so lonely sometimes," Loki cooed.

"Why? Are you no longer welcome in Heaven? I was under the impression you were in good graces with Odin again."

Loki laughed. "Actually, no. My welcome there was short-lived, as always. However, this time, I'm not likely to be asked to return. Unless Asgard or I are in pieces."

Thorgunna rolled over, facing Loki.

He was beautiful. Absolutely astoundingly beautiful. But such was the nature of evil. A beautiful, inviting trap.

"If I pray to you to make him stay, will my prayers be heard?" Thorgunna asked.

"Do you make this prayer?" Loki replied.

"No, I do not. I just want to know how you would respond should I pray to you."

"If he stayed … if he stayed…" Loki mused. "I could do it, but I'm not sure you would like my methods. Better you not ask that of me, Thorgunna," Loki responded, for once honestly. "Find comfort, Thorgunna. You bear his son. Ivar is dead. Olaf of Norway is without his trained dog sent to fetch the bone of Tiree, and your island is safe."

Loki moved his mouth close to Thorgunna's.

"I know you are lying. I don't know about what yet, but I will," Thorgunna whispered, not pulling away as Loki touched his oddly sensual scarred lips against her own, lightly licking her lips, urging them to open.

Thorgunna felt an infectious, hypnotic flood of desire sweep through her body. She opened her mouth, nearly accepting Loki's kiss, but asking instead, "Why in pieces?"

Loki smiled. "In pieces?"

"Why must either you or Asgard be in pieces before you can return?"

"I've been naughty," Loki murmured.

"More so than usual?" Thorgunna asked.

"Aye. I fulfilled my destiny, and once that is known, it shall cause more than a bit of commotion in the heavens," Loki replied.

Thorgunna sat up. "What have you done?"

"I've set in motion the hand that will send the sliver of death into the heart of the sun, itself," Loki said with an odd mixture of humility and pride.

Thorgunna, ashen, gasped, "The prophesy of the Final Battle. You have instigated the end of the gods, haven't you?"

"I have, yes. The death of Baldur is at hand. The Asgardian pantheon dies with him. Why do you think I've pressed you to erect my stone? I will live on as the protector of Tiree, while Odin, Thor, and Tyr rot in the memories of humankind. You know, dearest, I knew when Odin first came to me, begging for me to love him, that I was not only his one-time lover and blood brother, but also his destructor. It is an odd life we gods have led. Always knowing our end would come, but never knowing how, or by whose hand would we meet our demise. I do not want to die, Thorgunna. You have assured me I shall not."

"Before the gods fade into whatever form of death it is that takes them, you will be punished. The prophecies are clear in that," Thorgunna replied.

"The Vala, the Norse prophetess, was an old blind woman with little inner vision and only a dim inkling of how to interpret the vast tome of information she had access to. I interpret the prophesy differently. With more accuracy." Loki paused, again tracing his fingers along Thorgunna's tattooed upper arm. "And, Thorgunna, they will not catch me. The gods are even more blind than the Vala. I'm too clever for even Odin and his ravens of thought and memory to find me."

"What of the Christ?" Thorgunna asked. "How shall you fight Him when it is He whose image and priests now rule all but the most remote regions in the Norselands?"

"He stands at the gates of Asgard now, beckoning Odin to battle."

"He shall win," Thorgunna said.

"Yes, I know He shall win. By my own hand I have made Him King of Heaven and Earth. However, I shall be king on Tiree."

"By my hand," Thorgunna cursed.

Loki smiled.

Leif walked into the room.

"Thorgunna?" he asked, drawing his short dagger.

Entranced, Thorgunna turned her head, startled, glazed. "Leif?"

"Who is this, Thorgunna?" Leif asked angrily.

"Hello, Leif," Loki said mischievously. "Nice to meet you, at last. Of course, I hadn't expected to greet you in this form."

"Loki?" Leif asked.

"Of course! Hasn't Thorgunna discussed our relationship with you? We're very close," Loki teased, squeezing Thorgunna's left breast.

"Release her from whatever hold it is you have upon her. Now!" Leif commanded.

Thorgunna moaned softly. She wanted only to shake off the confusion and delirium of Loki's embrace.

"What do you want of her?" Leif asked.

Loki laughed. "Why, everything! And nothing!"

"You have Thorgunna in bed, and you want nothing!" Leif stormed. "Liar!"

"Oh, do calm down, Leif. We were merely discussing my plans for the isle. You don't mind, do you? You won't be here, anyway."

Laughing, the fire god faded into a thousand pinpoints of twinkling dark-light, momentarily blocking Leif's view of Thorgunna, alarming him.

"Thorgunna!" he cried, rushing to her side, cutting through the dissipating flecks with his dagger.

"Thorgunna, did he harm you?" Leif asked, mustering composure in the magnetic wake of a god.

"He did me no harm. He won't harm me, Leif. Not now. He needs me more than ever."

"Why?"

"By his actions he has unleashed the Everlasting Winter and sharpened the swords of the gods for the final battle. Ragnarok is at hand. Everything is going to change now. Everything."

"Everything changes anyway. Our faith teaches our gods will burn and die and out of their ashes shall rise a new world for mankind. It is so written. It is their time. Even that vile little Trickster shall perish. He is one of them, and he is not named amongst those remaining after the final battle."

"You are so calm in the face of this storm, Leif. Perhaps it is time for me to forsake the old gods and begin wholeheartedly worshiping the Christ. Confession and all that. I certainly have a lifetime of sins to confess," Thorgunna sighed.

"Many Icelanders pray to both Christ and Thor for protection, all the while looking to their kin for support," Leif said, climbing onto the pallet, holding Thorgunna. The linens where Loki had lain were icy cold and rough on his skin.

"You are so strong a woman to bear these things. Loki. Norway. My departure and the birth of our child. You are so strong, Thorgunna. No wonder even a god wants you."

"Christ, at least, respects His followers by listening to their prayers from afar. Should He guide our steps He does not trip us for amusement along the path as Loki does," Thorgunna said. "But it's too late for me. I am committed to Loki by my own pledge, in blood. Tiree is committed. It is not strength that runs through my veins, but folly."

"What have you done?" Leif asked, a feeling of dread washing over him.

"My actions are not important now. What matters is that Loki will be the last god standing, his cloven feet resting upon Tiree."

"If Ragnarok is at hand, even Loki will perish. Sacrifice to Odin, or…"

"Or what?" Thorgunna asked.

"Have Tiree blessed. But that would entail commitment to what you believe is a far more evil foe than the Trickster. Norway."

"Norway." Thorgunna sighed. "Never Norway."

Leif kissed Thorgunna's tattooed upper arm, gently tracing the encircling knot-work pattern. "I find your markings exotic," he whispered, changing the subject. I don't believe Loki has any true control. He's not that powerful. He only makes it appear he is."

"I found them painful," Thorgunna replied, recalling the hours lying still for needle and dye. "That's why I only have the designs on my arms and ankles. My mother had many designs. Beautiful, colored designs. Sometimes I miss her, Leif. And my brother, Helgi. I wonder where he is."

Leif, not knowing what to say, how to comfort, said nothing. But that was enough for Thorgunna. Just to be held in Leif's arms was enough.

For a brief moment, peace came to Tiree. But the war in Heaven was just beginning.

Chapter 19

The date was set. The Greenlanders were leaving Tiree. Thorgunna touched her belly lovingly. She had made no profit this summer. But the summer had changed her life, forever, nevertheless.

Ivar, dead. Leif, leaving. Loki, staying. And the child within her, growing.

Leif asked that no party be given in honor of their parting. "The men will drink your good beer and consort with your good women until the wee hours of the morn, and we'll never set sail for all their drunkenness. Please, no celebrations."

"As you wish," Thorgunna replied. "It's too soon. You cannot leave yet."

"An entire season has passed around us. I must fulfill my mission for my father before considering any greater purpose which awaits me," Leif said.

"Make love to me, Leif. When you sail from Tiree I am afraid I shall never love again. Until we meet and I put your son into your arms, I shall not love."

"We have never said the words, Thorgunna. Never said them aloud, to each other."

"I am not afraid to say them, Leif. I am afraid only I will never have the chance to say them again."

"Say it, Thorgunna. Say it so that, as I sail away from your embrace, I shall have something to look forward to hearing again."

"I love you, Leif."

"And I love you, Thorgunna. I love you."

****

The next morning Leif's longship launched, stalwart and seaworthy in its refit.

Thorgunna spoke softly as she and Leif walked the white sand beach of Gott Bay to Leif's waiting skiff, "I suppose there should be some blessing made as you depart. But I have no words to offer except 'Tiree bids you welcome,' in anticipation of your return."

"I cannot promise you I shall set foot on Tiree again. But hear me now, Thorgunna. I claim the child of your body as my heir. Let no man say otherwise. When my son comes to Greenland, he will be honored as my firstborn, and the grandson of the Jarl of Bratahild should be honored. This promise, I can make," Leif replied, squeezing Thorgunna's hand.

Spying Thorok, keeping his distance just out of earshot, but close enough to defend the Lady of Tiree if need be, Leif hailed the big *Tirisdeach*. "Thorok!" he called.

Thorok waved a response, walking across the beach to join Leif and Thorgunna.

"Thorok," Leif said placing a hand over Thorgunna's belly. "This is my child."

"Aye," Thorok replied.

"I regard you highly, Thorok. Even your threats to kill me only proved to me you are indeed, a man of honor and of a forthright nature. I ask you this, humbly, and with deep respect. Would you be uncle to my child? Watch over him and raise him in a fashion Greenland would be proud of?" Leif asked.

It was an honor to be asked to parent a child in the absence of the birth father. "Aye. I'll protect and raise your child."

Thorgunna smiled. "I welcome Thorok as uncle to our child."

Had they been in Norway, the ceremony would have lasted three days and been accompanied by feasting, sport, and boasting. On Tiree there was no need for such things. A man's word was a man's word.

Leif reached into his tunic, withdrawing a gold finger ring.

"I need you to accept this, Thorgunna," he said simply. "It was my mother's. She gave it to me before I sailed from Greenland. She knew, Thorgunna. She knew I would meet the love of my life on this voyage. What is a man to do with two women of sight who love him?"

Leif took Thorgunna's hand, placing the ring on her left index finger. His eyes said it all. There was no need for a final kiss, final embrace. Final words. His ocean-blue eyes, brimming with light and life, conveyed his heart to her soulful brown eyes surrounded by their long, black lashes.

Leif turned and waded through the bay to his skiff. He did not look back. Thorgunna would not have wanted him to.

Thorgunna looked at the gold band upon her finger. A perfect circle. Love without end.

"No matter where you go, Leif. No matter how vast the distance. I will find you. Someday," she whispered, wiping a single tear away.

A stiff gust of wind breezed in off the bay carrying a message only Thorgunna could hear, "And so shall I."

Chapter 20

The voyage was an easy one. As if a path had been lined with petals for them, the winds blew the Greenlanders north without incident. No storms. No leaks. No Thorgunna.

Leif and his crew had never seen such a site as Trondheim, Norway, home of King Olaf. Never before had they seen the likes of such a place. Sailing up a fjord flanked by the first tall trees any of them had ever seen, it was all Leif could do to keep his crew from gawking and staring like lovestruck youths.

The port was magnificent. Bustling and teeming with men loading and unloading great ships, not all of them Norse, Leif felt suddenly very, very small in comparison to the world of King Olaf Tryggvasson of Norway.

One great road stretched through the heart of Trondheim leading directly to a great stave house built upon stilts and connected by suspended walkways to numerous outbuildings. Behind the grand stave house, which Leif assumed was the king's residence and main hall, was an even more impressive sight. A church. Obviously so, for its construction was of fine stone and highly polished planks of good Norwegian fir, and it had glass windows. Rough-cut, thick, leaded glass windows colored in vivid shades of red, blue, and yellow, looking more like adornments against the throat of a lovely young woman than eyes of a fortress of the Holy Roman Church.

Leif forced himself to breathe. "So much to take in. So much. How can I focus on my mission when my heart pines for Thorgunna, and my eyes behold the wonders of the world? Drop anchor," he commanded.

Siggi placed a protective hand on Leif's shoulder. "Look there. The harbormaster rows out to greet us. Now there's a job, laddie. Think of the men he must meet."

"Aye. He's a rich one. Look at his garments. Red and gold and bearing the crest of Norway. Well, Sigurdur, let's show him Greenland's finest mean business," Leif replied.

"Hello the ship!" the harbormaster called, as his oarsman pulled alongside Leif's vessel.

"Come aboard, then?" Leif asked, extending his hand.

"No, no. Greenlanders, eh? How long in Trondheim?" the harbormaster asked.

"Long enough to complete my father's business with the king."

"Very well. Port fee up front, then, shall we?"

Leif nodded. "How much?"

"Three silvers for the stay. Do you need portage ashore for repairs? If so, that'll be another silver."

"We're in good shape that way. Made repairs over the summer on Tiree," Leif replied.

"Tiree? You came from Tiree?" the harbormaster asked.

"Aye."

"Well, you'll likely get an audience today if that's the truth of it. You didn't bring any of that *Tirisdeach* Gold beer did you?"

"Tireean Gold? No. We're not merchants. We landed for repairs only."

"Trondheim is a city that likes trade, boy. What business did your father send you after if not to trade?"

"Do you know Greenland, sir?" Leif asked.

"Never been there. Heard of it. A bit desolate, I understand. All that tommyrot about it being a very green place, rubbish!"

"Greenland, though not quite as vibrant a place as its name presents, is now a thriving community. We have good crops and fair fishing and hunting year-round. There is wealth to be made in ivory and fur. My father is the Jarl of Bratahild, and it is his wish Greenland be recognized as a part of Norway's realm."

"A well-prepared speech, I dare say. Greenlander, come ashore and prepare yourself to meet your king," the harbormaster invited.

Leif smiled. "Pay the man, Sig, and lower the skiff. I'm going ashore."

"Alone?" Sigurdur asked.

"Aye. For now. Dress down the ship and send the men ashore on a rotation."

"You're welcome to take your first man with you to the Hall of Olaf. It's your right," the harbormaster advised.

"I'll stay with the ship as my captain wishes," Sigurdur replied proudly.

"Very good, then. Come ashore when ready, sir. Come straight up the road to the gate. I'll announce you ahead of time. They'll let you pass."

"How will you announce me when we've not yet exchanged names?" Leif asked.

"You are the only Greenlander in Trondheim. That is all the guards need know, and that is how you shall be known to all."

Leif frowned. "My father would wish it otherwise, sir. We hail men by their given names on Greenland."

"You'll have ample opportunity to introduce yourself in fine Greenlandic style, sir. See you ashore." Then to his oarsman, "Pull away, boy."

Sigurdur dropped the coins to the harbormaster.

"Ashore, then, yes," Leif said.

"The token Greenlanders, we are. Out of touch and rough in manner we may be, but after this day, we shall be a part of the world, Sig."

"If all the world is full of pompous little men like that harbormaster, then I would be glad to be home at Bratahild, Leif," Sigurdur replied.

Leif slapped his friend on the back. "By my setting my rump on the bench of that skiff and my hands to the oars and my feet to the soil of Norway, I shall be opening up Greenland to many such men, Sig. Better we learn a bit of tolerance now, before our sisters marry the likes of the harbormaster or that half-wit oarsman of his."

"Get ashore, Leif. Norway awaits your conquering hand."

****

Difficultly pushing thoughts of Thorgunna deep into his heart and mind, thinking of father and country first, Leif unceremoniously set his feet upon the soil of Trondheim, Norway, the center of the Norse world.

A lovely young fishwoman looked up from her cleaver and block. A dusky beauty, no doubt the daughter of some seafaring man and a woman of Norse descent, she reminded Leif of Thorgunna. His dark beauty. Daughter of a fiery Rus and an exotic, tattooed Pictish woman.

Forgive me, Thorgunna. Please understand. Please. For you, Tiree always comes first. For me, at this time, Greenland must be foremost in my mind and heart.

Leif tied off his boat, forcing his sea legs to grow fast accustomed to dry land.

A little over a month ago I had considered abandoning my mission to Norway to forever remain in Thorgunna's arms, my face smothered between her breasts. But now all that seems so far away.

The sun, a bright, warm sun, was high above as Leif made his way through the throngs of merchants, stalls, sights and smells of Trondheim.

He forced himself not to dawdle. It was difficult not to be distracted by venders hawking wares from faraway places. Byzantine glass. British ironworks. Fabric rich in color sold by a man with skin as black as a starless night, calling for customers in an odd mixture of the Norse language and, no doubt, his own tongue. As the man barked to the crowd, his fabrics were displayed by a raven-skinned beauty with shining black hair and eyes. Leif managed a weak smile as he willed himself farther along the road to his king. The woman returned Leif's smile. A star shining in the night. A startling, brilliant smile, beckoning Leif to touch the fabric. To sit at the booth. To join her in the shelter behind their table laden with exotic goods looking mundane in comparison to her bright splendor.

"Another time, dear lady. Another time," Leif whispered, hurrying his pace.

The fence surrounding the enclave of Olaf of Norway was at least the height of two men, and solidly constructed of thick timbers ringed with iron bands. Heavy gates, emblazoned with the crest of the House of Tryggvasson, blocked Olaf from the hustle and bustle of his people.

"Through those gates, my destiny lies in wait."

"State your business, stranger," a guard called from an overlook along the fence.

"I am a Greenlander come for an audience with Olaf, King of Norway," Leif called.

"Your red sail in harbor?" the guard asked.

"Aye."

"Your ship stands out like a thumb hit by a mallet. We saw you pull in. The harbormaster has arranged for your stay within these walls. Are you ready to meet your king, Greenlander?"

Leif swallowed hard, his Adam's apple stuck in his throat. "I am."

"Then enter!"

Leif pressed his right shoulder against the gate. It slid open, deepening the groove in the earth by its passing.

A solitary man heavily robed in brown homespun held out his arm to Leif. "Welcome to Trondheim. May I show you to your quarters? The harbormaster said you are a dignitary from Greenland. King Olaf will be pleased you have come to pay tribute."

"I am Leifur Eiriksson."

"I am Baldur Jon Svensson, steward of the house of Olaf. Please, come with me."

Cautiously, Leif clasped wrists with Svensson.

As Leif followed Svensson, he again found it difficult not to stop and stare at the grandeur of Norway.

The main hall was grand, indeed. Three stories high, peaked with staves and intricate carvings of images Leif did not recognize, and made completely of wood. No thatch. No stone save for the flagstones of the walkway and main hall floor.

A young boy awaited Svensson and Leif at the landing of a great stairwell. "I'll leave you here. This boy shall be your escort to the guest rooms."

"Thank you, sir," Leif said, again clasping wrists with the steward.

The boy, a page of about twelve, escorted Leif to a room overlooking the harbor. Leif counted the turns and passages.

"How many live herein?" Leif asked the boy.

"The number of residents depends upon the number of guests seeking an audience with our king. In this wing there are seven rooms and a bath. Below us are the kitchens. Just wait until the scent of cook's bread wafts up from below. Mornings in the guest wing are glorious, indeed," the boy replied.

"A benefit of working and living in the home of Olaf of Norway," Leif agreed. "What's your name?"

"I am Mark, son of Magnus. My father is away on a mission for the king. My mother works in the gardens. I am in training to become a city guard."

"A noble trade, sir," Leif laughed, patting the boy on the head. "I am

Leif, son of Eirik, of Greenland," Leif said. *A fine boy, this. My son shall be so, too.*

"You have the red sail in the harbor, don't you?" Mark asked.

"Aye. Greenlanders bear red sails."

"Never before have red sails pulled to port. Your ship is the talk of the town, sir. Speculation as to your origins included the far east and Byzantium. As your ship grew closer, its square sail proclaimed you were of the Norse realm. Alessandra said no Byzantine would sail a Norse ship, red sails or no."

"Who is Alessandra?" Leif asked, enjoying the lively conversation with the page.

"She's your room attendant, sir."

"I have a room attendant?" Leif asked.

"Yes, of course. The king cannot see to your comforts personally, therefore, he has a woman of the court see to your needs."

"I have no needs save my need to gain audience with King Olaf."

The boy laughed. "All men have needs, sir." He stopped before a door slightly ajar. "This is your room, sir."

"Thank you."

"Will you be needing anything from your ship for your comfort, sir?" the boy asked.

"I'll fetch what I need from my ship, boy. Thank you, again," Leif said.

"A minister will be around shortly to give you your time to meet with King Olaf. He has been taking all callers lately. Sometimes he sees none. You are here at a good time, I think."

"Have you met Olaf, boy?"

"No, sir. My father says he attended my baptism, but of course, I was an infant," Mark responded.

Leif entered his chamber warily, a hand resting on the butt of his axe.

"No need for a drawn weapon here, Norseman. Welcome to Norway," a woman's voice sang from the shadows of the room.

"Are you my room attendant?" Leif asked.

"I am Alessandra. Our king wishes his guests to be well cared for, and I am a part of that care."

Leif looked thoughtfully at the kohl-eyed, raven-haired woman standing meekly before him. *She's no threat.*

"You're not from Norway, are you?" he asked, relaxing.

"No. I am from Byzantium. Olaf's men swept through a few years ago, collecting holy relics and treasures from the east. I am a small portion of the bounty they carried home to Norway."

A slave. "That explains your accent. Although your Norse is quite good," Leif complimented.

"How can I serve you?" Alessandra asked.

Leif smiled. "I really have no use for a slave girl."

"I come with the room, sir. You can sleep aboard your ship, and insult your king, or you can sleep here, and accept Olaf's gift."

"How many men have you served in this room?" Leif asked, sitting.

"As many as my king has blessed me with."

Alessandra took a step closer to Leif. She wore a simple robe of linen, tied at the waist with jute cords. Her full breasts moved seductively as she walked. Leif could see the outline of little erect nipples peeking at him.

The experienced Alessandra opened her robe, letting it fall to her feet. She was thin. Minute. A small woman with black eyes, dark skin and hair shining like water.

"I am here to comfort you, Norseman." Alessandra took another step toward Leif.

"I am Leifur Eiriksson. And you need not disrobe before me unless it is your choice. I will not command that of you. I have no love of slavery."

"I shall remain unclothed. It will be easier to help you bathe if I do," she replied.

"A bath?"

"Yes, of course. You cannot meet Olaf of Norway stained with salt and the sweat of a long ocean voyage. There is a lovely bath in this wing. Come. The door locks. I have the key. Your weapons are safe."

"A bath it is," Leif replied.

Unashamedly, the nude Alessandra led Leif down the corridor to the bath. Leif forced his arousal away, trying to keep his mind on one thing only: Olaf of Norway.

Alessandra slid back a gossamer curtain leading into the room. She smiled demurely at Leif.

Leif closed his eyes, concentrating upon the image of his father standing proudly at the shore as Leif sailed from Greenland. That was enough to keep him from growing tight of groin. Until he opened his eyes again, at least.

A great wooden trough lined with hard-baked clay sat in the center of the room. Under the trough was a small fire, lit to keep the water hot. Leif could see steam rising from the trough. "A bath. A hot bath. I shall enjoy this."

"Get in, Norseman," Alessandra commanded, helping Leif to take off his clothing.

As she unlaced his breeches, Leif felt himself harden. Alessandra seemed to ignore his partial erection, pulling the leather braies down and off.

Leif climbed the footstool and lifted himself into the trough, sinking into the hot water, sighing involuntarily.

"You like?" Alessandra asked.

"Oh, yes. I like," Leif responded.

Alessandra then entered the trough.

"Are you to bathe me or yourself, woman?" Leif asked, as the nude woman climbed onto his lap.

"I am too small to reach you if I do not join you! Besides, I think you'll enjoy this," Alessandra said, taking a coarse cloth from the edge of the trough and running a handful of soap slivers through it.

Leif could not stop himself from reaching his large hands around the woman's waist, encircling her small body in his grip.

Alessandra silently washed Leif. His chest and shoulders and arms. She lifted one leg at a time, washing his feet.

She then slipped behind him, her breasts, belly, and nether region going right over his face rather provocatively.

"I'll wash your back now," she offered. "Oh, my! A battle scar. And a new one, at that. The flesh is still prickled with stitch marks. Does it hurt?"

Leif coughed. "No."

"Would you tell me about the battle?" Alessandra asked.

Leif shook his head.

For a small woman, Alessandra was amazingly strong. Leif could not help but melt into the steaming water, relaxing for the first time in a month as she kneaded the muscles of his back, caressing away tension from his neck and shoulders.

"I've had a headache ... yes ... right there, at the base of my neck, for some time. Since I took Thorg— Oh, never mind," Leif stammered.

"Since you took Thorg's what? Thorg who?" Alessandra questioned, pressing harder.

"Thorgunna of Tiree."

"Thorgunna the Witch? The Jarl of Tiree? You've had pain since you took something from her?"

"Yes. I've not heard her referred to by that name, however."

"Thorgunna of Tiree is a witch. She brews magic ale. Ale which our king must have lest he become racked with the pain of his holy affliction. You are lucky you escaped alive from Tiree, sir. It is said she is a wicked woman," Alessandra said.

Holy affliction? Wicked woman?

A moment later Alessandra was astride his lap again, positioned so Leif's member shot up between her thighs, against her pubic mound.

She brought the cloth to that spot, pushing his member against her own silky ladies' fur, stroking it with her soapy hands.

"Is this a customary part of a bath in Olaf's palace?" Leif asked, ready to burst.

Alessandra did not reply. Her hand stroking rhythmically, she pulled her body forward, her mouth against Leif's.

"Allow me to show you what else is customary in Olaf's palace," she said, kissing Leif, her tongue sliding seductively into his mouth.

"No, please. Alessandra, you must stop this."

"A Norseman fresh from the sea who refuses a woman?"

"I am committed to another. If I were not, however, I'd have taken you already."

"You are a rare one, Leif of Greenland," Alessandra said, exiting the trough. "Here, a sheet to dry and cover you," she offered, holding out a large linen wrap.

Giggling, the tiny woman wrapped the large Viking explorer in the linen, in a toga-like fashion as Leif climbed from the bath. She then blotted herself dry with a second linen wrap, but did not cover herself.

"I'll send your clothing out for washing. You'll have it in the morning. Hungry?" Alessandra asked.

"Yes. Alessandra, are you to remain nude in my presence? Quite frankly, you look cold," Leif said, nodding toward the woman's hard, dark nipples.

"You make a joke! That's good, sir. A bath lightened your spirits. Too bad I could not do more for you." She shrugged. "Perhaps later?"

Leif smiled. "We'll see."

"I ordered food be laid out in your room. Bread, wine, cheese. Probably some fruit. Ever had a ripe apple, Greenlander?" Alessandra asked.

"No," Leif replied.

Alessandra laughed. "They're better than sex."

Leif ignored the comment, willing the emptiness of the ache in his breast to control the fire in his loins. "When do I meet the king?" he asked, changing the subject.

"Ah, that much I do not know. Soon, I should think. Once word reaches King Olaf you have been to Tiree, he'll likely send his ministers to retrieve you posthaste."

"I have mentioned my journey to Norway by way of Tiree to only you and the harbormaster. You have not left my side, and I am inclined to believe the harbormaster does not have Olaf's undivided attention day and night."

"The walls have ears, sir. Be wary of what you cry out in the night, or in the throes of passion. You never know who is listening."

Leif stopped. "Do you speak in jest?"

Alessandra smiled. "Alas, sir, I do not. This is the home of our king. He is aware of all that happens within these walls, one way or another. But on second thought, sir, since it is nearing Vespers, you'll likely be called to court tomorrow."

"Vespers?"

Alessandra stopped dead in her tracks. "Tell me, sir, is it the Latin word you do not understand? Vespers?"

"I do not know the word. Truthfully, I know little Latin."

Seemingly alarmed, Alessandra pulled Leif into his room, closing the heavy door. "Vespers is Latin for evening prayers. The act of making prayers. Prayers done in a Christian manner. Tell me, Greenlander, are you a Christian man?"

"And if I am not?" Leif asked, sensing the woman's alarm.

"Well, you have a lovely throat." Alessandra paused, reaching up to kiss Leif's throat. "I hope you make the choice to keep it attached between your head and your shoulders. Do you understand?"

"I believe so, yes."

"King Olaf is a good man, and a devout Christian. You shall learn that soon enough. But don't worry, Greenlander. More uncivilized men than you have sought audience and gained the king's favor. Sit and eat the fine repast cook has set out for you. I guarantee it is not poisoned or tainted in any way."

Leif sat, letting the linen fall across his lap. "Tell me, Alessandra, who has come to this court more uncivilized than I, a Greenlander?" He took a sip of the deep red wine poured for him at the small table.

"I recall a man who stayed in this very room once being a most uncivilized and vulgar bugger. He hailed from the heart of the eastern Norselands. He had bad teeth and the largest steed I've ever seen."

"He took you riding?"

Alessandra winked. "In a manner of speaking."

"Oh, I see," Leif replied, knowingly. "Did this one-time lover of yours have a name?"

"Ivar. Ivar Hestleggur. He did very well for himself after securing a place in the king's council."

Leif suppressed the welling anxiety in the pit of his stomach at hearing the name Ivar Horseleg. "What post did Ivar take in service of our king?" he asked. He reached to pour more wine. Alessandra quickly took up the pitcher, pouring it for him.

"You need not serve me. And please, take the time to dress. You look cold."

Alessandra smiled. "It is my pleasure to serve you. But I shall dress at your request. I am not cold." Alessandra reached into a small chest by the door, removing a bright orange tunic. She slipped it over her head, tying it off with a red sash.

"Very colorful," Leif commented.

"Maybe you'll notice me now."

"Oh, I noticed you before. Be sure of that. I am tortured as my eyes call my male parts to action while my mind fights against the natural instincts of a man in the presence of a willing, beautiful woman."

"Hmmm. Perhaps when you're more rested you'll feel less encumbered to she who has captured your heart so strongly."

"I cannot, Alessandra." Leif picked up a large reddish-pink fruit from the tray. He bit into it, savoring the sweet, tangy, crunchy flavor. The juice trickled off his chin. "By the gods," he moaned, his mouth full.

"Good, aren't they? The king relishes fresh apples. We have them all year round here. He imports them from warmer climates in the south. Ivar sees to that. His post with the council is a position of great importance to Olaf. Ivar is trade commissioner to the Crown of Norway."

"Apples," Leif said.

"And more. Ivar's ship transports the ale brewed by the witch of Tiree. He is due anytime. I am overjoyed you are with me, Leif. That man, Ivar, can wear a girl thin."

"So, if Norway agrees to open trade with Greenland, it is Ivar who will oversee the route and passage of ships?"

"I assume so, yes. But then, Ivar has the king's fleet at his disposal. Ivar, himself, sees to the king's beer."

"Because the beer brewed on Tiree heals the king's holy affliction?"

"That is so."

Not wishing to seem ignorant as to the health of the king, nor wishing to divulge Ivar would no longer be personally overseeing the collection of Tireean Gold, Leif simply nodded his head in agreement.

A light pealing of bells sang through the air.

"Vespers. You shall not meet your king tonight, Leif. But come the morn, be ready to meet your destiny."

"Well spoken, woman. My destiny is indeed at hand," Leif replied.

Night fell quickly. With the summer months fading into warm memories, the hours of daylight grew shorter and shorter each passing day.

Leif yawned.

"You are weary?" Alessandra asked, hovering about Leif, waiting to be commanded, directed, used or ill-used, as was her lot in life.

"I am. I must return to my ship before it is much darker, however."

"You will not stay here?"

"Yes, of course. I don't want to offend the king."

"Perhaps the page could run a message to your ship for you?" Alessandra offered.

Leif nodded. "Yes, that would be acceptable."

Alessandra bounced to the door, throwing it open. "Mark!" she called.

The dutiful lad trotted at her single call to Leif's chamber.

"Good evening, sir," Mark said politely. "Good evening, Alessandra."

"Hello, Mark. Would you run a message to the Greenlandic vessel and wait for a reply?" Alessandra asked.

"Of course, sir. What message may I carry for you?" Mark said, smiling brightly.

"Tell Sigurdur I shall stay the night within these walls. It is likely I shall have audience with the king tomorrow."

"Yes, sir. I'm away, then. I shall return promptly with any reply."

"There's a good lad. Tell Sigurdur to give you a few copper coins from my purse."

"Thank you, sir!" Mark turned on his heels, dashing off to carry Leif's message.

"I could get used to this," Leif said, sitting back in the chair, relaxing.

"Life in the home of a king has its rewards, true enough," Alessandra agreed. She closed the door, bolting it.

"And you said my clothing shall be here when?" Leif asked.

"At dawn. I promise. Work continues day and night within these walls."

"And what work will you see to tonight, Alessandra?" Leif asked, the bite of the wine seducing him.

"I am at your command. We can take a stroll about the compound. We could play a game. Chess, perhaps? Or is there another game you enjoy?"

"What can you offer, Alessandra?" Leif asked.

The diminutive Byzantine woman smiled. "Go to the bed. Lie on your stomach. I have strong hands. I will massage you to sleep."

"I snore," Leif replied.

"Does that matter?" Alessandra countered.

Leif moved to the bed, casting aside the linen wrap. Alessandra leaped upon Leif, resting her small frame against his, stretching out to completely cover him.

As she rose to her knees, straddling him, she raked her nails lightly down his shoulder blades, grazing the still-pink scar.

Leif shrugged. "You're tickling me."

"You want something a little harder?" Alessandra asked suggestively.

Leif rolled his eyes. "A massage, woman. Nothing more."

"Pity, that," Alessandra sighed, digging her incredibly strong palms into Leif's tight back muscles, moving her body rhythmically as she knelt over him.

Leif did doze off as the cares and worries of the long voyage from Greenland were massaged from him. He allowed himself to relax, truly relax under Alessandra's skillful touch.

"I must sleep now," Leif said simply.

"Of course, Greenlander. Slip under the coverlet," Alessandra replied.

Groggily, Leif rolled off the bed, immediately sliding under the heavy quilt. Alessandra slipped in with him.

"You sleep here?" Leif asked.

"I sleep where I can serve you best, sir."

"Very well. I'm too tired to argue with you. Your touch has placated me into a state of heavy fatigue."

"Good. We can keep each other warm. The nights can be cold in Norway."

"Do all the consorts of Olaf enjoy their job as you so obviously do?" Leif asked, allowing Alessandra's legs and arms to wrap about him.

"With the likes of you in bed at night, what more could a woman want?"

Thorgunna would say land, profit, and freedom, Leif thought. "But you are not free," Leif said.

"My freedom will come as my final reward in Heaven after a life spent serving the king."

"Ah, a well-rehearsed reply."

"What would you have me say?"

"Nothing but the truth. I'm going to sleep now."

Darkness fell upon Olaf's realm.

Leif was momentarily roused from slumber when Alessandra slipped from the bed to answer a light knocking at the chamber door. It was Mark returned from his ship, bearing a simple message. "All is well."

Leif did not feel Alessandra return to his bed. But he dreamed he saw her sitting before the window, hungrily eating the remains of his meal.

****

The room awash with bright sunlight, a deliberate, loud thud at the door awoke Leif from his deep slumber. Alessandra was nowhere to be seen.

"Greenlander, I bring your clothing," the voice of an old woman called from beyond the closed door.

Leif rose, walking nude to the door. He opened it, still surprised not to see Alessandra's small frame and large smile welcoming him to his first morning in Norway.

"Oh, my. You are a fine specimen. Maybe I'll give you a bath myself!" an old woman dressed in stark white chortled.

"I'm afraid you might prove too experienced for me, woman. I've opted for maturity over virginity a time or two, and women such as yourself wear me out," Leif replied. "Where's Alessandra?"

"Called away during the night. I'll be serving you this morning. I've a tray of tea and bread for you. You don't want to eat a heavy breakfast before meeting with King Olaf. And your clothes are washed, pressed, and mended. Shall I help you dress?" Without waiting for a reply, the woman moved into the room. She placed the tray on the end of the bed, then whipped Leif's clean tunic from her shoulder.

"I can dress myself, thank you," Leif replied.

The servant gave Leif a sharp spank on the buttocks as he turned to slip on his breeches. "Maybe I'll trade for this room, after all," she said aloud, but obviously to herself.

"If you do, you'll likely kill me with that smoldering passion of yours.

Better you find an old man with a bad heart. Give him a smile on his face at his burial," Leif said.

"I'll leave you to Alessandra. You couldn't handle me. It won't be long before you're called. Wait here," the old woman said, laughing her way out of the room.

Leif couldn't eat. He stood at the window, dressed and ready for what seemed like hours, awaiting his escort to the reception hall of Olaf, King of Norway. "My life is about to change. Greenland is about to change. I may soil myself in anticipation if I am not called soon."

At last, a forceful knock on his door alerted him to his mission. His audience with Olaf, King of Norway, Master of the Norse world, was at hand.

Chapter 21

Leif closed his eyes, not in prayer, but to muster all courage and strength possible as he stood erect and sturdy before the closed double doors leading to the main hall of Olaf the King. Doors he knew when opened, would set his feet on a new path. His actions, and the responses of the king to those actions, could make or break Greenland. Could make or break him.

Without fanfare or warning, the doors opened, pulled from the inside. Leif was ushered into the large audience area of Olaf Tryggvasson, King of Norway.

The room had a flagstone floor and finely milled wooden plank walls. Directly opposite the entrance was a riser upon which a large, heavy, solid wood chair sat. The throne of King Olaf.

Lining the wall above the doorway where Leif stood were several cut-glass windows. Byzantine craftsmanship, Leif assumed. Light filtering in from outside illuminated the large room without the need for hundreds of candles or torches.

Above the throne, suspended from a rafter, was an enormous, bronze-gilt T upon which hung a wooden sculpture of a man inflicted with a great many wounds, his head surrounded by thorns, and his wrists and ankles driven through with iron pegs.

Is this what Olaf does to those Norsemen who do not convert? Leif wondered, his throat going dry at the sight of the intense, painful suffering represented in the sculpture.

From a hidden area behind the riser and throne emerged a gray-haired man wearing a long black robe. He flowed across the floor so silently it seemed he floated above the flagstones.

"Greenlander, behold your king. Kneel," he commanded, doing so himself.

Leif dropped to one knee, head bowed, assuming he took the correct posture of genuflection as Olaf entered the room.

"King Olaf Tryggvasson, Ruler of Norway and those regions claimed by Norway, head of the Holy Church as decreed by Pope Gregory," the gray-haired man announced.

Olaf appeared to be wearing his bedclothes. Moreover, he muttered to himself as he eased unceremoniously into his chair.

"Is the king unwell?" Leif whispered.

The man in black turned his head toward Leif, shaking it in a silent *no*.

"Is the beer here?" the king asked.

The robed man stood, approaching Olaf slowly.

"No, King Olaf. This is a Greenlander, come to see you about something other than the beer," he said.

"Ah," staring sharply at Leif, "Did you bring the beer?"

Leif stood, assuming he should reply to the king. "No, sir. I did not bring your beer. I have other business."

Olaf slumped back into his throne. His left foot began to tap nervously.

"What does he want?" Olaf asked the robed man.

"The king wishes you to state your business," the man said to Leif.

"Sir ... Sirs—I am Leifur Eiriksson, son of Eirik the Red, founder and settler of Greenland," Leif began.

"Do I know this man?" the king asked.

"No, sir, you don't know me. I've just arrived."

"From Greenland?"

"Yes, sir. Though I did make port in the Hebrides for over three months before making the passage to Norway."

"Good beer in the Hebrides," the king replied.

Is he mad? Is his only concern for Thorgunna's beer? Leif wondered, but replied, "Yes, sir."

"The king has been expecting a shipment of beer from the Isle of Tiree for several weeks now. It appears our Rus traders have been waylaid, as you so aptly put it. Know you of Ivar Hestleggur? He is Norway's emissary to the Isles," the robed man said.

"I know of Ivar," Leif replied. *Know of Ivar Horseleg? I killed Ivar Horseleg!*

"Grimsson! Where's my beer?" the king called.

"It's coming, sire. Ivar sails now to Norway," the robed man replied.

Grimsson. Grimsson. Leif committed the name to memory.

"Please state your petition to the throne, now. You may approach," Grimsson said to Leif.

Leif took a step forward. "Olaf, King of Norway, Greenland would like to be recognized as a part of your realm and seeks the opening of a trade route between our two countries."

"Did I ask him about Greenland?" Olaf asked Grimsson, who immediately replied, "Of course, sire. Otherwise, he would not have mentioned it."

"Ah, yes. Young man, I know of Greenland. The outlaw colony begat by an outlaw. The wayward child seeks the comfort of the Father, at last. I prayed to God Greenland would kneel before me, and by His Holy breath, here you are. It is the Lord's wish that I recognize Greenland and open a trade route. I shall send merchants posthaste—and priests! Tell me of Greenland's church. Have you converted the heathen ice-dwellers and baptized all their children?"

Leif sighed. He reached up, nervously rubbing his throat at the spot

Alessandra had kissed. "Sir, we have no church on Greenland."

"Young Eiriksson, you are not yet then a Christian man, are ye?" Olaf asked.

"No, sir. I am not. Yet."

"Look above me. What do you see?" Olaf asked, suddenly taking on the countenance of a hardened, zealous man.

"I see a man of wood nailed to a tarnished bronze device for torture or execution," Leif replied, honestly.

"If that is all you see, then I am compelled by my faith in God to state I cannot take a heathen country into the folds of Norway."

"My father desires an alliance, sir," Leif responded.

"Is your father willing to sacrifice his life to the one true God, partake in Holy Communion, cast down all idols, and sanctify his land to Christ?" Olaf stood. Even in his nightshirt, he was an impressive man. An impressive madman.

Grimsson bowed his head slightly, raising his eyes to Leif. Leif could see the man tried desperately to convey something with those eyes. What, he did not know.

Leif then glanced up at the torture device above Olaf. It was dark, painful, and twisted. Yet, if he did not pledge his faith to the White Christ, Greenland's fate would be even more dark and painful than the image before him.

He took a long, deep breath, then spoke, "Sir, my father desires an alliance. In his stead I will sacrifice my life to your God, and in your name I shall sanctify Greenland to Christ."

Olaf sat back into his throne with a loud thud, laughing. Grimsson released a heavy sigh of relief.

The guards behind Leif, who had crept in as silently as fog, sheathed their swords. Leif shuddered as the shadow of steel upon his back slithered away. He knew he had narrowly escaped being slaughtered before the throne of Olaf.

"Young Eiriksson, go with these good men behind you, now. They will introduce you to those who shall instruct you in the ways of the Christ. Your catechism begins! When you're a Christian, come back and see me," Olaf commanded.

Leif bowed, then turned to his escorts.

"There's something special about that boy," Olaf remarked as Leif departed.

"Yes, Sire. Perhaps so," Jarl Grimsson replied.

"Do you have my beer, Grimsson?" Olaf asked, his dementia once again overpowering his kingly reason.

Leif was guided to another building in Olaf's compound—the largest. The most impressive structure Leif had ever seen.

Constructed of stone, the entrance doors were magnificent wooden behemoths, heavily carved with a depiction of Sigurd the Volsung and his battle with Fafnir, the dragon. Leif knew the story well. It had always been one of his favorites.

"Go in, Greenlander," a guard commanded, pushing Leif through a partially open door as it squeaked open.

Into the mouth of the dragon, go I, Leif thought, his hand lightly touching the carved head of Fafnir as he entered.

"So this is a church," Leif said aloud as the door closed behind him.

"Yes, it is. Have you never seen a church, laddie?" It was a priest. A Westman priest.

"Until this day, I thought I never would," Leif replied.

"But to keep your head you now stand in Olaf's own church," the priest said, extending his hand to Leif.

Leif clasped wrists with the priest.

"Sit down, Norseman. You're not the first to come blindly into this sanctuary, wondering if a sword is set to lop off his head. I am Petur."

"I am Leif."

"Do you wish to eat?"

"Eat? I thought I was here to be indoctrinated into Olaf's church."

"Aye. And you will be. But if you're hungry, let me give you a bowl of something hot. I'm a good cook," Petur chuckled.

"I'm not hungry. Thank you."

"Very well, then, on with it. You forced converts are such sullen company. Come on, then. Leave your cloak and armor, but bring your sword. It, too, shall be baptized into the service of the Church," Petur said, urging Leif to follow him to the front of the room.

Another idol of a dead man nailed to crossed planks of wood decorated what Leif assumed was an altar area. A stone bowl filled with water sat atop a table, flanked by a silver goblet and a tray of flatbread.

"What is this monstrosity?" Leif asked pointing to the statue of the man on the cross.

"It is a crucifix. The man is Jesus Christ."

"If he is your god, why is he not enthroned?" Leif asked.

"He is," Petur answered.

Leif scratched his head. "The Christ I see before me is dead and rotting, awaiting birds of prey to pick his bones clean. I see no evidence of godhood in this depiction."

"Aye, the body of the man that was the Christ is dead. But he was more than just flesh and blood. He *is* a living God, Greenlander."

Leif, uncomfortable, confused, and overwhelmed spoke, "Just get on with it. Do whatever it is you need do to me to make me a Christian."

Petur nodded. "Very well. Kneel facing me, here," the priest said, pointing for Leif to kneel in a spot before the bowl of water.

"Stretch out your sword across your raised knee."

Leif did so.

Petur made the sign of the cross, saying, "*In nomine Patris, et Filii, et Spiritus Sancti.* Young man, there are very important meanings behind these rituals you are about to undergo. I could explain a bit more, so you could gain some appreciation of the act of…"

"Just do it," Leif scowled, cutting off the priest.

"They never want to know why. I spend my life studying and never get to have formal discourse regarding the tenets of the Church," Petur said, placing his hands atop Leif's head. "I need to go back to Ireland—maybe to Rome."

Leif looked up. Apologetically, he whispered, "Should Olaf grant Greenland a treaty by my conversion, then I shall sit and speak of Godly things with you. You shall explain 'why' to me."

Petur smiled. "Then, Leifur Eiriksson, I baptize thee in the name of the Father, and of the Son, and of the Holy Ghost," Petur blessed, dropping water from the stone bowl onto Leif's head.

Leif shuddered. The water was cold.

"And further, Leifur Eiriksson, I mark thee with the sign of the cross and confirm thee with the chrism of salvation, in the name of the Father, and of the Son, and of the Holy Ghost."

The priest, dipping a finger into a small vial of oil, then made the sign of the cross upon Leif's forehead.

"And your weapon I baptize in the name of the Father, and of the Son, and of the Holy Ghost with the oil of God that it may be used in His name and for His glory alone."

Petur marked the sword with a cross.

Leif then watched as Petur poured wine into the silver goblet, quietly blessing the drink in Latin, then drinking. He then offered Leif the cup.

"Drink the blood of Christ and become one with the Holy Church," Petur commanded.

Leif raised a suspicious eyebrow. *It looks like watered-down wine. Does the Christ demand His followers drink His blood?*

Closing his eyes, Leif accepted the cup to his lips and swallowed. It was wine.

Petur then prayed over a flatbread, breaking off a piece, eating it.

"Eat the body of Christ and become one with the Holy Church," Petur again commanded.

It looks like bread, Leif thought, taking the proffered morsel into his mouth. It was, indeed, Viking flatbread. Nothing more.

"Now, Leif, you must make confession, make acts of contrition, and be absolved of your sins," Petur said, helping Leif to his feet. "Come, sit." Petur bade Leif sit at a small wooden table.

"As a Christian you have a duty to live morally. You may now ask forgiveness for any sins in your past."

"Forgive me, Petur, but what is a sin?"

Petur laughed. "I love this! I am priest to a king whose converts have no inkling what they accept save by submitting they will live another day! Leif, a sin is a word, thought, or deed against God's Holy Commandments. Let me ask you some questions to make things more clear. Have you prayed to false gods?"

"They did not seem false at the time. I prayed as I was taught to pray by my father," Leif responded.

"Have you always honored your mother and your father?"

"Oh, yes. Always. I would not be here before you if I did not honor my father so well."

Petur smiled. "Have you coveted another man's wife?"

Leif stirred in his seat. "Often," he replied, a broad grin on his face.

The priest frowned. "And did you have unlawful sexual relations with women not your wife?"

"More often."

"Have you killed?"

Leif nodded.

"Do you wish to make confession for these and any other sins and be absolved and be made one with the Holy Church?"

Again, Leif nodded.

Petur placed both his hands upon Leif's head from across the table. "Your sins are forgiven by the grace of God and the will of King Olaf of Norway."

"I am now a Christian?" Leif asked.

"Yes, Leif. You are a Christian."

"You say I am a Christian, yet I am unchanged. I am the same man I was when I entered this house. Priest, you wear a crucifix on your belt. Shall I then do the same to show my faith to Olaf? How will he know I am a Christian?"

Petur removed his own iron cross, handing it to Leif. "Leif, many men wear the symbol of our Lord Jesus Christ, but it is their actions, not their adornments, that show they are Christian men."

Leif fondled the thing carefully. In his hands he held the symbol of the Church his true love shunned and fought to ignore. "Thank you, priest. All the same, I'll keep this trinket. Since I am not versed on how I should now behave as a Christian, I think I'll need an outward sign. Or two. Tell me, Petur, why did the son of God die upon a cross? I cannot think of a more dehumanizing way to enter Valhalla." Leif asked, not realizing what he had just said.

Petur laughed aloud. "Christ died for our sins. He paved our way to Heaven with his own blood and sweat. I have not, however, heard he entered Valhalla."

"This is going to take some time, isn't it?" Leif asked.

"Yes, it will. But at least you'll be alive to enjoy the time. Had you not agreed to baptism, I'd be blessing your grave instead of your life."

Leif was silent for a moment. Then looking hard at Petur, he asked the question that had plagued him since the first moment he'd met Olaf, "Is the king mad?"

Petur nodded. "The Fire of God struck him. Struck from the heavens above he was. The rod of lightning entered his head like a ray of light from God's own eyeballs. Olaf struck the ground and writhed like a serpent, speaking the language of God's Angels. When he recovered, he was a different man. He does God's work now, Leif."

"And he drinks Tireean beer," Leif added.

"Our good king suffers pain in his skull where God kissed him. He says the beer alleviates the pain. Only the beer brewed by the Witch of Tiree, that is."

"He awaits his shipment, does he not?" Leif queried.

"He does. The Rus trader who brings the beer is long overdue. We fear the worst. If the beer does not arrive in the next few days, I fear the king himself will sail to the Hebrides. I pity the brewmistress on that Isle if Olaf does sail. He blames her for the traders' tardiness."

Leif sighed. Thorgunna. My Thorgunna. I did not help her by putting my axe through Ivar's body. I signed her death warrant in the man's blood.

"Petur, am I truly forgiven for the murder I committed?" Leif asked.

"Of course."

"By God and king?"

"Why do you ask this, Leif?"

Leif shook his head. "The man I killed was Ivar Horseleg. I opened his spine with my axe as he forcibly mounted my mistress, the Witch of

Tiree. He attacked me while I pissed, running a blade through my back, nearly into my heart. I defended Thorgunna before falling unconscious."

"God has forgiven you, Leifur. Our king, although a man of faith, is blinded by his pain. He may not understand why you killed his agent to protect the witch who makes his beer. In his pain, he may not recognize she is alive to brew further and that he can always find another Rus trader."

"How am I to protect Tiree? Thorgunna? Perhaps I should offer to fetch his damn beer," Leif suggested.

"Would you spend the rest of your life as the servant of Olaf, sailing between Norway and Tiree for beer? Leave that to the Rus, Leif. They were not born to greatness. The Rus follow orders—nothing more. Your mission lies with Greenland. Or is the scent of the whore of Tiree beckoning you to her bed?"

"She is no whore. Watch yourself, priest."

"I see. This Thorgunna, Lady Jarl and Witch, she was more than just your mistress, yes?"

"I've never thought about it."

"You should never lie to a priest, Leif. Do you love this woman?"

Leif put his head on the table. "She carries my child in her belly, and I love her more than I love my own life. I am torn, priest. I made a vow to my father I would woo the king for Greenland. By impregnating Thorgunna, I made a vow to her as well. I am not the kind of man who would leave a fatherless child behind on a distant, remote island. But now I have sworn an oath to a God I do not know."

The doors of the church burst open.

"Finished with him, priest?" a guard asked.

"Aye. Baptized and shriven this Greenlander is," Petur replied.

"Then back to Olaf with ye. Come along, then," the guard said impatiently.

Leif felt exhausted and drained as if he had just rowed all the way to Norway from Tiree.

Olaf sat upon his throne, casually eating an apple as any man might do, when Leif entered the audience chamber.

"You are now a Christian man, yes?" Olaf asked.

"Aye. I've been baptized," Leif replied.

"Good! I like you, Leif. I'm glad I won't have to lop off your head. It's so messy. I know I'll like Greenland, too. You have your alliance," Olaf laughed, his mouth full of apple.

"Thank you, sir," Leif replied.

"Tell me, son, that eastern wench who comes with your room, have you enjoyed having her?" the king asked.

"Yes, she's very nice."

"Small women like that are an easy mark, eh, boy? Though a large woman now and then helps keep a man healthy!"

Olaf is insane, Leif thought, nodding his agreement.

"Sir, if sexual relations outside of marriage are a sin which must be confessed, why send a concubine to my chamber?"

"Because I can! She is a slave and I am the king! And, because the priests who hear confession need something to punish themselves over later. If they didn't hear our confessions they would wither up and die as men. Although they are celibate, their whales still spout. They listen to our immoral acts upon the women of the court, then handle themselves at night seeking release from the lurid thoughts our lives provide them. Afterwards, they whip themselves with leather thongs until their backs bleed raw. Priests are an odd lot. But I need them. You will need them, too. When you return to Greenland, you will most surely need them." Olaf left his throne, walking toward Leif. "Don't worry, young Greenlander. Bed the woman, make confession, and win over Greenland for love of

Christ and Norway, and you will be a happy, wealthy man." Olaf stopped, holding his head. "Damn, my head!"

"I'm sorry, sir. Should I get help?" Leif asked, afraid to approach the king, but loathe to let the man stand barefoot in the middle of the stone-cold floor, holding his head, weeping.

"I need the potion. I need *her* beer. Oh, God! Where is Ivar?" Olaf wept.

Thorgunna has no idea why this man makes war for her beer, Leif thought.

"You didn't bring the *Tirisdeach* beer, did you? No. I've already asked you. Oh, God!" Olaf cried.

"Sir…" Leif began. Leif looked to the seemingly oblivious guards flanking the walls of Olaf's hall. "Will none of you see to your king?" he called frantically.

That moment, the doors burst open. In walked Grimsson, carrying a large tankard.

"Olaf, sir," Grimsson began softly, stroking the king's head, "Drink this."

Like a sick child, Olaf did as commanded, taking a long, slow drink, nearly emptying the flagon in one gulp.

Instantly, Olaf the Pained became Olaf the Mighty.

"He has arrived, your majesty," Grimsson proclaimed.

Leif felt a sudden wash of anticipation envelope him. *Who has arrived?*

Leif had his answer a moment later. In trod Ivar Horseleg.

Ivar bowed to the king, who bowed in return. Ivar then focused on Leif, a stunned look of disbelief turning his red face ashen. "You!" he cried.

"Ivar," Leif said flatly.

"I killed you," Ivar spat.

"And I, you," Leif replied.

"I lived," Ivar said.

"And as you can see, I am quite alive," Leif remarked.

"Not for long!" Ivar drew his axe, swinging it at Leif, who jumped away.

"Oh, my! A battle! Grimsson, bring a keg and a wench. I shall enjoy this!" the king said, scurrying to his throne.

Ivar's axe crashed down upon the flagstone floor, causing a stone to buckle and shatter.

"Oh, too bad, that," Olaf said looking at the crumbled stone. He stood. "Before you spill blood in my hall—and of course, I do enjoy a good blood feud, if that's what this is—I would like to know what we're fighting about," Olaf continued.

"He killed me while I bedded the Witch of Tiree!" Ivar spat.

"You look alive enough. I told you she was yours at any rate. Didn't you tell him that?" Olaf asked Ivar, nodding toward Leif.

"She is not his!" Leif called, drawing his sword.

"You were on Tiree before coming to Norway? And you didn't bring me any beer?" Olaf asked Leif.

"Yes."

"And you killed Ivar while he enjoyed the privileges of body I bestowed him?"

"I apparently did not kill Ivar, though I did strike my axe against his back as he attempted to rape Thorgunna," Leif replied.

"He made first passage with her. And you gave her to me!" Ivar whined.

"He beat you to her, did he? Good show, Leif! Oh, no," Olaf said. "I did give her to Ivar, Leif. You shouldn't have raped her. Why didn't you bring me any beer?"

"I did not rape her, sir. She gave herself willingly to me. Several times,

I might add," Leif said, winking at Ivar.

The Rus scowled, softly saying under his breath so only Leif could hear, "Recognize me, boy?"

"Ivar? Pay attention to me. I'm your king! You killed Leif because he bedded the witch. Yes?" Olaf asked.

"That's why I kissed him with the point of my blade in his back. He should have died from a wound such as that. The Witch healed him," Ivar explained.

"Yes, likely so. She used her beer. Her beer heals me," Olaf replied. "Where is my beer? And a woman!"

Leif defensively moved his sword to one side.

"I'll see you dead yet, Greenlander!" Ivar swore.

Leif quietly, yet firmly replied to the threat, "I recognize you. I've seen the face of the devil before, and I see it now masked by the man once known as Ivar Horseleg. Not dead, but not alive. Ivar is but an empty shell of a man filled with the hatred of one pathetic demigod who is naught but a frustrated child not being allowed to have his own way."

"I am more now than Ivar could ever have been. His hatred for you and his desire to possess Thorgunna were his undoing. It was easy to slip past his weak faith in the Christ and make him my own," Ivar whispered. "And I can do the same to you."

"Loki," Leif replied.

"And Ivar—though little of him remains," Loki paused, then speaking quite boisterously, so Olaf could hear, "You have vexed me so even God Himself could not deny me vengeance, Leif Eiriksson!"

"Vengeance is mine, sayeth the Lord!" Olaf chirped.

Ivar's possessed body raised its axe, swinging it violently above his head. Leif deflected the blow with his sword, the clanging of the weapons resounding in the large hall.

In and out of the streaming sunlight, the men fought. Leif, quick and young. Ivar, fierce, experienced, and saturated with Loki's venom.

"I'll teach you to rut with my virgin!" Ivar threatened, again crashing his axe to the floor as Leif jumped away.

"You're too weak a god or man to be able to breech her barrier with your own sword if the way you swing your axe is any indication of how great a lover you are!" Leif replied. He thrust his sword forward, nicking Ivar's shoulder.

"First blood, Leif! Good show! Where's my damn beer?" Olaf called.

"You may destroy this body, but you'll never destroy me, Leif," Ivar hissed, lunging at Leif, knocking the young Greenlander to the floor.

With Ivar's axe just out of his reach and his own sword now knocked far aside, Leif quickly worked out a defense, hoping to use it before his brains spilled out the back of his head.

In glima one uses his opponent's weight against him, Leif thought, recalling the numerous *glima*—traditional wrestling matches—he'd had as a child.

Moving quickly, Leif ceased his struggle to free himself of Ivar's hold, latching onto the Rus instead, pulling Ivar as close to him as he could, he bit the throat of his attacker.

Ivar screamed, sitting back, putting his hand to his bloodied throat. Leif spat the black blood from his mouth.

"You taste foul, Rus," Leif cursed.

"You shall die for that!" Ivar threatened.

Leif quickly crawled out from under Ivar. He stood, then backed away defensively.

Ivar, like a bull hoofing the ground before a charge, came at Leif with a berserker's cry, his eyes blood red with anger.

Bringing his battle plan to fruition, allowing the force of Ivar's rage to bring him down, Leif simply stepped aside, tripping Ivar as the Rus lunged.

Ivar's head cracked open hard against the flagstones, blood and brain matter oozing out. The gross pudding of gray and red spread out from Ivar's skull, its stench bitter and acrid.

"Finish him, Leif! Do not let a man suffer!" Olaf called.

Ivar rolled onto his back. "Kill me. Before *he* returns. Kill me," he whispered, blood choking his words.

"Ivar?" Leif whispered.

"Kill me. Kill me," the wounded Rus pleaded.

Leif retrieved his sword, standing ready to strike a killing blow to Ivar when the sunlight shifted, moving to the bronze crucifix above Olaf's throne. The glare from the reflective bronze caught Leif's eye, making him pause.

Bathed in the last light of day, the cross shone with a magnificence Leif had not noticed before. Never imagined before.

Suddenly the face of the tortured man, dying horribly for the benefit of the mankind, took on new countenance. In His pain, in His exquisite suffering, Leif saw something in the face of the Christ he had not before. Compassion.

Moving away from Ivar, Leif knelt.

Olaf crossed himself as a second ray from the setting sun burst into the room, bathing Leif in its yellow light. The Christ and the man, illuminated in a golden aura of sunlight that surrounded them and enveloped them and only them.

Leif stood, still ensconced in the glow, "I cannot strike the blow which shall kill Ivar. Rather I beg you to call your physicians to heal him. It is not my right to take his life. It is not what He wants me to do," Leif said, his eyes fixed upon the Crucifix. *And more, it is exactly what Loki would want me to do. To take a life after being baptized into the faith of the Christ. Clever, Loki. You've lost.*

From the shadows several bystanders appeared. Leif hadn't seen or heard them enter during the battle.

From the darker, blacker shadows, Loki laughed heartily.

"Spare the life of my Rus puppet, Leif. Do! He won't live long once I take my breath from his body. Follow your God. Love the Christ well. That love shall keep you far, far away from Tiree. I should thank Him myself for that blessing!"

"We'll take care of him," a man said, wrapping Ivar's head with his robe.

"Thank you," Leif said. Then to Ivar, "Let there be no fight between us, Ivar."

Ivar, unconscious, did not reply.

Leif dropped his sword. Its solid steel clanked against the broken flagstones, ringing like a bell throughout Olaf's hall.

"Your mission is clear, Greenlander. Wise it was to spare your life and lead you to Christ. You shall be my missionary," Olaf commanded.

"Aye. I am to bring the Christ to Greenland, and beyond," Leif agreed. "Teach me what I must know."

The king nodded. "I shall. You are dismissed, Greenlander. Go rest. Have some food. Pray for guidance. You shall dine with me tonight. I'll send a page to retrieve you," Olaf offered.

Leif bowed, and backed out of the room, his eyes firmly fixed on the image of Christ. "I am a Christian," he whispered. "I must share this wonder with Thorgunna."

But of course, Thorgunna was on Tiree, and he was most certainly not. Nor did it appear he would ever grace the Isle's shore again.

Leif found his way back to his chamber. His body shook and perspired. He had developed a headache. Such a day it had been!

A light meal of flatbread, cheese, wine, and fruit awaited him. Alessandra awaited as well.

"Are you hungry?" she asked.

"Oh, yes. I most certainly am," Leif replied. "I am hungry for so much more than just food. I thirst for answers. I hunger for the truth I beheld but minutes ago. I became a Christian today," Leif replied.

Alessandra poured wine, her breasts peeping seductively through the sheer fabric of her loosely tied robe.

"Baptism, communion, confession, and a short lecture on what sin is?" she guessed.

"Yes. That was it all right. But more happened to me than just the meaningless rituals. I learned—rather, I've begun to learn—what the faith of the Christ means. No priest could ever teach me that. When I battled Ivar before the king—who thought it was great sport, I might add—I saw in the face of the Christ hanging on the cross a peace I've never known before. I am curious now. I want to learn more," Leif shared.

"Is there anything else you want more of?" Alessandra teased, raking her fingers across the exposed flesh of Leif's tight belly.

"I cannot couple with you, dear lady. My heart is tied to another, and my mind is awhirl with the day's events. A poor lover I would be."

The chamber door, left ajar, pushed open. "Sir, the king has sad news for you," a page announced.

"Aye?" Leif replied.

"Ivar the Rus has died. The king wishes to spend the night in prayer and fasting for Ivar's soul. He wishes all Christian men to gather in the chapel at dawn," the page recited.

"Thank you," Leif said. "Please close the door."

The page backed out, shutting the door behind him.

"Well, Greenlander. Looks like it's just you and me, tonight," Alessandra giggled.

"I should have run him through with my sword and saved him from suffering," Leif said softly. *No. That's what Loki wanted. I need to remember this.*

Alessandra put her hand on Leif's shoulder, "That's not the Christian way, Leif. That is the Norse way. You did not kill Ivar. Ivar died from injuries sustained in a fall, yes?"

Leif nodded. "My blade was baptized to the service of the Christ."

"Many swords have been baptized to the service of Christ, Leif. However, I believe the true point of that is to not use them for killing, but as symbol of strength. The sword resembles the cross upon which our Lord died for the salvation of mankind. I know Byzantine men who have stopped in the heat of battle, knelt before their sword, its point buried in the bloodied earth, its hilt reflecting the light of Heaven, and prayed for strength," Alessandra replied.

"Strength to kill," Leif said.

"The strength not to kill."

"You are a wise woman, Alessandra. Thank you," Leif replied.

"Yes, and I'm saddened you want me only for my wisdom."

Leif smiled, "Your brilliance is the best gift you give me."

Alessandra drifted off to sleep long before Leif. He was too excited, too energized to sleep. Yet, as the hours passed and the dark of night sent its soothing, tranquil song to him, Leif did finally fall deeply, and soundly, asleep.

Leif dreamed he was in bed, entangled in the arms and legs of the king's concubine, just as he was in the waking world. The dream-Alessandra next to him encouraged his lovemaking as she stroked and fondled him. Normally such a dream was entirely welcome. However, when Leif pulled the woman atop him, ready to impale her small body, her face disappeared. In its place were flames. Red and blue flames. And he heard laughter. Foul, maniacal laughter. And within the laughter, Leif heard a threat. "She's mine now! She's all mine! You're too far away to stop it! Going to keep her from you, I am!"

****

Leif awoke with a start, leaping from the bed, taking his dagger in hand.

"By the gods, it was only a dream," he said aloud. Then correcting himself, he murmured, "By God. By God. This is most difficult. I am unsettled in the realization that the faith of my father is no more than stories told to children to explain thunder and tides. Accepting Christ to win favor for Greenland was one thing, but beholding the truth hidden behind the trappings of the Church and feeling the power that comes from that truth is another. If I am dedicated to Christ, will I continue to dream of Thorgunna's torment at the hands of that ungodly demon, Loki?"

It being near dawn, Leif dressed and went to the chapel. He was not the first to arrive. Olaf was deep in prayer, the body of Ivar lying in state at the front of the church.

A procession of nobles, laymen and priests were making a slow pass by the body of Ivar, their heads respectfully bowed. Leif joined the procession. The foul odor of death and decay hung heavy in the air of God's temple. An unclean, fetid aroma as if Ivar had been dead, buried, and exhumed. Leif removed a wad of cloth from the inner lining of his over-tunic. It was the virgin's blood-soiled blindfold he had claimed after making love to Thorgunna. It would now have to serve as a mask against the hellish smell of Ivar's rotting corpse.

When at last Leif came upon Ivar he recognized immediately something was quite wrong. Very wrong. The body, though wrapped in linen, was clearly visible through the gauze wrappings. And it was rotting. Rotting from the stink of worms and vermin. The leavings of Loki's kiss.

Leif looked around him. "Oh, yes, they see it, too. Will no one say something?" he whispered.

Leif gagged as he walked away from Ivar's corpse.

A tall, slender man, holding a black cloak snuggly about his body, accentuating its slightness, caught Leif's eye. As the stranger moved like a ghost toward Leif, he dropped his hood, revealing greasy fire-red hair and a twisted smile that unnerved the Greenlander.

"Poor, poor Ivar," the robed man said softly, falling into the line behind Leif. Leif shuddered and felt bile climbing up his throat as the man's icy fingers burned into his shoulder.

Without looking back, his stomach churning, Leif exited the building, vomiting.

Petur, seeing the demonic forces at work in the body of Ivar and the reaction of Leif, ran to his new friend's side.

"Ivar—I could not have killed him," Leif retched.

"He has been dead for quite some time. Our king prays for Ivar's soul, knowing the jaws of Hell itself must have snapped Ivar up betwixt here and the isles. Olaf may be quite mad at times, but he is also profoundly wise." Petur paused thoughtfully. "Leif, do you know the man in the black robe? I do not."

Leif shook his head, "I must not know him."

"But you do know him, don't you?"

"Aye. But he is no man."

Petur looked sternly into Leif's eyes, "You have a demon to defeat."

"The old gods die hard," Leif replied.

"Let us pray, Leif," Petur offered. "There's a special prayer we say in times of fear and hard decisions. We call it the *Paternoster*. Repeat with me, 'Our Father…'"

Together Petur and Leif recited the Lord's Prayer, Leif's first true prayer as a Christian man.

Again Leif retched, feeling as though his insides were fighting to free themselves and run away from the church and prayers of the Christian God.

"Poor Leif. You are so troubled by the apparition of an old one that you grow ill. It is the poison of a lifetime worshipping false gods seeping from you. Let me help you. Confess to me, here, under God's sky, before His holy church, what troubles your heart," Petur said, he and Leif sitting on a stone bench outside the entrance to the church.

"I am afraid I shall never see her again. That he may keep us apart."

"The Witch?"

"Thorgunna. My beautiful Thorgunna. My life has changed forever since pulling to harbor. My path seems to be set out before me in a direction opposite hers, and yet I am haunted by the demon she herself conjured."

"Pray, then. Ask God to reunite you, somehow. And pray when you do meet, she will accept the sacraments of the Church and find absolution from the minions of Hell that plague her, and shadow you."

"I can *ask* God?" Leif marveled. "This would be unheard of in the faith of my father. One does not ask the old gods for anything, lest you get more from them than you bargained for."

"Of course. You can pray to God to intervene in your favor, then continue to do service in His name, and see where your road leads you."

"Sir, you make this faith much less a mystery to me. I know Olaf wishes me to bring the Christ to Greenland. Will you accompany me and establish the Holy Church and minister to my people?" Leif asked.

The priest smiled. "I asked God for that very privilege. My prayer has been answered. My path lies with yours, Leifur. And I, too, shall pray our combined path crosses Thorgunna's."

Chapter 22

The church door suddenly burst open. Olaf moved slowly from the church, his entourage bearing the body of Ivar Horseleg.

Petur and Leif, rose and stood solemnly by as the procession inched passed them.

"Where is he?" Petur whispered to Leif, scanning the processional for the man in black.

"I don't know. I don't see him."

"He has fled God's light," Petur surmised.

"Or he's plotting how he might destroy me in the darkness of Hell," Leif responded. "Will they bury Ivar? Better his body be consumed by flames to eradicate any chance of re-possession."

"You are correct, Leif. Ivar will be cremated and his ashes mixed into hallowed ground. Not customary by any means, but this is a special case. Ivar was used by a demon. His body must never again be a vessel for evil," Petur responded. "The king, himself, meditated all night on the matter after first viewing the remains of Ivar Horseleg. It was divine inspiration. Olaf is truly blessed."

"Loki may not recognize your purification of Ivar by fire. He is a clever bastard," Leif said, sitting.

"What you do not comprehend yet, my friend, is there is only one God. And only one Devil. Loki is nothing but a petty, sodomite demon of Lucifer recognized as a godling by the Norse for centuries because an old woman once had a vision that Odin himself loved that wicked son of frost giants."

"Odin took an oath he would never drink from a cup unless a cup was also offered to Loki," Leif recalled. "It is true the All-Father once loved him."

"When the knowledge and love of Christ fills the hearts and minds of all men in Olaf's realm, Odin and Loki will no longer be recognized as gods, but as children's stories," Petur said assuredly.

"The old ones die hard, sir. Some places—Iceland, Tiree—and likely Greenland, are too far from the will of the church to have pure faith in the Christ. Those are wild areas where I have lived, and loved," Leif sighed.

"That is why you shall take the word of Christ to Greenland, Leif. You are an emissary of the king and missionary of our Lord. There is no greater task."

"My mind is a-whir, priest. To clear my mind, should I not pray to the Christ for clarity of thought? You said I can ask God for His blessings, for His intervention. I certainly need guidance right now." Leif paused, continuing quite emphatically, "Although a Christian but one day, I have more hope at this moment than ever I had in worshiping Odin."

Petur laughed. "God listens to our prayers, and never fails to make a reply. Sometimes the answer is *no*. And sometimes the answer is *yes*, seemingly at the most inopportune times. But God has a sense of humor and loves to set challenges before us. It's that lovely gift He gave us called free will. The Norse have this in abundance."

"Priest, I wish to pray now," Leif said.

"Then do so. You do not need my permission, my assistance, or the trappings of church and king to pray to God. Simply close your eyes, bow your head, and tell God what is in your heart. I'll leave you to your prayers, Leif. Come see me later," Petur said. "I'm making rabbit stew!"

"Are you a priest or a cook, Petur?"

"Come see me later, and you can decide which of my gifts you prefer. If you don't like my stew, I shall remain your priest."

Leif smiled. "I'll come along. I have much to learn."

Petur entered the church. Leif remained seated, taking the posture Petur had commanded for prayer.

He closed his eyes, blocking out the fear the shadow of Loki would pounce upon him in the darkness of the prayer.

Either I make a stand, and believe, or I am no better a Christian than Ivar was. I want to believe. I want to win this battle and have Thorgunna safe in my arms, and see our children baptized in Greenland's own church.

He bowed his head.

"God, I don't know you well. I saw Your light and feel there is a purpose for me, but need strength to follow it lest I return to Tiree and forget my pledge to my father, my king, and my home. The priest says You listen. I hope You do, for Odin and Thor never have. Lord, I want Thorgunna. As I want water to drink and air to breathe, I want her. I want to share this new faith with her, raise my children with her. Marry her in Your church. Yet, I burn with just as strong a fearsomeness to bring You to Greenland. To my mother and father. Further, Lord, rid me of the shadow of Loki. Show me which path I must take to cut my ties to the old gods, to serve You, and to fulfill my mission."

Leif felt pleased with his prayer. "I appreciate the ability to pray without having to make an offering or sacrifice. How clever is the Lord to make it so simple for men to pray."

He walked to his chamber. The time between early morning and late afternoon was but a fleeting memory, and that memory was now drowned by the foul air and acrid smoke from Ivar's cremation. Even in death the man was rank.

Leif rounded the corner of the main building which housed his quarters. A wisp of a black cloak turned a second corner just ahead of him.

"I know you! I know who you are!" he called. *It's him! It's Loki!* "Loki, show yourself! I am a Christian now! You have no power over me!" he called.

A foul smell wafted by. Leif gagged. It reminded him of milk long turned, souring in the belly of a Rus and expelled most ungraciously by natural means. In the same breath the sweet scent of honey filled the air. The honey carried a message. An undeniable message from Loki: "I'm about to."

"You are nothing without me, Loki! Nothing without the devotion of Norsemen. Go back to Hell!" Leif called, walking quickly away from the site of Loki's olfactory visitation. "You are a shadow of things past, and I choose to live in the light!"

****

Alessandra watched for Leif. Hanging out the window, she resembled a little girl waiting for her father to return from the fields more than a glorified concubine who came with the room.

"He comes, little one. Do not lean out so far lest you fall," a man's voice said behind Alessandra.

"Hello? I didn't hear you come in," Alessandra replied, not wary in the least of a strange man entering Leif's chamber. She was, after all, in the safest place in the world—the hall of the King of Norway.

"Sir, do I know you?" Alessandra asked, turning to drop down from her perch on the window sill.

"Not yet," the stranger replied.

"Are you lost?"

"No. I sought for you."

"Well, sir. You've found me. What can I do for you?"

"I am to be a guest in this room when the Greenlander sails," the man replied.

"Welcome," Alessandra said politely.

"I came to see if you are as tasty as Olaf says you are."

"It is not customary for me to serve men not yet guests in my room, sir."

"Just a kiss, little one. One kiss and then I shall return to my ship and await my turn for bath and bed."

Alessandra approached the man slowly, giving him a chance to feast his eyes on her diminutive yet womanly body.

She slid her arms around his neck, pressing her breasts against his leather vest. "You have the blackest eyes I've ever seen, sir. And yet there is a fire burning within your black eyes that burns hotter than even the sun."

"That fire burns for you, woman."

Alessandra raised her lips to the stranger's. She hesitated for a moment, taking note of several fine scars surrounding the man's mouth. Alessandra kissed the man, giving him a hint of what passions awaited him as a guest of Olaf.

****

Leif returned to his room moments later, pushing the door open to find Alessandra setting out a light meal for him. No vapor or scent of the beast lingered about.

"Hungry?" she asked.

"Aye. Very," Leif replied, removing his boots, cloak, and tunic.

She passed him a trencher laden with fruit, cold meat, and cheese.

"I need a drink," Leif said softly.

"Water? Wine? Tireean beer? Mead? Me?"

"Mead. And plenty of it."

"Oh," Alessandra sighed, pouting with disappointment, fetching the cask of mead from the table.

Greedily, Leif stuffed his mouth with meat, washing it down with a huge swallow of the golden liquid.

"I want to get good and drunk this night, woman. Pour me another."

Alessandra stepped directly in front of Leif, her robe open. Her pubic mound faced him as she poured another cup of mead for him.

Leif took the cup and drank, staring intently at her womanhood. He reached a finger into the thick patch of deep blue-black curls, twisting it.

"It's about time you noticed me," she said softly.

Leif took another mouthful of mead, swished it around in his mouth, feeling its sting and bite, but not swallowing.

"What else would you like to touch?"

Leif swallowed. "I shouldn't have done that, I'm sorry."

"Leifur Eiriksson, I'm beginning to think you don't like women! Every night I lie next to you, and you've never once touched me. I would do anything for you. Anything. Just tell me what it is you desire."

"Beautiful Alessandra, I am bound to another woman. She carries my child. I cannot take advantage of your offer, as much as I'd like to."

"Leif, may I ask one thing of you?"

"Yes, of course."

"Will you do me the honor of kissing me? Just once. One kiss to remember you by."

"I see no harm in one kiss. I can assure you, it will not lead to lovemaking, no matter how my body responds to your kiss."

Alessandra kneeled before Leif, her arms going around his neck. "Your strength of will overwhelms me."

Leif's hands went to her shoulders, his hard callused palms lost in the smooth, silky fabric of her robe.

Slowly, as if to make the moment last forever, Alessandra inched her mouth to Leif's.

Leif closed his eyes, enjoying the rush from the mead, the building excitement of the kiss, the sensation of a woman's warm flesh against his own.

Softly, skillfully to the point of professionally, Alessandra slipped her tongue into Leif's mouth, pulling him into a long, seductive embrace.

Alessandra moved her mouth to his shoulder, trailing her tongue across his throat, tasting his sweat. "Touch me everywhere," she begged.

Nuzzling and kissing his throat, she lolled her tongue across his jugular, flicking its tip across the big vein like a finger against a stringed instrument.

Her teeth nibbled, pleasantly at first. Leif felt a torrent of desire rush through him, until Alessandra bit down.

"Oh, gods! What are you doing?" he cried as Alessandra wrapped her arms and legs about him, digging into him like a parasite upon an oak.

A sharp odor, the scent of death, suddenly enveloped Leif's senses. "Woman, this is not pleasurable! Stop biting me so!" he cried, his chest in spasm as his lungs tried to expel the foul stench emitted from Alessandra's kiss.

"If I had a knife, I'd bite deeper, Greenlander," a male voice hissed.

Leif pulled away quickly, peeling Alessandra off him like wet clothing.

"Oh, don't go away, Leif. You would leave me unsatisfied and yourself as well?"

"I know who you are, and I command you to leave!" Leif demanded, dry heaving as he backed away from the form of Alessandra, now sparkling and aglow with the presence of Loki upon it.

"Oh, don't be ill because I chose this time to say hello and let you know I'm taking good care of the Lady Thorgunna. Good care of her, indeed."

"Leave her alone!" Leif screamed, pouncing on Alessandra's body, strangling her, strangling the Trickster.

"You'll kill the girl, Leif! Only my spirit is within her. This is her body! Do you wish to break God's law by murdering your whore?" Loki asked.

Leif continued choking Alessandra.

"You've hurt her, Leif. She is fighting for breath. She'll be unconscious in a moment. Let me enter you, and we'll have our way with her! Take her badly, Leif. Sodomize her!" Loki urged.

"You are insane. I will not rape this woman, or any woman. She has comforted me, served me."

"A god knows when to press his advantage. That is what makes me a god and you a simpleton. Go pray to your Christ now, Leif. Make your penitent acts of contrition, and I'll see you in your Christian Hell. But remember while you pray, it is I who hold Thorgunna at night. It is I who fill her each night. Even as your child grows within her, I take her."

"You want me to return to Tiree," Leif said, suddenly understanding the demigod's purpose behind the torment.

He released Alessandra.

"Do you not wish to save your woman from the savage love I bring? I give her no rest! I take her night and day. Then I enter her body in spirit and rape her soul!"

Leif bowed his head, concentrating on the image of Christ on the Cross, the golden image above the High Seat of the King of Norway.

"With Christ as my strength I see you for what you are. A desperate false god of lies and deceit. You do not harm Thorgunna. You mean to keep me from bringing the Church to Greenland. I vow now to fulfill that sacred task no matter what you say or do. Greenland is the last outpost of the gods. It is the final country in all of Olaf's domain still dedicated to the Aesir gods. You'd do anything to preserve it!"

The spirit of Loki rose from the bruised and barely conscious Alessandra. "You've not seen the last of me, Greenlander. Although men of

Christ erect churches in His name, I shall always reside in the hearts of those men."

"Go to Hell," Leif cursed.

Loki laughed. "I gave birth to Hel, Leif! She is my daughter!"

The Trickster vanished from the chamber.

"Leif, you nearly put me under." Alessandra coughed. "I don't enjoy rough sex play. Must we continue this?"

Leif held Alessandra, praying in his heart for forgiveness. Hers, and Thorgunna's.

*

Excellent! That is exactly what I want—his attention on Greenland, not Tiree! Loki said to himself. Greenland's destiny was long forged to Christ, you fool. Tiree, however, shall be mine. It is the last outpost of the gods. And it is mine!

Chapter 23

Life on Tiree returned to its slow, even pace after the departure of the Greenlanders.

Winter rolled in with a storm to match those of the summer months, belching out a rare sight on the Isle: snow. Relentless snow.

Confined indoors for a week, Thorgunna grew restless. She could not sleep. She feared sleep. With great drifts of snow outside her door, there would be no escape should the jaws of Hell come snapping at her like hungry wolves in the midst of a desolate winter. If Norway came calling. If Loki returned.

Her nemesis had been conspicuously absent from her life for weeks.

She dwelled on her fearsome thoughts. "It frightens me more to have him plotting in absentia than to have him making threats to my face. Of course, perhaps he's been caught and punished for his malicious acts. One can always hope. One can always pray. Pray. I don't pray. But Leif, most certainly does."

The day of Leif's baptism had been revealed to her through her sight. Images of water and light swirled in the mist of the knowing—and always, just off in the distance, blood and darkness.

Continuing her dialogue to herself, for there was no one to hear her, no one else with whom to speak, Thorgunna stomped about her house, to and fro, like a caged animal.

"I carry the child of a man who now belongs to the priests of Norway and the White Christ. He talks to the Christ as if he were talking to his own father. How ridiculous. The gods don't listen. If they cared at all about humanity, they wouldn't let the likes of Loki run amok upon the face of the earth."

Thorgunna peeked out her shuttered window to see only a wall of white beyond it. She touched her belly. Sometimes she felt a flutter from within. It would be many months before the baby was born. Before her son was born. Leif's son.

It was during the snowstorm that she longed for him the most. Missed his smile. The way his blond hair fell about his shoulders as he slept. The smooth, warm flesh of his tight belly against hers. His scent of salt and leather.

"How long did we really have together?" But the answer was clear: not long enough. From the end of spring to the end of summer she'd been his. His mistress. No—more than that. They both knew it. That knowing would bring them together, again. Weather and time against her, there was nothing she could do but wait.

****

The snow melted as a bright winter sun filled the sky near the end of the first month of the season. Her body changed rapidly as her child grew within her, though she stoically bore the discomfort to capture a single moment of freedom—the freedom of going on horseback. Thorgunna went riding, often. She drew strength from the horse beneath her. It quelled her fear, the pain in her broken heart, and made her surge with the power she'd thought lost at Loki's hands.

****

Leif sailed from Norway with the blessings of the king for Greenland, and for Norway's new missionary to Greenland, Leif himself. Three months he'd stayed in Norway. But the call of Greenland, and the call to bring Christ to that uncivilized land took him away from Crown and Church. Petur accompanied him willingly.

The voyage itself was unusually calm for early winter. Too calm. It unnerved the men, long accustomed to rough seas and howling winds.

"The Lord protects you, Leif. He sends a westerly breeze and calms the waters to take His new son home," Petur said, standing at the high prow next to Leif.

"I do not know the signs and wonders of God yet, Petur. I do know about the calm before a great storm. My men are afraid. They sense it, too. This is not right. The weather, the ocean. Something is coming," Leif said softly.

"You must put your faith in the Lord God, Leif. He guides you now. You have nothing to fear."

Leif laughed. "Except my father's reaction to you."

****

Eirik the Red, founder of Greenland's colony and Jarl by his own word, was overjoyed to see his son's ship pull into the fjord of Eirikstadr.

"It's good to see you, Father," Leif said, unashamedly hugging his father, kissing him.

Eirik embraced his oldest son warmly, "I missed you, Leifur. Your ship looks well. New strakes. You ran into a storm and made repairs?"

"Aye, father. A tempest like none other. We summered on Tiree, in the Hebrides, before sailing to Norway," Leif replied.

"Tiree? Never heard of it," Eirik laughed. "Who's this you bring to Bratahild?"

"A man sent from Olaf to teach Greenland of the Christ," Leif replied.

Eirik took a step back.

"Father?" Leif questioned, as Eirik's face turned as red as his hair.

Love's Second Sight 285

"You brought a priest? A Christian? Mark my words, this is the worst day in the history of Greenland! I send my son to Norway to make good with the king and what does he bring back? He brings a priest! Next time, I send your brothers! Bugger me!" Eirik cursed.

"Father, it is Norway's will that Greenland become a Christian land," Leif said thoughtfully. "This is Petur. He is a good man, father."

"Bugger Norway! And bugger the priests of Norway!" Eirik shouted.

Petur, about to speak in his defense, held his tongue as a stout, older woman smacked Eirik on the back of the head as she broke through the crowd gathered at the landing. "Be quiet, Eirik. All newcomers are welcome at Bratahild—Christian or no."

"Mother!" Leif cried, taking the woman in his arms.

"Petur, this is Thjodhild, my mother," Leif introduced.

"I am honored to meet you. Both of you," Petur said, directing his comment to Thjodhild, then to Eirik.

"Bah," Eirik muttered.

Thjodhild looked at the priest carefully. "There is a light shining in your eyes, priest. Is this the light of the Christ?" she asked.

"I would hope so, yes," Petur replied.

"I don't think so, priest. I see a bit of the Trickster in your eyes," Thjodhild teased.

"Dear lady, I hope to prove you wrong," Petur laughed.

Eirik stomped off, kicking away everything in his path. "A priest! My oldest son brings me a priest!"

"It would annoy Eirik greatly if I became a Christian woman. Priest, I believe I'd like you to stay in my house for the time being. Tell me of the Christ. Slowly. I'm an old woman with a short attention span. Too much too quickly and I'm likely to cut out your tongue," Leif's mother offered.

"I'll watch myself, madam. Thank you for the hospitality," Petur replied.

"I hoped Petur would stay in my house," Leif said softly.

"That will never do. It wouldn't annoy Eirik at all. No. The priest stays with me."

"As you wish, Mother," Leif responded.

"Your God requires a dwelling for worship, does He not?" Thjodhild asked Petur as she showed him to her house.

"Yes, dear woman. We call it a church," Petur said.

"And you, as an agent of your God, can consecrate the ground and make it a sacred place?"

"Yes, lady. I can."

"Would you have a church here, at Bratahild, then?" Leif's mother asked.

"I hope to, soon. Leif has offered to finance its building."

"No. My son should use whatever silver he has for a new ship. A vision came over me as I milked my goats shortly after Leif sailed from Greenland. He is destined to make a greater voyage than the one he has just returned from."

"You are a woman of sight?" Petur asked.

"Yes, I am. Does this frighten you, priest?" Thjodhild asked.

"No. An old woman's visions do not frighten me. What else did you see?"

"Leif will leave soon. He is born to greatness beyond the dreams his father has for him."

"Yes, this is so. Leif is a servant of God and king."

"More greatness than you know is my son destined for. He shall be remembered throughout history for…"

"For building the first church on Greenland," Petur interrupted.

Thjodhild laughed. "No. He shall not build your church. That is not

Leif's mission. I shall finance Greenland's first church. And its second if it will drive Eirik to distraction."

"Are you serious?" Petur questioned.

"Yes, I am. Leif must not be tied to this land right now. His path lies west. His destiny lies west. Priest, teach me of the Christ. I shall be your first convert," Thjodhild said.

"It is likely Eirik will be greatly put out should I baptize you," Petur replied.

Thjodhild smiled broadly. "Then we must waste no time!"

****

Early the next morning Thjodhild herself picked the location of the first Christian church on Greenland. She went alone, before dawn, wrapped warmly against the chill of Greenland's early spring. She knew where she wanted the church. On her land. Her rightful parcel of Greenland.

"You know me, Odin!" she cried, stomping her foot, marking the site with her heel. "You know I am a woman of honor even though I have been lax in my offerings to you. And I bear no guilt for keeping my kids and lambs for myself rather than burning them as offerings to you. This is Greenland! Our lives are harsher than in your other realms. But hear me now! This land, this small patch of good land, I'm giving to the White Christ. I mean to become a Christian. I am certain you will not be forgotten on Greenland, but you shall no longer be worshipped, at least by me."

Bravely, Leif's mother sliced open the palm of her hand, and in a very old tradition, placed the bloody palm against the earth. "My blood to the earth in promise this land shall be heretofore known as Kristness, Christ's Land."

A small act from an old woman, alone, at dawn, with vast repercussions.

Thjodhild's pledge in blood struck the final blow to the gods. The kiss of the old woman's blood to the land launched the great turning wheels of fate, calling them to action.

Moving with such force that nothing in all the nine realms of the gods could stop them, those great weapons of mass destruction pressed onward, announcing the last call of immortality for the gods.

The prophesy of the demise of the Norse gods was at hand. Odin, chief god of the Vikings, the All-Knowing, All-Seeing, Terrible One, upon recognizing the changes in his universe, uttered softly, "It has begun."

****

Petur took note of the blood-stained, hard-packed earth as he stood over the spot Thjodhild had donated for Greenland's first church. "Here shall be placed the foundation stone of Thjodhild's church," he prayed.

"Over my dead body!" Eirik cried, recklessly riding up to the site.

"Go away, Eirik. You weren't invited," Thjodhild smirked.

"Curse you, priest! Curse you!" Eirik continued.

"Father, you're drunk. Really, Father, it's just past dawn," Leif commented.

"I did not sleep. How could I sleep when my wife gives her land away to the Christ? I wanted only Norway's protection and trade, Leif. I did not ask for its God." Eirik coughed.

"Go home, Eirik. This is my land. I shall do with it what I wish. And I wish to build a church," Thjodhild said sternly.

"Why do you do this, woman?" Eirik asked.

"Ask your mistresses. They'll give you the answer. Now go away!" Thjodhild cried, tossing a stone at Eirik's pony.

The horse startled, reared, and bucked the drunken Eirik off.

The old Norseman landed with a heavy thud upon his backside, his right leg curling painfully under his weight.

"Father?" Leif asked.

Eirik tried to respond, but was unable to speak. Too drunk, too overwrought, and now winded from the fall, he waved a hand, dismissing any further questions, and passed out where he lay.

"Get on with this, priest. He won't stay out forever," Thjodhild said, showing no concern for her husband.

"Mother, I think father's leg is broken," Leif said.

"Ah. So it is," his mother replied.

"Mother?" Leif questioned.

"He's out cold. He won't notice if I splint it out now or afterwards. Does this meet with your approval, son?"

"Aye," Leif answered.

"Madam, perhaps you should attend to your husband. He is turning blue," Petur said, concerned.

"After," Thjodhild said sternly.

"As you wish, Lady," the priest replied, raising his hands to begin the blessing.

As the priest blessed the land, Thjodhild stood smugly by while Leif prayed silently, fearing for his injured father, yet overjoyed his mission to introduce Christ to Greenland was at hand.

Petur sprinkled Holy Water blessed by the Bishop of Norway upon the ground. Leif felt the droplets of water strike his own body as they kissed Greenland's earth, changing his home—changing him—forever.

****

Thorgunna stopped breathing.

Her heart slowed.

She fell hard into a vision, without warning. Without knowing from whom it sprang forth. There was no time to prepare. No time to interpret. The vision overtook her and ferried her away. She saw a drop of water splash in slow motion against hard-packed soil. Soil not familiar to her. A chill wind—a north wind enveloped her. She knew where the drop fell. Greenland. It fell in Greenland.

At the same moment, across the North Atlantic and southward into the British Isles, on Tiree, lonely little Tiree, she cowered as a vivid flash of lightning, followed by a crack of thunder joined the wind. The air around her became charged with the electrical current of the lightning. It was a dark and foreboding morning; the air was heavy, suffocating, and scratching at her like an uncombed wool blanket.

She stood in her home. The vision was so strong she felt ill from the force of it. She watched in horror and fascination as around her, the metal objects in her chamber began to glow. An eerie blue-green light wafted up from the iron joints of her loom, her father's sword, the brooches fastened to her apron—rising up and away—a glowing thread of light between earth and sky.

Something is coming! The hairs on the back of her neck prickled, standing on end. The voices of a thousand women of sight joined hers. She was not the only Norsewoman to feel the surge of energy wash across the vault of Heaven. Spindles and ladles and shuttlecocks and hooks fell to the ground or were cast aside. Thorgunna, entranced with the others, felt the change in their world as if it were their own bodies being molded by the hands of fate.

Still away from an earthly plain, Thorgunna ran outside, the wind whipping her cloak like a taskmaster's whip about her. Hundreds of pinpoints of light danced across the sky above Tiree. "The gods!"

She knew whose hand stoked the fires of heaven. "Loki! What have you done?" She beheld the simultaneous purification of Greenland's soil by the hand of a priest and the hand of a blind man wielding a dart of mistletoe. The lights above Tiree formed pictures, and she watched them tell the story she already felt in her bones.

Baldur, the bright god, around whom life revolved in all the worlds, lay dead. A sprig of mistletoe pierced his heart, coerced into place by the will of Loki with the hand of Baldur's own brother. But it was not that wound that took his life. It was the holy water of the priest which burned away the life force of the god.

Thorgunna turned and vomited as Loki's cries of victory reached her. "I shall be the last god standing!" he exclaimed. "And it is from your bed, Thorgunna, that I shall rule.

Thorgunna was completely lost to her second sight. Many times in her life, the sight had guided her, protected her, spoken through her. Never before had it completely engulfed her, removing her from her body, whisking her away on the streams of the heavens. She beheld the war of the gods from beyond the brewing storm above the world of humankind. In the midst of the battle was Loki, sword in hand, splattered with the blood of his kin, rapturous in the glory of the terror he'd created.

Thorgunna shuddered. The cold chill of the Everlasting Winter fell upon her, its icy tendrils cutting her as she succumbed to the horror of the death of the gods—gods she had never fully acknowledged until now, at the moment of their demise.

She saw the hands of a priest bless the sanctified ground, and saw strong hands she recognized well break the soil with a mattock. "Leif..."

He couldn't hear her. Mortified, she realized as the vision ended she was now more truly alone than ever she had been.

She had fallen to the floor, taking the contents of her table with her. She tasted dried blood on her lips and a deep ache in her side where she had landed.

No matter. The events shown her were not only playing out along the streams of time—she knew the physical world was about to be embraced by a war in heaven.

She pulled herself to her feet and dashed to the stable. The sky above closed in overhead, dark and menacing. She mounted her pony and as if being chased, she set off bareback across Tiree.

At Hynish Bay, Thorgunna dismounted, letting her pony rest. The chestnut mare reared and bucked against the gale-force wind. But this was where the storm had led her.

Creeping carefully over the stone slabs lining the high-water line of the beach, Thorgunna spied one large hook-nosed salmon trapped in some crags a few feet off-shore, having successfully avoided the nets. No, the salmon wasn't trapped—it was hiding. The large fish fought the wind-born current to remain secluded and hidden under the outcropping of rocks.

A bolt of lightning flashed. Then another. The salmon splashed angrily, thrashing against the current.

A long roll of thunder shook Thorgunna, the ground vibrating from the sound waves like an earthquake had struck. Her unborn child responded to the commotion with a strong kick to her ribs. She placed her hands atop her swollen belly, comforting her son, sharing her secret with him. "The gods are afraid."

The rogue salmon splashed again. For an instant, Thorgunna's eyes met those of the fish as it leaped high, then darted under the choppy water. The salmon had red eyes. Glowing, red eyes.

Another clap of thunder rolled across the sky. The salmon splashed furiously.

A brilliant realization struck Thorgunna. "The gods aren't afraid. They are angry! They are hunting!"

Thorgunna mounted her pony. Riding hard, urging her pony into the wind, she screamed into the tempest, hoping she was loud enough for all of Heaven to hear her, "He is here! He is here!"

The salmon ceased its struggle.

Thorgunna smiled. "So that's where you've been hiding, Loki. Thor's coming," she whispered.

The salmon, motionless, stared at her with its red fire-eyes.

"Thor's coming," she said a bit louder, in the direction of the salmon.

Thorgunna raised her head, shouting into the storm, "He is here!"

"I hope Thor guts you and dries your skin for shoes!" she cursed, finally allowing her agitated pony to gallop away … away from the capture of Loki by the gods. Loki would not escape punishment for his crimes, after all.

Standing alone in the wind and spray, drenched and shivering, Thorgunna felt a second powerful vision overtake her. This one was different. It was an embrace, not a horror.

She knew them. She knew them all and greeted them by name as the gods descended from the heavens to the wind-swept Isle of Tiree, ensnaring Loki in his own net, hauling him away to judgment. No longer shape-shifted into a salmon, but forced by the will of Odin to remain locked in his human form, the Trickster was bound with his own son's entrails to jagged rocks at the very ends of the earth. His neck, torso, arms, legs, and even his testicles were bound by the sinuous rope of his son's innards.

Thorgunna couldn't help but laugh at the helpless Loki, his mouth filled with his own tart, acrid, foul blood as he bit his lip to keep from screaming as the venom of a poisonous serpent suspended above his head dripped continually upon him, burning him with caustic acid.

There Loki remained bound. At least physically.

Even the last of the gods questioned the punishment. How can one truly control the mind of evil?

Freed of the visions, stunned, and in pain, Thorgunna wept. A great burden had been lifted from her already heavily laden shoulders. The shadow of any darkness within her soul had fled with the passing storm. "He is gone."

Chapter 24

Thorgunna was due. Overdue. False labor plagued her, keeping her from the fields, her weaving, and even walking along the beach or to the hill where she often watched the sea ... waiting.

Finally, the child of Leif demanded entrance befitting the son and grandson of Jarls. As with most babies, Thorgunna's chose to arrive at the most inopportune time.

Olaf of Norway had sent his priests to fetch his beer. They arrived on a Holy Day—the Friday before Easter Sunday—heading directly to the remains of St. Patrick's Chapel to pray.

Ignoring their arrival, offering no hospitality, Thorgunna was in a foul mood even Brigit could not quell.

"You cannot ignore us, madam! We have the authority of the king, himself! It is our duty to bring you to the Church and baptize your bastard child as well!" Father Tomasson called through Thorgunna's closed door.

Thorgunna cringed as a strong labor pain hit. "I refuse to submit to the will of the king, the Christ, or any man! And if you ever call my son a bastard again, I'll kill you!" she replied, fighting to speak through the hard pangs of labor.

"You damn yourself and your child," the priest replied.

"So be it. The Christ has not proved to me He is worthy of my adoration. When He does, I shall submit. Now, go away! Unless you wish to deliver my child, be gone!"

A long, great wash of pain overwhelmed Thorgunna. She squeezed Brigit's hand. "Brigit, get Thorok. I will give birth at the Ringing Stone. Please, hurry!"

Brigit nodded her head, unbolting the door to Thorgunna's house, nearly tripping over the waiting priest, her own pregnancy barely slowing her pace.

"You'd better leave, Father. The Jarl will not argue politics and religion with you as she pushes the child of Leifur Eiriksson from her body."

"The child is his?" the old priest asked, surprised.

"Of course the child is his!" Thorgunna screeched, overhearing the conversation. "Why? Do you know him?"

The priest peeked his head in the door, calling, "Yes, Lady. He is well-known, indeed. Leifur Eiriksson is the king's agent of God in Greenland."

"He is a Christian?" Thorgunna asked, already knowing the answer.

"Yes. Should not his child be baptized?"

A moment later water spilled from Thorgunna's body. "Not unless it is by his own hand! You shall not touch my child!"

Thorok burst into the house, pushing the priest aside.

"Your baby comes, Lady. We must be swift," Thorok said, scooping Thorgunna into his arms.

Brigit waited with a horse to carry Thorgunna across Tiree to the Ringing Stone. Thorok carefully placed Thorgunna atop the horse, leaping up behind her.

"The Stone, Thorok. I must give birth at the Stone," Thorgunna pleaded.

"We'll make it, Lady. Hold on to me. Hold on," Thorok encouraged, pushing the horse harder.

The midwife waited at *Clach a' Choire*.

Thorok, having witnessed the birth of several of his children, but uncertain he could deliver a baby himself, felt a great rush of relief overwhelm him as he lifted Thorgunna from the horse, placing her gently onto the birthing straw set out by old Aud.

"Leave us now, Thorok," Aud commanded.

"I shall stay. I stand here as the named uncle of the child," Thorok replied.

"You have that right. Take the Lady's hands and be prepared to hold her while she pushes the child from her."

Thorgunna screamed. "It's too quick! The child comes! It should not be this quick!"

The midwife lifted Thorgunna's dripping-wet shift, pulling the Jarl of Tiree to her knees, her legs spread. The baby's head had crowned.

"Thorgunna, I need to cut you. The baby is large and moving too fast. Lie back again. I'll bring you up to push the child from you after I've helped it along."

Thorgunna nodded her head, "He, not it. The child is male."

"Do as I say, when I command it. Do not push the child from you. No matter how much pain you are in, scream if you must, but do not push until I have made the cut, or you will tear wide open and bleed to death before I can deliver the child," Aud said.

Thorgunna panted, straining to keep her body from responding as it wished. Thorok held her, remaining calm and stoic, as always.

The midwife unwrapped a sharp, thin blade. Carefully, she made a cut along Thorgunna's perineum, making way for the child to exit.

Thorgunna, ready to continue, to complete the miraculous act of giving birth, felt nothing of the blade, so heavy was the pressure of the baby's large head against her flesh.

"It is done. Push, Thorgunna! Push!"

The baby came easily after that. One great push and Thorgunna delivered a red-haired, bright pink baby boy.

"Thorok, take the child and wrap him well," the midwife commanded, cutting and tying off the umbilicus. "Now to you. I'll sew you up like a virgin again."

Thorgunna, exhausted, covered in sweat, gazed at her baby. She laughed. "I have no lover. Sew it shut if you will!"

The midwife glanced at Thorok, cradling the babe, humming to the boy. "There will come a time when your child is fed and asleep and the arms of a man holding you will be welcomed."

"No. I shall not love again," Thorgunna replied.

"Ah, but your son you shall love." Aud reached up to take the baby from Thorok, placing the squalling child in Thorgunna's arms.

"Ring the Stone, Thorok. Ring the Stone and let my babe be baptized into the folds of Tiree." Thorgunna sighed, gazing into the bright blue eyes of her new son.

Thorok reached for the baby's hand. "Ah, he's a healthy one, Lady. Good color. The boy has large *hrethjar*. Just like his uncle."

"Oh, Thorok … do not speak so about my son's physical attributes. He will be a man's man, I promise, but for now, he is my baby boy."

"See if he's hungry," Aud suggested, skillfully stitching Thorgunna's incision.

Thorgunna pressed the child to a breast. The baby latched on quickly, calming as he nursed hungrily.

"What will you call him?" Thorok asked.

"I've thought of a good name. Thorgils. Thorgils Leifursson."

Thorok returned his attention to the Ringing Stone and struck it again, forcing the stone to sing its soft, yet powerful musical vibration, saying proudly, "All hail Thorgils, son of Leifur!"

"Thank you, Thorok," Thorgunna said, stroking her son's soft hair.

The midwife shook her head, paying close attention to her work. "You've lost too much blood."

"But I feel fine," Thorgunna replied.

"It's the rapture of birth, Lady. Soon enough, you'll want a sugar-teat for the boy and a soak in a hot tub. I'll see to the both of you. Shall I bury the sack or stew it?" she asked.

"Bury it. And plant something beautiful atop it," Thorgunna replied, not really listening to the midwife. "Will you consecrate the child to Odin or Christ?" Thorok asked.

"Neither. Thorgils can make up his own mind someday. I would prefer the gods leave my child alone. His life will be less complicated that way," Thorgunna replied.

"As you wish," Thorok said. He again took the child's small hand in his. "He is his father's son."

****

Thorgunna's infirmity kept the priests from her until well after their holy week, for which she was glad. "Let them make their prayers for my soul and the soul of my son—far away from me!" she said, as the last priest left Tiree.

Thorgunna, sore, but happy, her heart full of love for her child instead of longing for Leif, had never felt such contentment.

"He is a credit to you, Lady," Thorok said, peeking into the cradle where Thorgils lay.

Thorgunna beamed. "He is that."

"Thorgunna, may I make a request?" Thorok asked.

"Of course. Sit; we'll talk." Thorgunna sat, motioning for Thorok to take a place beside her.

"The boy, your son, needs a man to raise him up. Do me this honor, allow me to be his foster father. Leif called me uncle, but the boy will need more than that. While it is true I have many children, and more coming, I'll protect Thorgils as though he is my own son and you as if you are the widow of my brother. Your own father bade me protect you when you were born. To honor him, to honor you, I must therefore also protect your son," Thorok said, his voice steady, but heart pounding.

Thorgunna smiled. "I am honored to have you act as father to Thorgils. Perhaps you should move into my house. It would be easier than having you on the other side of the island. And, it is close to Brigit," Thorgunna replied.

"Lady?"

"Thorok, it is for my son's sake only. I do not ask you to share my bed. Only the raising of my son," Thorgunna cautioned.

"As you wish."

"Perhaps we should ask Brigit what she thinks, first," Thorgunna said, having second thoughts.

"She is not my wife, Lady," Thorok replied.

"No, she is not. But soon enough she shall birth your child, and you must not let her feel abandoned."

"I am a good father to all my children. Their mothers don't complain," Thorok defended.

"Why not marry one of them, Thorok?"

"Because my place is with you. There is no more sacred trust between Norsemen than to honor and protect the family of one's Jarl."

"You must promise me you will not neglect Brigit's child or any of your other children," Thorgunna demanded.

"I love my children," Thorok replied.

"Have you ever considered putting an end to the spread of your seed, Thorok? You have nearly a dozen children," Thorgunna laughed.

"My lovers do not allow me leave, Lady."

"Men are so arrogant."

"I fill a woman well. I make the passion in a woman sing," Thorok replied.

"Are you offering?" Thorgunna asked, catching Thorok's tone.

"No, Lady. I am not worthy of your bed."

Thorgunna studied the tanned, gentle slope of Thorok's face. "You are a good friend, Thorok."

"I shall always be here for you, Lady."

****

Leif enjoyed being home. His younger brothers and half-sister, Freydis, toasted him at every gathering. His doting mother fed him. His father forgave him—after the first ship from Norway arrived laden with mainland treasures of coal, candles, iron, and timber.

In Leif's absence, Greenland's population had grown. Colonists from Iceland had come over, and of course, those long Greenlandic winters were often filled with passion, the results of which were many new children each summer.

One newcomer, a man by the name of Bjarni Herjulfsson, intrigued Leif. Bjarni had sailed farther west than any other man. Accidentally, but still, it had been done.

"We sailed in fog—thick fog—from Iceland. We could only hope our ship sailed toward Greenland. When the fog lifted we did not see the great glacier in the distance, nor did we see any settlements. I knew we'd sailed past Greenland and were now in uncharted waters. Aye, we spotted land, but my heart was not in it to explore it. We turned the ship and came east, finding Greenland after three days at sea," Bjarni told.

"So, there's land west of here? About three days west?" Leif asked.

"Oh, aye. New land. Will you be the young buck to go conquer it?" Bjarni asked.

"Only if you sell me your ship," Leif laughed.

Bjarni laughed, "I may need it to return to Iceland if I cannot make a good home for myself here."

"Your ship's memory will serve as my chart, sir. Sell her to me. You shall have no reason to leave Greenland. This land is blessed by the Lord, and all those who work her land reap those blessings."

"Christian wisdom, young Eiriksson?" Bjarni teased.

"Perhaps this fire I feel in my belly when I think of the lands west of here is lit by God to serve His holy purpose. Sell me your boat, Bjarni," Leif replied.

Bjarni looked at Leif thoughtfully. Here is a man whose saga shall be sung by the skalds for centuries. How can I deny him his place in history? He held out his hand to Leif. "Done."

Chapter 25

Thorgils was a unique child. He failed to crawl, going to his feet and running wild, exploring everything within his reach before his first birthday. He began speaking in full sentences about the same time.

Thorgunna often took her son around the island on horseback. The boy loved the standing stone at Moss, which Thorgunna avoided. Yet every time they crossed western beaches, he insisted upon seeing it. Thorgunna had felt its haunting pull every time the wind blew from the west since erected by Sigfus and his sons. But she avoided it. Shunned it. It was a monument to sheer folly and ruination.

"It is a large stone, Mother," Thorgils commented.

"Aye, Thorgils, it is a large stone," Thorgunna replied.

"Who put the flowers around it?" Thorgils asked, pointing to several decaying lupines and thistles strewn about the stone's base.

Someone who doesn't know any better, Thorgunna thought, but replied, "I don't know, dear."

"Maybe it was Anna Kristjana. She loves flowers so," Thorgils said thoughtfully.

Brigit's daughter. Thorok's daughter. "Perhaps, Thorgils."

Thorgunna steered the horse away from the stone. She detested it, this solid, silent witness to the day she'd sold Tiree's soul to the Trickster to save Leif's life.

Holding fast to her son atop her chestnut mare, Thorgunna fell forcefully into the world of her second sight. She was pulled with such force that she could not catch a breath. Thorgunna panicked, trying to fight her way out of the fog of her otherworldly vision.

"Mama, where are we?" Thorgils asked.

Surprised to find her son had traveled with her into the realm controlled by the sight, she answered quickly, hushing the boy, "We're safe. We're safe, Thorgils."

"This is not Moss. I see the stone, but this is not Moss. I want to go home now, Mother."

Thorgunna pulled Thorgils tighter to her.

"A lovely boy, he is, Thorgunna."

Thorgunna's stomach lurched. Her heart began to pound furiously. "Loki."

"I had a lovely son, once. He's here with me now. It is his entrails which bind me. I must thank you for bringing us so close together, Thorgunna."

"Go away, Loki."

"Mother, I know this voice. It is the man who lives in the stone," Thorgils offered.

"It *is* I, boy. You are so bright for such a young lad," Loki replied in the haze of the sight.

"You have spoken to the stone?" Thorgunna asked.

"Oh, yes, Mother. The stone sings to me in my dreams. That's why I like coming here," Thorgils replied innocently.

"Such a delightful child, Thorgunna. I shall enjoy visiting with him in person very, very much. And very soon."

Loki laughed, a dark, sinister, sharp, and threatening laugh.

"I will never let you near him," Thorgunna hissed.

"There is no one left to stop me. Soon enough I shall be set free, Lady. Soon enough I shall return to Tiree. The time for me to profit from our broken contract is at hand," Loki said.

"I will stop you," Thorgunna said.

"I'll certainly enjoy your trying!" Loki replied.

Love's Second Sight

****

The vision ended. It had started to rain. Thorgils shivered in his mother's arms as she turned their pony toward Gott Hill.

Thorgils refused to sleep in his own bed that night.

Holding her little boy, stroking his shoulder-length red curls as he slept soundly in her arms, Thorgunna lay awake, ever-vigilant.

Thorgunna was not sure how to approach Thorgils regarding his conversations with *the man in the stone*. She rose from her bed to stoke her fire. To keep it bright and hot.

"I thought Loki was gone. Dead and gone. Why did they not slaughter him?" She paused. "They can't kill him. The blood of Odin runs in his veins. But if Odin is dead, what would it matter? Perhaps Odin lives."

Thorgunna searched her feelings. Does this give me comfort the All-Father may be alive and enthroned in Valhalla? No, it does not. No more comfort than ever it did.

"Mama?" Thorgils had awakened. She heard the thud of his feet hit the floor as he scampered from the bed.

"Yes, son. I'm by the fire," Thorgunna replied calmly.

"Mama," the little boy cooed, burying his face in Thorgunna's bosom as he climbed atop her lap. "I love you, Mama."

"I love you, too," Thorgunna paused. "Thorgils, can you tell me about the man in the stone?"

"He sings to me. When the night is very quiet," Thorgils replied.

"What does he sing?" Thorgunna asked, trying not to pressure her son.

"He sings songs like the Gothi from Coll sings. Only better."

"Ah, the man in the stone recites the words of the High One," Thorgunna said carefully.

"No. Not those songs. Other songs. The ones about the wolf swallowing the sun and the fires of Surt burning Tiree. Sometimes it frightens me. But at the same time, I feel excited. Is that all right, Mother?"

"Yes. That's all right. If the man in the stone sings to you again, will you let me know?" Thorgunna asked. *Damn you, Loki! Leave my son alone.*

"Yes, Mama," Thorgils replied.

"Do you want your breakfast now? The sun is just rising. Look, there—out the window."

"Yes! Can I eat with Anna Kristjana?"

"Of course, dear. Run along to Brigit's. I'll come shortly."

Thorgils pulled open the heavy door, straining to edge it open just enough so he could squeeze through.

"What's going on with the boy?" Thorok asked, emerging from his chamber.

"My son has the sight, Thorok," Thorgunna replied.

"That is a blessing," the big Norseman replied.

"Aye, it is. And it is a curse. Watch him closely now, Thorok."

"As I did you, of course. But he is his father's son, Thorgunna. The boy fears nothing and explores everything."

"More now than ever, I want to thank you for sharing our house, Thorok."

"It is my honor. I'm going to Brigit's. Coming?" Thorok asked.

"Aye. I'll be along."

****

Thorgils turned two. An adventurous toddler with bright red hair and a temper to match, he was the spitting image of Thorgunna's own father, Vagn.

For his birthday, Thorok had taken the little boy fishing, returning him home soaking wet, filthy, and asleep. "He's a fisherman, Thorgunna.

Look at this catch!" Thorok called, holding up a string of fish.

Thorgunna laughed, stripping her sleeping child of his wet clothes, and covering him snugly on his pallet. "Yes, and he caught them all himself, I suppose."

Thorok pulled a flagon from under his tunic. "I've brought a bottle of mead. Shall we celebrate the birth of your son?"

Thorgunna smiled. She had enjoyed Thorok's company for the two years he'd acted as foster father to her son. It was a comfortable relationship. Thorok lived in her home, yet continued his relationship with his children, including his daughter by Brigit, with ease.

They shared a bottle in honor of Thorgils' second year. Thorgunna became as drunk as she'd ever been, Thorok, not nearly as drunk as he had been himself a time or two before.

Thorok fell over, his head resting on Thorgunna's lap. She brushed wisps of hair away from his face with its creases and laugh lines.

"You're drunk, Thorok," she said.

"*Jae ja*," Thorok responded, a common Norse phrase used when no other words would do. "These peaceful times allow a man to get drunk and enjoy it far too often. We need Ivar back for a good fight."

"Oh, don't say that," Thorgunna replied. "The last thing I want is that. Olaf sends priests to collect his beer, now, and them I can handle well enough. I'm too tired to fight the Rus."

****

Thorgunna touched a large bruise on Thorok's left arm, "What is this?" she asked.

"A fly bit me today in the stable. Left quite a bruise, didn't it? It hurts," Thorok replied.

Thorgunna ran her fingers lightly over bruise. "This is terrible."

Thorok winced. "Did my touch harm you?" Thorgunna asked.

"No. My left arm is tingling. It does that sometimes. I'm getting old, that's all. Oh, no…"

"What is it?" Thorgunna cried as Thorok convulsed in pain, clutching his left arm.

Thorok sucked in one final breath, unable to exhale. Unable to move as the pain of his exploding heart ripped and tore throughout his limbs.

Thorgunna panicked, screaming, slapping Thorok across his bearded face, pounding on his bare chest with her fists.

Thorok was dead.

A fly buzzed around Thorgunna's head. She absentmindedly shooed it away. It returned. Again, she brushed it aside.

Spittle drooled from Thorok's mouth, and he had released his bowels and bladder at the moment of his death. There was no mistaking it. Thorok, her protector, lifelong friend, and foster father to her son, was dead.

The same bothersome fly lighted on Thorok's chest.

Thorgunna watched the fly. It watched her as well.

Thorgunna nodded her head. "I know who you are."

The fly buzzed around Thorok's corpse.

"Of course you do!" the fly replied, an eerie glow and unholy shadow of dark light radiating from the insect.

"Why kill Thorok?" Thorgunna asked.

"Because it hurts you. You condemned me, Thorgunna. You traitorous bitch!"

"Give me a moment to get my fly swatter, and I'll make you suffer more than the gods did for your crimes, Loki. I'll punish you myself," Thorgunna replied.

"Glib, as always, aren't you? Hear me now, woman. I mean to sever

Love's Second Sight

the head of Tiree and serve it up cold at Hel's table!"

"Liar," Thorgunna replied, her mind frantically working to unravel Loki's plot.

The fly buzzed aggressively about Thorgunna's head, then flew out of the main room, and into Thorgils' room.

"Thorgils!" she cried, running to her son.

The fly was on her child—no, the shadow of Loki was upon her child. Like a blanket it covered him, smothering him. "Living in fear and desperation is your lot now, Thorgunna. As you suffer, so shall Tiree!"

"No!" Thorgunna cried, lifting Thorgils away from his bed.

The pink-cheeked little boy awoke, his arms going about his mother's neck.

Loki, a pestilence in fly form, flew off.

****

Mourning fell upon Tiree as the news of Thorok's death spread. From Coll and Mull and even as far away as Islay, men and women came to witness the pyre of Tiree's protector. Thorok had eleven children by nine women. Six sons. Five daughters. They stood huddled together in the rain as Thorgunna lit his pyre.

Brigit knelt in the wet sand, crossing herself, praying. A few others of the Christian faith joined her. Some clutched Thor's Hammers. Some, like Thorgunna, stood silently as the flames consumed the linen-wrapped body of Thorok, praying to no god. Asking for no solace. No divine intervention.

The stillness broke as, one by one, the men of Tiree and Coll and Mull began the low-pitched cry of death, warning Valhalla a warrior approached. "Odin!" they cried in unison, invoking the name of the All-Father, beseeching Odin to open the gates of Heaven for Thorok.

It was an empty plea, for Thorgunna knew Odin could not hear the prayers of his scattered followers. Odin had passed on. Thor, too. Ragnarok's final battle had been fought and lost by the gods. Only Loki remained.

Thorgunna looked at her son. His eyes were red and swollen from tears and smoke. He looked tired.

Thorgunna looked at her people, the *Tirisdeach*. Drained, tired. Without heart. They were as gray as the rain-filled sky.

She closed her eyes, looking inward. Loki's poison had spread. A blight was upon Tiree. She could see his spider-like fingers gripping the soil, devouring the heart of the isle. Devouring its soul.

Thorgunna saw the roots of Tiree. They were unhealthy. Weak. Infested. And within the twisted, struggling courses she saw herself.

"When a stalk of corn is dying, what does one do? Cut off the bad shoot to save the strong. I am the weak stalk. I need to leave. It's time for me to leave."

Chapter 26

Though sometimes overwhelmed with grief, Leif gave himself no time to think about Thorgunna and his child, his son, for thoughts of them made him feel empty, hollow, and lifeless with grief. It was too painful a memory.

The church built on Greenland and a good, solid ship now his, it was time for him to move on. To sail westward.

Where once Leif busied himself with affairs of the Christ, he now made ready a sailing to those uncharted lands sighted by Bjarni.

"For God, king, and Greenland I shall claim new lands," Leif boasted to his father as he sounded his ship, checking each strake, each iron rivet.

"And I'd be going with you if I hadn't broken my damn leg. It healed poorly, and I am too lame to *fara iviking*!" Eirik moaned.

"No matter, Father. I'll wear your seal—the great seal of the Jarl of Tiree..." Leif paused. "I mean the seal of the Jarl of Greenland when I go ashore. That way, you'll be with me."

"Miss her, don't you?" Eirik asked.

"Who?" Leif replied, embarrassed.

"The woman you met on Tiree. The Witch. You could turn your ship south and sail to her, you know," Eirik said. "It's no crime to love a woman, son."

"My destiny does not lie south, Eirik. Thorgunna's does not lie north. She is bound to Tiree just as I am bound to my faith and mission to claim new lands for God and king," Leif replied.

"As you wish, Leifur. Still, I see your loneliness. Even when a woman is in your arms at night I wager you think only of *her*."

"I have taken no women since last I held Thorgunna."

Eirik laughed in disbelief, "None?"

"None."

"Leif, that's not right. That's just not right," Eirik replied. "Even with a lame leg I've managed to bed a wench or two!"

"Good for you, Father. I have not had the time or inclination to woo a woman into my bed. I certainly won't now!"

Eirik limped off, shaking his head. "The boy has gone celibate!" he cried.

No. Not celibate. Just wiser, Leif thought, tying off a loose rope.

More passion did Leif feel for this sailing than he felt for his family, his home, or even his God. Only unbidden thoughts of Thorgunna put a damper on his burning desire to explore the new lands west of Greenland. But adventure called—and it was a stronger force than even that of the Witch of Tiree.

Alone, as he had been every night since returning from Norway, Leif lay awake in his bed. He'd left the door open purposely. "I need to see the stars. She may be looking at the same sky this night. It is as close as we shall be for some time. Please, Lord, let Thorgunna be looking at the stars this night and let her know I love her."

At dawn, Leif and a crew of thirty-five stout Greenlandic settlers sailed west.

"We sail into magic, young Eiriksson. I feel it in the pit of my stomach," Tyrkir, a robust Germanic settler to Greenland, said.

"Aye, friend. There's more to this sailing than just the founding of new land in the name of Olaf and Eirik. The All-Mighty Himself steers this vessel," Leif responded.

"We shall make a fine colony and come back for our women, yes?" Tyrkir laughed.

Leif sighed. "Yes. We shall, indeed."

Leif mulled over the length of time it would take to develop a new colony, take care of his father's estate as Eirik's health grew poorer, and how to sail to Tiree to fetch Thorgunna and their child to settle them in the new colony.

"My Thorgunna. My raven-haired siren. I wonder how she is. I wonder how my son fares. I must return to them, someday. I'll bring them to a new home where we shall never be separated ... again." Horror suddenly struck Leif. "What if she won't leave Tiree? Oh, dear Lord, she can't leave Tiree. She is bound to that isle as if her own flesh was the soil and sand."

His heart sank. Suddenly, the longing for Thorgunna overpowered the excitement of being on *iviking*.

Leif's thoughts turned to the moment he first made love to Thorgunna. He felt himself harden, but unashamedly did not try to conceal the bulge in his breeches as he looked out to sea, fantasizing, recalling, replaying over and over in his mind the moment he entered her body, burning past the barrier between girl and woman, plunging into her with a passion he'd never felt before. He recalled the way she responded under him—hesitantly at first. *But as I moved within her she opened up like a summer blossom and met my thrusts willingly—joyfully.*

In his mind he replayed how he had kissed her nipples in the moments after her passion had welled. Her large, dark pink nipples, responding to her own orgasm and the delicate flicks of his tongue. He recalled his own seething climax. How hard it had been to pull away. How good it felt to be in her, atop her. With her.

Leif chastised himself for such lurid thoughts at a time he needed to remain focused on the mission at hand.

****

Four days of eerie fog and little wind set Leif's men to the oars. They listened for sounds of land—waves crashing, birds singing. Leif dropped his lead sinker often, testing the depth of the sea. The water was deep and calm. The fog was thick, yet oddly comforting at times.

"We sail within the breath of God," Leif commented.

"Aye. But I wish the Lord would hold His breath for just a moment. Not knowing what's on the horizon unnerves me," Tyrkir responded.

"Do not let fear envelop you like this fog, old friend. I feel changes in the air and in the movement of my ship upon the sea. Land is close. Land like we've never seen before. I can smell it," Leif said.

"Holy Mother of God!" Tyrkir exclaimed.

Leif turned toward the direction an excited Tyrkir pointed. The fog had lifted ahead of them. Through the lifting curtain of chill fog there appeared land.

"Land," Leif said softly. "Praise God. Land."

"A land of stone," Tyrkir commented, surveying the rocky shoreline.

"Aye. But look there, in the distance, I see what could be green hills, or trees. I say we sail toward that patch of green, Tyrkir," Leif said.

"You're the captain, laddie," Tyrkir responded. Then to the oarsmen, "Turn the ship south, men! The captain would have us set our sights on that patch of green at the horizon!"

As a bright mid-autumn sun shone down upon the vessel, Leif could not revel in the warmth of its glow. His men were jubilant, giddy with excitement. Although he felt that familiar knot of anticipation growing in his belly, a fog of loneliness engulfed his broken heart.

A twinge of guilt stabbed Leif. If only she were here, beside me—to share this adventure. I was a fool not to have fetched her after leaving Norway. I should have never left her. She should be here. Had I not journeyed to Norway, would I know the love of the Christ? Or would

I have continued to live my life without His grace? God's will took me away from Thorgunna, and by His love for me, He shall reunite us. I must concentrate on the mission at hand.

A hoarse, throaty voice interrupted Leif's thoughts. "Rationalize it all you want, Greenlander. God has deserted you, and I rule Tiree."

Leif turned to his men. "Tyrkir? What was that you said to me?" *I'm hearing things, or I've garnered the attention of an unwelcome shipmate.*

"I said nothing, Leifur," Tyrkir replied.

At the ends of the earth, from atop jagged rocks, bound by the now hardened entrails of his own son, Loki laughed.

Leif shook off the feeling of dread welling up from the deepest recesses of his being. He knew the feeling, oh, yes. All too well. *I am running afoul of Loki. Dearest Lord in Heaven, protect me from this minion of Hell.* Then directing his thoughts outward, hoping the Trickster would hear him, Leif added, *I'll not be swayed from my mission, Loki. Not your lies of harm you wreak upon Thorgunna, nor anything else will sway me from the holy path I tread in the name of the one true God.*

****

Leif and his shipmates passed by, but did not land at the patch of green, a dense forest. It had no suitable inlet to come ashore. Disappointed, they continued south along the coast of this new land.

They finally pulled their skiff ashore at a rocky beach banked by rolling hills and a vibrantly colored meadow. Leif spent the next three months exploring his newfound land of wine, so called because of the grape vines growing in abundance just beyond the first hillock from the shore.

"I have fulfilled my mission, Thorgunna," Leif said softly into the night sky on the eve of his departure. "A colony we've made here, at Vinland. A colony of good men ready to build homes and settle down in the name of Norway and under the banner of the Jarl of Bratahild. I sail now to bring their women to this new land. Will you join me, here, so far away from Tiree?" The night sky made no reply. "I'm coming for you, Thorgunna," he called.

Again, there was no reply. But he was certain she had heard him and was making ready their son for the trip to Vinland.

Leif sailed at dawn, leaving six of his crew behind to prepare houses of stone and sod and hunt game to fill the larders for the coming winter months.

It was on this sailing, this return trip to Bratahild that Leif happened upon survivors of a shipwreck off Greenland's southern tip. Leif rescued the lost colonists.

Eirik, still lame from his broken leg, was ecstatic. "I don't know what makes me happier! You claiming a new land or your rescue of the missing colonists!"

"I'm glad I've done something for you to be proud of. I thought you'd never forgive me for bringing the priest," Leif chortled, clasping wrists with his father.

A stout, balding man with a pox-marked face approached Eirik, "I am Thorir, come to settle. This is my wife, Gudrid. My crew, or what's left of them, will settle here as well."

Eirik nodded. "What's your trade, sir?"

"I was a merchant in Norway, Jarl Eirik. Here, I intend to claim a tract of land and farm it as a man will," Thorir replied.

"Aye. Welcome to Greenland," Eirik said. "You and your wife can make your home with me. I can house your crew with my servants for the time being."

Gudrid smiled seductively at Eirik from beyond her husband's shoulders, pursing her lips in a semblance of a kiss.

Eirik raised a questioning eyebrow at the woman. What a smoldering bitch she is. I wonder if Leif has put her to the planks while her husband slept. No. Leif is still bewitched by his Hebridean mistress.

Leif escorted Thorir and Gudrid to Eirik's house. Unique in design, the main house had two smaller attached homes on either side. Leif lived in one of the ante-houses; Thorir and Gudrid were put in the other.

"You have a fine house," Gudrid said, looking about her new temporary home.

"My father has worked hard to make Greenland what it is. He imports what he needs, but we make do with Greenland's own resources for the most part. We waste nothing here. Your roof beams come from a shipwreck. The straw in the mattress will comfort your sleep for a time, then will go to the livestock. My mother oversees the rotation of goods from place to place," Leif said proudly.

"We are grateful," Thorir said.

"I'll leave you now. Come out and join us after supper. Your experience will enliven the otherwise dull stories of my father and his men," Leif offered.

"I shall tell them of Leif the Lucky, our savior," Gudrid smiled. Her eyes picked up the dancing flames in the fire, bringing an eerie glow to her face.

"Thank you," Leif replied, blushing.

Thorir nodded, giving Leif an odd look. Leif took that as a sign the old man wanted him to leave. Such a sour old Norseman to have such a vivacious young wife.

Gudrid and Thorir joined in the drunken storytelling after dinner. Gudrid wore a borrowed shift. She had tied it at the waist, gathering the extra fabric in a cascade at her hip. The V-slit from neck to bosom was unclasped, exposing her ample bosom whenever she moved. Eirik could not help but watch her.

Such breasts! he marveled, feeling a familiar tightening in his groin.

Eirik, not too drunk this evening, could tell Gudrid watched him as well. Her smoking eyes told a long, naughty story to him. A story of seduction, passion, and clandestine kisses beyond her husband's knowledge. Gudrid beckoned Eirik to sexual union with those hypnotic eyes, while at the same time stroking her husband's leg softly, running her hand under his tunic every now and again, then looking back at Eirik, licking her lips.

What a whore she is, Eirik thought, watching Gudrid's hand stroke her husband's leg, while her eyes smoldered and beckoned to Eirik. *I must have her. I must have her tonight.*

Thorir shook his head. "Your ale is stronger than I'm accustomed to, Eirik! I like it! But, I'm going to bed. Wife, attend me," Thorir said possessively.

Gudrid looked at her husband with her fiery eyes, her lips brushing against his, "I would stay a bit longer, husband. If it is all right with you, of course."

Thorir pressed Gudrid to him briefly, "I can refuse you nothing. You know this."

Gudrid smiled. "I'll be along shortly."

Eirik was not the only Greenlander who had noticed Gudrid's beckoning-to-the-hay looks at Eirik. As soon as Thorir was inside and the shutters closed, Leif, Bjarni, and Tyrkir left, leaving only Gudrid and Eirik by the fire.

"Now we're alone, is there something you want to say to me, woman?" Eirik asked.

"Aye, there is," Gudrid responded, taking a deep breath, expanding her chest, making her breasts seem even fuller.

"Then speak before I am too tired to listen," Eirik suggested, moving one stone closer to Gudrid.

"May I speak plainly?"

"By all means." Eirik moved to another stone, leaning in to hear Gudrid better.

"My husband is an old man and in poor health. The time at sea, waiting to live or waiting to die, did him no good, either. I'd divorce him except I am not only his wife, but his bondwoman. He paid my debts in Iceland, and until I have repaid him, I cannot legally divorce him."

Eirik nodded. "How do you intend to repay him?"

Gudrid smiled, sliding her fingers along the V opening of her tunic, pulling it open to her navel.

"I thought as much," Eirik said, feasting his eyes on the round edges of Gudrid's breasts.

"I've two years left under him before we can call the debt paid. He is a poor lover, Eirik. Two years more under him and I shall go mad. That is, two more years of *just* him shall be my undoing."

"You don't mince your words, do you?"

"Why should I? You are the perfect solution to my problem."

"What does that mean?"

"I see no reason why I should not take a lover from amongst the men of Greenland to at least have something to look forward to in this *gods*forsaken place."

"Which man?" Eirik asked, knowingly.

"I want a man who has proven his virility. A man with many happy women milling about him. I want a man with courage enough to make love to me here, within earshot of my sleeping husband. I like a life fraught with danger. Do you know such a man, Eirik?" She pulled open one side of her shift to expose a breast.

"Aye," Eirik responded, reaching for that exposed breast, holding it in his large hand, putting his red beard to its delicate pink nipple.

Gudrid moaned, pushing Eirik's head deeper into her shift.

He pulled the dress up to her waist, then unlaced his own breeches while Gudrid let herself fall backwards onto the ash-covered soil.

With no further delay by way of foreplay, Eirik mounted Gudrid, pushing into her hard and fast. Gudrid welcomed the old Viking, moaning and panting beneath him, her hips thrusting to meet his, until she sang with the surge of sweet release.

Eirik, completely spent, pulled away, wanting to see the look of satisfaction on the face of the woman beneath him. If Gudrid was not flushed, not swooning from the orgasm he'd brought her to … then he had not done his job. He brushed his coarse red beard over her lips, kissing her. She responded weakly to his embrace.

He kissed her again, this time noticing small indentations around her lips. Little scars.

"What happened about your lips?" he asked, rolling off Thorir's wife, tucking his still-steaming beast away.

"A childhood accident. But don't worry, Eirik, my lips can do your bidding well enough," Gudrid replied, standing, straightening her borrowed dress, now covered with dirt, ash, and sweat. "I haven't felt truly filled by a man in some time. You're quite the Viking invader, Eirik." Gudrid paused. "When shall you conquer me again?"

"There are more things to discuss than just where and when we shall rut, woman. What if your belly grows? What then?"

"Thorir and I have relations often enough. He'll think it is his child."

"What if I don't want to share you?"

"I am using you to make my sentence bearable, Eirik. Nothing more. I will have you and then straddle Thorir wet with your seed if I so choose. In two years when my debt has been paid, we will be free to discuss other arrangements. Now, when will I see you again?"

"You are a vixen whore," Eirik commented.

"If cursing me arouses you, then please continue. Name the place and time."

Eirik laced his breeches, nervously looking about. "Tomorrow."

"Fine. I'll come to you. Where shall you be?"

"In the mornings I'm at my son's ship. My leg prevents me from other work right now. Thorvald, my second son, sails it to Vinland, to Leifsstad, the colony Leif created in a fortnight."

"No good. Why would I have business aboard Leifur's ship? What about the church your estranged wife built? Does your priest work in the fields by day?"

"Aye. The church will be empty. I've never set foot inside it."

"All the better. We can consecrate the place to the god of our choice and cast out that imposter Christ."

Eirik nodded. She was a forceful woman. A tryst in his wife's church? A marvelous idea!

Gudrid smiled a devil's smile, then went in to her sleeping husband.

Eirik limped to his Thjodhild's house, hoping she'd let him sleep there for the night. He was in pain and did not want to be alone. Although legally divorced, Thjodhild did not kick Eirik from her pallet, but neither did she respond to his embrace. "Go to sleep, Eirik. Only for your leg's sake do I allow you in my bed," she said, rolling over and away from him.

He sighed. He had truly loved his wife at one time. Now she loved the Christ and their children, and he found love wherever he could. Tonight it had been with Gudrid. Gudrid Scar Lip. Gudrid Ember Eyes. Gudrid, wife of Thorir and mistress of Eirik. He felt his loins twitch. Perhaps Thjodhild would consent to a quick coupling for old time's sake.

****

The next day Eirik entered Thjodhild's church, sheepishly, like a child afraid of the dark.

The shutters were closed, making the one-room building of sod and stone dim and uninviting. The far wall held a crude wooden crucifix, the painted face of Christ staring out into the darkness. Below that was an altar of sorts, covered with a linen shawl. Upon the altar rested a silver cup, box, and plate. The room had two benches of squared sod blocks upon which a plank was placed.

The hard-packed earthen floor was clean-swept, and the structure looked solid enough. Eirik could see no droppings of mice or water damage on the walls or roof. "Solid. Hmmm. That's too bad."

As Gudrid entered, latching the door from the inside, an aura of anticipation and dread enveloped Eirik. He felt cold.

Without a word, again only her smoldering gray eyes speaking, Gudrid cast off her wrap and pulled her tunic over her head. She passed Eirik, going directly to the altar, standing naked before it.

"I've never met a woman who wasted less time than you," Eirik said, himself nearly undressed. He was battle-scarred and furry, his red hair covering his back, shoulders, and chest.

Gudrid and Eirik met, crashing into each other in their passion. Eirik wanted time to explore this woman's body, but again, she urged him into immediate union.

"Not yet my beauty. I want to savor and explore you. A woman such as you shouldn't rush to complete the act. You've too much to offer a man's senses," Eirik said, refusing Gudrid's pleas.

"In the name of what god will you take me, Eirik?" Gudrid asked, holding the old man's head to her breasts.

"What god?" Eirik murmured, slathering Gudrid's breasts with kisses.

"Here, before the altar of the pretended god, name your allegiance."

Eirik paused, "Is this pleasurable for you? You talk too much."

Gudrid rolled atop Eirik, hovering her ready womanhood above his own throbbing member. Slowly she slid herself onto Eirik, driving him deep into her body, grinding her hips atop him. She lowered her mouth to his ear as they coupled furiously, breathlessly asking, "Which god does Eirik worship?"

Barely able to speak, Eirik responded, "Thor."

"Does Thor come to your aid when called upon?" Gudrid cooed.

"Never," Eirik responded, trying to hold his release.

"You should call upon another god for protection," Gudrid said.

"Woman! How can you talk right now! I'm about to explode!" Eirik cursed.

"You may not release until you agree to let me choose your god," Gudrid said.

"Yes, yes, anything you say!" Eirik rolled over, pushing Gudrid to the floor under him, putting his body to her with great force until they erupted with simultaneous orgasm.

"Now tell me, wench, what god am I to call upon?"

"You want to fight Christ's hold upon Greenland?"

Eirik nodded, "Greatly."

"Then you must call upon the Trickster to guide your steps and actions."

"Loki? He's not powerful enough."

"Oh, yes. He is. He is, indeed."

"What must I do?" Eirik questioned, playing along with Gudrid's game.

"Sacrifice to him. Call upon him. Make an offering of flesh to him. And he will be ours to command."

"How would he help drive out the Christ?"

"He is the Trickster. The most clever of the gods. He would find a way. Will you follow Loki?" she asked.

"Aye," Eirik responded, still playing her game, turning his attention to Gudrid's flat belly and golden mound. "You make me burn with desire."

"I am fire, Eirik. I am fire to burn a trail of desire across a man's heart," Gudrid responded, opening her legs to again accept Eirik's hard, probing member.

"You worship Loki?" Eirik asked. "Are you a consort of the Trickster?"

Gudrid's hips moving in time to Eirik's thrusts, she thrust her tongue in his ear, then pulled away, whispering, "No, I am not his consort. I am Loki."

Unable to stop his body, Eirik climaxed as he beheld the face of Loki before him. He pulled away, sickened. "I'll kill you!" he threatened.

"You cannot kill what you cannot catch!" Gudrid's body with Loki's face vanished. A single horse fly buzzed about the church, lighting always just out of Eirik's reach.

Eirik trampled about the church, swatting at the fly, naked and slow for his crippled leg. Heaving, unable to catch his breath, his leg buckling under him, the fly landed on Eirik's back and bit him.

Several hours later the priest entered the church. There he found the place in a shambles, and a dead, nude Eirik the Red slumped over a sod bale, his body bloated and swollen with death.

Shortly thereafter, a corpse washed ashore west of Bratahild. It was that of Thorir's wife, Gudrid. It went unnoticed. Unshriven. Unburied. Forgotten.

Leif held his head sorrowfully, prayerfully, "My dreams, my plans, my life. My life is now over. By the death of Eirik, Lord, I am now bound to Greenland as the eldest son of the Jarl. I pray you watch over my colony on Vinland that she may thrive in my absence."

My brothers and half-sister will see to Vinland, he told himself, his heart heavy as his own ship pulled away from Bratahild, without him. It is my duty to take my father's place as Jarl of Greenland. I must be content with this lot. I have brought Christ to my home and the fortune of Norway with Him.

Thjodhild patted Leif on the back. "You're a good son, Leif. You're the chieftain now. Time you took a wife and raised grandsons of Eirik to follow you."

Leif shook his head. "I want no wife, Mother."

"She's so far away, and still she bewitches you. Leif, listen to me. Set up your house here on Greenland. Take you a young wife. Have you a son. Then, sail to that little island in the Hebrides and bring that woman here. Make her your mistress."

"A wife in the eyes of God is a sacred thing, Mother. How could I take her as my mistress when she is my one true love?"

"I pray you will not sail from here until a child of your body is born, Leif. Eirik worked too hard to leave Greenland to a council of men not his kin."

"Yes, Mother," Leif replied.

Thjodhild smiled. "You're a good son."

And a lonely one, Leif thought sadly.

Chapter 27

"I am leaving, Brigit. I must. We must," Thorgunna said hotly, wrapping hard yellow cheese and bread in a cloth.

"You cannot leave Tiree," Brigit sobbed. "You cannot leave me."

Thorgunna sighed, "Do not be overwrought, Brigit. Tiree is my home. When the tide of my life turns, I shall return."

"Are you certain you will be well-received at the home of Finn MacLean?"

"Aye. I am his rightful widow. They'll take us in and give us shelter and likely try to kill me before too long just to make sure I cannot squander his wealth—but at least it will be away from Tiree. I mustn't stay here any longer," Thorgunna replied, thinking, *I have no intention of sailing to Oban, Brigit. But even you must not know my true whereabouts.*

"We can fight him, you know," Brigit suggested.

"Fight whom? I'm tired. I don't want to fight any longer. That's why I'm leaving Tiree," Thorgunna said flatly.

"Who else? Loki," Brigit sighed. "He is why you are leaving, yes?"

"He torments my son, Brigit. And he killed Thorok. One by one, the people I love will be taken from me—have been taken from me. If Loki cannot find me, he cannot harm me. He'll lose interest in Tiree because there will be no one left who recognizes him." *That's why I am telling no one, not even you, where I am truly going.*

"You do not have to leave, Thorgunna. You must simply call upon the strength of the Lord to protect you," Brigit whispered through her tears.

"Should I put my faith in your God, Brigit, I would become a party to Norway's reign of terror. If I call upon the old ones, I might as well sing into a grave. They are as dead to me as Thorok."

"I loved him, too," Brigit replied weakly.

"He would have married you," Thorgunna offered.

"Aye, he would have. But not much of a husband would he have been. I did not want to be a second wife," Brigit said.

"Thorok died unmarried," Thorgunna replied.

"No. He was indeed wed to a most demanding woman. You know her well, Thorgunna. She calls upon you often enough," Brigit said.

"Of whom do you speak?" Thorgunna asked, puzzled.

"Why, Tiree. Thorok loved Tiree."

"As do I. And now she will be without us both." Thorgunna sighed, returning to packing her son's possessions for the voyage.

Standing upon the beach of Gott as they waited for the skiff to row ashore, Thorgunna forcefully tore Thorgils from the arms of his playmate, Anna Kristjana. "I don't want to leave her, Mama! I don't want to go to Scotland. I want to stay here!"

Thorgunna, herself heavy with grief, felt her temper rising. Without forethought, she slapped Thorgils. "Do as I say and get in the skiff!" she commanded.

Stunned, Thorgils did as ordered, sobbing to himself, holding his stinging cheek.

"Thorgunna," Brigit sighed. "You have never before struck your son."

"This is hard enough without him making such a fuss. I have been poisoned by the blight upon Tiree, Brigit. I am the blight. I must be away lest I wither and die and take Tiree with me."

"I love you, Thorgunna," Brigit said, embracing her mistress.

"And I you," Thorgunna replied, pressing her lips to Brigit's in a loving kiss.

"Good-bye," Brigit whispered. "Go with God."

Thorgunna smiled, "I hope to escape the notice of any god by leaving. But thank you for the blessing. I know you mean it sincerely."

"Aye," Brigit said, picking up her weeping daughter and turning her back to the skiff as it rowed Thorgunna and the son of Leif Eiriksson to a waiting longship.

"I don't want to go to Scotland," Thorgils continued.

"Neither do I, Thorgils. Neither do I," Thorgunna responded with a bit more patience. "I'm sorry I struck you, baby."

Thorgils looked up at his mother, his bright blue eyes—the eyes of his father—shining with love. "That's okay, Mama. And don't call me baby. I'm nearly a man now."

Thorgunna laughed, holding her son. "Aye, that you are."

"Lady Thorgunna! Welcome aboard!" a weatherworn old man called from the boat as the skiff slid in next to it.

"Captain Fridriksson. Hello," Thorgunna replied.

"Are you that man taking us to Scotland?" Thorgils asked.

"Scotland?" the captain asked, helping Thorgunna aboard.

"Yes, we are sailing to *Scotland*, aren't we, Captain?" Thorgunna emphasized her words by making firm eye contact with old Fridriksson.

"Oh. Yes. Scotland it is, son," the Captain responded, picking the little boy up. "Do you think you'll like Scotland? You know, we're going to sail for nearly a week and I bet we'll see whales! You'll know we're near Scotland when you see a shining white glacier in the distance, rising above the waters like the jewel in a crown."

"Whales!" Thorgils returned, ignoring everything else.

"Yes, whales! Now go ye into the shelter and take a nap. I'll need a man on night watch, and you'll do just fine for the job," Fridriksson encouraged.

"Yes, sir!" Thorgils obeyed.

Thorgunna, never having been long aboard a longship, was unable to sleep. Thorgils grew accustomed to the rocking motion and sounds of the oars being pulled as if he had been born at sea. He loved everything about the voyage. From the way the ocean peaked and foamed as an oar chopped through it, or how the sail billowed out like a heavy white cloud when the wind was strong enough to harness, he obviously loved it all. The son of a sailor, he was.

"He's a good boy, Lady. And smart. I taught him how to read the waves as a map, and I believe, even at his tender age, he understood the lesson," Fridriksson said.

"He is a good boy. Thank you for making his voyage so enjoyable. I hope he shall fare as well in our new home," Thorgunna replied.

"*Scotland*, Lady, is not the farthest point away from civilization, but it is so far that you are likely to be quite shocked by the frugal lifestyles of the place," the captain said softly. "For you, I would turn this vessel and sail her to the Rhineland or France. I fear you will grow bored and your son dull, *in Scotland*."

"Thank you for your concern. Let me ask you this, however. Is there work to be done at my destination? Hard work. And families with children Thorgils' age?"

"Aye. All work is hard in this place. And there are children in abundance because there's no other entertainment save making them during the nine months of winter!" Captain Fridriksson laughed at his own joke. "I don't understand why a Lady such as yourself would want to settle in such a godforsaken place."

"I pay you for the voyage, sir. Your understanding of my purpose for said voyage is inconsequential," Thorgunna responded. *Godforsaken is exactly what I need.*

"What would change your mind? Say a handsome sea captain made you an offer of marriage? What would you do then?" Fridriksson asked.

"Row faster," Thorgunna replied.

Fridriksson laughed. "You'll have no problem finding yourself a husband in Iceland—I mean, Scotland—with that sense of humor."

Thorgunna shot the captain a look so sharp he felt it cut him like a razor. "I asked you to never intone our destination, sir. I paid handsomely for your silence, did I not?"

"Yes, Lady. Forgive me. I'm sure the boy didn't hear," Fridriksson apologized.

Thorgunna feigned a smile in forgiveness.

The ship bearing Thorgunna and her son from the Hebrides pulled into the harbor at Olafsvik, Snaefulls Peninsula, Iceland, in early summer.

Thorgunna had specifically chosen Olafsvik for its close proximity to kin of Eirik the Red. Thorgils would be welcomed, and they would live amongst family in Leif's line.

Thorgunna surveyed the turf farmhouses and weary-looking inhabitants of Olafsvik. "Greenland is too obvious a choice. Loki will look for me wherever Leif is. This is where I belong. Where Leif once played as a child," she said softly.

As Thorgunna waded to shore, her son in her arms, her passion for Leif, anything of Leif's, grew stronger. Even a distant cousin was more of an icon to her than all the saints of the Holy Church.

A single tear rolled down her cheek. *Oh, how I miss him. How proud he would be of his son. Where is he now?*

"Welcome to Iceland. I am Kjartan of Froda Farm. Have you kin here?" a round-faced smiling man said to Thorgunna, helping her to shore.

"Aye. My son is grandson of Eirik Rautha by his son, Leifur. There remains kin in this place, no?" Thorgunna asked.

"No, Lady. Eirik has some family remaining inland, but no longer are any here at Olafsvik. When he moved his family from Ox Island, many of his kin left the peninsula."

"Then I shall have to travel to Greenland, though I don't relish another journey at this time. I can work for room and board. Is there a house that can keep us?" Thorgunna asked.

Thurid, Kjartan's wife, hanging about her husband's arm like a leech, could see Thorgunna was a woman of high status. "With us, dearie. Stay with us. You and your little boy. Kjartan and I have a large farm by the river. We have the only house of stone in all Olafsvik. Three rooms have we, plus an outbuilding for servants. It sits empty right now, and it is yours if you wish."

"Thank you, Lady," Thorgunna replied.

The farm at Froda River was very nice by Iceland's poor standards. Built into the earth with a foundation of basalt, it was roomy and clean. Thick sod walls plastered with mud kept out the chill, and a fine stone hearth, whose fire never died, kept the place dry and warm.

Thurid gave Thorgunna the outbuilding as her own. The hearth area could be easily separated from the bedbox and privy with a drape, making two rooms. Thorgunna immediately unpacked the tapestry that had separated her room from the main house on Tiree, hanging it as she had before, as a barrier to the outside world.

"Oh, this is fine work. Yours?" Thurid asked, running her hands over the weaving.

"Yes," Thorgunna replied, continuing to unpack.

"Linens!" Thurid cried, handling Thorgunna's bed sheets enviously. "There's nothing this fine in all of Iceland. I'll take these linens and those bed curtains for payment. That's a fair trade," Thurid said sharply.

Thorgunna laughed. "I shall accept your offer of the house, but I will work for my board. Would you have my son and I sleep on bare straw?"

Thurid shot a glance at Thorgunna that could have frozen a raging fire. "As you wish, Lady."

Chapter 28

Life at Olafsvik was hard. As hard as the worst of times on Tiree. The weather was foul, the food plain, and even though summer approached with its never-ending hours of daylight, Thorgunna felt darkness crowding her into a corner. Nightmares plagued her. Her second sight had abandoned her.

She watched her son play with the children of Thurid and Kjartan. Gentle Kjartan. A man akin to her own Thorok. *I am so out of place here. Yet, Thorgils thrives. His roots go to Iceland. Mine never will.*

Thurid moved closer to Thorgunna as they raked hay in the field. "I'll buy the linens from you, Lady. With silver," she offered.

Thorgunna straightened her back, stretching. "I have nightmares every night sleeping upon the linens. How restless would my sleep be without them? No, Thurid. My linens are not for sale."

Thurid scowled. "You've lived with us for nearly six months now, Thorgunna. True, you work harder than most in the fields and take your turn at the hearth, but I tell you, I need those linens and will have them as compensation."

"I'm too tired for this, Thurid. Go rake in the north field. Leave me alone," Thorgunna responded.

A clap of thunder silenced the bickering women. The sky clouded over a menacing gray as it prepared to rain down upon the hay.

"Damn!" Thurid cried. "We must cover the stacks!"

The women ran to the stack yard, hoping to beat the rain. Wet hay would rot quickly and be of no use in the winter.

The rain clouds burst open with a fury, drenching the field hands.

Only Thorgunna remained outside, desperately trying to pull the sheepskins over the hay mounds. It was then she noticed the pure drops of rain had changed. Not into hail or snow or mist or any other godly form of rain. It was blood which fell from the sky.

A heavy, pelting rain of blood poured from the heavens, drenching Thorgunna, and only Thorgunna. Soiled with the red, viscous liquid, Thorgunna collapsed.

Kjartan ran to her aid, carrying her inside his house.

"Is Mother unwell?" Thorgils asked, concerned. "Why is she red? Why did red rain fall?"

Thurid calmed the boy. "Mother got too wet in the rain, dear. Sometimes the rain is red in Olafsvik, that's all. Go sit by the fire now."

But Thorgunna was quite unwell, and Thorgils knew it. He looked over his shoulder at the limp body of his mother as Thurid and Kjartan washed and tended to her, speaking in whispers, holding her hands, patting her face.

"Mother has never taught me how to pray. What am I to do? Brigit often prayed to the God of Norway. But I don't know how to pray to Him." Thorgils sat silently by the fire, his young mind racing. "I know! I'll ask the man in the stone to help mother get well."

Mimicking Brigit, Thorgils attempted to cross himself. He then bowed his head, praying so silently barely any breath escaped his lips, "Man in the stone, I miss your jokes and games. My mother is very sick, and I'd like you to come make her better if you can. A red rain fell and I think it hurt her. I'm afraid. Please, can you help?"

From the jagged stones at the ends of the world of humankind, Loki smiled, sending his thoughts on the wind to the little boy.

"One prayer will keep me alive. One prayer is all a god needs to be reborn, to flourish, to be worshipped. I hear your prayer, child. I hear your prayer all the way from Iceland. You're in Iceland. Your mother is in Iceland," Loki cooed. Although bound with the intestines of his own son to razor-edged boulders with the venom of a terrible serpent dripping upon him, Loki with his insane thoughts of vengeance, self-importance, and glory, for the first time in a very, very long time, became aroused.

"Sigyn," he whispered to his loyal demigoddess wife. "I need you. Pleasure me. I am in need."

Obediently, the haggard and oblivious, simple-minded Sigyn set aside the bowl in which she collected the dripping venom, mounting her godly husband solely for the sake of his pleasure. The stinging venom dripped onto the back of her head, neck, and shoulders as she sat astride Loki. She gained no satisfaction from the act, only more scars for a life married to the Father of Lies.

Chapter 29

Autumn, 1004

Iceland

Leif sailed into Reykjanes harbor gleefully, full of anticipation. "I missed you, Iceland," he said, as his ship sailed past the steam spout in the middle of the bay. "It has been too long since I left this wondrous land of my birth. I've been quite tied to Greenland with Eirik's passing. I need this trip. This voyage. It shall bring me back to life."

"Ah, you're just waxing poetic over a little island, Leif. You're certain he'll be here? Greenland's new priest, more's the pity," Sigurdur asked, still with Leif after the sailings to Tiree, Norway, Greenland, and Vinland.

"Aye. He's likely already here and waiting."

"I'm ready to return to Norway," Petur said. "I love Greenland, but it's time. It's just time. Thank you ever so much for accompanying me to Iceland."

"Good timing is all, Petur. You wished to return to Norway—and we get word a replacement priest for Greenland is to meet us in Iceland within days of your wish. Good timing, indeed," Leif replied.

"A new, young priest who may be more willing than I to travel to the Vinland colony," Petur said.

"When Thorvald returns, I'll see if I can coerce our new priest to make the journey," Leif agreed.

"You will not return to Vinland, will you?" Sigurdur asked Leif.

"No. My place is on Greenland. With Eirik dead, I'm needed there more than ever. My brothers and half-sister can manage the colony in my stead. This voyage to Iceland is necessary to facilitate the exchange of the priests, but I am glad for the journey. Call it a fever, but I felt I would go mad if another ship sailed from Bratahild without me at its stern," Leif replied.

"I can see in your eyes you've missed Iceland, Leif," Sigurdur said.

"Only the abundant hot water!" Leif laughed, realizing he'd said the exact same words before to Thorgunna. *I wonder how she's getting on. Has she moved on with her life? I should turn this vessel now and sail to the Hebrides and claim her. And my son.*

Reykjavik, a thriving community and quite populous since Leif had last seen it nearly twenty-five years prior, was busy and noisy and crowded. When last Leif saw Reykjavik, there were but a few sod houses, no proper roads, and little commerce. Now, to his amazement, Reykjavik had many shops and homes of turf and stone flanking one long dirt path marred heavily by the wheels of carts and the hooves of the horses that drew them. The natural harbor at the edge of the town brimmed with vessels from all over the Norselands. England. Ireland. The Baltic Regions. Even some Leif did not recognize.

They disembarked, tying their skiff off at the pier. A few short strides up the dirt trail, and they were in the middle of Reykjavik, the hub of life in Iceland.

"I love this town!" Sigurdur remarked, passing the township's whorehouse.

Leif laughed. "I'll see you later, then. What? In a week?" *How long will it take you to have every doxy in Reykjavik seduce you out of your silver, Sigurdur?*

"I'll see to the priest with you first—then go a'whorin'! I brought plenty of coin," Sigurdur replied.

"You'll both go to Hell," Petur smirked.

"Be quiet, Petur. I took no oath of celibacy. Your eyesight would improve if you had a woman," Sigurdur scolded.

"Before I joined the Church, I had enough women to ensure I shall never go blind," Petur replied.

"And you gave up women for God?" Sigurdur asked, stunned.

"There is a love beyond the physical that only knowing Christ can bring to a man. I chose that love, over *that* love," Petur replied, nodding toward the brothel.

"This is it, laddies," Leif said. "The Inn of the Lamb. Herein shall be Greenland's new priest."

The three men boldly entered the inn, a good-sized, smoky building of stone. A dour woman stirred a pot at the hearth, while a red-faced man served cups of frothy beer to the Inn's guests sitting at small tables near the fire.

"Good sir, I seek a priest come from Norway named Helgi," Leif said to the innkeeper.

"Aye. He's here. Are you the son of Eirik the Red come to fetch him to Greenland?"

"Yes, I am," Leif replied.

"You're late, lads. Your priest should return to the harbor. King Olaf's fleet sails at dawn," the innkeeper said.

"Oh, my. I must away. I don't want to miss the sailing. God bless you both," Petur said excitedly.

"I'll never forget you, Petur," Leif said.

"Nor I you. Go with God," Petur said in blessing. "Do take good care."

"Aye. We'll continue to watch each other's backs. I promise ye this," Sigurdur replied.

"And I shall watch out for his soul," a young priest said, emerging from the shadows to join Petur, Leif, and Sigurdur.

"Helgi? Father Helgi?" Leif asked.

"I am he," Helgi replied.

Petur embraced his fellow priest briefly, then ran out of the inn to find the ship that would give him passage to Norway.

"Sir, I am Leif Eiriksson, come to take you to Greenland. This is my shipmate, Sigurdur."

"I am honored to meet you," Helgi said, extending his arm to Leif for the customary clasping of wrists.

The new priest was young, freckled, and red-faced.

"How long have you been in the service of the Church?" Leif asked, motioning for Helgi and Sigurdur to sit at one of the tables.

"I left home at fourteen and joined a monastery in Ireland. I traveled to Norway a few years ago. Now I go to Greenland."

A disturbance from another table, and a splashing of ale against the floor piqued the attention of the Greenlanders and their new priest.

"I tell ye she's possessed! The blood rained upon none but her, and my own sister was in the field with her. I'm riding to Skalholt to fetch a priest. He'll exorcize the demon posthaste. We'll have no truck with Satan at Olafsvik, no, sir," a drunken man said, his voice growing louder with each word.

"You said she's nobility?" the drunken man's tablemate asked.

"Aye. A Rus princess in hiding, I understand. Owns four islands in the Hebrides and brews beer so fine it has bewitched even Olaf, himself."

Helgi stood, facing the boisterous, excited men at the neighboring table. "Sir, surely the Lord has guided your steps on your journey to Skalholt. This inn is a way station for servants to Christ and king."

The man was too drunk to understand. Having been in the same situation a time or two himself, Helgi rephrased, "I am a priest. What can I do to help you?"

"Exorcism!" the man choked.

Leif spoke up, "I knew a Hebridean woman once ... from Tiree. A Jarl, not a princess. She was a brewmistress, however."

"Yes, Tiree. That's her home," the drunkard replied. "And as for you, priest—where are your vestments and cross?"

"I've travelled for days by ship and on horseback. I have priestly vestments, but why ruin them with the dust of the road?" Helgi asked.

"Then if you be a priest, come to Olafsvik and cast out the demon in the woman before she dies and leaves her restless shade to haunt the land forever!"

Leif felt his chest tighten. He dared not breathe. It could not be so. He stood. "Sir, is her name Thorgunna? The possessed woman from Tiree now living at Olafsvik? Thorgunna Vagnsdottir?"

Helgi the Priest's face went ashen. His eyes widened in disbelief. "Leif, I am Helgi Vagnsson, Thorgunna's brother," he gasped.

"Oh, my God." Leif sighed.

Seeing Leif's distress, Sigurdur handed Leif a horn of beer being offered to another man, at another table. "May I?"

"Aye," the man whose money had bought the beer replied. "Looks like he needs it more than I!"

"Drink, Leif. Then breathe," Sigurdur ordered.

Leif downed the contents of the horn. As the smooth, frothy liquid reached his belly, a gentle calm came over him. "Helgi. You are Helgi—her brother."

"You know my sister! But when were you on Tiree? Why would she leave Tiree? No matter. We'll have time to discuss these matters on our way to Olafsvik. How miraculous we should meet here and now at a time when Thorgunna needs us the most. But what *is* she doing in Iceland?" Helgi queried, crossing himself. "Thank the Lord."

"Looking for me, or perhaps bringing our son to Greenland," Leif responded.

"Your son? Your son—by the body of my sister? God be praised and His miracles abound! Looks like she'll find you, then. Dearest Lord, thank you," Helgi replied with a knowing grin. "What is my nephew's name?"

Leif shook his head. "I don't know. When I sailed from Tiree, Thorgunna was only just quickened. But I know I have a son. She foresaw his birth."

"We shall meet him together, Leif," Helgi smiled.

Leif turned to the drunkard, "Sir, we go with you to Olafsvik. When can we leave?"

"At dawn suits me just fine," the man replied.

"Tomorrow at dawn," Leif confirmed. *Thorgunna is here!*

Chapter 30

Wafting in and out of consciousness, Thorgunna fell into a nightmare born of fever and pain. Her lungs were on fire. The slightest breath was laborious. Blood sometimes oozed from her mouth as she struggled to take air into her lungs. Her skin took on a purplish tinge. The good people of Froda were afraid and ignorant of how to treat Thorgunna's illness.

Only gentle, kind Kjartan ministered to Thorgunna by squeezing drops of water into her mouth, mopping her fevered brow, burning sulfur and herbs said to cleanse the lungs in the room. Thurid hovered about timidly, still coveting the bedclothes and linens Thorgunna rested on.

Thorgils wandered aimlessly about the farm, dirty and confused. No one brought him meals. No one helped him dress. He stole bread from Thurid's hearth and had his ears boxed for his effort. Even at his tender age, he knew the vacant-eyed, fearful adults should be caring for him. The other children shied away from him as word spread his mother had fallen to demonic possession. And when he asked what "demonic possession" was, they ran from him. Only his prayers to the Man in the Stone eased his suffering.

"If she dies, I'm not keeping the boy, Kjartan. I'll not pay his passage inland to the kin of his father, neither," Thurid said, growing jealous of Kjartan's attention to Thorgunna's infirmity after the passing of over a week.

"Thorgunna has already spoken her wishes regarding the boy and disposition of her things, Thurid. No blood will pour from you for the well-being of Thorgils," Kjartan replied. "Now, quit being an old dried-up sow and fetch me some clean water."

"How dare you speak to me in such manner. She has bewitched you! Thorgunna has possessed you even in her ill state!" Thurid cried. "And how do you know her wishes? Has the witch's spirit come to you as you slept on the floor at her bedside?"

"Thurid, I am tired. I am very tired. I do not have the patience to deal with your jealousies or arrogance. This woman lies dying, and it is my duty as a Christian man to comfort her as best I can in her last hours. Now, get me the water, or I swear, I shall take my horsewhip to you."

"I could divorce you for that, you know," Thurid replied, unafraid.

"Don't make idle threats, Thurid. You came into this marriage with no dowry, and there's not a man on all the peninsula who would take you in."

Thurid softened. "How do you know Thorgunna's wishes, Kjartan?"

"Very early this morning, she awoke briefly. She spoke to me before falling into an even darker abyss of fever and death."

"What are her wishes?" *I must have her linens!*

"She said she knew she was dying. She directed me to burn all her possessions—the linens, the bed curtains, her clothing. Everything except the mantle of Greenlandic homespun. That, she wishes to be buried in. She made me promise to carry her body to Skalholt for burial. She wishes a Christian burial as she said she fears Christ less than the wrath of the old gods."

Thurid pursed her lips. "All her things are to be burned, then?"

"Aye. And I'll see to it, too. I know you covet Thorgunna's finery. But hear me, woman, all of it goes. All of it shall burn. She does this so her illness shall not spread further."

"And the boy?" Thurid asked, suppressing her sharp tongue.

"Thorgils must be placed with his father's family. With his father if I can find him. Thorgunna told me where her silver was hidden. I'm to use it to portage the boy to his kin, and to pay the Bishop to sing Mass over her grave."

"Thorgunna has silver?" Thurid asked.

Kjartan stood. "Thurid, I married you because it was my father's wish that I do so. You are kin to his own half-sister and therefore, not only my wife, but kin as well. If you were not kin, I would put you out. You have never been a good wife, and now that I see you are more vulture than woman, I feel nothing but contempt for you. Have you no Christian compassion for this woman?"

Thurid shook her head. "I have none, sir. I hate her."

Kjartan turned back to Thorgunna, not looking up at his wife. "Very well. It is said. Go fetch me the water now, Thurid."

Thorgunna did not die during the night. The rise and fall of her chest was barely evident, and as if bound by unseen ropes, she lay rigid and stiff, yet alive, throughout the dim hours of night in a season when the sun never set.

Kjartan felt as if he were suffocating as he awoke on the hard-packed earthen floor of the sick house. The sweet, warm, comforting perfume of death hung about the room.

He opened the shutters and door to allow the warm late summer sun in to refresh and cleanse the air. "Let the sun chase the dark from her."

A golden ray of light streaming in from the open door fell upon Thorgunna's sleeping body, illuminating her for a moment. A shadow fell upon her just as quickly as the light had, as a figure entered the room, blocking the doorway. "Hello inside the house," the stranger said.

"This is a sick house, stranger. It is not wise to enter," Kjartan said sharply.

The visitor ignored the warning, making straight for Thorgunna's bed. He pulled back the privacy curtain and spoke softly to Kjartan, "I must see her. I must."

Kjartan balked, "The Lady is dying, stranger."

"Nevertheless, I must hold her. I must try to speak to her. I am Leif Eiriksson."

Thorgils, who had found refuge in the far corner of Thorgunna's room during the night, spoke as quietly as a mouse, "Father…?"

Leif turned to see the soot-covered, thin, but beautiful little boy standing by the hearth. "Are you the son of Thorgunna?"

"Yes. Thorgunna is my mother. Are you my father come from Greenland?" Thorgils asked.

"Yes. I am he, son. What name did Thorgunna give you?"

"I am Thorgils."

"A good name. I am Leif, your father. Come stand by me, my son," Leif said, reaching out for the boy.

"Mother is dying," Thorgils said softly.

"Lung fever?" Leif asked toward Kjartan. *She must not die, Lord.*

"Aye," Kjartan replied.

Leif dropped to one knee beside Thorgunna's bed.

Crossing himself, he prayed softly, "Thank you, Lord. Thank you for bringing us together again. Bless Thorgunna and let her live to know you and your works. Let her live that we can raise our son together to do Your service."

"Leif? Are you here?" a second man called, entering the house.

"Yes, Helgi. We are here," Leif responded.

Helgi stood silently for a moment, a single tear rolling down his cheek. "Let us pray," he commanded.

Kjartan crossed himself.

"May the Lord bless and keep you all. May the Lord heal Thorgunna that she live to glorify His holy name."

Helgi passed the sign of the cross over Thorgunna's bed.

"Amen," Leif whispered, compelled by a love he thought he had forgotten to kiss Thorgunna tenderly upon her forehead.

"Wake up, beloved. Wake up," Leif whispered, lowering his kiss to her lips.

Thorgunna's eyes fluttered open.

"Christ All-Mighty!" Kjartan exclaimed.

"Leif?" Thorgunna whispered. "I heard your voice in a dream."

"I am here, Thorgunna. I am here at Froda River, with you."

"I am dying," she whispered.

Leif stood. "Good steward of Froda, by chance and the will of God, we met your man in Reykjavik. We stopped his journey to Skalholt, for I travel with a man who is both priest and physician."

Thurid made a loud *humpf* from the door.

"Helgi, I put her life into your hands. Heal her, I beg of you," Leif pleaded.

"I will do all I can," Helgi replied.

Helgi looked into the face of his sister. "Thorgunna, it is I, Helgi. Trust me now, my dear sister. Let God work through me and heal you."

"Helgi?" Thorgunna cried softly.

"Don't talk now," Helgi replied.

Thorgunna could not speak further. She was again unconscious.

Helgi ushered everyone out of the house. He removed his travel clothes, donning vestments for prayer and healing. "I must be alone with her. Go now. Pray."

Leif scooped Thorgils into his arms, carrying his son lovingly.

"We can go to my house," Kjartan offered.

"Thank you," Leif replied, kissing his son.

Helgi closed the door behind them, then turned back to Thorgunna, speaking aloud. "The sky rained blood upon thee, and death comes. Your lungs are filled with fluid, and you burn with Hell's fire. But I wonder what is it that truly ails you, sister?" He placed his hands on Thorgunna's brow. "The fever must come down and your lungs be made clear before life can gain hold of you."

He took the linen compress Kjartan had been using, wetting it again. He placed it on Thorgunna's forehead. "Too slow. Too slow. I need to bring your fever down, now. I need a tub of ice," he said, standing, milling about, pacing the room.

He walked to the window, gazing at the perfect view of the Snaefullsjokul glacier through the open shutters. His eyes wandered down the horizon to the Froda River. A glacial stream. Ice cold. Ice-cold salvation. It shimmered like the purest of gems in the cool light of fall's evening sun and jealous pale moon.

"Yes. Of course," he whispered.

Carefully, Helgi took Thorgunna in his arms, carrying her from the house. Dead to the world with fever, Thorgunna did not move nor speak.

"What are you doing? You'll kill her if you move her!" Kjartan scolded, dashing from his house and into the priest's path.

"Stand aside. I mean to lay her in the water to cool her body so life's breath will jump in and take hold. If I can bring her fever down thusly, her life may be saved," Helgi replied sternly. Kjartan stood aside, dumbfounded. "Why did I not think of that?"

Leif, still cradling his beautiful son, watched nervously as Helgi waded waist deep into the Froda.

The water was frigid. Helgi felt the sting of icy numbness course up his body. "God help me," he prayed, lowering Thorgunna's limp body into the Froda River, submerging her so only her face remained exposed. He smoothed the cold water over her face. Reminding him of baptism, he then cupped his hand and poured the chilly water over her forehead.

"Should I say the words? Has Thorgunna received the sacrament of Baptism? I must proceed without her consent. Should the Lord take her, she cannot be properly shriven or receive Last Rights without Baptism."

Gently trickling water over Thorgunna's brow again, he recited, "In the name of the Father and of the Son…"

"Father, look at the moon!" Thorgils cried, so vehemently Helgi ceased the act of baptism.

The moon shifted from pale yellow against a dusky midnight-sun drenched sky, to blood red before their eyes, dancing in between the clouds with an eerie glow.

The farm animals, reacting to the celestial oddity, stomped and shuffled their hooves nervously in their fields. A rooster crowed, and a dog returned the cry with a long, frightened howl.

"*Tunglid vedur i skyjum*—the moon wades through the clouds, Kjartan. An ill-omen. An omen of death," Thurid said fearfully.

"Give me strength," Helgi continued, trying again to bless Thorgunna with baptism. Trying to ignore the phenomenal red orb hovering overhead. It did him no good. The moon was not the only force of nature acting against him. The waters of the Froda suddenly swelled as if a great downpour had occurred, the river surging around him, the current rapidly turning swift and dangerous. Helgi struggled against the swirling torrent, nearly losing Thorgunna in his battle against the raging influx of water.

"Help!" Helgi cried, desperately trying to climb up the now-muddy slope leading into the Froda. Still unconscious, Thorgunna fell limply onto the bank.

"The Froda is too pure for the likes of her. It spits her out just as the moon bleeds across the sky in anger," Thurid hissed.

Helgi coughed. "Be silent, woman. Thorgunna is not evil. Nor are the workings of the heavens and waters of the earth controlled by demonic forces. God, Himself, sets these things into motion for a purpose. A grand purpose we must not dismiss, but respect and follow."

"You must go to the fire, sir. You and Thorgunna. Please. Hurry," Kjartan offered.

"An odd night it is when the sun shines cold light in the west while the moon dances red in the east," Helgi replied.

Leif handed Thorgils to Kjartan, then scooped Thorgunna into his arms. "Beloved, Thorgunna. Awaken. Awaken," he whispered.

****

Abed before a raging fire in the main house, Leif dried Thorgunna and wrapped her warmly in a pile of skins and woolens. Thorgunna's dark, erect nipples peeked out through her wet chemise, teasing Leif into memories he had long suppressed.

"Live, damn it. Live that I may love you as you deserve to be loved. I should never have left you to raise our son alone."

As the midnight sun-lit night passed, the Froda continued to swell until it breached its banks, threatening Kjartan's fields.

Thorgunna, however, slept soundly. Her fever had broken. Color had returned to her cheeks, and her breathing was even and steady.

"Never before has the Froda overrun its banks. And never before has the moon bled across the sky. It is a wonder of great magnitude," Kjartan said.

Thurid whispered to her husband, "The old ones are angry that she lives. Thorgunna is a witch, I tell you. She touches the river, and it overflows. She grows stronger as she pulls the stars from the sky and the light from the moon."

"I thank you for sheltering Thorgunna and my son during her stay, but heed my words, woman, I will not stand for slander," Leif said, overhearing Thurid's rude remarks.

"It is a sign, I'm sure of it. I shall memorialize this event, calling it the Froda River Wonder, and send word to the Bishop about it," Helgi said.

Leif agreed. He knew it was a sign, too. And he had a good idea whose it was.

Two more days passed with the Froda swelling and breeching her banks before calm returned to the river. That night the moon waxed golden. Thorgunna slipped in and out of death's sleep, seemingly fighting some unseen force to remain conscious, but always descending again into oblivion after but a moment at the surface of her life.

Leif carried her to the outbuilding. Good Kjartan had boiled Thorgunna's linens and swept out the house. The lingering scent of death vanished with the dust and soot swept away by his broom.

Helgi and Leif stood at the door, watching Thorgunna sleep, waiting for her to again regain control over the opponent keeping her from them by way of death's sleep. Helgi sighed. "There is nothing more I can do. She is in God's hands. I pray He grants her the strength to fight her way back from wherever it is she is trapped."

Thorgunna sighed and shifted in the bed. Weakly she spoke, barely above a whisper. "Leif?"

"Thorgunna?" Leif cried, leaping to her side. "I'm here, Thorgunna. I'm here! Awaken!"

Her eyes fixed shut, Thorgunna fought to speak. Her body tightened, and her head arched backwards against the down pillows. "Loki."

"Yes, I know. I assumed as much. What must I do?" Leif asked, lifting Thorgunna into his arms, cradling her.

Thorgunna bolted upright, eyes wide open. Her complexion took on a sallow tinge, accentuating the hollows of her cheeks after such a long confinement. Spittle and blood seeped from her mouth as she formed one simple word in a voice far from her own. "Die."

She then collapsed exhausted onto the bed. Like a mist rolling in off the sea, Thorgunna's face and body shed the pallor of death, becoming awash in her own natural, healthy beauty.

As if she had not been ill, but only sleeping in the arms of her lover, Thorgunna awoke. "I live." She pushed herself up to a sitting position. "Thorgils?"

"He is well, Thorgunna. He is beautiful," Leif replied. "You are beautiful."

Thorgunna smiled. "Leif. It is so good to see you again."

"Thorgunna," Leif whispered, pulling Thorgunna to him, kissing her gently, yet passionately. "I've missed you."

"And I, you," Thorgunna replied. "He found me, Leif."

"Yes, I know. But I'm here now. We're together. There is no greater force in the universe than the love of a family."

"Helgi is here, is he not? I vaguely recall seeing his face shining above me as he…"

"I am here, sister," Helgi called.

Thorgunna raised her arms beckoning her brother to her. "Dearest Helgi, I remember little of my nightmare, but I do recall you carrying me into the river. Your face shone like the sun above me. It warmed me. You began to speak. I recall the words piercing me with a goodness that filled my heart and soul with a love I cannot describe. Then the moon bled, and I was whisked from the goodness of your arms and cast down into the bowels of Hell once again. But I carried your words with me. I carried them in my heart, and it was the strength I gained from them that helped me climb out of the abyss. Helgi…" Thorgunna paused. "Not only did you save my life with your wise ministrations, but you have saved my soul as well."

"What do you mean, dear?" Helgi asked.

"I've never been baptized. I fought the priests on Tiree. I would not submit. As I lay in the water, unable to move or speak, I wanted you to say the words over me—I heard you begin them. And, Helgi, the words were good. They felt good. They felt so right. But when you were forced to stop your priestly act, the great light filling my heart dimmed. Brother, I would be baptized. I believe it was a sign from the White Christ that it is time for me to accept Him. Not for king or Tiree, but for *me*," Thorgunna said.

"Praise the Lord," Leif whispered, bowing his head.

"Then, sister, tomorrow at dawn, you shall be baptized," Helgi replied. "Now, rest. I'll bring you something hot to drink and let Thorgils know his mother lives."

****

Leif and Thorgunna were alone in her small house as evening fell. A fire had been built and tallow lamps lit, giving the cottage a warm, romantic glow. The dwelling smelled sweet from wild flowers picked by Thorgils for his mother.

Thorgunna reclined against the eider duck-feather bed, pulling the privacy curtains about her. Leif sat on the edge, smiling.

He brushed her hair and regaled her with tales of Norway, the Christ, and finding new land to the west of Greenland.

"You've changed little," she commented.

"Nor have you," Leif said. "I should have never left you."

"Would you have discovered Vinland and founded a new colony had you stayed, or had I traveled with you?"

Leif shook his head. "Vinland was a great adventure. Colonies now fight to survive there, but I am too humble to think my name shall be remembered as the man who found the land of grapes. Had you sailed with me, I would have farmed my father's land and kept you having babies for years. I would not have sailed far again."

"Thorgils is a good son, Leif," Thorgunna whispered.

"Perhaps we shall have another," Leif replied.

"Yes, perhaps," Thorgunna agreed.

"I love you, Thorgunna. I've always loved you. I shall never part from you again."

"Nor shall I let you leave," Thorgunna replied.

"I prayed to God to reunite us. It was my first prayer. His Grace overwhelms me, Thorgunna. He has taken you from the jaws of Hell, placed you into my arms, and on the morrow, you shall be baptized. I am truly blessed."

"Hold me, Leif. I am loath to sleep for I have slept enough to last a lifetime, yet I can no longer remain awake. Hold me as I sleep." Thorgunna slid under the heavy wool wraps, urging Leif to join her.

Entwined, they fell asleep.

Thorgunna awoke drenched in sweat. The room blistered from an unnatural stifling heat, and a heavy odor of decay clung to the air like a coating of honey.

Thorgunna looked at the fire. It was low-banked. "Why is it so hot? Has my fever returned?" she said, pulling away from Leif's embrace.

"Because fire makes light enough to see the cowardly grovel, and its heat burns the wicked to ashes," a voice said from the darkest corner of the room.

Thorgunna turned toward the voice, a wash of fear enveloping her.

Blue and red flames danced threateningly in the corner, gathering together, merging together, forming the bane of her existence and the image of the beast itself. Loki had returned.

"Be gone!" Thorgunna hissed through her teeth, not wanting to awaken Leif.

Loki laughed. "He's grown fat. What did you ever see in him? He fondled you as you slept, you know. Pinched your nipples, cupped those round breasts of yours in his hands. He wanted to take you. But he could not. Morality overwhelms him, Thorgunna. He has no sense of adventure. The Christ has warped his soul, leaving him without imagination. I do, however, know how to imagine, and act on those imaginings. My imagination is about to run wild, in fact."

Thorgunna bolted from the bed, running to the door. Loki followed, moving across the room like a will-o'-the-wisp. His flames enveloped her, pinning her to the wall. The flames became hands. The hands grew claws, cutting into her flesh.

"You're hurting me. Let me go," Thorgunna begged. Her skin rent, her lifeblood flowing into little rivulets, soaking her gown, Loki's talons only pinched harder.

"Run from me will you, Thorgunna? After all our years apart?"

"Loki, no," Thorgunna pleaded.

"You force my hand by consorting with that weakling priest-brother of yours. I wanted to wait a bit longer—to keep you hanging between life and death. You hid from me well, here, at the ends of the world. But I found you the day of the red storm. The day Heaven bled upon you. My crimson tears of anguish from the torment you put me through. My tears of joy at knowing you will never, ever escape me again. I made you ill, Thorgunna. If only you had crossed over! But that damned priest saved you! I hate the Christ and his minions! Do you know how I found you? Your son prayed to me—the man in the stone—for assistance. The purity of his prayer was like a trail of breadcrumbs, Thorgunna. Your son has no idea with whom he has been singing in his dreams."

Thorgunna frantically searched her mind for a solution. The pain was excruciating, yet she could not, she dared not call out and awaken Leif. Loki would kill him. *Loki acts now because Helgi is near, he said it himself. He must take me before I am made a Christian woman! Helgi! I must awaken Helgi! To fight a god, I need another God.*

"Here and now, Thorgunna, I shall have my way with you. On the very hillside where I caused blood to fall from the sky, you shall submit to me. If I must kill you in the process, so be it. For betraying me to the gods, for revealing my hiding place to them, for giving them the opportunity to snare me and bind me with my own son's entrails, I shall rape you, body and soul, for all eternity." Loki hissed at her, his tongue forked, his eyes red and glowing with insidious pleasure.

Thorgunna spat at the demigod, and pulled away. She felt her flesh tear as she forced herself away from Loki's razor-sharp embrace. *No matter. I need to get away!*

She ran.

Laughing viciously, Loki gave chase.

Weak from her long illness and slowed by loss of blood, Thorgunna had not the strength to run very far. She fell to the ground, and Loki fell upon her. He struck her. He kicked her. Stunned, bleeding from nose and mouth, her breathing labored from freshly broken ribs, she could not fight back.

Loki delighted with each blow. Dancing about her fallen body, he spat and hurled curses upon her. He exposed himself, pissing upon her as she rolled into a ball in an effort to protect herself. "You had your masons defile my stone, Thorgunna. Now, I defile you!" he cursed, remembering his rage when the stonemasons soiled his monument with their foul body fluids as they carved it out of the heart of Tiree.

Loki spread himself atop her like a shadow, tearing open her gown with talons and claws, ripping at her flesh with his unholy hands. Darkness moved about her wrists and ankles, encircling them, pinning her securely to the ground.

He dragged his beastly talons down Thorgunna's belly to her legs, opening her flesh in great rifts as if he were plowing a field. His shadowy form forced her legs wide open, then quickly shifted into a grotesque plunging phallus.

Thorgunna screamed.

Before the sound of her scream ceased, Leif ripped the piercing darkness from her. He fought to hold the beast of shadow and fire, to keep it away from his love. He fought the very substance of night, knowing it could be his last battle.

The shadow wound its terrorizing claws and jagged teeth around Leif, pinning his arms to his side, shattering his ribs from the force of his own arms used against him like a vice.

"No!" Leif cried, fighting to free his arms, to pull the beast away. "Lord give me strength to defeat this devilish function of the old ones. Lord give me strength!" Leif freed an arm, then the other, ripping Loki from him, casting the flaming shadow to the ground.

Like a dog about to strike a rabbit, Loki crawled about on all fours, shifting from shadow to light and back again, growling angrily, baring his teeth, black saliva dripping from his canine-like teeth.

"Be gone!" Leif commanded.

"Never!" Loki replied, lunging at Thorgunna, shifting into white-hot flames—laughing, maniacal white-hot burning flames.

Thorgunna yelped in pain and terror as the flames enveloped her, sizzling her hair, setting fire to her blood-soaked, tattered clothing.

"Leif, I'm on fire!" she screamed. "Oh, God! Leif, help me!"

Ignoring his own burns, Leif scooped Thorgunna up and out of the unholy fire, diving into the still-swollen Froda River. They doused Loki's unholy fire in the cold, clear waters of the Froda River. Steam rose from their bodies. Leif stood mid-stream, nearly waist-high, and held Thorgunna tightly.

Loki approached even as Leif waded through the water to the far bank. His shape changed over and over with each step, morphing from one vile creature to the next, his rage apparent.

Thorgunna felt a trickle of water run from her forehead across her cheek. That simple, gravity-generated event showed her the way to defeat Loki. "Leif, I know what he wants. I know what must be done to stop him," she said.

"Speak now, Lady, for the beast approaches," Leif replied.

"Baptize me, Leif. Baptize me now. That's what he wants to stop!" Thorgunna cried.

Leif hesitated for only a moment. Growling like a berserker, his focus steady upon Loki's own red gaze, Leif lifted a cupped hand of water above Thorgunna's head. His voice booming, he called out, "I baptize thee, Thorgunna Vagnsdottir, in the name of the Father, the Son, and the Holy Spirit."

Loki halted his attack, and resumed human form.

"Damn you! Damn you, Thorgunna!" he screeched, stomping his feet like a spoiled child.

Thorgunna, the remnants of her burnt shift clinging to her flesh, pulled away from Leif and stood alone in the river, "I'll not be damned by the likes of you ever again! I accept the Christ as my savior! Do you hear me, Loki? I accept Christ! And by virtue of my acceptance of Him as my Savior, Tiree shall become Christian if His grace has not already embraced the land and people."

Loki lifted his head, and howled like a wolf. From a clear sky, a loud crack of thunder pierced the night. He cowered at the sound. "No! I won't go!" he cried. "I don't want to die!" His beautiful human form began to fade like dust picked up and dispersed by the wind. "Another time, Greenlander. And another lifetime for you, Thorgunna!"

With a final twinkle of fading dark light, Loki vanished into the world of memories with his fellow gods, leaving only a glimmer of fireflies of red and blue lights twinkling in his wake.

"*I* became his last refuge, Leif. In my absence, Tiree must have fallen to the Christ. Now I, too, have fallen to the God of Olaf, and by doing so, my life has been spared," Thorgunna wept as Leif lifted her from the river.

"You have not fallen. You have been raised on high by the Lord of Hosts," Leif replied.

Chapter 31

Morning's light found only some of the apprehension lifted about the farm at Froda River. Loki's appearance was not unknown to the people of Snaefulsness, but none had seen him appear with such fury.

"Leif, before we go to Reykjavik, I'd like to stop at Skalholt. I must report the appearance of the Trickster to Bishop Thangbrandur," Helgi said. "Even though Iceland is God's country now, the old ones die hard in these wild places. The Bishop must be informed."

Leif nodded his agreement.

"I was to be buried at Skalholt," Thorgunna replied.

"A more joyful sacrament than burial, I can re-baptize you there if you wish. You can receive Holy Communion and make confession."

Thorgunna laughed. "I have a lifetime of confessions to make!"

Leif, looking quite thoughtful, added, "Helgi, can you marry us in the eyes of the Church at Skalholt? It is time we become a proper family in God's eyes."

Thorgunna smiled. "Oh, Leif. Yes! Yes, please, let's wed."

Epilogue

Thorgunna, heavily veiled in lace from Gaul and wearing a heavy, crisp linen dress, entered the chapel of Skalholt. She knelt gracefully before the high altar. Leif, splendidly dressed in his chain mail and a crimson cape, knelt beside her.

As he had so many years before while making his silent promise to Thorgunna, Leif again placed the gold band on Thorgunna's finger, this time proudly proclaiming, "You are my land, my home, my hearth."

Thangbrandur, priest of Skalholt, and king's emissary to Iceland, blessed them both, marrying them. "Let us pray…" he said, beginning recitation of the *Paternoster*.

"…but deliver us from evil…" Leif said, turning to Thorgunna.

"…Amen," Thorgunna prayed in unison as they completed the prayer with Thangbrandur.

"Amen," Leif whispered again, taking Thorgunna in his arms, kissing his new wife.

Thorgunna fought to keep her eyes open, still fearing the flames of Hell licking at her in the darkness, but she could not. Leif's kiss flooded her with a purer love than ever she had known. Blissfully, she closed her eyes, surrendering to his embrace. She needed no defense against this Norseman or his God. Her God. There was nothing in the darkness except realization that change had indeed occurred. But the changes were good. She was warm. She was safe. And she was loved.

Her nightmare was over.

About the Author

Darragha Foster is the author of the award-winning paranormal romance novel, *The Orca King*, as well as several other novels of a similar nature. She loves scary movies, her miniature dachshund, and her iPhone (which she claims changed her life). She has been married for over twenty years to her mate from the infinite past, a very patient man who doesn't mind being her crash-test dummy for love scenes. Her favorite quote is from the writings of Nichiren Daishonin: *Many raging fires are quenched by a single shower of rain.* Darragha is all about joy, and hopes she shares a bit of the same with her readers at every turn of the electronic page.

Made in the USA
Charleston, SC
27 July 2016